Praise for *A Small Life*

"*A Small Life* isn't small! It's a compelling historical fiction full of brilliant imagery and vivid characters, so real that on the final page, a reader will linger to savor the story and revisit it again. A truly enchanting novel."

Cherilyn DeAguero
Writer

"Magical. With intelligent and graceful prose reminiscent of Alice Hoffman, Roxanne Z. Kind emerges as a female voice worthy of our attention. Her characters come to life so vividly and fiercely. Yet, Ms. Kind takes you by the hand and lovingly walks you through this tale of three disparate women, who, once upon a time, touched and changed one another's small lives forever."

Sara Wood
Actor/Director/Producer/Founder of Actors Space West

"Roxanne Z. Kind's *A Small Life* had me enthralled from the very first paragraph. It is a magically beautiful recounting of her family lore, drawn with nuances that, imagined or otherwise, seem both real and mystical. It is a novel, a history and a poem all combined."

Gila Zalon
Screenwriter/Film Producer

Cover paintings by Elly Zambrano · Cover design by Rolf Busch

Library of Congress Cataloging-in-Publication Data

Kind, Roxanne Z.
A Small Life: A Novel

p. cm.
Paperback ISBN: 978-1-947708-70-9
Ebook ISBN: 978-1-947708-73-0
Library of Congress Control Number: 2023919470

10 9 8 7 6 5 4 3 2 1
First Edition, October 2023

State College, Pennsylvania, U.S.A.

(828) 585 - 7030

Publisher@CitrinePublishing.com

www.CitrinePublishing.com

ROXANNE Z. KIND

A SMALL LIFE

A Novel

CITRINE PUBLISHING

For my Mother

Acknowledgments

There are too many wonderful souls to name who read parts or all of this book and who gave me so much inspiration to keep writing. To all of them, I will be forever grateful.

To my husband, Keith, thank you with all my heart for your patience putting up with me while I hid in my office for endless hours, and when I came up for air, my mood and thoughts were still on the characters of this book.

To my late agent, Stanley Corwin, a publisher for several major book companies, former president and CEO of Pinnacle Books and president of Stan Corwin Productions, without whom, I would not have the resolve to bring this book forth. I'm sorry the world lost you and cannot thank you enough for your encouragement and conviction.

Table of Contents

The Foundling Wheel

Santiago, Chile, 1929

The man carried the baby in a woven basket. The woman followed a few steps behind, buried her face in a large shawl and tried to stifle her sobs. As they approached the *iglesia*, her cry turned to animal-like wailing. He placed the basket down and wrapped his arms around the woman's shoulders, attempting to calm her. From her cheeks, he kissed the tears that were falling faster than summer rain.

"Shhhh! We'll wake someone," he whispered.

Unable to take another step, the woman froze. She stared at him, her eyes pleading.

"We don't have a choice! We cannot keep her!" The man said as he had a thousand times before.

"There must be another way! I beg you, please!" as she fell to her knees.

"I'll finish this!" he said harshly, which did not come from unkindness, but fear—fear so visceral it cracked his voice. Fear so overwhelming it filled him with emotions not allotted to his gender. But he reasoned that not completing their mission would prove worse, so he pressed on.

The man's hands shook, but he walked forward as though what he was doing was an ordinary event. The woman, still on her knees, hugged herself, rocking back and forth. She could not watch as he took the small bundle farther and farther from her reach.

Under her breath, she cried, "Lilia, my Lilia."

A path led him toward the convent entrance. Pink jasmine, although dead on the vines, still released its intoxicating scent. The heavy perfume nauseated him. He felt wobbly like he had during his first day of work on a fishing boat. He steadied himself and walked on.

The man contemplated the tall convent wall of black and grey volcanic stone and thought how ugly the structure was. It surrounded the convent, protecting the building and its courtyard. On the front wall was a double door with hinges of forged iron wide enough for a horse-drawn carriage to pass through. It also included a smaller door with an embedded turnstile large enough for a person to walk through without having to open the great doors. The oddly shaped turning door was used as a foundling wheel to leave unwanted babies safely behind convent walls in the hands of caring nuns. The convent was fortress-like, able to keep the outside world from peeking into the mysterious life of the sisters as well as the sisters from looking out.

Thankful the baby was asleep, he pushed aside his impulse to kiss her rosy cheek and risk her waking. He placed the precious infant in the turnstile and gritted his teeth as he rotated the baffle gate. It groaned, echoing a call to the specters buried in the church's yard. As he completed the spin of the turnstile, the infernal machination forever separated the infant from her family.

The baby was gone.

For a moment he was relieved. *It's done! The good sisters will know what to do.* His relief was fleeting as guilt crept in and he recognized himself to be a coward, a man without dignity, a man who could not help by providing a little extra food for the child.

He returned to the woman still crouched on the cold ground, her ashen face covered by night. Shadows played on her swollen eyes, making them appear lifeless. *Has she turned to salt as Lot's wife had?* The man touched her. She did not move. He walked around her, fearing she would fall into a heap at his feet. The cross on the steeple glowed as if reflecting the morning sun, yet it was not dawn. *Has God punished me already? Is this a warning that I have forever blackened my soul?*

The woman took a breath—the spell broken. He sighed with relief that she was still one of Earth. She stood, teetering, as a searing black grief filled her heart.

"It's better this way," he whispered as he took his sister's hand and guided her home.

The Convent

The first glimmer of dawn broke through the windows of the damp convent. August, the coldest month, was usually dismal and grey. Sister Agata hoped that today there would be enough food to satisfy the children. She was thankful that at least Santiago did not suffer extreme cold winters like her childhood home in northern Spain.

The rays of the winter sun played with the water in the sister's washbasin, casting shimmering reflections on the wall. "Time to rise: one, two, three!" Agata mimicked the words her father had used to wake his children every morning—those youthful days were never far from her thoughts. She shivered as she splashed cold water onto her flawless skin. She dressed, didn't bother with her morning prayers and rushed outside toward *El Infierno*, as the sisters jokingly called the hellish kitchen. The nun prepared breakfast every morning for the orphans living in their convent—the staple was hominy. To the delight of the children, today she would simmer the gruel in milk instead of water as she did every Sunday.

On the holiest day of the week, work details were not much different from all other days, but the disposition of the sisters changed as they welcomed parishioners to mass and relaxed a little from their rigid routines. Most of them loved singing in the choir, treasuring Sundays.

Knowing the children were about to wake with ravenous appetites, Agata quickened her pace across the chilly courtyard. Before reaching the portal, she prayed to the Virgin that today would be the thirty-two-day record of finding the turnstile empty. But her heart sank as she glimpsed a basket—thirty-one days it would remain, after all. She murmured to herself, "Another little soul who will always wonder why."

Sister Agata quietly approached the basket, peered inside and saw the infant awake and sucking on a blanket. "How unusual—you're not crying," she said to the angelic baby. "Look at you, so darling with your wavy hair. Let's get you inside, away from the winter's chill."

Most babies living in the convent had dark brown or black straight hair with matching dark eyes. They were most often the offspring of either very poor indigenous people called *Indios* or the "half breeds" that often resulted from rape or prostitution between a European and an indigenous person. This child's hair formed ringlets like the Spaniards of Agata's homeland. Her eyes were golden brown with specks of green. Unlike the usual newborns abandoned on the foundling wheel, this baby was at least three months old.

"Poor little thing, you'll be all right." Agata rushed into the kitchen, out of the wind, and set the basket a few feet from the massive stove. She lit the stove, pumped the bellows stoking the fire to life and heated milk in a large cast iron pot. Worried that the child still had not cried, the young nun took the serene baby and cradled her in her arms. For a moment, holding the baby made Agata feel peaceful and calm.

Agata unfolded the tight swaddle cloth and pressed her palm against the small frail body. The baby's temperature felt normal. Agata scooped some milk from the pot, poured the liquid into a glass, attached a rubber nipple to it and fed the baby who sucked vigorously.

"Slow down, little one!"

Once the baby was full, Agata peeked into the diaper to check the baby's gender.

"Of course, you're a girl! We have so many girls here. It must be harder to abandon boys. Is that true, sweet baby?" The infant cooed and grabbed Sister Agata's pinky. The nun placed the baby across her chest and felt the sweet exhale on her neck. She patted her back and a burp escaped.

Needing to stir the hominy into the boiling milk, Agata laid the baby in her basket and noticed a folded crinkled paper between the blankets. She unraveled it and read the inscription: *Please take care of my Lilia.*

Another Girl

Agata tasted the coarsely ground corn and deemed it soft and ready to serve. The baby had fallen asleep, giving Agata time to carry the heavy pot to the dining room. A group of children sat at the table waiting for their breakfast.

"Sisters, can one of you help me? A child was left on the turnstile this morning. Please fetch her from *El Infierno* while I serve breakfast," Agata said to Sisters Bene and Lucia.

"I wish parents would not use that horrible turnstile contraption to leave their babies. They should ring the bell. Last night was too cold to leave a baby unattended," Sister Bernadette said as she shook her head in disappointment.

"It's easier to leave a baby without having to show your face," Sister Lucia replied.

"I'm sure the baby is a girl—most of them are," said Bene, her French accent making the words sound like a caress.

"Yes, it's a girl," admitted Agata as she placed the pot of hominy on a sideboard. "I read about a time in the Roman Empire when Romans discarded infants into the city's rubbish pile if they were female or born with a deformity."

"How cruel. Sad to say, things haven't really changed," Bene lamented.

"Later, the senators contracted wet nurses to visit the dump and feed the babies in hopes that some would survive. Even the brutal Romans had some compassion, and yet two millennia later, the cycle continues," Agata complained as she searched for a ladle.

"Why do girls have such little value? Is this God's plan?" Bene asked.

"We cannot understand God's plan, that is not our prerogative. Bene, please fetch the child before she wakes, and Lucia, will you notify Mother to contact the welfare department and report we have another resident?"

"Of course." Lucia left immediately.

"I'll see to the girl and make..." Bene didn't finish, as she realized Agata was too deep in her thoughts while scooping out the hominy to hear her.

The eighteen-year-old nun had never come to a reasonable conclusion why male babies were more desirable. How easily her parents had sent her to the novitiate, even though she objected and cried endlessly. She could still hear her mother's voice retaliating against her objections, "What importance are your tears compared to the honor of serving God?" They sent her away regardless, proud of their conviction. That was what honorable families did to daughters in Catholic Spain.

It was easy for Agata's father to marry off her older sisters, but yet another dowry for his fourth daughter was too much to bear, as it jeopardized her brother's inheritance. Her father would not put his son and heir's fortune at risk by subdividing the farm and selling it off in pieces. Sister Agata, born Caterina Luz Zamora de Elizalde, was only eleven years old when the door of her family home shut behind her and she entered the convent as a novice in the province of Navarre. Years later, nearing her sixteenth birthday, she took the oath and married Christ, never to see her family again. Hence, she volunteered to go with the Franciscan Brothers and head to the upside-down part of the world. Agata hoped that in Chile, where seasons are reversed from the Northern Hemisphere, she might find a speck of freedom and adventure.

However, Agata's life in the sisterhood did not afford freedom or adventure. At a young age, she was responsible for the daily care of children, all under the age of six. Agata, along with the other nuns, played the roles of mother, father, cook, nurse, and even make-believe ponies—crawling on all fours to entertain the children.

Twenty sisters called the convent home, but only thirteen performed the entirety of chores. The non-working nuns were frail, old or ill. Mother Superior excluded herself from the mundane jobs of childcare and housekeeping. She was absent most of the day, hiding in her office, shuffling paperwork or praying in the chapel, but was always present at the dining room table when the dinner bell rang.

Sister Bene returned holding the basket. "She is sound asleep, poor child."

"Her name is Lilia. I found a note between the blankets," Agata explained.

"Like the sweet flower—what a beautiful name." Bene stared at the child.

"It makes me sad when a child is brought here. I'm always shocked at how their lives change in an instant." Agata dabbed away a tear.

"Such loss. Not many are lucky to find parents through adoption. She'll live here for only a few years and if not adopted, she'll leave to an institution."

"Bene, what happens to the children after they've moved to the institution and still can't find a home?"

"They are kept there until age sixteen, then are released to the world."

"Where do they go?"

"They look for jobs in farms, factories or the military. There are always positions in fisheries in Southern Chile. Although it is beautiful there, life is harsh and lonely in the inlets so close to Antarctica. I hear many choose their own deaths by jumping into the icy water of the fjords. Some go to the mines in the North, also in harsh conditions. They go wherever they can to forge a living."

Agata's Promise

Santiago, Chile, 1931

Time passed quickly at the convent, and the little foundling from the turnstile became an inquisitive toddler. Although Sister Agata doted on all the convent's children, she forged a special bond with Lilia, and the two became inseparable. If she left the children's room to handle other duties and had to leave Lilia with others, the tiny girl cried inconsolably until she was again close to her favorite nun.

Agitated by the noise from the tiny tot, the sisters tried to distract Lilia but rarely managed to do so. The distressed nuns, tired of hearing the high-pitched wail, often commanded Agata to take the child with her. Lilia was happy to hold on to the skirt of Agata's habit and toddle alongside her.

On one such occasion when Lilia would not stop howling, Sister Bernadette begged, "Agata, that child is upsetting the other children with her constant demands for your attention. She's loud and bothersome! Please take her away so we can have peace."

"I'm sorry, Bene, but I can't take her now," Agata peered out of the window at the darkening sky. "The wash is still on the line. I must fetch the linens before the downpour."

"I'll handle the laundry. Take Lilia to the library where we won't hear her," Sister Bernadette commanded in her heavy French accent.

"Thank you, Bene."

Agata carried Lilia to the library. She placed her on a small rug on the floor where a few toys lay strewn about. She eyed the meager bookshelves and looked for something new to read. She had read almost everything on the shelves except for some insipid free reports and manuals that arrived via mail from government agencies. She spotted a new booklet from the Department of Welfare for Children. It seemed boring, but because it was new, she sat to read. Flipping the pages quickly and seeing the many statistical graphs affirmed her suspicion that the pamphlet would not be entertaining, but the title intrigued her: *Orphans and the Perils They Still Endure.*

"Da, dada, mmm, da," Lilia babbled as she played with a tin toy tiger.

The child absorbed in her play afforded Agata a few moments to read. The writing revealed useful information, but the facts were hard to digest. She was surprised that Santiago's first orphanage opened as early as the year 1756. She learned that eighty percent of abandoned children are under one month old and born out of wedlock.

"Oh, Lilia, this is very sad," the nun spoke to Lilia as if the child understood.

Agata's reading confirmed her beliefs that many of the convent's children came from unwanted pregnancies, adulterous relationships, rape or incest. These pregnancies were culturally shameful and burdened the family both socially and economically; therefore, the infants were abandoned.

The more Agata read on the subject, the further she became depressed and blurted out loud her conclusion, "Not only do parents commit such horrific crimes, but God is a participant in allowing such things to happen to the innocent."

The indisputable facts included the survival prospects of institutionalized orphans scarcely improving in the last sixty years. Agata learned that many people were combating this dilemma and had sparked the Rights of the Child movement.

Sister Bernadette entered the room holding a large laundry basket, tiptoed over Lilia who was now asleep on the rug and dumped the linens on the couch next to Agata. Bene wondered what had caught Agata's attention so completely that she did not greet her nor even look up.

"My sweet Sister, why are tears streaming down your cheeks? What are you reading that's moved you so? You didn't even hear me come in."

"Bene, the truth is horrifying."

"What truth? Put your reading down. Biographies of martyrs are too depressing. Help me fold the sheets, please?"

"I'm not reading about Saints."

"What has put you in such a mood?"

"What I have just read! The children aren't safe. We can't provide enough for them." Agata put the booklet down and rose to help Sister Bernadette fold.

"What do you mean? We have sufficient food and clothing."

"Not nearly enough! Of course, our children live in grandeur compared to government institutions where orphans die at alarming rates. Did you know the mortality rate between newborns and eight-year-olds is seventy-four percent in those places?"

"No, it can't be! That figure must be incorrect."

"These are government statistics."

"If true, it's because the government is stretched to its limit. At least in our convent, we can thank the Vatican for its help," Sister Bernadette said as she grabbed another sheet.

"But we too have had our share of loss without explanation for why these children died. We shrug it off and say, 'It's the Lord's will!' I can no longer accept that! God should not test children!"

"Be careful, Agata. Don't blame God!"

"It's how I feel, Bene."

"It's blasphemy; don't say such things! Sickness happens everywhere. When our children are severely ill, we summon the doctor, but death happens everywhere. It doesn't discriminate."

"But the doctors don't tell us the child could have been saved with better food or perhaps by an earlier intervention. We can do better for these small lives." Agata swallowed her tears.

"We inherit these problems—they're too great for us to solve. When things are tight and Rome stops sending money, our priests help. They collect more alms. Although with the economy in a downward spiral and their commitment to the elderly or the sick and poor, the Sunday collection isn't enough to come around to our little charges."

"Yes, Bene! The priests do try, but they have their own agendas and problems. When things go especially wrong, when both the government and Vatican stipends dry out at the same time, we can count on the women of Santiago. They always come through with their bake sales."

Bene smiled, "And their *brazo de reina* cakes always sell out at the bazaar. I love their generosity. They even bake some for us."

"I wish I had a slice of it right now with extra filling of *dulce de leche*." Agata could almost taste the butterscotch cream filling.

"Bene, children often come with tokens like bracelets, right?"

"Yes, they do."

"Is it because these trinkets might help establish identity and give the orphans a chance to find and reclaim their families?"

"I assume so."

"But there is a flaw in that?"

Bene looked puzzled.

Agata continued, "Such tokens present problems. Do you remember there was a note in Lilia's basket? I assume it was scribbled by her mother. It only said, 'Take care of my Lilia' and nothing else."

"Then there's hope she can find her family."

"No, there wasn't a surname."

"And perhaps it's because the family doesn't want to be found."

"How could that be, Bene? How could a mother not want to find her child? I bet after a short period of time, her remorse is great and her heart aches with regret."

"Not everyone feels the same way or wants to bring them back. A child out of wedlock brings such shame to the family."

"I know, but it doesn't make sense to me. The child is so much more important than the shame."

"I've seen infants come with gold religious medallions around their necks with names and birthdates engraved on the back. The poor mothers want to leave a loving clue to their offspring." Bene shook her head and lowered her eyes.

"Those babies are lucky to have a connection."

"No. Mother Superior sells all the trinkets to help buy food and necessities. The children never keep their tokens." Bene looked pained.

"And to think those gold medallions were probably the last thing of value owned by the mother."

"Stop thinking about it; it does no good. The children have us and we love them. We are now their mothers." Bene picked up the neatly stacked laundry basket. "Cheer up. It isn't as bad as you think." She winked at Agata as she left the room.

Agata placed the booklet on the shelf and knelt by Lilia, who still held the toy in her hand while sleeping. She stroked the child's hair. "Lilia, my little angel. I'm sorry you've lost your family. It'll haunt you forever. I too was abandoned by my parents when they forced me into sisterhood, but I suppose it is not the same thing. No, it isn't. I know where I come from."

Agata picked up the sleeping child, sat back down on the couch and rocked her. The child's steady breathing was soothing, but it could not stop the deep sorrow growing within the young nun. She noticed that Lilia was still too thin. "What a beautiful child you are. What will become of you?" Agata's tears fell and disappeared in Lilia's wavy hair. "I love you so much, my little sliver of a girl. I love your curls, your tickly toes and every tiny bit of you. I wish I were your real mother to love and protect you forever." The nun searched the ceiling as if God were looking down on her and spoke in hushed tones, "I baptize Lilia as my own. I choose to be her godmother forever." She hesitated, a little ashamed of her declaration, and then added, "Amen."

The Rights of the Child

Señora Gertrudis Alvarez, a social worker, agreed with the new idea germinating among teachers, doctors and civil workers that advocated for the social, medical and educational needs of minors. The movement was called *The Rights of the Child*. She understood what was important and necessary for a child to grow up healthy, educated and a valuable member of society. A new law was proposed to the federal government to dictate that all orphans under six years of age be transferred from convents and orphanages and placed in foster homes. They reasoned that growing up in a family environment would prove a better start for orphans than in institutions or convents. The bill came to the president's desk at the *Palacio de la Moneda*. Humble volunteers along with Señora Alvarez begged for action.

The compassionate social worker became well acquainted with elite leaders and teachers of the capital city. She followed the teachings of Italian physician and educator Maria Montessori and paid attention to those who promoted the rights and betterment of children, such as delegate Cora Mayers, pediatrician Luis Morquio and the great writer Gabriela Mistral. Señora Alvarez studied what was necessary for her orphans to thrive unencumbered by lack of nutrition or education. The notion that a boy is a small man and a girl is a small woman no longer applied. A child is not a small adult but a different entity altogether, and they deserve different rights.

After delivering a compelling speech to government officials and merchants, Señora Alvarez went to a nearby café. She caught a glimpse of the tall Spaniard, Don Manuel Villavicencio, sitting alone at a nearby table. He recently had stepped down as chief manager of McKenna Enterprises for a new prestigious role as Minister of Transportation. Señora Alvarez walked toward his table and put on a warm smile. "Don Villavicencio, congratulations on your appointment. I read about it in this morning's paper."

"Good morning, Señora *Capitan*! I enjoyed your speech this morning." Don Villavicencio rose to greet the woman.

"Thank you, but please, Señor, don't use that awful nickname. I'm only a widow, certainly not a captain. I don't deserve such praise or to be included in the same category as our brave military men."

"I'm sorry, Señora Alvarez, but you've managed to push the most stubborn magistrates to your way of thinking better than any captain I've ever known. I was impressed with your speech, and I could see so was the President. Will you join me, please, for a cup of tea?" He rose and pulled out a chair for Señora Alvarez.

"Thank you. It is I who am impressed with your new position of Minister of Transportation," Alvarez said as he graciously helped her into her seat.

"My wife is not happy! She's upset that I'm not retiring and our plans for travel are put on hold yet again. I couldn't turn down the honor. Unlike her, I've had enough of traveling. Shall I order you a tea?"

"No, thank you, I'll only be a minute. I understand her yearning to travel. I too would love to see a small part of the world."

"I agreed with parts of your speech, Señora. Proposing legislation for every child to have the right to a good education and to start life in a family setting is a grand idea. I hope it will become law. Let me give you my card. Perhaps we can discuss this further." Don Villavicencio reached into his pocket and pulled out a calling card.

"Thank you. I'm happy to hear that you side with the children. I heard wonderful things about your previous firm, McKenna, being responsible for funding the building of the school. And they say there is already a waiting list. Imagine, even before the foundation is poured. What will it be called?"

"The McKenna Academy."

"Naturally, I should have guessed it. The McKennas have given so much to the people of Santiago. We appreciate their devotion to our fair city."

"It will not be built in Santiago."

"In Valparaiso?"

"You're close. It will be in Viña del Mar."

"How wonderful!"

"Did you know it will be a school for girls?"

The social worker was surprised. "A lovely change from the norm."

"We already have great schools for boys."

"I'm delighted, Señor. Equal footing for the girls. I hope that some of our underprivileged orphans will have a chance to attend your school.

Perhaps the McKenna brothers will offer scholarships for our girls in the orphanages?" The tireless social worker never missed an opportunity to help the children under her jurisdiction.

"You'll have to ask the Ministry of Education. The McKennas are only paying for the building; they have no jurisdiction over tuition or scholarships."

"I'm sure you still have influence."

"Not really, Señora Cap...pardon, I mean, Señora Alvarez."

"We must fight for every child to have rights under the law and not to differentiate between children of different social status. We must give every child an education. Don't you agree, Don Villavicencio?"

"You mean the illegitimate?"

"Señor! 'Illegitimate' is such a barbaric word, it should not exist in our vocabulary. Children are children regardless of how they show up. But yes, I'm speaking of them."

"I tend to agree somewhat, but the system cannot afford to give everyone a great education."

"We must not continue to be guilty of how we treat the abandoned." The social worker's voice grew louder. The people at the next table turned their heads to stare at the couple.

"I'm not guilty of anything, Señora, and please lower your voice."

"Children should not be punished because of the circumstances of their birth. They don't choose! They find themselves here and should not bear the fault of their parents."

"Do we agree that their parents share the blame, and bad seeds sire bad seeds? After all, children are so much like their parents, perhaps it is something that they are born with."

"Nonsense! Surely you don't believe that!"

"It's Catholic doctrine we are all born with sin." Don Villavicencio took a delicate sip of tea.

"With all due respect, Señor, I'm a devout Catholic, but I don't give credence to everything priests say. I do not believe a baby is born with sin."

"Are you claiming to be a Catholic and not believe in original sin?"

"I'm not educated in the clergy, but I feel God has blessed us with free will, and I don't believe he burdened us. Sin is something we acquire when we understand right from wrong," Señora Alvarez tried to soften her tone.

"The archbishop is joining me on Sunday for dinner. I'll share your modern ideas with him and ask for his opinion on the matter," Don Villavicencio spat out his words, rose from the table, tipped his hat and walked out of the café.

Señora Alvarez was stunned but resolved to continue her talk with the powerful man. She followed him out and yelled after him. "Sir, I'm reminded of what Paulo Freire said about this matter."

Don Villavicencio turned to the short, stubborn woman.

Señora Alvarez's gaze bore through the man. "Freire said, 'Washing one's hands of the conflict between the powerful and the powerless means that you side with the powerful, and it does not mean that you are neutral.' Señor, I believe in Freire's words. You must take the side of the powerless. Children rely on us. You cannot remain silent."

"You are an idealist." He nodded and walked away.

A week after her speech, President Arturo Alessandri Palma signed the legislation agreeing that all orphans of pre-school age would be placed in foster homes. The decree was a great win for the social worker.

It took only six months from the law's enactment to the removal of children from the *Convento de San Francisco,* where Agata and the sisters lived. The convent, now empty of children, saddened the nuns who felt as if they had lost their purpose. The Vatican quickly assigned new jobs to the sisters. The younger nuns with aptitude became elementary school teachers or nurses. Agata was designated to become a nurse.

The nursing students reported to the largest hospital in the city. They worked alongside certified trained nurses and doctors and learned their skills directly from them and by close observation. They spent mornings at the hospital and afternoons in classrooms at the University of Santiago. The nuns who would be teachers, attended a smaller teaching college and after only a year of study, were granted a license.

Sister Bernadette found herself working with terminally ill patients who languished in their family homes. Her job was to ease the sick into the afterlife as well as provide solace for their families. The older nuns were not assigned to any profession but were still capable of tasks such as collecting clothing, food and money for the poor. They spent most of their day knocking on doors and begging for alms.

Agata did not like nursing and would have preferred teaching but was grateful for the opportunity to learn any profession. Mornings trailing the medical staff at the hospital were difficult for her. The afternoons were easier, as she enjoyed studying the medical vernacular and biology at school. The Vatican's goal to turn nuns into working members of the community while serving their faith was a brilliant idea. After two years, they received a nursing certificate. The program afforded the sisters a life-long skill while filling Chile's void of medical personnel. Their salaries helped bring money into the convents. After a long day at the hospital and school, the nurses returned to the convent and completed additional household chores.

Agata was happiest when patients recuperated as she watched their frowns turn to smiles. She relished bringing meals to those whose appetites finally returned. The most joyous of chores was discharging a patient. With the severely infirmed, Agata was emotionally overwhelmed. She loathed tasks such as cleaning infected wounds or scraping burned skin, but most horrific was listening to the lamentations of people in pain. Her suffering for them made her body tremble. The stench of bodily fluids, gruesome open wounds and vermin in stools caused her to run to the lavatory and vomit. The staff laughed at her, mocked her sensitivity and nicknamed her the "princess nun."

Even the vile smells and groans of the sick were easier for Agata to withstand than when patients clung to life and then, exhausted, finally gave into death. At these moments she could feel her blood drain to her feet, and she became dizzy and sometimes faint. More than once the staff sent her back to the convent in shame.

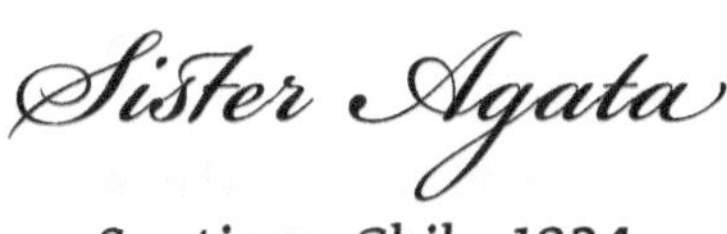

Sister Agata

Santiago, Chile, 1934

The exhausted nun spent most of her nights twisting and turning in bed. In the wee hours of the morning when Agata finally succumbed to sleep, she dreamed of her childhood in Spain.

"Rojelio, where are you?"

"Silly goat! I'm right above you, on our branch."

"No, you're not. I can't see you, it's so dark."

"It's not dark. It's morning."

"Hold my hand and help me climb." Agata extended her arm and felt Rojelio's grip as he boosted her up the apple tree.

A loud knock startled Agata awake. She disliked coming out of her dreams in such a brutal manner and finding herself in her dreary bedroom.

"Sister Agata, wake up, it's late! It's the second time this week. Please come down and set the table!" Sister Bernadette knocked again.

"I'm sorry!" Agata yawned. "I'll be right down. Thank you, Bene."

"You'll be in trouble with Mother."

"I'll hurry."

So many nights, Rojelio crept into her dreams. The languid summer days of her youth, playing games among the groves and vineyards, were so far in her past that she was not sure what was real and what was now fantasy.

The son of the family's washerwoman, Rojelio, was her companion. While his mother washed her family's clothes and linens in an outdoor tub, the children roamed the fields. He was Agata's only friend. In her dreams she could never see him clearly, as his face was always obscured. When awake, she was unsure she remembered what he looked like, as she tried to age him and not think of him as a boy. In her shadowed dreams, they played a game of hide-and-seek or climbed high above the ground in their favorite tree. She was sorry that time had blurred his image.

Agata remembered parts of his face—the most vivid was his nose. It had been upturned and covered with freckles. Some of the orphans in her care reminded her of his features, like those with oddly protruding ears or rust-colored hair. Lilia had sparked Rojelio's image into focus by having the same color eyes. She fantasized that she had given birth to her favorite child with him as the father. Her daydreams were sacrilegious and betrayed Catholic doctrine, but Agata could not help it.

The nun missed her childhood friend, but even more than him, she missed Lilia. Three years had passed since the government officials took the children away from the convent. Most sisters felt the same emptiness, but Agata spent hours worrying about Lilia and whether she had found a good home. Agata lost weight, became pale and began to appear much older than her years. When she awoke from dreaming, an uneasy but pleasurable feeling made it difficult for her to rise from bed. She did not know of wet dreams, and after such an event, fear took over her body and she trembled. She would lie still until the feelings eased. One such time, lying in bed with her eyes closed, she wondered if Rojelio had taken a wife and if he had sired children. She preferred to imagine she was his wife and that he kissed her over and over again.

*****

Navarro, Spain, 1921

Overheated from playing in the hot afternoon sun, Rojelio and Agata cooled themselves on a branch of the apple tree. The tree's leaves and blossoms of white with pink edges gave plenty of shade. The young boy climbed to a higher branch and Agata followed him. They stood teetering side by side, precariously looking downward while giggling with fright.

Rojelio kissed her cheek causing a frown on Agata's face, "What are you doing?"

"Kissing you. You'll need seven more for luck. It's tradition on your birthday." Rojelio kissed her closed lips.

"Yuck! Not on my lips!" Agata wiped her mouth with her hand.

"My brother said girls like kisses."

"I don't care what your stupid brother said!"

Agata shot him a dirty look and climbed down the tree. She ran home ashamed but dared not tell anyone what had happened.

***

Santiago, 1934

Agata had pushed him away but now wished she had not. The thought haunted her as she relived the memory of it throughout the day. She became obsessed about what a real kiss would feel like. Even though such memories brought desire, she prayed that these random thoughts would cease tormenting her.

She thought about broaching the subject with Sister Bernadette in private but remembered Mother Superior's rattled caution: *Devils and imps play on young women in the witching hours of night. Be warned! Bridle your mind. Think thoughts of purity and pray continuously.* Although it was against the rules, Bene often sneaked into Agata's bedroom where the two talked throughout the night as they lay side by side on the small bed.

A second knock jolted Agata. "Sister, did you fall back asleep? Breakfast is on the table!" Sister Bernadette's voice was breathy from having run up the stairs.

"Yes, Bene, I'm up. I'll be right down." Agata jumped out of bed.

"Hurry! I thought you'd be downstairs by now!"

Skipping her morning toiletry routine to save time, Agata dressed in her habit. *It's better to be unwashed than late. I hope Mother doesn't notice.*

Sister Agata hurried downstairs to the dining room where the other sisters were already eating. Luckily, Mother Superior was busy spreading jam on her roll and ignored Agata's tardiness. Sister Bernadette winked at the tardy nun. Agata was grateful that someone had completed her chore and set the table, abating Mother Superior's anger.

The frazzled Agata sat down and began praying silently before reaching for the teapot. She stirred milk and sugar into her cup and took a bite of unbuttered toast. A knot formed in her stomach. Feelings of terror returned and made it difficult to swallow the dry bread so she used her napkin to spit it out.

Agata was overcome with a feeling of wanting to run. She placed her teaspoon on the table very quietly, trying not to rattle the silverware and alerting the sisters. A cold tingling sensation crawled up her spine, making her feel as if she might lose control of her bowels. She felt an unseen danger about to manifest itself. Looking to her left and then to her right, she was unable to decide which way was safest to leave the room unnoticed. *I can't go right towards the courtyard because I'd have to pass right by Mother's all-seeing eye. If I leave on the left, Sister Bernadette will notice and might stop me as well. I don't like how she sometimes devours me with her gaze. I love Bene, but I wish she'd mind her own business.*

Sister Agata chose the left and managed to leave the dining room without any interrogations. On her tiptoes she climbed the dark wooden stairs and tried not to stumble, holding the rail and steadying herself with every step. An unspeakable fear gripped her chest, making it hard to breathe. The same recurring malaise that had begun when the children were taken away returned, randomly and without reason. The long hallway seemed to sway from side to side, reminding her of the scary carnival ride she endured as a child. Arriving at her bedroom, she collapsed on the bed.

As the room spun, Sister Agata managed to pull open her nightstand drawer and search for rosary beads. She found them and clutched them in her palm but quickly placed them back in the drawer. Staring at her crucifix hung on the wall, she said in a loud voice, "I will not pray because you remain silent." Agata's heart palpitated in irregular beats. The quiet was shattered by the clicking sound of footsteps approaching as she realized it was too late to bar the door with her chair against the doorknob.

Sister Bernadette did not knock and ran into the room. "Are you ill? Has the dizziness come back?"

"No, Bene," Agata lied. "I'm fine but need to rest."

Sister Bernadette ignored Agata's plea and took her shaking hands in hers and held them. "I'm here to help you."

"Give me a moment to compose myself."

"I'm not leaving. I don't care what you say!" Bene rubbed Agata's cold hands. Feeling Agata's tug to free them, Bene squeezed tighter, refusing to let go. Bene proceeded to kiss the younger nun's fingers and moved her lips slowly down to the wrist. Agata flinched and tried to pull away but stopped at the feel of Bene's soft lips. It was comforting, so she allowed the kisses. Agata liked the pleasurable sensation. Sister Bernadette lay down next to Agata and made herself comfortable. Their bodies touched as they stared into each other's eyes. Bene searched for acceptance; Agata was confused.

The twenty-three-year-old virgin knew nothing of love, nor much about anything concerning sex. Bene was not new to love, and her touch sparked desire in Agata while she tried to resist. She desired Rojelio. *Rojelio, what do you look like now that you are a man? Climb the apple tree and kiss me!* Agata flushed at her thoughts. Bene, seeing Agata's cheeks turn rosy, became confident. Both women desired intimacy, but they were not a pair. Agata wondered if men's lips were different from Sister Bernadette's. Agata did not move.

"You're beautiful, Sister." Bene's voice was melodious.

"Stop, Bene, please!" Agata pushed Bene away. The bewildered Bene rose from the bed but did not leave the room. Brazenly, she moved to the head of the bed, climbed behind Agata and sat up against the headboard. She placed Agata's head on her lap, untied the strings of her stiff cap and slowly ran her fingers through her short hair. An involuntary moan escaped Agata's lips as she let herself melt into calming sensations. Agata released her fear. Sister Bernadette noticed the change in her friend's breathing and smiled.

"I want to be near you," Bene whispered.

Agata did not respond.

"Share your secrets with me," Bene continued in a breathy voice.

"My thoughts are garbled! I miss the children." Agata allowed Bene to massage her scalp. Bene moved her hands lower and rubbed Agata's neck.

"Children do not occupy my mind, but you do."

"I can think only of them."

"You've carried on too long over the children. Stop talking and enjoy my touch."

"I miss my Lilia, and the pain of losing her doesn't go away. It feels as if it were only yesterday when they were removed. If only I could be sure that she is safe in a good home. I worry about all the children."

"I'm certain they are happy and feel lucky to have parents. Perhaps they even have a sibling or two. It's more than we could ever give. Now be quiet and relax." Bene traced tiny circles with her finger along Agata's arms.

"Without children, I no longer feel this convent is home. I'm not the only one affected by this. Haven't you noticed how somber the other sisters are—such little laughter? They go about their business as if they were machines, hardly acknowledging one another, performing their duties in a trance-like state."

"You've misread the signs. They are quiet and serve the Holy Spirit. I suggest you pray more. God will grant the happiness you seek."

"Do you remember the feel of their chubby arms around your neck?"

"Of course." Bene slid out of bed and motioned for Agata to turn over.

Agata turned on her stomach. "I can still hear their giggles in my ear. Why couldn't they keep this convent as an orphanage?"

"It's better for them." Bene rubbed Agata's back. "It's important for the children to be with families. What could we teach them of the world? We nuns are more like mice than women, huddled together in this dark and ugly place. Now stop talking and enjoy." Bene dragged her hands on Agata's lower back, moved them over her buttocks and caressed her thighs.

"Stop! Bene, do not go further!"

"I want to love you."

Agata gasped and turned to face Bene. "I'm sorry, but I can't be with you. Not even if you were a man. I've already sinned by such thoughts from which I may never be able to atone. I will keep my vows intact."

Seeing the hurt on Bene's face, Agata softened her voice, "But I do love you, although differently. All people need human touch, but we cannot fall from grace. My nervous affliction is probably caused by such solitude, but that is our chosen life and the only way for a nun."

Bene rose and left the room. Agata felt guilty for what transpired between her and Bene but even more so from how she had failed her vow to protect Lilia forever.

The River

Maipo Valley, Chile, 1934

Lilia ran through fields of yellow mustard bushes and wild artichokes. The landscape gave way to a field of red poppies growing on the rocky slopes towards a meandering river. The sky was painted light blue with white and grey clouds while the mountains wore garbs of purple crowned in snow. Lilia did not notice any of this. Her singular thought was to reach her favorite spot and sit. She ran and did not stop until she was hardly able to breathe. Her bare and callused feet did not feel the pebbles and roots beneath them. There was her rock, glistening as the sun hit its granite surface. She sat in triumph, having succeeded in running away from Mamita's ubiquitous eyes.

Slipping a hand into her dirty dress pocket, her small fingers felt the still warm *pancito*. Lilia caressed the prize she had stolen from the clay bowl, pulling it from her pocket as her eyes widened with pleasure. She giggled when she placed it on her lap. Salivating, she admired the beautiful round roll with the cross Mamita had slashed on its top prior to baking. She opened her mouth wide and tore into the soft bread. It was gone in a few bites. Searching her lap for crumbs, she spotted a few, picked them up between her fingers and put them in her mouth.

The small treat did not placate Lilia's hunger. She rose from the rock to hunt for berries that might be left on raspberry bushes. Seeing none, she wondered if the pretty blooms all around her tasted as delicious as the ones Mamita used on salads. The beautiful red-petal blooms looked as if they were crinkled paper. Her stomach grumbled.

Searching for the biggest and brightest bloom, Lilia snapped the stem of one, delicately pulled out a petal and placed it on her tongue. It tasted bitter, but she enjoyed chewing and swallowing. Running her tongue on the seeds before biting into them, she was surprised they were crunchy as she chomped them between her teeth. It appeased her hunger.

Lilia loved the beautiful river that lay ahead sparkling in the sun. She skipped towards it and remembered the stern caution from both Mamita and Bernardo. *Stay away from the river's edge.* The child hesitated for a few seconds and entertained thoughts of returning to the rock but chose the riverbank, as the gurgling water's song was mesmerizing.

The five-year-old did not like spending most of her days alone. She entertained herself but wished she had a friend. The *ranchos* in the valley were distant from one another, too far for Lilia to scout a playmate. Whenever she asked her older siblings to play, Ana and her brothers were quick with excuses and denied her attention. The family worked long hours in the fields and by the end of the day were exhausted.

Why does Ana get angry when I call our mother Mamita? Why don't I call Bernardo Papá? Lilia snapped the stem of another poppy and ate the seeds while pondering her family but could not formulate what troubled her. A memory began to take shape in her mind of a woman wearing a black dress singing as Lilia sat in her lap.

"I'm dizzy," Lilia said aloud as if she were addressing the trees. She pulled a petal from the crimson poppy and popped it in her mouth and smiled, as she now liked the acrid taste. She heard the river babbling furiously over rocks and call to her above the cacophony, "Lilia!"

"I'll see what the river wants," Lilia kept conversing with no one. A wave of nausea came upon her as her knees threatened to buckle. She stopped and regained her balance. She felt as if the ground moved and yelled out, "*Temblor!*"

Lilia became apprehensive when her legs wobbled and realized it was not a tremor but her own body causing the uneasiness. She again steadied herself and said, "I'm thirsty."

Walking closer to the river, she heard it again call her name. She answered, "I'm coming, River." She walked in a zigzag gait with outstretched arms, pretending to be a bird.

Lilia sauntered around the rocky terrain and felt her skin warmed by the sun. Breathing in the earthy scent of the hills, the gentle wind made her twirl and laugh with delight. Continuing to spread her arms, she imagined she was flying through the clouds. She joined a chorus of crows. "Squawk! Squawk!" No longer hungry, she felt happy. The river lay a short distance ahead in its azure colors, mirroring the sky.

Lilia froze as she caught sight of a woman standing in the middle of the river. In an instant, her memory crystallized in photo-like stills, recognizing the figure as the visitor to her dreams who sang lullabies.

"Hello," Lilia addressed the woman and walked closer to the river's edge. She walked faster to greet her but tripped on a rock and nearly fell. "I know you. You've come from my dreams. Are you an angel?"

The image smiled at the girl, then rose from the water until she hovered in midair.

Lilia continued, "Will you sing to me again? I remember your songs. I hear them when I go to sleep. Will you tickle my feet and make me laugh?"

Walking knee deep into the river, Lilia reached out to the figure, who stooped down from her stance and reached for her hand. The apparition ordered, "No, my child, I wish for you to sing to me the song of St. Francis."

The words and melody immediately came to Lilia's mind, and she sang out.

All creatures of our God and king
Lift up your voices and with us sing
Alleluia, alleluia
Thou burning with golden beam
Thou silver moon with softer gleam
Alleluia, alleluia, alleluia, alleluia, alleluia,

Thou rushing wind that art so strong
Ye clouds that sail in heaven in a long
Alleluia, alleluia
Thou rising morn in praise rejoice
Ye light of evening find a voice
Alleluia, alleluia, alleluia, alleluia, alleluia

When Lilia finished, she gleefully screamed out, "Sister Agata!" The child felt happy that the woman had come to comfort her. Lilia knew she loved the woman as much as she now loves Mamita. The ghostlike figure let go of Lilia's hand and floated higher into the air and blew a kiss as the skirt of her habit swayed back and forth. The woman then began to sink, descend into the rapid river waters and disappear.

The landscape seemed to spin as Lilia gasped for air. The cold river water needled her legs, making it difficult to walk. Wanting the river to release its grip, she struggled to the bank. With stiff legs, the child managed to reach the pebbled shore before her world turned black.

The Social Worker's Visit

Myrta, or Mamita as the children called her, searched for Lilia. She checked the barn and the chicken coop but could not find her. She ran around the house calling her name. Myrta had not seen the child since breakfast, and it was now noon. She thought it unusual that Lilia was not underfoot pestering her when lunch was almost ready. Myrta scanned the hectares of her land, hoping to see her husband and children coming home for the midday break. Finally spotting them, she was discouraged that Lilia was not with them and became more agitated. At least, she thought, they could help look for the child.

"Have you seen Lilia?" Myrta yelled loudly, cuffing her hands around her mouth.

The family was too far to hear Mamita's words. They hand-signaled her to wait until they were closer. Impatient, Myrta ran towards them. Bernardo saw his wife's deep frown and addressed his children, "Lilia must be missing again." When Myrta reached them, Bernardo could see tears forming in his wife's eyes.

"I was hoping Lilia was with you. She's nowhere to be found. Please, scatter about and let's all look for her!"

"Give us a minute to wash off the dirt and sweat," Bernardo said with disappointment in his voice.

The family quickened their pace to the outdoor basin and took turns washing. Myrta tried to rush them, "Hurry, fetch your horses, she might have traveled far. Spread out in all directions. I'll stay here in case she returns."

"We left the horses in the field. They need to graze and rest. We'll go on foot," Bernardo said.

"You've got one in the barn," Myrta corrected.

"Muchacho is still healing from *mal seco*."

"I don't care—take Muchacho!"

Ana, the middle child, whined, "Can't we eat first? I'm hungry and the food will get cold. Lilia's safe. She's playing and running in the fields as she always does!"

"I'm not going to look for her until I've eaten," a disgruntled Rafael, the third and laziest of Myrta's children, declared. The eldest son, Rodrigo, stayed quiet.

"You're right, Myrta. I'll take Muchacho. He should be healed by now. We've much work to do this afternoon. There's no reason we all should waste time looking for her. I'll find the troublesome child. Let our children eat," Bernardo ordered.

"Thank you," Ana said as she entered the house.

"Hurry, Bernardo. I'll keep your soup warm on the stove," Myrta said gratefully.

Inside the small house the teenage siblings served themselves. They tore the buns into small pieces and dropped them in the soup. As they ate, they heard Muchacho galloping away.

Myrta looked out of the window, checked the big stallion's trot and was pleased to see the horse had recovered and regained his natural gait. A sense of relief overtook her as there was one less problem to deal with. As she watched the handsome animal break into a run, she noticed a car racing up the hill creating a billowing dust trail. Very few cars traversed the unpopulated valley, but one such vehicle was a Model T belonging to Señora Alvarez.

As Bernardo rode away, he also noticed the dust rising in the distance and deduced the social worker was paying them an unexpected visit. He kicked his horse hard, spurring the great animal to gallop faster. *I should beat that child for always wandering away. The little money we get fostering isn't worth the trouble.* Another much more sinister thought crept into his mind. *What if she's fallen into the river? What legal problems would rain on my head?* He calmed himself. *No one would fuss over such a tiny problem, an orphan, when Chile was suffocating from so many of them!*

Mamita, her distress rising, screamed at her brood, "Get up from the table! Señora Alvarez is coming! Spread out and help your father search for Lilia. Now!" Then she murmured to herself, "Oh God, why do these things always happen to me?"

"Just our luck! She decides to pay us a visit just when the brat is missing," the youngest son grunted as he picked up his bowl and placed it on a shelf for later consumption. Ana placed her bowl beside her brother's. Rodrigo slurped his soup directly from the bowl and, in a few gulps, emptied it. He grabbed another bun and ate it as he went outdoors to search for the annoying child who continually tormented their peaceful lives.

Mamita was first to greet Señora Alvarez. "Good day, Señora Alvarez. What a lovely surprise!"

"*Buenas tardes*, Myrta. I realized this morning that I haven't checked on Lilia in almost six months! It is hard to come so far, but I thought today was a beautiful day to drive to the country."

"It is. Come in, Señora."

The women made small talk. Myrta served while thinking how lucky it was that she had baked *pancitos* this very morning and had something good to serve the social worker. They sipped tea as Myrta bragged about how well Lilia was and how the child had gained weight.

"Myrta, you said that Lilia would be here shortly, and it's been almost an hour."

"She's out with Bernardo," Myrta lied. Señora Alvarez smiled, elated that the child was finally receiving attention from the father figure of the house.

"Nothing to worry about. You know how children are when they're having fun." Mamita felt heat emanating from her flushed cheeks and hoped the social worker did not notice her deception. She was relieved when she heard the horse's hooves racing up the pathway.

"Myrta! Come quickly!" Bernardo yelled.

The women ran outside.

"I don't know what happened," Bernardo's voice cracked.

Mamita screamed. Lilia lay unconscious in Bernardo's arms. Myrta took Lilia in her arms, carried the lifeless girl inside and placed her in the matrimonial bed, tucked in a corner of the room. The children slept upstairs in an open loft.

"What has happened?" Señora Alvarez kept her demeanor calm. She touched Lilia's cool forehead. She then patted the child's thighs and called her name, but Lilia did not respond. She placed her ear on the girl's nose and felt air. With a sigh of relief, she said, "Thank God, she's breathing."

The bottom of the child's dress was drenched. Señora Alvarez wondered why Myrta would lie about Lilia being out with Bernardo and surmised she had gone into the river alone. She also had seen a horse ride away as she approached the house and was now sure it had been Bernardo.

"Was she alone by the river?" Señora Alvarez tried to contain her anger.

"I found her on the riverbank. I couldn't wake her," Bernardo confessed.

Señora Alvarez's suspicions that the foster parents were not properly caring for Lilia were confirmed. Hoping the child was not severely injured, she scanned her body for open wounds. Finding none, she relaxed. She wanted to berate the couple but realized it was not the time for accusations. The child needed immediate medical attention. She forced herself to stay calm as she felt a sharp pain in the middle of her chest. Her doctor had warned her that stress and high blood pressure could prove problematic. He had begged her to consider early retirement, but she had refused. Disregarding her health, she decided to continue working for the children who needed her. Retirement was not an option.

"Help me get Lilia into the car, and we'll go into town to the doctor's office."

Bernardo pleaded, "No, please leave her here. The doctor is rarely in his office. He makes rounds during the day and could be anywhere in the valley. Find the doctor and bring him here. She'll be more comfortable here."

"You're right. Lilia can rest, but do not leave her side. Not even for a moment. Keep her warm under blankets and if she wakes, give her milk."

The drive to town was narrow and the hills steep. The twists and turns of the landscape along with unpaved roads made the drive treacherous. It was arduous for Señora Alvarez to travel faster than twenty kilometers per hour. Last year's rains turned insignificant potholes into detrimental ones, forcing her to maneuver around them. She hoped the doctor was not on a house call in the vast valley, for if so, she might wait hours for his return. The grueling roads, the pressure in her heart and worry about Lilia made the drive feel even longer.

Upon reaching the main road, *El Camino Real,* and turning right, Señora Alvarez headed straight for the doctor's office. The doctor was her longtime friend. He cared for all the children placed in the valley under her tutelage. Before placing a child in a home, the doctor examined each one from head to foot. If the child did not receive a clean bill of health, the child was sent to a government institution or a hospital.

The elderly doctor was kind and dedicated his life to helping the poor. No one remembered his name—he was simply addressed as *el doctor*. He spoke to the rural residents of the Maipo Valley with a loving tone, no matter their social status. The emphatic social worker worried for the overworked doctor, as he was the sole medical practitioner within a fifty-five-kilometer radius.

The grey-haired, balding doctor helped everyone, even the poorest farmers who hardly managed to squeeze out a living from selling their produce. The rural inhabitants traded with one another and rarely did a peso exchange hands. The doctor, along with carpenters, sheepherders, cheese makers and anyone with a trade or product, used the barter system. All products were currency and welcomed in exchange for services or commodities.

The most impoverished of his patients were the foster children, yet because of these orphans, the doctor earned a little money from the government. This allowed him to purchase medicine and equipment from Santiago. As Señora Alvarez approached the doctor's small clinic, she was relieved to spot his car.

When Señora Alvarez returned to Bernardo's farm with the doctor in tow, Lilia was awake and sitting up on the couple's bed. She looked tired and weak and did not remember what had happened. The doctor examined the child and found a poppy petal between her teeth and cheek. He and the social worker deduced immediately what had transpired. Señora Alvarez noticed Lilia's still thin frame. Because of this, and in addition to the lie Myrta told as to Lilia's whereabouts, she made the decision to find a more suitable and permanent home for Lilia. But for now, and until she could find such a home, Lilia would have to remain at Myrta and Bernardo's farm.

Master Puppeteer

The return trip from Maipo was a blur for Señora Alvarez. She was astonished when she realized she was already at the city limits. It felt as if the car had driven itself. She was focused on finding new parents for Lilia. *The girl deserves better than what the poor farmers provide.* Trying to recall the names of people in her circle of influence and jarring her memory as to anyone who might be encouraged to take in a child occupied her mind. Checking off a mental list of possible prospective parents, she wondered why there were always more children in need of parents than couples willing to foster. There were so many children in even worse circumstances. The Señora tried to stop thinking of Lilia and calm her mind, but the incident had so agitated her that she was resolved to quickly find a solution.

Standing on her front porch, Alvarez fumbled in her old black-leather purse and searched for her key. Looking between the papers, notes and handkerchiefs cluttering the inside of her purse was to no avail. Brushing her fingers against paper bills and coins, she finally felt the heavy key. When she pulled it out, a calling card fell on the porch step. She picked it up and glanced at the printed name: *Don Manuel Villavicencio.*

Wondering why she had not placed the card in her index box, Señora Alvarez entered the dark house and turned on a lamp. She kicked off her shoes and went into the kitchen to make a cup of chamomile tea. Taking a match from her matchbox, pressing the match head onto the striker and quickly dragging the match several times, it finally sparked into a flame. The act of lighting the burner reminded her of her endless votive offerings in church, and out of habit she began to pray aloud. The devout Catholic always followed this ritual, especially when there was a special favor that needed filling. St. Jerome Emiliano was a favorite target for her prayers as he was known for granting wishes dealing with children's welfare.

Alvarez began to pray. "Dear St. Jerome, mighty warrior. Your grace. Help me find a better home for a tiny girl who is but skin and bones. She's like a baby bird fallen from a nest."

The Señora stood trance-like in front of her stove until the teapot's whistle startled her, and she realized that St. Jerome had already answered her prayers. The falling card from her purse was the divine solution that had come to her even before she prayed to the loving saint. The misplaced key, the card hiding in her purse, were messages from heaven. "Thank you, St. Jerome."

Spending the rest of the evening considering how to approach the conceited, overconfident Don Villavicencio, Alvarez devised a plan. Rehearsing her proposal in front of a mirror, she found answers to questions he would inevitably ask. She prepared retaliations to all objections the condescending man might spew forth, studied all possibilities and sharpened her rebuttals. Señora Alvarez spent an agonizing night in bed, rehashing her plan and never succumbing to sleep.

When morning light peeked through the small parting of her drapes and Alvarez heard the newspaper hit the front porch, she rose and dressed. As habit dictated, she took the paper to the garden and read it while sipping tea and savoring the quince jam thickly spread on her toast. After a second helping, she glanced at the comics and then folded the newspaper. Señora Alvarez was ready to execute her plan and meet Don Villavicencio. She knew he was a regular at the cathedral's Sunday mass. Not knowing which of the three services he preferred, she decided to attend all of them and not budge from her seat in the last pew until she found him. Executing the surreptitious meeting with Don Villavicencio, she would become a master puppeteer and make him a father to Lilia.

The Nation's Crisis

(Santiago, Chile, 1935)

Ten months had passed since Señora Alvarez met Don Villavicencio at the cathedral. It was finally time to reap the rewards of her labor. She had played the game superbly and won. She would remove Lilia from her foster home and bring her to the wealthy and childless couple. The social worker was immensely proud of her manipulations because Lilia's future now held the prospects of a good education and economic security.

Gertrudis Alvarez sat at her breakfast table, unfolded the newspaper and read. After only a few sentences, she became angry at the article. She did not need to read that the League of Nations declared Chile to be the nation most devastated by the Great Depression. That was obvious by the number of orphans entering the system. The export of saltpeter and copper had come to a standstill; therefore, money from the great banks of New York ceased its flow into Chile.

Her country was not a leader in weapons or science, but it held great assets. Its climate was worthy of paradise, with volcanic soil high in mineral contents and with a population who considered work a great privilege. This formed a perfect trifecta for agriculture. Vineyards grew in numbers from vines brought over by the Spaniards in the mid-sixteenth century, and starting in 1909, wine producers shipped wine to Argentina via the Transandine Railway. Fruits and vegetables were abundant in the warm fertile valleys, like those of the Mediterranean and California. Three thousand miles of coastline along the cold Pacific waters made it a fisherman's haven for the finest fish and crustaceans.

Overnight, though, the Depression had turned industrious and upstanding citizens into homeless vagabonds. Due to inflation, money was almost worthless, but the community would not let its people starve. Fishermen and farmers donated surplus stock. Doctors, lawyers, teachers, street cleaners and merchants joined long lines in all the Chilean major cities to receive a bowl of *Caldillo de Congrio*, a Chilean fish stew served free for those who could not pay. The savory stew simmered in giant black cauldrons over burning logs was abundant on city sidewalks.

Money was devalued and families became homeless. It was common to witness families move from stately homes into the hundreds of caves dotting the foothills of the Andes. It was not unusual to live in a cavern decorated with richly furnished tables from Florence and dishes from England. These strange days were unprecedented in Chilean history.

The grandfather clock struck eight, nudging Señora Alvarez to start the long drive to the Maipo Valley. After sipping the last of her tea, she gathered her things, locked the front door and walked to her car carrying a small lunch tote filled with empanadas and fruits for the long drive. She had filled a thermos flask with *maté*, not only to quench her thirst but also for the caffeine that would help keep her awake and alert throughout the day.

The beat-up Ford proved to be a dependable friend, almost never failing to run. Although the tires had been replaced many times and the engine overhauled, it faithfully delivered her to her destinations. Señora Alvarez relished the freedom of driving. Every night in her prayers, she thanked Carlos for teaching her to drive. He had been an unusual man, atypical of his time. She could still feel the weight of his arms in his embrace. The pain of his loss had lessened but was not gone. It took years to learn to block her tears. Time had finally taken away the blazing sting of death and replaced it with a softer, kinder pain.

Though Señora Alvarez longed to find a man to fill the void in her heart as well as her bed, she remained faithful to her husband. Remembering a day from childhood when discussing the subject of marriage with her mother, she could still hear her mother's singsong voice speak from the recesses of her mind, cautioning her.

***

Santiago, Chile, 1898

"Marriage is eternal, Gertie. Share your body but with one man."

"If something should happen to my husband, why wouldn't I marry again?"

"Don't say such things—you'll put a curse on yourself."

"But why would I live alone for the rest of my life?"

"Gertie, what will you do when you arrive at the gates of heaven and there are two men waiting for you? How would you choose?"

"I would choose them both if I had married both!"

The belligerent reply stunned Agustina. She slapped her daughter's face with the palm of her hand, shocking them both. In Gertie's nine years of life, she had never been hit by anyone. Now her mother's handprint lay visible on her cheek.

"Oh, dear God, what have I done?" said the distraught Agustina. She knelt by her daughter and with the hem of her apron, wiped the tears from Gertie's eyes. "I didn't mean to strike you, but your words were blasphemous. Forgive me, please. It's not your fault you're young and don't understand. You'll learn to be a good Catholic and not stray from our morals or canon law."

"Mamá, I don't care for religion." Gertrudis found it hard to fight back tears.

"Gertrudis," Agustina's voice raised an octave higher, "how dare you say that? Leave my sight. I cannot look at you. Help your grandmother peel potatoes. Go!"

"But—" Gertrudis could not think of anything to say.

***

Maipo Valley, Chile, 1935

Señora Alvarez pondered if her mother had foreshadowed a curse. *Have I prompted the good Lord to test my faith?* As an adult, she now understood what her mother had tried to instill. As she neared the Maipo Valley, she thought of her husband. Thinking that tears for Carlos had finally dried, she was disappointed that they came again, and unable to see through them, she pulled the car to the side of the road. She sat with the windows rolled down, trying to regain her composure and stop the flood of memories. But instead, she found herself remembering the day Carlos surprised her and what happened after.

*****

Santiago, Chile, 1909

"Gertie, I've news," Carlos said, barely able to contain his excitement as he entered the house.

"What news?"

"Let's eat first and then we'll talk."

"Why wait?"

"Because I love to keep you in suspense."

They ate and Gertrudis cleared the table.

Carlos was surprised Gertie was not needling him to spill his news. "Well, aren't you going to ask me?"

"Oh, I forgot already," Gertrudis pretended.

"I'm going back to check the mines," he said with a smile on his face.

"Again? More concerns over safety issues? Which mine—copper or saltpeter?"

"It's the Tesoro Mine—saltpeter, the one near Antofagasta."

"I'm sad you're leaving again, yet you have a smile on your face."

"Gertie, my beautiful Gertie, it's my job." Carlos laughed and looked into her large brown eyes. He grinned even wider and said, "This time, you're coming with me."

"I'm not in the mood for jokes."

"It's true."

"Stop, Carlos!"

"I'm not joking! We're going to the Atacama."

Gertrudis stepped behind him, wrapped her arm in a chokehold, pretended to strangle him and said in a make-believe villain's voice, "I'll kill you if you're teasing me."

Carlos laughed, faced his wife and planted a kiss on her pouting lips. He kissed her a few seconds longer than usual, savoring her sweetness. He repeated, "I'm not joking!"

Gertrudis screamed with joy and covered his entire face with tiny kisses. Her actions filled Carlos with desire, and he thought about taking her to bed. Unfortunately, he had an early afternoon meeting.

"The desert is maybe a thousand kilometers away. Will we take the train?"

"No, we'll go by ship. We can have a few days' respite. And there is more." His eyes twinkled like children's when they are about to spill a secret.

"More?" Gertrudis' eyes widened, and she bit her lip in anticipation.

Carlos stared at her and was pleased that his wife still had a childlike quality. He remembered the first time he saw her when they were children. It was outside of a local bakery where she was enjoying a Napoleon pastry. The cream oozed out and dropped onto her school uniform. She had wiped the cream from her skirt with her finger and then licked it with her eyes closed to fully savor the delicacy without distractions. He had fallen in love with her at that moment and remained so ever since. She had not changed but remained the same—a girl waiting to taste everything life offered.

"Gertie, it's the seventh year!"

Gertrudis gasped, "Is it? The desert is blooming?"

Carlos nodded.

"I can't believe it. I will finally see it!"

"They say it's a miracle." Carlos spun her around in a dance-like motion and kissed her again.

***

Tesoro Mine, Near Antofaghasta, Chile, 1909

Carlos was anxious to perform a preliminary check of the mine and meet the crew so upon arriving, he left his wife in the small visitor's cottage. Gertrudis finished unpacking their suitcases and was excited to walk to the local grocery and have a peek at the town. She found a small butcher shop and bought two lamb cutlets. Then she crossed the street to a small grocer and bought a small bottle of oil, wine from the Maipo Valley, eggs, bread, a head of cauliflower and cherries for dessert. On the way home, Gertrudis picked a sprig of rosemary from a large bush growing wild alongside the road to cook with the lamb. Hearing sirens in the distance, she assumed a fire had broken out and scanned the sky for smoke. Surprised the sky was clear with not a trace of smoke or even a cloud, she thought nothing more of it.

Gertrudis returned home and prepared Carlos' favorite dinner. She hummed as she carefully beat eggs, mixed them with steamed cauliflower and was about to pour the batter into a hot oiled pan when she heard a gentle tapping. Assuming it was the wind, she ignored it. A minute later a loud knock startled her. She turned off the stove and wiped her hands on a kitchen towel as she opened the front door.

The happy wife and first-time visitor to the Atacama Desert wondered why four miners stood outside her threshold. Directly in front of her, the setting sun caused her to squint, and the backlight obscured the men's faces. She shaded her eyes with her hand to see them clearly. They held their hard hats in front of their chests with eyes lowered to the ground and remained still and silent.

A man mumbled, "Señora Alvarez, I'm so displeased to…" The miner choked on his words. A shock coursed through Gertrudis' body, warning her that her life would never be the same. The miner regained his composure and continued, "Señor Alvarez squeezed through a newly carved tunnel, and within minutes of his entry, the shaft gave way. I'm sorry…hundreds of tons of earth buried him. We come with heavy hearts bearing this news."

Along with Gertrudis' beloved, fifteen miners lost their lives. Death, an uninvited guest, had paid a visit and turned wives into widows, robbed children of their fathers and birthed pain to many.

Forever buried deep in the Atacama Desert, Carlos was enshrined in his makeshift grave in a desert where above him flowers bloomed.

Separation

Maipo Valley, Chile, 1935

Señora Alvarez, still parked on the side of the road, inhaled deeply and wiped her tear-stained face with an old handkerchief. She wondered why her memories were haunting her this day, making her work more difficult. The widow knew that taking Lilia away from her foster family was the cause of her renewed sadness. It would be a devastating day for all as loved ones made of flesh and blood would turn into fading memories. Although the poor farmers were not educated and didn't know how to properly take care of children, they were managing to raise three strong teenagers, and Lilia loved them. But the near poisoning had sealed their fate. There was no choice but to sever the relationship. The social worker knew how tough this day would be but was resolved to follow all the protocols.

There was no need for Señora Alvarez to knock on the door of the farmhouse because it was wide open. The parents, along with Rodrigo and Ana standing at the threshold, silently waiting for her. They greeted her with a smile, but their stiff demeanor and sad eyes told a different story. The social worker entered the tiny house carrying a box with a large pink ribbon and placed it on the table. She scanned the room for Lilia.

"Where's Lilia?" Señora Alvarez skipped the normal greeting protocols, worried about not seeing her ready.

"She's playing on her swing. Rafael is pushing her," Bernardo said in a hushed voice.

Mamita's sorrowful tone chimed in, "The boys built the swing. She loves it very much."

Señora Alvarez heard pain in Myrta's voice. The social worker empathized. "I'm sorry it has come to this, but it is for the best. Isn't it thrilling that Lilia's new family can afford so many things and they live in our great capital? Such a superb city to grow up in. Think of all the things she will have, especially a great education. This should be a joyous occasion."

"You're right, Señora. I'm thinking only of our loss. It will be hard not having her around. I don't think she remembers any other place as home. Please sit down and let's have a cup of tea." Mamita tried to stall the inevitable, as she was afraid of how quickly the moment of Lilia's departure would arrive.

"No, Myrta, thank you. We need to leave as soon as possible. It's a long ride to the capital, and I'll want to deliver her to the Villavicencios before sunset. Fetch Lilia for me and say your quick goodbyes."

"Of course, Señora," Bernardo said but made no effort to get her.

Mamita could not restrain herself and began crying, prompting Ana to embrace her. Bernardo looked at his shoes. "She doesn't know she's leaving us. We didn't have the heart to tell her."

"You should have prepared her! I warned you to tell her so she could get used to the idea. Your responsibility was to make this transition as easy as possible. You didn't do that!"

"We're sorry, Señora, please forgive us. We were afraid to tell her. She's too young to understand what's happening." Myrta's eyes were red and bloodshot.

"And now I'm expected to take her? It will be a shock for the girl." Señora Alvarez shook her head. "Dry your eyes, Myrta. Make Lilia feel excited that she will go on an adventure with me. Don't mention anything about having new parents. Tell her she's visiting an aunt and an uncle. Please, someone go and get her!"

Rodrigo, seeing his parents and sister motionless with grief, took it upon himself to bring in Lilia. A minute later Rodrigo, Rafael and Lilia entered the house.

"Good morning, Señora," Rafael said sheepishly.

"Good morning, Rafael. Hello, Lilia. I'm so happy to see you looking so pretty."

Lilia did not reply but eyed the cardboard box on the table.

"How sharp you are. You've spotted my gift for you. I hope you like it." Señora Alvarez placed the package on the floor in front of Lilia.

"For me?" Lilia's mouth formed a circle as she inhaled a breath of surprise.

"Yes. Let's open it together because it could break if you are not careful." Señora Alvarez untied the ribbon.

Lilia pulled the box top off and squealed with delight. A beautiful baby doll wearing a white gown and bonnet lay inside. She picked it up and the doll's blue eyes popped open, prompting Lilia to cradle it in her arms. Rocking the doll, she hummed a lullaby. Mamita wondered where she had learned the new melody—she was not familiar with it.

"Lilia, what do you say to the Señora?" Mamita prodded.

"Thank you so very much, Señora Alvarez." Lilia smiled as she looked at Mamita and waited for approval that she had remembered all the proper words to say. Mamita nodded proudly.

"My baby! I love her!" Lilia turned to Señora Alvarez, "What's her name?"

"She doesn't have one—it's up to you to choose the name," said Alvarez, pleased with her choice of gift.

"Her name is Ana, like my sister, but because she is little, we'll call her Anita." Lilia's baby teeth showed through her smile.

Ana felt a wave of guilt at the honor Lilia had bestowed her and that she had always pushed the little girl away. Finally understanding that Lilia would leave forever, a feeling of unbearable regret descended upon her. She hugged Lilia tightly and kissed her on both cheeks. It was uncharacteristic for Ana to behave this way, but Lilia enjoyed it and giggled. Lilia thrust the doll's face near Ana's lips and demanded, "Kiss her!"

Ana kissed the doll. Mamita burst out in sobs she could no longer stifle. She fell to her knees and hugged Lilia. Lilia sensed something was not right and asked, "Mamita, what's wrong? Don't you like my baby? Don't be sad. Do you want a dolly too?"

"No, my angel, I don't want a doll. But I want you to always remember that we love you very much."

"Lilia..." Señora Alvarez paused, not knowing how to continue, "we're... uh...going on a special trip to visit Santiago! Remember you told me you wanted to ride in my car?"

"Yes, I want a ride. Are we all going?"

"No, just the two of us are the lucky ones to go. Isn't it exciting?" Señora Alvarez's smile was wide and fake.

"I want Mamita to come, and Ana too."

"Oh, that would be fun, but not this time. They must feed the goats, chickens and especially the horses."

"The boys always take care of the animals," Lilia said.

"Mamita and Ana must help with the farm. This trip is only for us. What fun we'll have riding in my car all the way to Santiago. Won't that be great?"

Lilia looked at the faces of her family and noticed their sadness. "I don't want to go to San-san-tigo."

"San-ti-a-go," Señora Alvarez corrected.

Rafael, feeling a lump in his throat, rose, stared at Lilia for a few seconds, attempted a smile and hurriedly left the house before losing his composure. Rodrigo decided to follow and when he reached the door, he too turned for a last look at the girl. "Lilia, be a good girl and..." He could not finish his sentence, was surprised he felt sorry for her, turned and ran after his brother before he risked shedding a tear.

"Wait!" Lilia screamed. "I'm coming with you. I'm not going to Santiago."

Lilia clutched her doll and headed towards the door, but Alvarez grabbed her arm. The now frantic girl tried to break free but could not. She wailed, "Let go of me! I'm not going with you."

Mamita sobbed harder and soon her quiet sobs were loud, heightening Lilia's distress.

"Say 'goodbye' for now, sweet girl, you'll be back soon. We're going to visit a new Mamita and Papito." Señora Alvarez tried to smile as she forgot her plans to refer to them as Aunt and Uncle.

"No!" Lilia screamed and kicked Señora Alvarez in the left shin. Bernardo, seeing the furious kick, came forward and swatted Lilia on her buttocks. Lilia froze. This was not the first time someone had spanked her, but previously it had always been a light pat from Mamita and never by the heavier hand of a man, especially one as strong as Bernardo. Feeling the sting, she caught her breath and cried out. Bernardo again swatted her. At this new assault, Lilia's wail grew louder.

Señora Alvarez stepped between Bernardo and Lilia. She yanked on the girl's arm, causing the doll to slip from Lilia's clutch and drop to the floor. The porcelain head shattered into pieces on the cement floor, and the dislodged glass eyes stared at Lilia. Ana ran to pick up the broken shards of the doll's head and didn't know what to do with them. This caused Lilia to cry even louder.

"My dolly! My Anita!" Lilia screamed as she struggled to break free from Alvarez's grasp. Mamita brought an old canvas tote out from under the bed to place in the car. Lilia recognized her green-and-white sweater spilling from the top and understood that her belongings had been packed.

Bernardo helped Señora Alvarez drag Lilia outside, the small child resisting every step. They reached the car and pushed her onto the front seat. He tried to shut the car door, but Lilia stretched her legs out, and he could not close it. She swung her arms to strike Bernardo, but her arms were too short and missed him. Seconds later, as the social worker took the driver's seat, Lilia lunged at the social worker and bit her forearm. The social worker gasped. Bernardo wanted to strike Lilia again, but the social worker intervened, "It's fine. She did not break the skin."

Bernardo, furious at Lilia's action, bent over the child and in a harsh steady voice reprimanded, "You'll sit quietly in the car, and you will not dare move. You will not bite. You will not kick. If you misbehave, the Señora will tie you with rope she keeps in the trunk. Do you understand, Lilia?" He pushed her legs back inside the cab and slammed the door.

The stunned, terrified five-year-old sat quietly as her tears fell. She did not know why this was happening but understood her days with Mamita and the family had come to an end. The social worker started the car and slowly drove away on the bumpy dirt road. Trembling, Lilia kicked the dashboard, and her eyes locked on Señora Alvarez. "I will run away! I'll come back. I hate you, Señora Alvarez!" Lilia's world turned black as it did the day she ate the poppies—her body limp in the seat of the old Ford.

Joyless Ride

The ride from Maipo to Santiago proved stressful for both the social worker and the child. When Lilia fainted, Señora Alvarez did not use the smelling salts she carried in her purse, deciding the ride would be easier with the child asleep. When Lilia woke, she curled into a fetal position and whimpered. Her wish of riding in a car had become a reality, but it was joyless. This day was forever etched in her memory as one of contradictions.

Lilia watched the scenery and noticed the landscape changing. The lush green hills gave way to an imposing city. The noise of speeding cars, buses and horse-drawn carts crowding the street unsettled her. A garbage strike in its second week left trash baking in the summer sun. Lilia pinched her nose to stifle the reeking air. She watched hurried pedestrians on the sidewalks and wondered where so many people came from and where they were going. She let go of her nose and placed both hands over her ears to shut out the clatter.

Shops had set up their wares on the sidewalks to tempt customers not entering their stores, their tables overflowing with merchandise. Food vendors yelled out as appetizing scents enticed customers.

At an intersection, Lilia saw a car on the left jump the stop sign and nearly clip a horse-drawn wagon. Startled, the frightened horse whinnied. The alarmed brown *criollo* mare stopped in the middle of the intersection, and not even the lash of the driver's whip could move her forward. Traffic ceased while waiting for the animal to move.

While the car idled in place, a toy store caught Lilia's attention. She scanned every detail of the large window display of dolls, cars and even doll houses filled with miniature furniture. She spotted a cradle with a doll like the one she had received a few hours ago. Longing to hold it again—and at the same time reliving the anger of losing it so quickly—caused Lilia to cry out, "My dolly. I want that dolly!"

"Hush! I can't afford to buy another doll. Don't worry, your new parents will buy you one. We're almost there," the tired social worker reprimanded.

Lilia's eyes continued to peruse the shop window and spotted another doll at the center of the display holding a stuffed bear in her arms. There were so many, even a lady doll, complete with a purse, lace gloves and a string of pearls around her neck.

Lilia's eyes widened, and she stared at the shop window as if taking a photograph of the wonderful toys to store in her memory. A smiling girl strolled out of the shop pushing a baby carriage containing a doll with hair the color of sunflowers. Her proud father walked behind her. Lilia felt a new emotion overtake her, a strong desire to jump out of the car and strike the girl, perhaps push her to the ground and run away with the stolen doll. Although impossible, Lilia relished the thought.

Traffic resumed. Señora Alvarez shifted gears and made a left turn. Lilia lost sight of the store and the girl. She closed her eyes and remembered every doll she had seen in the window, never to forget the magnificent shop.

The car slowed as the social worker pulled to the side of a tree-lined street. "We're here!" Alvarez adjusted the rear-view mirror to catch her reflection. She reached for her purse and pulled out a lipstick, dabbed her cheeks with it and rubbed her fingers in tiny circles to spread a little color on her pale cheeks, then applied a thin layer on her lips and tightened her bun.

"Oh, my goodness, look at you!" Señora Alvarez shook her head. "I can see streaks of tears on your face. Let's get you looking a little better." She opened the glove compartment, pulled out a clean handkerchief and began to wipe Lilia's face. The dry fabric did not help dislodge the tear marks, so she moistened the cloth with her tongue and wiped the child's face. Lilia flinched and glowered.

"We'll have to do something about your hair," the Señora said as she pulled a wooden bristle brush from her purse. She tamed Lilia's wavy hair. Lilia, frustrated, did not have the will to fight and let the woman fastidiously groom her.

"There, that's better now. You look presentable for your parents." Alvarez realized she had again inadvertently erred by mentioning the new parents, but now it was too late to hide the truth.

Lilia narrowed her eyes but kept silent.

"When you meet the Villavicencios, please tell them how happy you are to be their new daughter."

"No! I want to go home!"

"If you're a good girl, I promise to come and drive you to Mamita's house for a visit real soon." Señora Alvarez felt guilty for lying.

Lilia folded her arms and lowered her head, pretending she did not hear.

"Remember to use words such as 'thank you' and 'please' as often as possible." Alvarez smiled and tried to get Lilia's consent, but the child remained obtuse. The Señora continued to beg, "Don't be like a mule on a hot day! I understand you are angry with me, Lilia, but one day you will no longer blame me. I do this for you because I care that you have a better life."

Lilia gave her a menacing look.

Alvarez stepped out of the car and removed Lilia's tote from the trunk. She walked around to the passenger side and helped Lilia out of the car while holding her hand firmly.

A Room with Six Walls

Santiago, Chile, December 1935

A tall wrought-iron gate surrounded the house. Lilia noticed the metal roses entwined in the rails, but the need to protect such a small yard mystified her. She peeked through the gate and saw a trickling fountain. Señora Alvarez released the child's hand to pull a chain on the iron post. The sound of clanging bells rang out.

A middle-aged woman sprang out of the front door wearing a welcoming smile while drying her hands on a dishtowel. She unlatched the gate and kept her smile as she spoke, "*Bien Venidos*! I'm Susana. We've been anxiously waiting for you."

Susana's warmth prompted Lilia to ask, "Are you my new mother?"

"No, sweetheart. I cook and clean for your parents. They are so eager to meet you, Eliana."

"My name is Lilia."

"Hush!" Señora Alvarez threw Lilia a stern look.

"Come in, please." Susana walked ahead and held the door open for the pair. They entered the massive foyer. Lilia stared at the high ceilings and oversized furniture and whispered, "Do giants live here?"

"Not giants but a wonderful couple," replied Alvarez.

They walked into a large room. Lilia did not like the cavernous room and dark red furniture, preferring Mamita's house where the family lived in a simply furnished one-room cabin.

"Please sit down and make yourselves comfortable. I'll let the Villavicencios know you've arrived." Susana left the room.

Señora Alvarez sat on a large sofa and patted the cushion beside her, coaxing Lilia to join her.

Lilia sat and bounced, "This is a very soft bed."

"Sit still! This is not a bed, it's a sofa. Don't forget your manners when the Villavicencios come in."

"I want to go home!"

The sofa was so unlike the rattan chairs Bernardo made for the family when he replaced the long uncomfortable benches around their table. Lilia remembered how Bernardo had worked for weeks in the barn, hiding his surprise and then sneaking them inside on Christmas Eve and pretending the chairs were a gift from *Viejito Pascuero*.

An old, wrinkled-faced couple entered the room followed by Susana. Lilia noticed the man was tall and was startled to see the whites of his eyes were almost yellow. His hair was white. The woman was short with dark almond eyes and eyebrows even thicker than his. Her hair was a dull grey. Alvarez rose and tapped Lilia's shoulder, hoping she would rise, but Lilia continued bouncing on the springy sofa.

"Good day, Señora Alvarez. Thank you for her. Today is a blessed day." Don Villavicencio shook hands with the social worker and stared at Lilia. Carmen stepped in front of her husband and nudged him with her elbow, prompting him to say, "Forgive me for not introducing my wife, Carmen."

"A pleasure to meet you, Doña Villavicencio," Señora Alvarez nodded.

"Enchanted, Señora Alvarez. I must admit that it is odd to finally have a child at this age."

"Susana, bring refreshments," Don Villavicencio ordered. Susana nodded and left the room.

"I'm so excited to introduce your new daughter." The social worker pulled Lilia up from the couch and stood behind her, anchoring her hands on Lilia's shoulders.

"Welcome home," Don Villavicencio smiled.

"Thank you for your kindness in allowing me to bring this angel for you to raise during your golden years. Your generosity is extreme." Alvarez pushed Lilia towards the couple.

"On the contrary, it is God's generosity." Doña Villavicencio leaned on her cane and craned her neck forward to inspect the child. "You are tiny for a five-year-old."

Lilia didn't respond. She missed Mamita and did not want to stay with strangers who thought they were her mother and father. She scrutinized the couple's faces and wondered how old they were.

"Give Doña Villavicencio a kiss and properly thank her," the social worker coaxed.

"What is a Doña?" Lilia asked while taking a step back.

"It is how we address and respect important women, just as we do for Don Villavicencio. Now go on and kiss her." Alvarez tried to push Lilia forward for a second time, but Lilia's feet were firmly planted on the floor, and she did not budge.

"No! I want my Mamita!"

At the child's outburst, Don Villavicencio immediately began to wonder if the adoption was a mistake. The scowl on his face terrified Lilia, and she tried to hide behind the social worker.

Señora Alvarez appeased him, "You must forgive her. She's had a most difficult day."

"A difficult day is the way our Lord teaches us," Doña Villavicencio spoke directly to Lilia.

Lilia glanced at the front door in the foyer and noticed it was still open. Without hesitating, she bolted out of the house.

Alvarez's voice was shrill, "Lilia! Stop!"

The befuddled grownups, shocked at the speed of a five-year-old, stared motionless. Susana, hearing the commotion, ran into the room holding a tea tray with tiny sandwiches. She put the tray down and reassured them, "Don't worry, I'll bring her back."

Lilia tried to open the garden gate, but lacking the strength to release the rusted latch, she was trapped in the small yard. Susana reached the child and dropped to her knees. She wrapped her arms around the tiny girl and kissed her head and cooed in a whispering voice, "Eliana, everything will be fine, I promise you."

The housekeeper's warm brown eyes and soothing voice caused a lump to form in Lilia's throat, and she tried to hold back her tears. Susana hugged the child, and the softness of the woman's arms lifted some of the stress from Lilia. She released a sob. Susana kept the child in her embrace until the sobbing stopped. She rose from her kneeling position and picked her up. Lilia's head rested on Susana's shoulder, her body limp, resembling a rag doll.

Susana bypassed the adults in the parlor. She headed straight into the kitchen and whispered in Lilia's ear, "I've spent the morning making a zoo, right here in the kitchen. I have zebras, tigers, a snake and other animals, just for you. The llama is my favorite. Would you like to see it?" She placed the child on a chair, poured a glass of milk and removed a napkin covering a large gold-edged platter filled with animal cookies. She placed the milk before Lilia and watched the girl's lips shape a smile.

After the Villavicencios had gone to bed the previous night, Susana had iced the treats with colorful details. The llama's face was bare of icing except for a dot representing an eye, while yellow frosting swirled on the body imitating the animal's curly hair. Lilia studied a zebra with alternating stripes of white, vanilla and blackberry frosting. Enchanted by the menagerie, she calmed.

Susana pushed the plate closer to Lilia, "Choose and eat your pick of an animal."

"They're too pretty to eat."

"I can always make more."

Lilia chose a bear and bit off its head. She ate quickly and took a sip of milk. Her eyes widened with surprise. "The milk is so cold!"

"Yes, it's been in the icebox." A quizzical look appeared on Lilia's face.

"We keep our food cold so it will not spoil easily."

Doña Villavicencio entered the kitchen. "Very well done, Susana. The child has settled."

"Yes, and she's delightful." Susana placed a napkin by Lilia's dish, but she ignored it and wiped her mouth with the sleeve of her dress.

"Get her acquainted with the house. We'll finish our tea, and I'll send Señora Alvarez to say her farewells."

Susana nodded, removed Lilia's empty glass and washed it in the sink. After drying it, she placed it in a giant built-in cabinet with leaded glass doors. Lilia eyed the massive display of table service neatly stored and wondered why anyone would need that many dishes. She remembered Mamita methodically teaching her to count the plates and cups in their small cupboard and had counted nine plates and twelve cups. A smile came across Lilia's face as she remembered how proud Mamita had been. She thought it would be impossible to count the endless number of dishes in Susana's kitchen.

Señora Alvarez opened the kitchen door partially but did not step inside. She didn't want to agitate Lilia with a fussy goodbye. "Thank you, Susana, for everything. I'm leaving now and wish you both well. Be a good girl, Lilia." She stepped back and closed the door, not giving Lilia a chance to utter a word. Lilia was left wondering if she would ever see the Señora again.

Susana extended her hand, and Lilia reached for it as she rose from the table. They walked together as Susana showed her the house. "This room is your parent's bedroom. It's attached to Don Villavicencio's study. You may not enter these rooms unless you are invited." Susana then showed her the Villavicencio's bathroom.

"The outhouse is inside the house?"

"Yes, Lilia. But this bathroom is also only for your parents. We use the hall one."

When they reached the hall bathroom, Susana saw Lilia's perplexed face and taught her how to flush the toilet. She also warned, "This tap is for hot water, and you should not use it; it can burn you."

"Hot water?"

"Yes, turn that one on and wash your hands. Use that bar of soap, and lather as much as you like."

Lilia washed her hands and giggled as a soap bubble floated into the air.

Susana surmised that Lilia's previous home had a hole in the ground rather than a toilet in their outhouse. She continued the tour of the house and was pleased that Lilia asked intelligent questions about the strange new things she saw. As the sun brushed the horizon with orange and pink colors, the house took on a daunting air with shadows casting long in the semi-darkened rooms. When they reached the library, Susana flicked a switch, and the room glowed from the chandelier above. Lilia was startled and wondered how lights turned on without lighting lamps or candles.

"It is magic."

Susana chuckled, "Not magic. Here, flick the lights yourself and see."

Lilia played with the light switch, turning it on and off many times.

"When the light is on, it makes the ground shiny."

"Oh, you mean the floors. I wax them at least once per week."

Lilia remembered when Bernardo put in the cement floor covering the dirt in their tiny home. She could hear Mamita exclaiming, "It will be so easy to keep clean!" and recalled how tightly Mamita hugged Bernardo.

Susana reached the end of the hallway, "And this is your room."

Lilia stepped inside and found herself in an oddly shaped room. She pointed her finger at each wall and counted, "One, two, three, four, five...It has six walls!"

"Yes, it's special and different, like you." Susana fluffed Lilia's hair.

Matching windows graced each side of the brass bed that was covered in a crocheted blanket. The dresser was tall, and the top drawer was beyond Lilia's reach. A nightstand matching the dresser had a lamp that looked like a tree with a multi-colored glass shade on top. A crucifix loomed above the headboard and was too large for the size of the room. Each wall had wallpaper in stripes of purple and grey. Lilia preferred the simple whitewashed stucco walls of her previous home and thought the room with six walls was ugly.

"Will I sleep here with you?"

"No, it's your room."

"I can't sleep alone. I sleep with Ana in my bed, and the boys sleep in the next bed. I'm scared of the dark."

"There's nothing to be afraid of. I'll be next door. If you need me, call out and I'll come right away. Now open that door," Susana pointed to one of the walls.

"What door?" Lilia stared at the wall and saw only stripes until she squealed, "Oh, I see the doorknob."

"Open it!"

Lilia turned the knob and pulled on the heavy door. "It's an outdoor room."

"It's a courtyard. You can play here any time you like. Isn't it wonderful?"

"No."

"Why don't you like your very own playground?"

"There are walls all around," Lilia shook her head, feeling like a caged animal. "There isn't dirt or grass, only a stone floor." She stretched out her arms, "I can't feel the wind. How will I fly like a crow?" A pout crossed her lips. "I don't see mountains. I cannot hear the birds and crickets."

Lilia wondered how far she was from her beautiful farm and the giant eucalyptus trees that stood tall, spilling their fragrance throughout the valley and gracing the banks of the clear blue river. Her lips quivered. She longed to be back in Maipo, sit on Mamita's lap, place her head on her ample bosom and fall asleep.

Empty House

Señora Alvarez returned home from the arduous day of bringing Lilia to the Villavicencios. She was hungry but too tired to prepare a snack and dragged herself directly to bed but stayed awake. She questioned her decision to place Lilia with such elderly parents. *The child has been in Maipo for three years with the only family she knows. Tearing her away was painful for everyone, but what else could I have done? Bernardo and Myrta are responsible for Lilia running free in the countryside, and she was almost poisoned.* The Señora concluded that the sacrifices made were for the benefit of the child, and she tried to dismiss her regrets.

But Alvarez continued to have doubts, remembering a particular conversation she had with Don Villavicencio when he said, "Since we don't have children, Lilia will eventually become our caregiver." When he first spoke these words, she thought it normal as it is the duty of all children, but now she feared she had made a mistake. She tried telling herself that it was a miracle he had agreed to the adoption at all. The child was already of school age, would not present the demands of an infant and she would attend boarding school at summer's end at the McKenna. *Why do I feel so bad?*

She eased her worries by thinking of the countless orphans who never found a permanent family—all would readily trade places with Lilia. This reasoning along with knowing that Lilia would inherit their estate helped ease her guilt. The decision was final, papers were signed and she hoped the nagging thoughts would stop. Señora Alvarez, angry at consuming so much time thinking of only one child, vowed to concentrate on something else.

The *something else* always turned out to be memories of her husband. Not a day passed that she did not think of him. He had left her as a young widow, alone and like the Villavicencios, childless. His death was the catalyst that culminated in her choice of helping children and becoming their voice. Pleasures of the first tingles of life in her womb or a baby at her breast were unknown to the surrogate mother of hundreds. Though it was painful not having an heir to carry on the Alvarez name, the social worker knew God was great and just. The Almighty had been fair and compensated her for losing her husband by giving her love from many helpless orphans strewn throughout the city and valleys. Her loneliness was counterbalanced by thousands of wet kisses from children who finally dared to risk loving another person.

She was their mother. *Oh yes, God was good!*

On such solitary nights, when sleep was impossible, the Señora read her worn and dog-eared Bible. When her eyes could not focus on the verses, she put the Bible back on her night table and thought about the peculiar but amiable nun she had met at the hospital and jogged her memory to recall the nun's name. *Oh yes—Agata.* She smiled as she remembered the nun known for her squeamish ways and who did not fit the mold of a hospitable nurse. Alvarez enjoyed hearing Agata's accent because it reminded her of her mother's—the charming lisp inherited from a long-ago King that separated the Spaniards from the Latin Americans.

Alvarez, peeking out of the parlor window at the gloomy sky and feeling the usual current of loss ripple through her body, tried to combat the darkness that threatened to drown her. Sometimes such thoughts were a welcome reprieve, allowing her to wallow in memories of love. Looking out at the encroaching early winter darkness, the sadness deepened. *Stop it, Gertie! Be strong!* She knew rainy days made her susceptible to depression and, therefore, turned on the lights in every room of the house to help lift her spirits. The light managed to bring a little semblance of happiness.

When not visiting children, Alvarez spent most of her days working on reports and stopped when the clock chimed five. On this day, she made tea and thought about how she would pass the evening. Instead of reading, she decided to go out. She thought about befriending Agata, who was likely now working at the hospital. She planned to invite Agata to dinner on Sunday and kindle a friendship. Feeling good about her decision, she was proud she had stopped herself from sulking at the thought of her fallen husband and decided to join the living instead. Breaking her usual pattern of frugalness, Señora Alvarez left the lights on when she left for the hospital.

The tired woman climbed into her car and closed her eyes before starting the engine. Alvarez felt the soft leather seat. Carlos had taught her how to keep them soft and supple. She inhaled deeply to smell the turtle wax and was lost in her thoughts of Carlos dipping his chamois into the leather polish, applying the cream in tiny circles until it melted and then taking a clean rag and buffing. "Carlos, you'll always be with me, but I must put you aside until the day we meet in heaven. I must continue my journey, *mi amór*," she whispered. With her eyes still closed, she puckered her lips and blew a kiss into the air. Filled with resolve, she started the engine.

Señora Alvarez found Agata not in the emergency room but in the trauma unit. She was scraping dead skin off a man who had survived a house fire. A large heavyset nurse held the man down as he groaned in pain. Agata soothed him as a mother soothes children and told him a story, attempting to deflect his pain. The social worker watched the nurse perform the difficult task and knew it was not the right time to interrupt. Moved by the scene, she returned home without ever connecting with Agata.

The pair would never meet again. There are times when worlds come close enough to change each other's trajectories, but this was not the case between the lonely social worker and the equally lonely nun. If they had spoken, certainly the lives of both women would have been very different.

Fear

Agata spent another night staring at the ceiling. She had not felt well for the past two weeks. Her decision to stay home and not work at the hospital caused more stress. The dizziness, tremors and nausea worsened. Sister Bernadette reported to Mother Superior that Agata would miss work again and suggested it was time to send for the doctor.

That afternoon Sister Agata's body trembled, her mouth was dry and she was disoriented. Mother Superior ordered the doctor's visit to take place in Father De Soto's office because men were not permitted to enter the convent. Mother and Sister Bernadette helped Agata out of bed and noticed how thin she had become.

"You've lost so much weight; you look like a plucked chicken!" Bene chided.

"It's so," said Mother Superior. "Agata, your arms are slender like chicken wings."

"And did you notice the goosebumps on her skin?" Bene added.

A smile appeared on Agata's face, "I know how awful I look, and I'm glad that mirrors are not found in convents. If I caught my reflection, I'd be even more frightened."

The short excursion to the first floor was unnerving as Agata's legs wobbled. It was hard to stay balanced as she shifted her weight and grabbed Bene's arm to keep from falling. Sister Lucia was waiting with an old wheelchair.

"I'm embarrassed to be carted around like an old woman but ever grateful."

They traversed the courtyard and entered a side door of the church. Not having to exit the convent, they entered directly into the vestibule. They reached the transept where Mother Superior and the sisters stopped to genuflect and cross themselves. Agata made the sign of the cross but did not get up from her chair. The church was cold and empty, with only the burning candles providing a semblance of warmth. The familiar smell of melting wax helped Agata relax.

The nuns walked behind the altar and sacristy into an ambulatory to reach the office of Father De Soto. He greeted them with a nod. This was Agata's first visit to the father's side of the church. Only Mother Superior had cause to speak with the father and venture to his domain. The father's office, opulent in contrast with Mother Superior's, had walnut shelves lining the walls filled with leather-bound books. Agata was surprised at how beautiful the book covers were. As she passed them, she tried to read the small print on their spines. They were great works of literature and art, but she noticed books of Catholic doctrine were missing. She wondered why the convent's book-shelves did not include Don Quixote or the cataloged paintings of the Louvre.

A crucifixion hung from the ceiling in front of a stained-glass window and directly behind the father's grand desk. A statue of the Virgin guarding the father's door was glorious. Agata noticed the details; the marble veins on Mary's hands seemed life-like. The beauty of the sculpture proved the statue was made by an accomplished artist and probably came from Italy. Mother Superior also had a statue of the Virgin in her tiny office, but hers was not chiseled from stone but poured into a mold with inexpensive clay, probably by an unknown artisan.

Father De Soto closed the door to keep the office warm and surveyed Sister Agata. He wondered what demons had taken over her body. The once young and healthy nun now looked distraught. Her skin was ghastly white, dark rings encased her eyes and her habit hung loosely on her frame. He smirked, thinking that an exorcism might ameliorate her symptoms better than a doctor's visit.

Father De Soto pulled his chair out from under his desk. "Mother, please sit down." He pointed to a small divan and asked Sisters Bernadette and Lucia to sit as well. Agata trembled in her wheelchair and prayed for the shaking to stop. The awkward silence was broken by rhythmic footsteps approaching followed by a knock.

Father De Soto opened the door, "Good day, doctor."

"Good day, Father, Mother, Sisters." Dr. Herrmann's smile was all-embracing.

"Doctor, I'm sorry you are taking precious time away from the hospital to see me," Agata whispered.

"I'm much sorrier to see you ill and in a wheelchair. What's wrong?"

"I can't seem to keep food down. I'm always nauseous," Agata's voice trembled.

"What else?" The doctor opened his notebook and pulled out a pen.

Agata was embarrassed and did not answer. Sensing the nun was uncomfortable talking in front of the priest, the doctor addressed Father De Soto, "Thank you for the use of your office, but can you please excuse us for a few minutes?"

Father did not like being dismissed from his own office and huffed, "We do not allow our sisters to be alone with a man. I'm here to protect their virtue."

"I understand your concern, but I am usually alone with this very sister when we are working at the hospital." Dr. Hermann did not release his smile.

The father, taken aback at Dr. Herrmann's retort, only stared.

"Mother Superior and the sisters will protect Agata's virtue. We wouldn't want to embarrass her, would we, Father?" Dr. Herrmann ended his question with an even bigger smile.

"Very well." Father De Soto exited his office but left the door open.

Dr. Herrmann watched until the priest reached the sacristy and then closed the door behind him. He took out a cuff, pressure meter and stethoscope from his bag and placed the equipment on the father's desk. He placed his hand on Agata's wrist and checked her pulse.

"Good news! You have a heartbeat!" The doctor joked and the sisters chuckled. "I've seen you at work when you seem agitated. Tell me how you feel at that moment."

"Perhaps, Doctor, I'm not sure. These feelings are indescribable and can happen anytime."

"Do they happen more often outside of the hospital?"

"At first, they happened only in the hospital, but now they happen anywhere. I am becoming more afraid of them as I fear fainting."

"Is there a particular sign when you feel it coming on?"

"My heart races causing me to feel off balance. I can't think of any reason why. Sometimes it all goes away quickly, but other times my heart races for a long time, and it's as if it wants to jump out of my body. I perspire even when

I have not exerted myself." Agata raised her hands to show the doctor her sweaty palms. "When I am overcome by it, I think I might die."

"Is there a trigger causing these spells?"

"What do you mean?"

"Perhaps a field mouse comes indoors and runs over your feet?"

"That has never happened, but it would not frighten me."

"Do you have any phobias you are aware of?"

"No. I'm not even afraid of snakes like the ones that slithered around my childhood farm. I've always felt the Virgin watches over me. Now I'm not sure I can rely on her."

"Are these episodes random?"

"Yes. When they happen, I cannot force myself out of bed."

"Have I told you, Sister, that my father is a psychiatrist?"

"No."

"He still practices in Berlin."

Sister Agata wiggled in her chair. "Do I have a mental disorder?" She hid her face with her hands. "I'm so ashamed."

The doctor pulled them away from her face. Agata, a bit startled by the doctor's gesture, stiffened. She relaxed when she saw his compassionate expression. He reached for the blood pressure cuff and proceeded to put it on her upper arm.

"There's nothing to be ashamed of. I'll check your pressure."

The timbre of the doctor's voice was soothing. His pronunciation of Spanish came off as staccato and not musical the way it is spoken by the natives. Although he had mastered the language, he sometimes placed the accent on incorrect syllables and could not shake the idiosyncrasies of his native German tongue.

The accent brought her back to a splendid summer of her youth. Agata's parents had taken the family on a once-in-a-lifetime holiday in Bavaria. The highlight of the trip was visiting the magnificent Neuschwanstein Castle in the middle of the Black Forest. She had been enchanted with castles ever since.

It had been a vacation like no other with every day an adventure. After a long day of sightseeing and sampling a different cuisine, Agata and her siblings hunted fireflies to add to their glass jars. The children pretended to be Teutonic Knights, riding horses and wearing chainmail. They knew all about the knights from reading books their father bought. They applied their new knowledge to the games. The girls borrowed their mother's dresses and pretended to be princesses held captive in tall towers, guarded by fiery dragons and saved by handsome golden-bearded men. The boys made cardboard swords and fought to the death until their weapons were pulverized.

"Your blood pressure is slightly elevated."

As the doctor put his instruments back into his bag, Agata wondered why he had left his homeland and traded such a fine country for the remote and raw land of Chile. Agata missed her childhood home and felt a desire to be in a home again with family surrounding her. Once again, she thought of Lilia. The baby had brought such fulfillment to her life from the moment she retrieved her from the foundling wheel. The day the officials moved the children out of the convent had been the worst day of her life, worse even than leaving her family for the sisterhood.

No reports ever came of their beloved children. It was the not knowing that caused Agata's angst. Her nervous disorder started when the convent was emptied of children and she began to question her religious beliefs. No longer could she find comfort in attending mass, her job or even in her favorite pastime—singing in the choir. The once-relished ensemble was now lackluster. Even the ritual of lighting candles and sending messages to heaven seemed trivial.

Although Agata questioned her faith constantly and fought silently with God, she always prayed to the Virgin. On such a day while praying to Mary, Agata imagined a gale wind from the South Pole catching the Holy Book in one of its squalls, pulling the spine apart and sending pages flying across the skies before they morphed into doves that flew and disappeared into the horizon.

The doctor closed his bag and addressed the sisters, "I think I know what the problem may be." Dr. Herrmann's voice brought Agata back to the present moment.

"What does she have?"

"Patience, Lucia!" Sister Bernadette scolded.

"Pantophobia."

Lucia could not contain her curiosity, "What?"

"It's anxiety neurosis. I have a remedy, but it will need Mother Superior's permission." His splendid smile wormed its way into the hearts of the nuns, making them feel as if they were young girls at a *quinceañera* party.

"Of course, Doctor, whatever you say," Mother Superior smiled while nodding her head in agreement under the spell of his charisma.

"First, she'll need to rebuild strength with physical and mind exercises."

"And how so?" Mother Superior lost her grin.

"By getting a library card. I have books that will help her psyche," the doctor spoke directly to Mother Superior.

"What books? Wouldn't it be easier to simply prescribe a tonic?"

"No, Mother. Tonics can sometimes have side effects that can do more harm. There has been research on this condition," replied the doctor. "I'll insist on a daily two-hour outdoor walk, and she'll read books that I'll personally prescribe." He patted Agata's shoulder but continued to address Mother Superior. "They are designed to help her understand her melancholic tendencies."

Sister Lucia, excited by a chance to gain free time, volunteered, "I'll walk with her."

"That's very thoughtful of you, but I prefer she walk alone to contemplate her life without chatter of any kind."

"Yes, Doctor," a deflated Lucia agreed.

"What books do you speak of?" Mother Superior was apprehensive.

"I'll leave a list with the head librarian—I know her well."

The mother asked, "Which library?"

"The one adjacent to the cathedral in the center of town. The other libraries are too small and will not have all the books I require. Now, Sister Agata, after you read your first set of books, stop by the hospital and let me check your progress."

Sister Agata nodded. The doctor once again flashed his luminous smile at Mother Superior, "I'll advise when she's ready to return to work."

The Library

The day after Dr. Hermann's visit, Agata mapped out a route to the library to begin her remedy. The long walk to the center of the city invigorated her. She climbed the marble library steps with reverence, as if she were entering a holy place. The entry gave way to polished granite floors and wooden tables set up in rows. Each table was equipped with a green-shaded lamp in its center. She patrolled the shelves while inhaling the scent of books. In the stillness and solitude of the library, she sat in a chair enjoying the moment while waiting for the appointed time to seek out the head librarian.

Agata approached the reference desk, asked for the head librarian and was pointed to an office at the back of the great room. She walked through the stacks with her index finger extended, rubbing each book as she passed. She reached the office and knocked lightly, her knuckles barely tapping the door.

"Come in!" a melodic voice answered.

Agata entered and saw a beautiful woman with dark hair coiled tightly in a bun. She wore a simple white shirt and a mid-calf blue skirt.

"Thank you."

"I'm Elsa Herrmann, I've been expecting you," she said, extending her hand.

Agata admired the librarian's firm handshake and asked, "Are you Dr. Herrmann's wife?"

"Yes."

"I'm so pleased to meet you. I didn't know the doctor was married. Everyone loves his bedside manners and brilliance."

"Thank you, Sister." The librarian grinned and said, "I've heard about you and your...sensitive nose."

Agata flushed.

"I find the stories he tells of the hard-working nurses quite charming. He is fond of the entire staff and has the greatest respect for the sisters. Please, sit down."

Agata sat on one of the two guest chairs and noticed a stack of books neatly piled on the librarian's desk. Elsa placed her hand on the stack, "Here is the first set of books." Elsa picked the top book off her stack and handed it to Agata.

A look of surprise showed on Agata's face when she read the cover and placed it on her lap. "*Little Women.* How odd."

Elsa grabbed the next book and added it to Agata's lap. "This is by the Chilean writer, Gabriella Mistral, titled *Desolación. Do you know this?*"

"No. A poetry book? This couldn't be the doctor's remedy—a novel and a book of poems?"

"It is exactly what he prescribed. Roland also wanted to warn you," the librarian pulled her chair close to Agata, sat and lowered her voice, "should Mother Superior question you about the selection," pointing to the books on Agata's lap, "you are to show her this." She reached for the third book on her desk. "Roland says healing begins with the mind. Use this psychology book as a decoy, but you don't have to read it. He asked for your pledge that this is a secret between the three of us. Do we have a deal?"

"Lie to Mother? I cannot."

"It isn't a lie! It's avoiding unnecessary turmoil. He knows Mother Superior will not understand. We want you to get well by reading these books. They will be a respite from your daily chores; he is certain of it. It's good medicine."

Agata was intrigued and hungry to read the books.

"All right, you have my word. I won't tell Mother, but if she asks, I'll have no choice but to spill the truth."

"We are agreed! The psychology book is written by Sigmund Freud. If you don't want to lie to Mother Superior, simply read the book. Roland says his father has studied every word of the text!"

The excitement Agata felt about reading soon turned to apprehension, as she feared she had sinned in forming a clandestine relationship with the doctor and his wife.

"I've worked in many dire situations by your husband's side, and I've seen him perform miracles with his medical knowledge. I'll trust him and follow his orders. What other books will I read?"

"They will be a surprise. Finish these in a week or two, and more will be waiting on my desk."

"Oh, Señora, I'll be back much sooner, as I'll devour them."

"Very well, Agata, come whenever." Elsa placed the books in a paper bag.

"I can't wait to see you again. Thank you. Good day, Señora Herrmann."

"Please, call me Elsa."

"Thank you, Elsa." The sister exited the office, hugging the bag close to her chest.

"Good day, Sister."

Señora Herrmann looked out her window, caught sight of Agata walking up the hill, and noticed a delightful skip in the nun's step. The librarian was proud of her husband's wisdom and thought to reward him. She walked home for lunch and told her housekeeper, Beppina, to bake her husband's favorite chocolate torte.

Agata could not wait to get back to her room and discover what mysteries the books would unravel. She felt lighter, as if she had received the Eucharist. Her excitement and gratefulness grew as she neared the convent. Such was her anticipation to read the books that she wanted to run but curbed her impulse and walked at a rapid pace. She remembered that she would not be able to read immediately upon returning, as there were many chores to complete before the evening meal.

"Sister, is there an emergency? I can give you a lift," a concerned man in a delivery truck stopped to ask.

"Oh, no thank you, sir. All is well."

Agata knew the citizens of Santiago always kept a loving eye on nuns; it was customary to acknowledge and greet them. She also knew that any odd behavior might be reported to Mother Superior. Therefore, Agata slowed her pace and put on a stern expression, giving the appearance she was entertaining serious thoughts and should not be disturbed.

Sister Lucia was waiting at the convent gate. "Agata, you are sweating, and your face is flushed. Are you ill again? Please go to bed immediately, and I'll alert Mother that you're not well and cannot attend to your chores."

"Thank you, Lucia." Agata felt a pang of guilt, as she was not ill and had lied.

Sister Catalina heard the discourse while sweeping the courtyard. "Don't worry, Agata. I'll handle your chores. Rest and get well."

"Thank you. I will get to bed immediately." A second pang of guilt coursed through Agata as she continued the lying. *How sweet of Catalina;*

she is old and can barely see through her thick glasses, yet she volunteers to do my chores. Agata resisted the impulse to confess to both sisters and beg forgiveness but did not turn back and continued to her room.

Closing the door behind her, Agata removed her veil, shoes and habit and took time to fluff her pillow and hide the poetry book underneath it. Sitting on her bed with the psychology book on her lap, she opened *Little Women* to the title page. She read the author's name aloud, "Louisa May Alcott," and turned to the first page. Before she completed the second paragraph, Agata was already immersed in a different world. The book played in her head as if it were a film. Unconscious of the typed words, she soon fell under the spell of the compelling and gratifying imagery the book conjured and was lost in the days of the American Civil War.

When she was on page forty-five, Agata heard footsteps in the hall. She hurriedly placed the novel under her pillow next to the poetry book and opened the psychology text at a random page. Three quick taps told Agata it was Sister Bernadette, but before she had a chance to grant her entrance, the door swung open and Bene flew into the room carrying a tray.

"Sister Lucia said you were sick. I just heard the news, otherwise I'd have come sooner. I've brought you something to make you feel better."

"Oh, you shouldn't have. Thank you."

Bene placed the tray on Agata's lap. The aroma of cabbage soup along with freshly baked *maraquetta* bread awakened Agata's hunger, and she realized she had skipped lunch in her eagerness to read. Tearing the bread into small pieces and dropping them into the soup, she then spooned a piece of the soaked bread and was about to take a bite.

Bene shrilled, "Sister, you haven't said grace!"

"I'm sorry, it is because I am feeling faint."

What is the matter with me? Lies upon lies! Agata spilled the contents of the spoon back into the bowl and placed the utensil on the tray. "Join me in prayer, Bene."

"Of course, but first, let me kiss your beautiful head." Bene kissed the cloth wrap she wore under her veil.

"Before I eat, I need contrition and will recite the rosary."

"I should not have said anything about grace. The soup will be cold after a long rosary! No, Agata, a simple prayer will do, and I will begin."

Sister Bernadette prayed aloud. As Agata listened, she saw herself tethered to heavy chains. The chains constricted like yellow Amazonian anacondas, choking and strangling. Then she envisioned a small drop of the soup spilling on the links, immediately peppering the metal with hues of orange and crimson. More drops turned the ore to rust, as if the soup were eating the chains in a frenzied feast. Agata foresaw that one day she would break free from the chains of sisterhood.

Valparaiso Express

Santiago, Chile, February 1936

"Tickets, please!" commanded the train attendant. Don Manuel Villavicencio waved a silver-plated ticket with the emblem of the Department of Transportation embossed on the front. The startled attendant stood at attention as he viewed the rare ticket. "Thank you, Señor," he nodded and did not bother to check for the girl's ticket. "Is there anything I can ask the steward to bring you, perhaps a cup of *maté*?"

The old man muttered, "Earl Grey," and placed the card back into his wallet, not bothering to look at the attendant's face.

The sheepish attendant asked, "And would your granddaughter like a beverage?"

Don Villavicencio, annoyed by the attendant's assumption that the girl was his granddaughter, did not correct him but threw him a stern look and ordered a hot chocolate.

"Yes, Señor!"

The attendant stopped collecting tickets and immediately headed for the dining car to place the order. He turned for a second to eye the strange duo and wondered what powerful position the man held, as he had only heard of the silver ticket but had never seen one. The exclusive thin card gave the bearer free transportation and food anywhere on the line. The attendant noted the quality of the tailor-made pinstripe suit adorned with a heavy gold chain tethered to a pocket watch and deduced the passenger was probably the Minister. The girl seated next to him wore the elite McKenna school uniform, leaving no doubt that the condescending man was a person of importance.

Lilia, oblivious to the power of the silver ticket, was nervous, restless and frightened to enter school for the first time. Susana had explained to Lilia that the McKenna was no ordinary school but an incredibly special one. Built high on a hill in the small sea village of Viña del Mar, the two-year-old institution already had an exclusive clientele. The school's reputation was growing as the finest school for girls in Chile. Its patrons were the children of foreign dignitaries, wealthy business owners, famous artists, writers or anyone who wanted the best for their daughters and could afford the tuition. Girls from families of average income attended at a reduced cost, but they were only the daughters of people employed by the McKenna brothers. Lilia was too young to understand what it all meant.

Before acquiring the job of Transportation Minister, Don Manuel Villavicencio was the right-hand man of the three McKenna brothers. After years of dedicating himself to the McKennas, he was considered part of their family. Many of the McKenna employees originated from Scotland. If they were not recent immigrants, they had Scottish ancestry. Don Villavicencio was the exception.

Prior to immigrating to Chile while still in his early twenties, Manuel Villavicencio had dropped out of the University of Salamanca due to the pressure of his father's passing. As the eldest son, Manuel tried to save the family's foundry business, but it was in too much debt to resuscitate. His younger siblings blamed their older brother for the loss of the business. Angry at his family's accusations, Manuel left his homeland for a new life in the Americas. Chile and the United States both attracted him, but he chose Chile because he did not want to learn another language.

Upon arriving in the country, the local priest suggested Manuel apply for work at McKenna Enterprises. The firm was founded in 1905 and was owned by the Scottish family. The McKennas were not yet industry magnates when Manuel was hired. He proved to be a worthy employee by diligently working into the long hours of night and arriving at work before sunrise. The brothers admired Manuel's work ethic. He impressed his superiors, and the brothers took notice. Realizing his potential, the McKennas rewarded the young man with a scholarship to their alma mater, the University of Edinburgh. They primed Manuel to complete his education in civil engineering and sent him for his degree to their glorious home city, Edinburgh. How ironic that Manuel completed his studies in Scotland and was forced to learn English after all.

Manuel worked on the new railroad line. He had an uncanny ability to spot hectares of wasteland and procure them at insignificant costs from peasants. The terrain was used for the new railroad that extended from

Antofagasta to as far south as Puerto Montt. They also built an East to West line traversing the Andes from Santiago to Buenos Aires, Argentina. Later, the railroad was sold to the government at an exorbitant profit.

After a few years of employment, the brothers promoted Manuel to head engineer and manager. Manuel grew into his job, becoming an invaluable member of the McKenna firm. While there, he modified the entire system, including building new bridges that spanned over steep ravines. It was to the McKennas that he pledged his loyalty, paying homage to them by hiring mostly young Scottish immigrants. The McKenna brothers and Manuel gave thanks to their new country by funding the private school for girls, and Don Villavicencio insisted on naming it after the brothers.

The three-hour train ride from Santiago to Valparaiso felt like an eternity, and Lilia's fearful anticipation of the first day of school caused her stomach to somersault. Although anxious, she was thankful the monotonous summer was finally over and glad to start an adventure away from her new parents. The Villavicencios had short tempers, and their demands for quiet never ceased. They constantly reprimanded her for singing or humming, as everything irritated them. Lilia already missed Susana but hoped that going to school would provide her with a friend.

Don Villavicencio was eager to drop his daughter off at boarding school and restore calm to his life.

Lilia had many books to keep her amused. She could not yet read but enjoyed looking at the illustrations. The Villavicencios had delegated Susana to read to Lilia from these books. The precocious child memorized them and recited them back to the delighted housekeeper.

The long summer had been an ordeal for both Lilia and her parents. The elderly couple refused Lilia's pleas to play in the street. When she heard other children playing on the sidewalk, Lilia plotted ways to escape and join them.

Lilia always thought of Mamita, Ana and her brothers in Maipo and wondered what they might be doing. She tried to remember every detail of her old home: the fields, the farm animals, the horses, especially the big stallion named *Muchacho,* and even the crows that swept the fields for food. She realized she was losing her memories of the beloved central valley and now could hardly recall Mamita's earthy scent.

Lilia thought about the dolls in the shop she had glimpsed the day she arrived at the Villavicencios. She had solicited her parents to buy her one, but

Don Villavicencio refused, saying, "Dolls are worthless trinkets, wasting time from little girls."

Lilia had tried to ward off boredom. One of the games she invented was *busca amigos*. The object of the game was to escape the confines of the house and climb over the front gate to where children played in the street and find friends. She managed to escape eight times within three weeks, enjoying her freedom before a double-key lock was installed on the front door.

While out on her jaunts, Lilia usually befriended stray dogs. The mangy mutts became instant friends. Lilia snuck food from Susana's pantry and delighted in their wagging tails as they gobbled up pieces of dry meat. Lilia also met some of the neighboring children. She found it easy to converse with anyone on the street, regardless of age. One day, two sisters taught her how to play hopscotch and jump rope.

Lilia's new mother, Carmen, did not spend much time getting to know her and delegated most responsibilities of caring for the child to Susana. Lilia bonded with the housekeeper, who worked hard to make the house feel homey. The two became inseparable. Lilia understood the McKenna School would be her new home until she graduated many years later and that she would return only for summer break and long holidays.

"But Susana, how often will you come to see me at school?"

"As much as possible. It's hard for me to travel so far from Santiago."

"You can visit on church day."

"You mean Sunday?"

"Yes."

"It takes time to travel to Viña del Mar and back and still be able to serve your parents."

That morning Susana was sad at the thought of missing Lilia and cried while serving breakfast. Don Villavicencio noticed the tears and ordered, "Susana, don't walk us to the train station, as I'm afraid you'll make a scene."

The remainder of the train ride was uneventful as Lilia watched her father read the newspaper in its entirety without ever addressing her. Lilia did not dare disturb him and occupied herself by looking out the window as the countryside unfurled.

The Color of Music

Valparaiso, Chile

When Don Villavicencio and Lilia arrived at the Valparaiso train station, they rented a taxi to Viña del Mar. To calm her growing anxiety, Lilia opened her satchel and counted the colored pencils in her box. She fingered the eraser and examined the pencil sharpener. A large steamer trunk packed the week before with her clothing and toiletries had been shipped to the school and was already waiting at the dormitory. The car stopped at the front gates of the McKenna.

"Wait for me. I'll return in a few minutes, and then you may take me back to the station," Don Villavicencio commanded. The driver did not argue. The humble driver knew that men dressed as fine as his passenger did not run off without paying and graciously agreed to wait.

Father and daughter walked side by side onto the campus. As they turned a corner and Lilia caught sight of the ocean, she gasped at its enormity. She inhaled deeply at the briny, aromatic sea air. She then gazed at the magnificent school and felt awed by its imposing appearance. The school consisted of four buildings—a chapel, a dormitory, a classroom building with an office for the administration and a dining hall. All the structures complemented each other in their motif. They walked inside the main door by the offices.

"Close your mouth or you'll catch a fly," Don Villavicencio reprimanded.

Lilia's jaw made a snapping sound as she clasped it shut and added, "Yes, Papá."

The old man grimaced as he grabbed his daughter's hand and pulled her toward the principal's office. Lilia did not see any students, as classes had already begun. She tried to conquer her nerves by looking at the tiles on the floor. Adding a skip to her walk, causing the A-line pleated blue skirt to shift from side-to-side, distracted Lilia from her fears. She much enjoyed wearing the new uniform and especially her black patent-leather shoes. The only part of the uniform she did not like was the embroidered emblem on the left side of her vest. The delicate flames woven in threads of orange, red and yellow, forever engulfing St. Joan as she burned at the stake, made Lilia shiver.

As the pair entered the office, a woman spotted them and rushed to greet them. "Don Villavicencio, we've been waiting for you and your precious little girl."

"Thank you," the old man nodded. "Eliana, this is the principal, Señora Albert."

Lilia looked quizzically at her father.

"Señora Albert is the most important person here—please greet her."

Lilia stared at the floor and did not speak.

"Don't be rude. Please shake her hand," Don Villavicencio spoke in a severe tone, and Lilia complied.

Señora Albert smiled and shook Lilia's limp hand. "A pleasure to meet you, Eliana."

"My name is Lilia, not Eliana!"

"Don't fuss about the name. We've discussed this already." He softened his voice when he addressed Señora Albert. "Please excuse her, she was raised by *campesinos*!"

"It's to be expected! She's young, and we should not expect so much from a little girl on the first day of school."

"Please remember we need an English tutor for her. I'm sure all the other girls are proficient in the language. She has only been exposed to Spanish, and I did not have time to teach her this summer."

"Of course, I've already set it up. I also took it upon myself to place her with second-graders for roommates. I think it's better that they are a year older and can help her acclimate."

"Splendid! Thank you," Don Villavicencio nodded.

"Class has already begun, so I should show Lilia her room in the dormitory, and then I'll take her to her classroom. Will you like that, Eliana?"

Lilia forced a nod.

"Give your father a big kiss and say goodbye."

Lilia stood motionless, not knowing whether she should obey. She knew Don Villavicencio was not an affectionate man and was not in the habit of kissing.

"Go on," the principal coaxed.

"Goodbye, Papá," Lilia managed to utter.

"Thank you, Don Villavicencio, for bringing us your daughter. She'll be a wonderful student." The principal turned to the child, "Now, dear girl, your father is waiting for his kiss."

Before Lilia could take a step forward and plant on her father a kiss, Don Villavicencio had already started to walk away and turned, "I've a taxi waiting. Good day, Señora Albert, Eliana!"

Señora Albert could not understand Don Villavicencio's behavior. It was not typical of a father. Most parents lingered for a long goodbye during the child's tender years. The principal shouted, "Goodbye, Señor." Turning to Lilia, she added, "As I was explaining to your father, your roommates will not be in your regular classroom, but they can teach you the rules and become your friends."

Lilia smiled at the thought of finally having friends. When they reached her room, Lilia recognized her trunk at the foot of one of the beds. "Is this my bed?" She was thrilled when the principal nodded. "I like it. It's small and cozy. I have a big bed at home that I don't like."

"Your clothes are already put away in the dresser. Now that your trunk is empty, you can use it to keep the books your teacher will give you and for keeping special things."

"What special things, Señora?"

"Gifts your parents will surely send."

"They will send me gifts?"

Señora Albert wondered if she had made a mistake by assuming the child would receive trinkets and toys. The way her father had behaved gave her concern. She tried to correct her error. "They may, but that is not important. The school will give you everything you need."

"When will I meet the other girls?"

"When class is over. You're the only one who arrived today. School started yesterday. I told your father to bring you a day late because the second day is much quieter. Are you ready to go to your classroom and meet your teacher?"

"Yes."

The principal and Lilia held hands and chatted as they walked towards the next building and into the first-grade class. Señora Albert introduced

Lilia to Señora Rosales and the students before excusing herself. The teacher pointed to an empty seat in the front row and then continued her lecture. Lilia eyed her classmates but was soon bored and spent the next hour playing with the hem of her skirt while trying to stay awake.

Lilia thought the teacher was pretty. It did not matter to her that Señora Rosales was almost as wide as she was tall. Her roundness and rosy cheeks gave her a comforting look and reminded her of Mamita. Lilia felt at ease in the classroom, and the dread from the train ride receded. Señora Rosales smelled like the soap Mamita would make from rendered fat and lemon zest, and this pleased Lilia.

The pudgy instructor sang the alphabet in the center of the room. Lilia listened intently to the melody. When finished, she asked her students, "If you already know the alphabet, can you sing it back to me?"

Most hands rose quickly and some murmured, "I do."

"Very good. Now sing along with me." The teacher sang again and was joined by most of the children. Lilia listened.

When they were done, the teacher approached Lilia. "Eliana, do you know the alphabet?"

"I am not Eliana. I am Lilia!"

"Oh, I see. Is that what you wish to be called?"

"Yes."

"That is fine. Now Lilia, do you know the alphabet?"

"No."

The class broke out in laughter. Lilia sank in her chair.

"Quiet, children!"

The six-year-olds fidgeted in their seats. Lilia averted the teacher's eyes.

"Lilia! Please look at me when I speak to you. The alphabet is a set of letters we need to know to learn how to read."

Lilia interrupted, "Yes! I know what letters are, but I don't know all of them."

The class once again broke out in laughter, and the teacher stopped the misbehavior with a stern look. "Can you repeat some of the letters we sang?"

Lilia sang the first five letters and then stopped. "I don't remember the letters, but I love the song." Lilia hummed the song in its entirety in perfect pitch.

"Very good, Lilia. You have musical memory and a lovely voice."

The church bells chimed signifying it was time for mass. Señora Rosales smiled at the welcomed break.

"Girls! Line up two-by-two. Please remember to be very quiet on the way to the chapel. Do not talk or fidget during mass. The sisters will be watching you, so you must be as quiet as mice."

Lilia grew apprehensive. She had liked church when she had attended with Mamita but did not like it with the Villavicencios. With her previous family, mass had been peaceful as Lilia laid her head on Mamita's soft thighs and usually dozed off. In contrast, her new parents would not allow her to nap. They would give her a hard tap on her thighs, jerking her awake if she showed any signs of drowsiness.

The idea of spending a long hour in a new church did not sit well with Lilia, especially since her stomach gurgled from emptiness. She followed her classmates to the church and sat in the third pew. Señora Rosales watched her pupils sit and then left the chapel.

Lilia, now thinking only of food, fiddled with her hair and tried to chat with her neighbor to the right, but the girl shushed her. She tried again with the girl on the other side but was greeted with another hush. Closing her eyes, she was lulled by the insipid voice of the priest and had almost fallen asleep when the world seemed to explode. Loud and harmonious music jolted Lilia out of her seat. Her foot caught the edge of the kneeling stool, and she fell forward smashing her head onto the shoulders of the girl sitting in front of her.

"*Ooouch!*" screamed the startled girl, causing a cackle of laughter amongst the students. The giggles continued to rise from girls glad for the distraction. A nun came rushing towards them, pulled Lilia out to the aisle by her elbow and forced her to sit with the nuns in the last pew.

Lilia, under normal circumstances, would retaliate from such humiliating treatment. She thought about running away if the opportunity arose, but the glorious music calmed her, and she listened intently. The music resonated through her. She felt as if the sounds were waves caressing her and melting her anger and boredom. The continuous stream of divine notes captivated her, and she felt each note throughout her body, even to her toes. Her brain transformed the sound from her ears into vivid colors and patterns that formed and reshaped themselves.

Lilia did not know that the instrument making the music vibrating through her was a pipe organ rescued from a Bavarian church and transported by ship across the ocean to Chile. She also did not know that the composition had been recently rediscovered. Its creator was a composer named Pachelbel. She *was* aware that the magical stringing of the notes and chords registered deep within her, and she would never forget them.

When mass was over and the music stopped, everyone rose and left for the cafeteria. The nuns tried to stop the students from pushing each other on the way to lunch. But Lilia remained seated while the church emptied. She sat motionless, closed her eyes and heard phantom tones of the glorious sounds that had radiated throughout the church. She hummed the notes.

"Crazy girl, what are you doing?" interrupted a high-pitched voice from an altar boy borrowed from a nearby Catholic boy's school. He had a quizzical look on his face. Lilia, embarrassed by the intrusion, shot him a disdainful look. "None of your business, funny boy wearing a dress. Why are you in a girl's school?" She stuck out her tongue and ran toward the aroma of beans and rice.

A Disciplined Life

Viña del Mar, Chile

Lilia's search for a friend on the first day did not come to fruition. Her classmates refused to speak Spanish. They kept their distance and mocked her as they glanced in her direction. Lilia did not know why they behaved this way or why they did not speak Spanish. She wondered why so many students had light hair and blue eyes. Lilia felt different from them.

That evening Lilia's roommates, Monica, Elizabeth and Georgia, segregated Lilia with their constant chattering in English. One of the young housekeepers responsible for keeping an eye on the younger girls intervened. She pulled the girls aside and told them to speak Spanish and include Lilia in their babble and games. The girls still ignored Lilia, but Señorita Isabel had the idea to tell the girls that Lilia had an immensely powerful and rich father. It made all the difference, and the girls took an immediate interest in Lilia.

Elizabeth, or Lizzie, as she was nicknamed, whispered in Lilia's ear, "Have you met the house mistress, the old spinster?"

"No, but what is a house mistress?"

"The house mistress is the chief of the housekeepers. You'll need to stay away from her; she's mean and scary," Lizzie warned.

"Who?" Lilia sat on her bed.

"Señorita Silva! She looks like this." Lizzie contorted her face.

Monica, overhearing the conversation, added, "If you need anything, talk to Señorita Isabel, but never the spinster."

"Why?"

"We can talk about it tomorrow. It's time to turn the lights off and be in our beds before she cracks open the door and finds us awake."

Lilia fell asleep, happy to have company at night. Early the next morning, she was awakened by the loud chimes of the chapel bell. Drowsy, she forgot where she was and was about to call for Susana when she saw the silhouette of Monica's body in the next bed and remembered she was far from home. She listened to the bells and did not like their somber timbre, unlike the happier higher-pitched ones that sounded from the cathedral in Santiago. She felt the depth of the bells vibrate in her bones and counted the chimes. Bong. *Four.* Bong. *Five. Is it only five in the morning?* She hugged her pillow and was about to fall asleep again when the rain began to fall and a flash of lightning lit up the sky followed by a clash of thunder.

Rain splattered on the roof. Every drop made a thump, and hundreds of thumps together created an unusual rhythm. The drum-like rhythm spun a melody in her head. The rain falling on the eaves had a different tone than those falling on the roof. She spun a story around the sounds and imagined the droplets of rain were green-clad toy soldiers. She saw them marching in rows of perfect formation in endless columns.

The wind picked up, knocking the shutters against the exterior wall. *Clip, clip, clip. The cavalry arrived, men riding horses of many colors— yellow, green, striped and some even polka-dotted. Ready! Ready for war!* Lilia heard the battle cry. Her mind exploded once again with vivid patterns playing on the screen of her closed eyelids.

Soon the bells chimed again, announcing it was six in the morning. Lilia heard the door to the room open and someone pounding on the dresser. Señorita Silva entered the room and clapped her hands twice. "Morning! It's time to get up!"

The girls, accustomed to the drill, jumped to their feet. Lilia thought it odd that they could function so quickly after only seconds from being asleep. They greeted the house mistress in unison. "Good morning, Señorita Silva."

The girls climbed out of bed, grabbed their towels and left the room to stand in line for the hall bathrooms. Lilia languished in bed, stretched and yawned.

Señorita Silva approached, "Get up, girl!"

Lilia gave her an insolent look and did not move from her cozy bed. The woman's stance was rigid as she stared at Lilia.

"Did you not hear me?" the woman screamed.

"Yes. Please don't yell. My father says talking loudly is rude," Lilia said in a soft voice.

"Do not speak to me like that. Do not put on airs around me, orphan!"

"What is an orphan? Are you Señorita Silva?"

"Get out of bed."

Lilia climbed out of bed.

"You are a child without parents, fetched out of a farmer's hovel to live with the Villavicencios."

"I have parents. I have a mother and a father, even brothers and a sister in Maipo, and I have another mother and father in Santiago. And I have Susana—she is my third mother, and she says I'm a princess. I have many parents."

The woman laughed, "You are not a princess! You're a *guacha* and come from a bad seed."

"I don't understand you. What is a *guacha*?"

"An urchin."

"I don't know what that means either."

Señorita Silva smirked. "Have you ever met a stray dog?"

"Yes, of course."

"A filthy, homeless mutt who hunts trash in the street."

The words confused Lilia. "I like the dogs that live in the streets. They are not lucky to have owners to bathe them and brush their fur. It's not their fault they don't smell good. I would be proud to be a street dog!" Lilia held her tears. She had cried enough throughout the summer and forced herself not to shed a tear. The memory of the homeless dogs she had loved and befriended paraded through her mind. She remembered feeding and petting them on the days she managed to escape from the house. She loved all dogs.

"Dogs are kinder than you!" Lilia knelt on the floor, posed like a dog, growled and barked at Señorita Silva.

Shocked at the child's unusual behavior, Señorita Silva retorted, "If you behave in this manner again, you will be punished!"

"R-ruff, ruff, grrr," Lilia growled and barked and remained on all fours. "I'm going to tell my father what you said! Grrrrr."

Stunned at the child's threat, the mistress realized she might have made a mistake but promised herself, *Eliana will pay for her insolence.*

Señorita Isabel, hearing the commotion from the hall, ran into the room. She smiled at the mistress, hoping to calm the situation. "I'm sorry, I should have been here to help Lilia with her first morning's routine. I'll help her get ready."

"Do so!" Señorita Silva stormed out of the room.

The compassionate young housekeeper motioned Lilia to get her towel and then offered her hand and helped Lilia off the floor. Lilia forced herself to skip to the washroom, pretending she was not hurt by the mistress's words. Señorita Isabel stayed by Lilia's side during breakfast and watched Lilia eat only one spoonful of oatmeal.

"Lilia, I'm always here if you need me," Señorita Isabel consoled.

Lilia blew her a kiss and picked up her tray. She threw out her food and placed the dishes in a large aluminum bin before walking slowly to her classroom. She remembered Señorita Silva's harsh words and felt that something was amiss. Her stomach ached.

Señora Rosales was pleased when she watched Lilia quietly take her seat and was eager to get to know the child. When lessons began, Lilia found it difficult to concentrate and fell into a daydream. She played in her memory the beautiful chapel music from the previous day. Her mind toggled between music and the ugly exchange of words from the house mistress. More than once, Señora Rosales reprimanded Lilia for not paying attention.

After lunch, the principal visited the first graders. When she entered the room, Señora Rosales asked the students to rise. The students stood at attention and said in unison, "Good morning, Señora Albert."

The principal scanned the room. "What wonderful students we have this year in our first-grade class. Don't you agree, Señora Rosales?"

"Yes, I do."

The principal tried to make eye contact with every child. She spoke with a soothing voice. "I'm so happy we're starting a long journey together. I know it is hard to be away from your family, but now we are each other's second family. The McKenna family. It's large and strong. This family will help you do great things in the world. Raise your hand and tell me what you want to be when you grow up."

A braided girl raised her hand. The principal nodded, prompting the girl to smile shyly and say, "I wish to be a teacher like Señora Rosales!"

Another girl pouted and said, "That's what I was going to say."

"Wonderful choice, both of you. We need teachers. Who else would like to tell me?"

No one raised their hand.

"Are there any future artists in the room? How many like to color and paint?" A few girls raised their hands as excited whispers circulated the room.

"That's why I'm visiting you today. We're going to choose fun things to do."

The principal announced the school's offerings: drawing, singing, painting and dance. She jotted the names of students in her notebook by the activity they liked. The first graders, soon bored of the chore, became restless until she mentioned ballet. Their whispers now turned to excited exclamations of glee when the principal showed photographs of ballet dancers wearing tutus. A flurry of students begged her to write their names down.

Lilia did not know what a ballet dancer was and was not enthusiastic about any of the activities. She stifled a yawn and wondered what the morning snack would be as she salivated thinking it might be butter cookies.

"And lastly, who is interested in learning to play the piano?"

No one raised their hands.

"Is there anyone who has not signed up for an activity?"

Lilia raised her hand.

"Would you like to study piano?"

"Huh? Piano? Is it what I heard yesterday?"

"Heard where?" Señora Albert asked.

"The music I heard yesterday at the church."

Señora Rosales interrupted, "She means the organ, Señora Albert."

"Well, the organ is very much like a piano."

Lilia jumped from her seat and ran to the principal. "I want to study the organ. I like how loud it was."

"I'll put you down for piano, as we don't offer organ lessons. You'll start today after lunch."

Lilia smiled, showing her missing two front teeth.

Professor Goretsky

Lilia wolfed down her lunch and waited in anticipation for her piano lesson. Señorita Isabel came to escort her to the music room, but the principal took her instead. Lilia reached for Señora Albert's hand and skipped to the music room. Outside the practice room, Señora Albert released Lilia's tight grip.

"We're here. Knock and then enter. Introduce yourself to your piano teacher."

Lilia knocked, giggled, peeked inside, was astounded at the tall black instrument and flew into the room. Such was her excitement that she forgot to thank Señora Albert for walking her to the studio. Lilia did not see the piano teacher kneeling behind the door, perusing a set of beginner's books.

"Hello," a grey-haired man in a three-piece suit and bow tie welcomed her.

"You're a boy teacher. I thought teachers were only girls."

"No, they can be men. My name is Professor Goretsky," he extended his hand, and Lilia shook it.

"Is that the piano? Señora Albert says it's like the one in the church?"

"You mean the organ?"

"Yes."

"The keys are similar, but the organ has many more of them. I'll explain the difference another time."

"I like the organ very much. I can't wait to play it."

"You will. First let's learn the piano."

Lilia nodded.

"Come and sit on this bench. The organ and piano sound a little different. Have you heard the voice of this instrument?"

"No."

Professor Goretsky sat next to her. He played Mozart's *Ah, Vous Dirai-je, Mamám*. Lilia heard the sweet sounds of the instrument and they too coursed through her body. She felt it was more playful sounding than the organ. The hairs on the back of her neck tingled in agreement.

"Well, Lilia, I want to teach you the names of the notes." He rose from the bench, and she centered herself on the seat. "You'll need to learn, step by step, but I think you need to be propped up a bit to reach the keys better."

The professor placed a pillow under her. "And speaking of steps, let's make-believe this keyboard is a set of stairs. Did you ever walk up the stairs in a tall house that has more than one level?"

"Yes. I went to a doctor's office that had three sets of stairs."

"Well, the piano is like a building that is set on its back. It has eight floors. Each floor has seven steps with their own names. Let me show you." Professor Goretsky played a scale, singing each note, "Do, Re, Mi, Fa, Sol, La, and Si. Today we'll pay attention only to the white steps and ignore the black ones. Let's go up another flight—Do, Re, Mi, Fa, Sol, La, Si," he sang as he played the keys of the next octave. "Now, can you repeat the names of the steps when I play the note?"

Lilia named them all correctly. The professor nodded and continued his lesson. "The Do always guards the two black steps—that is how you find it."

Lilia pointed to all the keys representing Do. She then played the scale exactly as the professor had, even folding her thumb under before striking the Fa. She looked at Professor Goretsky and seeing his approval, smiled wide.

Professor Goretsky was stunned at Lilia's astuteness. He was surprised that such a young girl had even noticed the nuances of his hand positioning. No other student had paid that much attention. He wondered if the girl might be gifted but feared it was too early to tell.

Lilia enjoyed the private lessons with Professor Goretsky twice per week. Even though she practiced daily, she still had to manage her homework and leave time for fun. None of her friendships equaled that of Professor Goretsky's. He grew to love Lilia as if she were his daughter, and she was in awe of him, constantly desiring his praise. He made her feel special. His constant applause fed Lilia with inspiration. She grasped everything easily and was never bored. The Professor was careful not to show his preference toward her in front of other students as well as teachers. He hoped his lifelong wish of discovering a prodigy would materialize and prayed she was the one. It was difficult for him to contain his joy with each new lesson she mastered.

After her lessons ended, Lilia would ask the professor to play something new for her. He complied and chose a multitude of varied composers. He knew exposing her to as much classical music as possible would help train her ear. She absorbed every detail and could easily decipher different composers' styles. To the professor, her mind was a riddle he did not understand. She loved to hear about musicians' lives, even the tragedies that followed them. She cried when learning that Beethoven was deaf but still composed, and she was especially pained to know that Mozart died young and poor. Lilia was the professor's most capable student.

The little girl who began her life abandoned on a foundling wheel found happiness at the McKenna and especially learning to play piano. More importantly, she found a nurturing relationship with a father-like figure. She memorized everything the professor presented. The piano teacher wondered how Lilia understood complicated music structures without much explanation. As time passed, he began to think she could be his prodigy. Still too early for optimism, the professor was careful not to raise his hopes, but he could not stop thinking that Lilia was destined for an exceptional piano career. He indulged in his daydreams.

For Lilia, music was a puzzle to solve and enjoy. Every musical composition was like a painting of many colors, each with a secret pattern. Each aria or sonata was a gift from a composer for her alone. When she practiced, she experimented with sound, texture, volume, duration, form and emotion, all expressed by the way she touched the keys. She practiced whenever she had spare time.

Dark Days

Viña del Mar, Chile, 1937

The year passed quickly for Lilia. She endured an overwhelming amount of work for a first grader. She was an average student in schoolwork but exceptional in piano studies. Although not required to practice on Sunday, Lilia refused to skip even a day. She became obsessed with the instrument. Graduating to second grade, she thought less about running through the fields of Maipo and more about learning new music. It was still not easy for her to conform to the strict rules the McKenna required, but she tried.

Señorita Isabel monitored Lilia and worried that she did not play outdoors enough and would rather be at the piano studio. Señorita Silva was not as positive towards the well-being of the child. She would punish Lilia by forcing her to stand in the hallway and face the wall for hours. Professor Goretsky heard of these punishments and intervened by bringing it to the principal's attention. He begged Señora Albert to make concessions for his gifted student, and she agreed. More than once she called the house mistress to her office and warned her to ease her comportment toward Lilia. Señora Albert had much respect for Professor Goretsky and did not want news of the mistress's behavior to reach Don Villavicencio.

Lilia learned to avoid Señorita Silva as much as possible. The mistress envied Lilia's musical talent. She was secretly angry at Professor Goretsky, furious that the principal was not on her side and ordered the house-keeping staff, "Make sure Lilia makes her own bed daily and cleans her side of the room without help, for she needs the discipline." She especially warned Señorita Isabel, "Befriending Lilia is against school policy, and if you continue to show favoritism, I will be certain to recommend your dismissal." Señorita Isabel agreed not to help Lilia, as she was frightened of being replaced during such harsh economic times.

Señorita Gloria Silva had come from a well-to-do family. Her father died from tuberculosis when she was a child, leaving his wife and four children under the age of ten. Her mother sold their assets to keep the family afloat, and when those funds ran out, she was forced to sell their house and place the children's futures in peril.

Seven years after her father's death, Señorita Silva was a teenager with a lackluster education. Forced to find employment, she acquired a supervisor's position at a private school dormitory. Many years later when the McKenna School opened its doors, she applied as mistress and was dumbfounded when they hired her. The now middle-aged woman had lost all hopes of marriage. Jealousy caused her to resent the privileged girls, who mocked the severe woman and called her "old spinster" behind her back.

Often wondering why circumstances had robbed her of a rich life, Señorita Silva was forced to play the role of school mother to rich girls. Most students at the McKenna could trace their lineage back to the Old World but now were the prominent families integral in building Chile. Out of all the students, the house mistress disliked Lilia most. She believed that orphans were the worst human beings. Señorita Silva assumed that Lilia's biological mother must have been a prostitute and, therefore, the sins of the parents are the sins of the child. She decided it was her duty to make the odious Lilia miserable. Such an opportunity presented itself on a Sunday while the girls were at mass. She noticed Lilia's roommate, Monica, had not been wearing her watch. Señorita Silva entered their room and spotted Monica's watch resting on a nightstand. She tucked the heavy gold watch in a back corner of Lilia's dresser drawer under a rolled-up pair of socks.

Señorita Silva knew Monica would eventually miss the watch and ask about it. Monica did not mention it until the fourth night. Approaching Señorita Silva, Monica asked, "I haven't been able to find my watch. Has anyone turned it into the lost and found?"

"Not that I know. I'll ask the help," said Señorita Silva, happy that her plan was working.

"My father gave it to me for my Saint's Day. He warned me not to lose it."

"Did you check with Señorita Isabel and your roommates?"

"I did. No one has seen it."

The mistress smiled, "I'll supervise a search of your room. Gather your roommates and meet me upstairs in a few minutes."

"Thank you."

Señorita Silva went through the motions of asking both staff and students about the watch with concern in her voice. After dinner, she went to the room where the girls were already looking under beds and furniture.

"Girls, pull out every drawer from your dresser and dump the contents onto your bed," the mistress ordered.

"Señorita Silva, please, it's my practice time in the studio. May I leave now? I don't want to lose my time slot," Lilia pleaded.

"You can skip practice for today."

"I cannot. I've a new piece to learn." Tears welled in Lilia's eyes.

"No. When all the contents are on the bed and you've folded everything back into the drawers, then if there's time, I'll let you go."

The mistress's left eye twitched involuntarily. She sat on a chair and did not stop staring at Lilia, never glancing at Lizzie, Georgia or Monica. Lilia pulled out the top drawer and heaped everything onto the bed. Señorita Silva spotted the watch as it tumbled out along with a dozen white socks and underwear. Lilia did not notice it and struggled as she slid the empty drawer back into the dresser. She began folding her underwear. The mistress hoped Lilia would be frightened by finding the watch in her possession and try to slip it back in the drawer when no one was looking. She relished the thought of accusing Lilia of the theft, and it would mean Lilia's expulsion from the school.

Lilia gasped when she saw the watch. She grabbed it and held it over her head and announced with glee, "Monica, I found it. I don't know how it got into my drawer, but I'm happy it is not lost. Can I practice now, Señorita Silva?"

"No!" Señorita Silva said through clenched jaws.

"How did it get in your drawer? I always keep it on my night table," Monica asked.

"I don't know," Lilia answered.

Señorita Silva grabbed the watch from Lilia's hand. "You should be so ashamed! Why did you steal Monica's watch?"

"Lilia is my friend and would not take my watch." Monica spoke to the mistress and then turned to Lilia, "I know you didn't take it."

"I wouldn't." Lilia's lip quivered.

The mistress grabbed Lilia's arm and marched her to the principal's office. Lilia fought the tears welling in her eyes as she tried to keep up with Señorita Silva's long stride.

A hard knock on the office door alarmed Señora Albert. "Come in."

"Señora Albert, excuse us. I'm sorry to disturb you, but we need to address a situation immediately."

The principal read Lilia's distraught face and greeted her with a smile, "Hello, Lilia." She turned to the mistress, "What's wrong?"

"Lilia stole Monica's gold watch. It was hidden in her dresser. This behavior is most disturbing."

"Is that true?" Señora Albert looked disappointed.

"I'm as shocked as you, Señora. Imagine one of our girls committing such an intolerable act."

"Let's remain calm. Lilia, what do you have to say?"

"I didn't take the watch. I don't know how it got into my drawer."

"She stole it!" Señorita Silva shouted.

The principal shot the house mistress a stern look. "Lilia, have you ever taken anything that didn't belong to you before coming to this school?"

"Yes." Lilia felt her face flush. "I stole bread from Mamita when I was hungry."

"Was there anything else?"

"Yes, Señora Albert. I stole from our pantry because there were hungry dogs in the street."

"Did you ever take anything that was not food?"

"No. Never! I would never steal a watch."

"Lilia, I will forget this incident as there is no proof. I'm sorry, Señorita Silva, we must let this slide."

"We must send word to Don Villavicencio of what has happened. He needs to know." Señorita Silva folded her arms.

"Can you explain why it was in your drawer?" Señora Albert's voice was soft.

"No." Lilia stifled a sob.

"Perhaps Señorita Silva is right. We should tell your father."

"No, please don't. Monica is not angry. She knows I didn't take it."

"Monica is not upset?" Señora Albert asked the mistress.

"Monica is a child and does not realize the gravity of the situation. I'm sure Monica's parents would like to know what has happened, and they'll demand that Lilia be punished."

"Well, if Monica is not blaming anyone and we don't have proof of what happened, we'll call this an unfortunate event and not trouble any of the parents."

"But this is absurd! We cannot encourage our students to steal!"

"Señorita Silva! Have you forgotten your position in this school? Am I not the principal? I take offense at your tone." Señora Albert turned to Lilia, "Go on, child, leave us."

"Thank you, Señora Albert." Lilia ran out of the office straight to the practice room.

"I will forget the way you spoke to me just now. I appreciate your loyalty and desire to do what you feel is right, but why would she want such a trinket when Don Villavicencio is her father?"

Señorita Silva did not respond.

"In the future, I expect my staff not to question my decisions, especially in front of students. I beg you will not hold a grudge towards Lilia for what happened today."

The house mistress nodded.

Señora Albert reached for her purse and walked towards her door. "It's late. Turn off the lights and lock up for me."

Premonition

Santiago, Chile, December 1939

Gertrudis Alvarez scrubbed and filled the birdbath. Even such a dirty job was pleasurable on such a sunny day. The birds flapped their wings as if to thank the kind woman for the clean water. She sat in her usual place to sip her morning tea, surrounded by flowers in the minuscule garden. She loved the chatter of birds and inhaled the dewy fragrant air.

While in her garden, she prayed for the children under her growing auspices. Her geographical zone ranged from Santiago to the central valley. Señora Alvarez's numerous tasks were detailed and planned in her outdoor sanctuary. Whenever possible, she liked to bring little tokens of joy to her children. It might be a used toy donated by the church or a pretty comb to help a preteen feel special for not having to share one with many other girls. When she collected donations, she enjoyed filling small bags with such trifles that meant so much to children who owned nothing.

Unfortunately, there were never enough trinkets for all her orphans. The endless visits to them proved to Alvarez that every year the situation worsened with more children entering the system. Children in institutions were often disheartened in their austere buildings. Those who were fostered were also unhappy sometimes because their new families refused to treat them like real sons and daughters. Parents who had their own biological children seemed to care only that the government stipend arrived on time. It was needed to help with monthly household expenses.

The overextended social worker felt hopeless as a heavy feeling of discouragement descended upon her. She felt uneasy reading the extremely bleak news about the growing rancor in Europe and a second world war starting. Germany had invaded Poland. She sensed the war would be the beginning of hell on earth, much worse than the first global war.

Señora Alvarez picked up the paper and read another article about Germany's land grab and Italy's dreams of glory. Disgusted, she shook her head wondering why the Europeans loved war. Thinking there might be another prolonged conflict, along with the constant distress over her orphans, caused her endless angst. She often felt her heart fluttering out of rhythm. Doctors warned her blood pressure was rising to dangerous levels and she should retire. She did not heed their warnings but pushed onward and tirelessly aided the children. She experienced premonitions during sleep-like trances. One such presentiment was that the current disastrous events in Europe would not unfold quickly. Terror filled her as her mind agonized over what might happen. She prayed constantly, hoping the burning sensations in her stomach would cease.

Although Señora Alvarez's sixth sense of impending doom sent an alarm to every cell of her body, she could not guess how future events would play out. At the end of her prayers, she always thanked her mother, who watched from heaven, for teaching her the rigid Catholic dogma and forbidding her to deviate from its strict rules of conduct. Faith helped her remain strong.

If someone had been sipping tea by Señora Alvarez's side, they would have been astounded at her clarity. She perceived that World War I had not ended—it was merely on hold. Lessons had not been learned from that war.

As was her custom, she folded her newspaper into a square and placed it under a vase in the center of her patio table for protection against the wind. It would wait for her return from an arduous day to reread the articles and contemplate the state of the world.

A Link Breaks

Santiago, Chile, 1941

After a long convalescence, Sister Agata returned to her normal schedule at the hospital. Although the nun tired easily, her mood improved. Both clinic and convent chores became tolerable. Dr. Herrmann kept his eye on Agata, fearful that overwork might cause her to slip back into depression and anxiety.

On weekends, the nuns took shifts at the hospital. After Sunday's mass, the sisters laundered and caught up on the convent's never-ending chores. When tasks were completed, they had an afternoon of respite. Agata read the books the doctor and his wife continued selecting for her.

Agata's eyelids drooped, the words blurred and she dozed in her chair. Not even a book falling from her lap would awaken her. When she was not sleeping, she fantasized about being married to her childhood friend, Rojelio. She envisioned children of various ages playing at her feet. Her mind transformed the gawky boy into a robust man, but his loving and kind nature remained. Agata daydreamed of a cold night where she would be warm in Rojelio's arms. Ashamed of her thoughts, she jumped out of bed, knelt and prayed for forgiveness.

As her fantasies became commonplace, Agata spent less time kneeling. She no longer ran to the chapel for redemption but allowed herself to wallow in bed. During one such moment, a knock intruded and she disapprovingly answered, "Come in."

"Surprise, dear Sister!" A jubilant Bene entered holding a tea tray. Under her arm she held jasmine vines that bloomed by the turnstile.

"Agata, grab this bouquet from under my arm; I'm about to drop it. This tray is heavy."

"Has Mother allowed you to cut the jasmine?" Agata took the vines and brought them to her nose.

"She didn't see me snip them from our front gate. Place them in your water pitcher, please."

Agata grabbed the crystal pitcher. "Why all the fuss, Bene?"

"Today is San Esteban Day, which I know is the same day as your birthday. So, happy birthday!"

"You remembered. Thank you for the fanfare." Agata arranged the long strands of jasmine as Bene placed the tray on the bed.

"I've already added milk and honey to the tea."

"The scent of jasmine is divine, but the steaming hot empanada is even better."

"A leftover from dinner. I hid it in the cupboard before Sister Lucia made her nightly rounds."

Agata admired the beautiful tray. "The way you placed the pomegranate seeds in a glass goblet looks like hundreds of rubies. You're so clever, Bene."

"I wish they were real gems for you."

"You can't eat stone. This is much better!"

"I wish I had a treat befitting a birthday. I wish it were an éclair or a *baba-au-rhum*. How I loved it when my Papá would buy them at the *Petit Patisserie* in Strasbourg. Chile doesn't have such fine bakeries."

Agata's eyes widened. "It's a perfect treat, but speaking of pastries, do you remember Linzer torte?"

"The velvet texture of it. Yes. I hunger for its sensation on my tongue."

"A slice of Linzer with a strong espresso would be wonderful right now! It's been years since I've enjoyed them together."

Agata sat on the bed. "Sit on the other side of the tray, and we can split the empanada."

"No, it's only for you. Sister, how old are you?"

Agata hesitated, "Thirty. It is so old."

"You still look nineteen."

"It feels like only yesterday that I took my final vows and traveled to Santiago."

"For me as well," Bene frowned. "When I arrived from France, I thought I'd run back home in a year or two, but fifteen years have passed, and I'm still here."

"I hate being thirty," Agata sighed and took a bite of the empanada.

"Thirty is not old. I'm thirty-six, but I feel like an adolescent. Age is an illusion. Thankfully, it does not exist in our eternal life."

"You feel young because you're happy. While my health has improved, I've not regained...joy. We lost our beloved children."

"Love is still in our hearts, regardless that the children are gone," Bene scolded.

"Love doesn't exist. We don't know what it's like to be real women." Agata took another bite of her empanada and covered her mouth to speak, "This is better the second day."

"We are real women. Just because we are celibate doesn't mean we are not what we are born with!" Bene smiled mischievously and continued, "I have experienced love, even in a place like this."

"Quiet, Bene! You know how I feel about carnal knowledge."

"I've shared my body."

"You have said, but then you were a mere teenager! Now that you are mature, you can control your impulses. We sacrifice secular pleasures for a higher calling. We serve our Lord and that is enough."

Agata felt a sour taste in her mouth. Forbidden conversation, even with her friend, caused her anxiety. Agata took a sip of tea. Her hands trembled, and the cup clanked on its saucer as a little tea spilled. Embarrassed that Bene noticed her shaking hands, Agata forced them still and realized she had not completely healed from her nervous disorder.

"Agata! You're turning pale before my eyes! Do you feel faint?"

"No, I don't, and I forbid myself to faint." Agata gripped the sheets to steady herself. Bene removed the tray and placed it on the dresser. She sat and stroked Agata's hair.

"It's been months since I've had an episode. I'm afraid I'll slip back into the abyss."

"Breathe, yes, breathe the way I do." Bene inhaled deeply. "Slow...the way the doctor showed us. Remember his words." Bene held Agata's clammy hands. "Inhale and count to five. Hold your breath. Now exhale slower and count to eight. Let's do it again. Slower...that's it." Bene's cooing helped steady Agata's breathing.

"You're magical, Bene. I'm feeling better, thank you." Agata tried to dislodge Bene's interlocked hands, but Bene tightened her grip.

Bene stared at the wall. "Look at the way the sun's rays shine through the crystal vase. It's creating rainbows."

"It's a sign. God is love and love is touch and touch divine." Agata bowed her head and kissed Bene's hand.

Bene's face showed surprise. "You want...me?"

Agata shook her head. "Through you the Virgin has reached out. Even in this dark moment of fear, she's sent me a message as she's done for women throughout the ages."

"I don't understand!"

"She said to leave."

"Leave where?" Bene let go of Agata's wrists.

The mantra repeated in Agata's head, *God is love and love is touch....* Staring at the spectrum of colors, she saw what seemed like light melting the ore of an imaginary link in a chain that wrapped around her body. "I'm leaving the sisterhood," Agata whispered.

Bene stood in disbelief.

Agata knew she could not love a woman and could not phantom any other love than that between a man and a woman. Time would not shroud her in a tomb before she could explore a range of human experiences. She would divorce Christ and venture out and feel the texture of a slice of Linzer lingering in her mouth.

Leaving All Behind

Santiago, Chile, 1942

"You're a disgrace to this order thinking you can break ties easily without regard to reason and abandon your vows on a whim! If you insist on this folly, I will not stop you!" Mother Superior looked down at the papers on her desk and avoided looking directly into Agata's eyes.

"Mother, please! I want to do this the proper way. I need dispensation from the Holy See, but I need it done as soon as possible, as I cannot wait." Agata reached for her arm, but Mother Superior pulled away.

The senior nun immediately regretted her offensive behavior. She tried to make amends by walking around the desk and placing her hands on Agata's shoulders. "I'm sorry. The correct thing to do is to be patient and not be in such haste. There's no harm in waiting a few months when making such a dire decision. It is worth the wait."

"If it were a matter of months, then, yes, I'd gladly wait. But Mother, I've heard it could take years!"

The mother removed her hands from Agata's shoulders. "Yes, it can, especially now with a war raging in Europe. The Vatican will not rush to work on your insignificant case when Pope Pius is worried over an entire continent...but why not spend your time here in the meantime? Take the time you need for this decision, as it deserves much attention. Breaking your vows is the work of the devil."

"I'm running out of time. I've been a nun for half of my life. I'm afraid that if I don't do this now, I'll never again have the fortitude to do so."

Mother Superior walked back around her desk and dropped into her chair. She took a deep breath and gathered her thoughts. "But if you wait and your heart sees the enormity of this mistake and you decide to stay, then nothing would be lost. You would still be here and continue your life as a sister as if nothing happened. All would be forgiven, my dear child."

"I've made my decision, Mother! I will leave without dispensation."

"Are you certain?"

"Yes!"

"Very well, then. If you cannot wait, it's done."

Agata nodded. Hearing the word "done" aloud and spoken with such gravity gave Agata the urge to run back to her chambers and hide. The moment felt surreal.

Mother Superior paused and spoke slowly, assuring that Agata understood every word, "You will leave tonight. You'll not tarry nor loiter around the convent. Most of all, you will not mention a word of your departure to any of the sisters."

"But Mother—"

"Quiet!" Mother Superior regained her rigid stance. "After midnight mass, when the sisters have gone to bed, you'll wait for the clock to strike two and meet me in the courtyard."

"Mother, I cannot leave so soon. I'm not ready. Please, I'll need a few days."

"It must be this night. Your attitude cannot fester among the sisters, nor do I wish to witness tears from you or anyone else."

"Mother, I have no personal effects. I need clothing, money and time to sort things out. I don't know yet where I'm going. Please, Mother, give me a fortnight to get ready. I beg you."

"Go to the dispensary. Along with bandages and medical supplies, you'll find clothing and toiletries. Take what you need. There are old suitcases for you as well."

"Mother, those are things collected for the poor. I cannot take them. I'd feel guilty."

"You are now the destitute this order serves; take what you need. Tonight, you will be one of the poor without the church behind you for support and sustenance. Go and be amongst the sheep you so desire!"

"Yes, Mother," Agata trembled.

"Remember my words. You will not tell anyone of your plans. I request that you will not be seen by anyone. After collecting items from the dispensary, stay in your room. I'll tell the sisters you are not feeling well and need to be left alone. Do not attend supper tonight. The next time I see you will be by the foundling wheel."

Agata took Mother's hand and kissed it, "Thank you, Mother. I've heard the Virgin's voice. It is with her blessing I make my choice."

"I doubt very much that you have heard the voice of our Blessed Mary. You're still sick and need to overcome your paranoias. Accept your illness, and do not pretend to be St. Catherine! The fainting spells, the trembling, the crazy ideas you derive from books you dare read behind my back! Your focus was never on anyone but yourself. I'll pray that you find inner peace in the daunting outside world."

Agata's eyes were bloodshot and filled with tears. She knew Mother lived a secluded life, never belonging to or understanding the outside world. Agata left the office and gently closed Mother Superior's door. Sister Bernadette grabbed Agata's arm and startled her.

"I heard every word. It isn't true! You cannot leave! You cannot!" Bene whispered frantically.

"Shush! Come with me! Don't let Mother hear you."

They hurried down the hall to the stone steps leading to the cold cellar that was now the dispensary. Agata opened the door and stepped into darkness. She hunted for the light cord and pulled it. The room brightened. Bernadette followed her inside, and Agata shut the door.

"I won't let you leave! I can't bear it!" Sister Bernadette's voice cracked, and her face paled.

"It's done. I've failed my parents' dream of the sisterhood. I can now choose my own destiny. I will never be captive again—not by anyone, especially the church."

"Agata, I love you. I won't live without you. I promise to never ask for anything that is not in your capacity to give. Life outside isn't as rosy as you think. The sisterhood gives us a roof and provides every meal. That guarantee does not exist anywhere else. You are too timid, sometimes afraid of your own shadow, so how can you leave this haven and venture outside?"

Agata put her arms around Bernadette and pulled her close. She felt Bene's body sink into hers with her breasts heaving as she sobbed.

"Why are you holding me now when you never let me hold you before? Do you finally love me?"

"I do, as I always have, but in a sister sort of way."

"I'm going with you."

"No! Dearest of all my sisters, I must find my way alone. Bene, this is your home. It's where you belong. You have said that the sisterhood is your calling."

"Maybe it was at one time, but not anymore. I love you too much."

"It'll be alright." Agata held Bernadette's chin with one hand and with the other wiped the tears from her cheeks. "You know who you are and what you were meant to be. Your blissful face shows me during prayers, and your contentment shines through your work with the dying. I see how you lovingly hold them in your arms and guide their passing. And your patients are so grateful. You are their bridge to the ever after with one foot on Earth and the other in Heaven. My love, you are perfection sent by God."

"I don't care about them as much as I want you, Agata."

"Shhh, dear, sweet love. Leave me now, I beg you. Close your eyes."

Bene closed her eyes, and Agata kissed her lips. Bernadette stood motionless, her lips quivering.

"Keep your eyes closed. Don't open them until you are out in the hallway." Agata opened the door and guided Bene out. "Bene, don't look back. Let my kiss be the last you feel from me. Know that I love you."

Bernadette whimpered, "No."

Agata gave Bene a gentle push and closed the door behind her.

Bernadette opened her eyes and ran up the stairs to hide in her room lest any of the sisters see her storm of tears.

Agata let out a sob but stopped herself from crying. She found a worn valise and checked that it was sturdy. Hunting through a pile of clothing for something to wear proved harder than finding the case. Most fabrics were too thin, nearly shredded by the amount of wear, or too large for her slender body. Finding a cotton floral skirt that reached mid-calf, she wondered if she would look like other women who wore such skirts. She had been fascinated by how they twirled their bodies, sending their skirts afloat and showing off their shapely legs through a pair of nylons. *Would I dare to wear such hosiery?*

The distraught soon-to-be ex-nun assembled a small wardrobe, folded the clothes and placed them neatly in the valise. While latching the case, Agata noticed an old purse strap sticking out of a cardboard box. Her heart skipped a beat as a purse is something she had never owned. She pulled it out and was delighted to find it in good condition and made of leather. She left the dispensary and was grateful that she did not run into any of the sisters on the way to her room.

Agata pulled her chair and placed it under the doorknob to stop anyone from entering. She took off her habit and tried on the skirt, which fit loosely but would do. Pulling off her veil and running her fingers through her short hair, she hoped it would grow quickly and one day be long enough to wear braids. From her stash of newly found clothing, she pulled a scarf and wrapped it around her neck to see if she could feel comfortable dressed as a woman of the outside world. Wanting to see her reflection in a mirror, she was instantly ashamed and promised herself never to become vain.

Agata added her personal belongings to the valise. They included a framed photo of her family and Lilia's rag doll. She wrapped the bar of soap from her sink in a cleaning cloth and placed it in the purse along with her rosary beads. She did not own a wallet and stuffed her handkerchiefs in the purse to fill it up. After folding her habits and veils, she stacked them on the dresser, leaving them behind for the sisters to use.

Time seemed to stand still as she waited for nightfall to meet Mother at the appointed hour. Minutes felt like hours. She opened the window, felt the dewy night air and caught sight of the foundling wheel reflecting the moonlight. Thoughts rushed her mind of the morning she had found Lilia, and her body ached to feel the child once again in an embrace.

Agata agreed that Mother's decision to miss supper had been a good one. Mother had realized it would be hard to keep her emotions in check while dining together with the sisters for the last time. Her stomach gurgled from emptiness but not from hunger. She sat on her bed and waited for midnight mass. Contemplating how she would manage without a job, money or anything of value to sell, she worried. Throughout the evening she heard Mother Superior and the sisters going about their usual business of completing chores. More than once, a sister knocked on her door and asked if she was feeling better. They all volunteered to bring her tea or soup, but Agata thanked them kindly and refused to open the door. She was surprised that Bene stayed away.

The bells for the matins tolled at midnight. Listless, Agata listened to the shuffling of tired feet heading for the chapel. Mass lasted over an hour. Finally, the appointed hour came, and the bells broke the silence of the night. It was time for Agata to leave the convent. She pulled the long purse strap over her shoulder and grabbed her suitcase. The door squeaked, and she looked back at her room for the last time. The hallway was dark and empty. She did not turn on the lights but descended the stairs carefully to not hit the rails with her valise. A moment of apprehension swept over her as she grabbed the banister and steadied herself. Reaching the front door and stepping into the courtyard, she stopped to listen for any movement from the rooms above. Hearing none, she stepped out and closed the door.

The air was unusually still. She paused again to listen if Bernadette would come down and plead with Agata to take her along. Mother Superior stood by the portal and watched the wayward nun approach. She prayed silently that the parting would be tearless and absent of drama. Agata was both sad and relieved that Bernadette restrained herself and followed her wishes, but in her mind, she pictured Bene awake with her ears pressed to the door, listening for Agata's departure and then crossing the hall to Agata's room for a better view of the courtyard.

"I prayed that your heart would change." Mother Superior shivered in the moonlight.

"I'm sorry, Mother." Agata put down her suitcase. "Thank you for your kindness. It's hard to leave, but please understand I do this *not* from malice."

Mother Superior nodded and spoke hurriedly, "Goodbye, Agata. I hope you find what you are looking for. I pray."

Agata kissed Mother's hand and genuflected before slipping into the turnstile portal of the foundling wheel. She ducked her head to fit through but before she could complete the pass, she looked up at her bedroom window and saw Bene, exactly as she had imagined, staring down at her and holding a lit candle. The tiny flicker illuminated Bene's smile and sent Agata a message of love. Agata pushed the gate and heard the wood and iron door groan as it turned and shut the convent out of her life.

Night Streets

Fog settled over the street, hugged buildings and dispersed around Agata as she walked. It wrapped around the kerosene lamps, creating a halo and casting an eerie glow. The wind, gentle and soundless, brushed her cheeks. Night engulfed the newly emancipated nun. The ghostlike city, usually full of life and color, spread out in front of her, beckoning, yet foreboding and unrecognizable in the dark. Agata walked without a clear destination.

She heard the scurry of tiny feet and edged closer to an alley to see if rats were causing the noise. She saw streaks of grey, a dash of black and even yellow jump from one roof to another. Lonely feral cats were the originators of the hustle, living on rooftops to protect themselves from dogs that hunted them on the streets.

Tightening her thin wool shawl against the wind, Agata quickened her pace. As a youngster, she had always found herself safely cocooned at home surrounded by family when day turned to dusk. The same was true as an adult living in the convent. Nuns did not venture into the night. She walked uneasily through the macabre streets, feeling uncomfortable as if someone was watching her. She reassured herself that it was only the circumspect four-footed creatures that eyed her.

A strong stench of whiskey wafted from a man coiled on a bus stop bench, snoring vociferously near puddles of vomit splashed on the ground. Agata walked briskly, channeling thoughts of sunny days. She ran through all the possibilities of where to go and how to earn a living. None of her ideas seemed feasible. Needing comfort or a sign, she searched the sky for the Southern Cross, but fog cloaked the stars.

Agata decided to head to the hospital and resign from her job. It didn't matter it was night, as someone would be there to carry the message to Dr. Hermann. She continued at her hurried pace, barely able to catch her breath when she arrived. Stepping through the hospital threshold, she inhaled the familiar odors of alcohol and disinfectant, nodded to the night guard at the front desk, and walked to the emergency room.

Agata noticed the oldest of the nurses hunched over a patient. "Good evening, Maddalena, or should I say good morning?"

"Agata, what are you doing here at such an hour?" Maddalena noticed her street clothes and inquired, "Why are you not wearing the habit?"

"Oh, Lena, it has been a difficult day. And why are you working the night shift? Isn't it too much for you?"

"I switched shifts with Rosa, the new mother, for her baby's sake. But dear, what brings you in?"

"I've come to see the doctor."

"Doctor Borja is upstairs napping in one of the empty beds."

"No, I was hoping to see Dr. Herrmann."

"I'm sorry, Dr. Herrmann is not on tonight. He's on the morning shift. Is there something I can do?"

"No. Thank you, Lena. I'll wait in the lobby for him."

"Sister, I'm about to go on break. Would you share a tea with me at the lounge?"

"Yes."

"Why don't you start the tea, and I'll be but a few minutes."

"Thank you, Lena."

Agata walked past the sick rooms and noticed her labored breathing. She entered the empty lounge and filled the tea kettle with water and placed it on the burner.

The elderly nurse arrived and removed her dirty apron. She added tea leaves to the cups, and both women waited for the water to boil.

After the women talked about Rosa's new baby and there was barely any tea left, Agata told her story.

"There is no need to quit your job. Why not stay employed at the hospital and save money you will surely need for your next destination? And, if you change your mind, you can return to the convent. It's easier, don't you think?"

"I cannot stay here alongside the other sisters. Mother Superior would not like it, and I don't want to answer endless questions. I will wait for Dr. Hermann and resign."

"Why not resign to Dr. Borja?"

"Because I owe Dr. Hermann my gratitude for helping me through my rough times."

"If you are worried about running into the other sisters, they will surely be here in the morning. Why not go and see him at his home? He lives only blocks away."

"Does he?"

"Yes. We attend his Christmas Party every year. The entire staff is invited."

"Really?"

The nurse blushed, "I'm sorry, I've forgotten we are not to mention the party to the sisters. Your Mother Superior never allowed the doctor to invite the sisters to any social gatherings. I should not have mentioned it; it was an error in judgment. Of course, all of us at the hospital wanted the sisters to be part of the celebrations."

"Mother is correct. Parties are not for nuns. I think I will go to the doctor's house so I won't run into any of the sisters. What is his address?"

"I can't remember the number, but it's on O'Higgins Street. It's very close, and you can't miss the house. I'll draw a map." Maddalena tore a sheet of paper and scribbled on it.

"It's too early to visit. I'll wait at the train station."

"Wait on his front porch so you don't have to backtrack with your heavy luggage. He has a lovely bench out front."

"Thank you, Lena." Agata secured the note in her purse.

Agata, no longer afraid to walk in darkness, confidently walked toward the doctor's house. Hearing the familiar rooftop patter, she smiled knowing it was only cats. She had no problem finding the house. She sat on the bench and found the lovely front yard a congenial atmosphere. Its lemon trees hugged the exterior walls, and camellias lined the path to the front door. Fragrance filled her nostrils as she waited patiently for dawn.

When the sun rose, Agata pushed the round doorbell. Through the door she heard the distinct voice of Dr. Herrmann complaining to his wife, "Stay in bed. I'll get it. I'm sure it's someone from the hospital wanting me to help Dr. Borja. Why can't they ever wait just one more hour? *Cristo Santo!*"

Agata regretted ringing the bell so early.

"Who is it?" Dr. Hermann demanded from behind the door.

"Dr. Herrmann. I'm sorry, it's Agata." She placed her hand over her mouth, afraid she would cry. The doctor opened the door and stood surprised. His belt to his robe hung on its loops, exposing his green-and-white checked pajamas. Agata could not face him as shame forced her to keep her eyes on the ground.

"Agata! What are you doing here? Is something wrong?"

"Roland! Let me, please!" Elsa stepped in front of her husband, her forehead wrinkled in a worried frown. "Agata, come inside. You look cold and scared." Elsa placed her hand on Agata's elbow, pulled her inside and noticed she was not wearing her habit. "Agata, what has happened?"

Dr. Herrmann yawned, "What's going on?"

"Darling, go back to bed. You can sleep for at least another hour. Agata and I need to talk."

"But, uh..." Dr. Herrmann nodded his agreement, "Yes."

Elsa escorted Agata to the kitchen. Seeing her husband still standing in the foyer watching with a befuddled expression, addressed him, "*Mi Amor*, can you put some clean towels in the guest room? Agata will be spending time with us."

"No, I couldn't possibly. It's so very kind, but I cannot stay. I wish only to give the doctor my resignation and to thank both of you for all the help you have given me."

"Dear Sister, please sit down." Elsa's voice was soothing. She turned to face her husband who still stood in the foyer. "And Roland, don't forget the towels."

"Right away." Doctor Hermann ascended the stairs.

"Señora, I'm so sorry and ashamed to have rung your bell so early!"

"It's no problem. Please, tell me what happened."

"I've left the convent."

"I see."

Agata's posture was stiff, clutching the handle of her suitcase tightly. Elsa unclasped Agata's fingers from the suitcase and placed it in the hallway. She sat next to Agata and patted her hand. "Your hands are cold. I'll brew a *maté*."

"I am no longer a nun. I've wanted this, but it happened so fast."

Elsa lit the stove and placed a heavy copper teapot on the grate.

"Thank you, Señora Herrmann."

"Please, don't be so proper with me. We have been friends for a while now, and we shall continue to call each other by our first names. Are we agreed?"

"Of course."

Elsa gathered two cups, filled each with a teaspoon of *yerba maté* leaves and pulled two *bombillos* from a drawer. She reached for a tin cookie box. "I hope you like Maria cookies."

"They are my favorite."

When there was only one cookie left in the box, Agata retold her story for the second time that night.

"You'll have to stay with us for as long as you need."

"No, I must not! Thank you with all my heart, but I will not be a burden to anyone."

"Don't be silly. It would bring us joy. We would delight in your company, and besides, I must fatten you up before you can have the strength needed to face a new life."

"Elsa, my gratitude is endless, but I need to find my own way."

"It will not hurt you to stay a few weeks, just until you figure out your next move."

Agata sat quietly, staring through the window at the slivers of gold and pink pushing away the morning fog. "Yes, I'll stay but only for a very short period of time."

Both women felt a sense of relief.

"Now, my friend, it's time for you to get some rest. It was a long night, and you must recover. I'll show you to your room."

"Thank you." Agata bowed her head and kissed Elsa's hand as was the custom when thanking Mother Superior.

"Agata, the first rule of freedom is that you never bow to anyone."

They rose from the table. Agata grabbed her purse, and Elsa carried the valise upstairs.

"It's already time for Roland to rise, and both of us need to get ready for work." Elsa stopped at the end of the hallway by a closed door. "Make yourself comfortable. We'll be back at noon for lunch."

"I'll have a meal ready for you."

Elsa laughed, "Beppina would not like that."

"Beppina?"

"She was once my nanny and then our housekeeper. Now she is part of the family. She's getting on in years but still insists on doing the cooking. It's our turn to take care of her as she has taken care of us. I'll let her know we have a guest."

Overwhelmed, Agata could not find enough eloquent words to express her gratitude and settled on a simple, "Thank you."

"Beppina will be excited to have you. She's lonely during the day when we are not here. She'll chatter the day away and tell you wonderful stories. Well, go on in, and get some sleep."

Agata entered the room and pulled a nightgown out of her suitcase. She bounced on the mattress, tested its springs and sighed. She stretched out, her body melting into its softness. The room was a celebration of an English garden. The bedspread, pillows and curtains were made of the same fabric—roses that exploded in shades of red and pink, intertwined with shades of green for leaves. She pinched the fabric between her fingers but could not determine if it was damask or brocade. Too many years had passed since she and her mother shopped for fabrics.

Agata removed the pillows and folded the bedspread and placed them on top of a chest at the foot of the bed. Feeling the softness of the sheets between her thumb and index finger, she compared them to the rough fabric made of the jute plant that priests had bought for them in giant bolts.

Exhausted, Agata prepared for a few hours' nap but first retrieved the photograph, stared at the fading images of her family and rested it on the night table. She also pulled out the ragdoll and remembered the day she sewed scraps of material to make it for Lilia. Putting the doll's mangled yellow yarn hair near her nose, she inhaled deeply and imagined she could still smell the girl's sweet scent. The day the children left, Agata had crept into the nursery room where Lilia slept and cried over the empty crib. She had spotted the doll hiding behind a diaper pail. Even though it should have gone with Lilia, she thanked the Virgin for leaving her a small token of the beloved child.

Still holding the toy, Agata removed the cross from her neck. She knelt by the side of the bed and prayed. "Mary, Mother of God, thank you for guiding me to this safe place. I promise not to stay long." Agata stopped in mid-prayer, rose and looked out the window to the now clear and glorious sky. "Are you there, my Virgin Mary? Are you real?" Agata shook her head and said, "Mother Superior is right—I've gone mad!"

The Sandwich

Santiago, Chile, 1943

Dr. Herrmann and Elsa hugged Agata on the platform of the train station. Elsa dabbed her eyes with a handkerchief.

"Agata, can't I convince you to stay with us a while longer?"

"Doctor, I would love to stay, but six months is more than enough for both of you to bear. If I stayed a minute longer, I'd never be able to pull myself away. Both of you are now my new siblings and Beppina, a beloved aunt."

"Agata, please let us know if you ever need anything," Elsa said loudly over the train engine noise.

"I'll always be grateful that you found a place for me to work these last few months. I would not have been able to save money and stand on my own feet otherwise."

"All aboard!" the conductor roared.

"And you shouldn't have bought this new suitcase when the one I had was perfectly suitable."

"I couldn't let you leave with that old thing to start your brand-new life," Elsa replied.

Dr. Hermann pleaded, "Agata, please write to us as often as possible. I want to know where you are and how you are doing. If things don't work out as you expect, promise us that you'll come back."

"I promise! Don't look so scared for me. I'll be fine. I've never felt this free."

Elsa embraced Agata for the second time as the train's whistle gave a final warning.

"The train will leave without me. *Adios*." Agata hurried towards the train where a conductor offered his hand and helped her navigate the steep metal steps.

"Wait, I almost forgot." Elsa ran to Agata, "Beppina made a snack." Elsa took a bundle out of her large purse. "It's your favorite, so promise not to share your sandwich with anyone."

Agata nodded.

"No, promise us. Say the words!" Roland begged.

"I promise," Agata replied and placed the napkin-wrapped package tied in twine in her purse and blew them a kiss.

The train slowly left the station. The couple followed Agata through dirty windows as she navigated to a seat. The train rolled by them as they continued to wave. The doctor and his wife watched the train until it disappeared around a curve in the tracks.

Agata's compartment was almost empty. A lone elderly man slumped on his seat was sleeping soundly. He snored loudly, and the whiskers of his mustache quivered when he exhaled. At the next stop, the man's eyes fluttered, and he woke up. He looked around as if he had forgotten he was on a train and then finally seemed to remember. He greeted Agata with a nod. She returned the greeting with a smile. A moment later, he was again deep in sleep.

The train picked up speed as Agata tried to dispel her anxiousness about traveling to Valparaiso and beginning her search for employment. She planned on saving more money for a ticket on a ship to what was still an unknown destination. She knew all would fall into place when God decided it was time.

Agata had been too nervous to eat breakfast, and her empty stomach was making her queasy. Grateful Beppina had packed a sandwich, she pulled the butcher's string and unwrapped the package. Assuming the sandwich would be her favorite ham and cheese, her mouth watered. Agata removed the top half of the baguette and lifted a large drooping lettuce leaf to verify its contents, shocked to see that instead of ham, there was a neatly folded stack of money on the bottom side of the bread. Barely able to breathe, Agata quickly covered it with the lettuce. She glanced to see if the man had seen the money and was relieved he was still sleeping. She rewrapped the sandwich and placed it in her purse, hurried to the lavatory and locked the door.

In the privacy of the small water closet, Agata dismantled the sandwich again and noticed the insides of the bread had been hollowed out to make more room for the bills. Counting the *pesos*, she was astonished at how much it was. Agata felt a wave of embarrassment at the extravagant gift but was also euphoric. She promised herself to repay the doctor and his wife every cent they had gifted her.

Agata placed the money in a side pocket of her purse and was about to throw away the remaining bread and lettuce but realized that a pickpocket might rob her and, therefore, decided the best way to keep it safe was to keep it disguised. Once again, she reconstructed the sandwich, wrapped it with a double-knot, and placed it at the bottom of her purse. She returned to her seat and very afraid of losing her wealth, clutched her purse so tightly that her fingers ached.

Because she was not familiar with Valparaiso, Agata assumed most of the hotels were by the port, so she walked toward the sea. She admired the colorful city, especially how the bougainvillea grew everywhere and bestowed a charming atmosphere. The city, with its houses perched on hilltops above the turbulent tints of greens and blues of the swirling ocean, might be a contender for where she would live.

Having extra money, Agata also considered returning to Spain and reacquainting herself with her homeland and family. She quickly dismissed the idea, because the war was not officially over in Europe, and she feared that since her parents were deceased and her siblings no longer answered her letters, she had no family eager to have her back. And lastly, she guessed her childhood friend, Rojelio, was probably unrecognizable as an adult and most likely married with many children.

Agata was incredulous at how many different types of ships crowded the bay. There were ocean liners, merchant vessels, fishing boats and even Chilean Navy ships. Her eyes could not move away from the majesty of the Pacific Ocean, and she realized how much she missed the sounds and smells of the sea. Inhaling the salt air, so much cleaner than the air of Santiago, she heard the roar of the waves and felt at home. In that moment, she swore to herself that she would never be far from the ocean again. An idea began to take shape—*I could find work on a ship and see a small part of the world.*

Spotting a large stucco hotel painted in a flamingo-pink color, she pulled herself away from the view and went to inquire about a room. She felt uneasy about approaching the building because she had not stayed in public lodgings since her childhood vacation days. Determined, she placed her fears aside and headed for the Hotel Reina Victoria.

The entrance doors of the beautiful edifice were open, allowing fresh ocean breezes to cleanse the air of the lobby as patrons sat reading the newspaper and smoking cigarettes. She strolled inside covered in a facade of confidence.

The man at the front desk smiled. "*Buenas tardes.*"

"*Buenas tardes.*"

"May I help you?"

"Yes, please. I would like a room with an ocean view if it's not too expensive."

"All our rooms have a direct view. The architect was brilliant when he designed the hallway on the opposite side and a single row of rooms for each floor facing the sea."

"What a marvelous idea."

"How long is your stay, Señora?"

"I'm not certain, but I shall stay at least a week."

The man continued smiling as he spoke, and Agata daydreamed of how exciting it would be to share dinner or a stroll on the beach with a man. She stared at his dark piercing eyes.

"Did you hear me, Señora? Is the price acceptable?"

Agata had not heard his words but trying not to sound foolish answered, "Of course."

When he asked for payment, she smiled, as the price was reasonable. The inexperienced traveler was grateful that the transaction was easy and the man did not look strangely at her or ask multitudes of questions as Mother Superior always had.

Climbing four flights of stairs to her room, lugging the heavy suitcase, exhausted Agata. Hunting for her room number, she noticed an elevator and felt foolish for not accepting the porter's help. As she turned the knob of her room, a strong breeze blew the door wide open, and Agata gasped at the sweeping panorama of the crystal blue ocean.

The small room had a private bathroom—a luxury for Agata. She caught sight of a Victorian claw-footed tub and nearly screamed with excitement. She touched the soft cotton bathmat draped over the side of the tub and placed it on the floor. Not wanting to step on the pristine white mat, she removed her shoes, kneeled and thanked the Virgin.

Agata searched the room for a safe place to hide her money and decided that between the mattresses was safest and she would open a bank account later that morning. Satisfied with the money's hiding place, she dumped the contents of her luggage onto the bed and found her yellow shawl. Wrapping it around her shoulders, she grabbed her purse and stopped in front of the dresser mirror to examine her appearance. Satisfied, she walked out of the room feeling as free as if she had grown wings.

The Fisherman's Boat

The cheese empanada was so delicious, Agata regretted buying only one at the small *panaderia*. She ate it while she walked toward the rocky coastline and followed a path along towering cliffs that dropped to the roaring ocean with jagged rocks standing like monoliths below. Her gaze was settled on the horizon of the great ocean, where she marveled at the curvature of the earth.

A boat anchored about a hundred meters from shore appeared to be about to sail for a night of fishing. Two men were busy moving traps stacked onshore to the boat on a dinghy so tiny that only one trap could be loaded per trip. The boat showed wear, with many patches proving numerous attempts to stop rot from disintegrating it. The vessel seemed too fragile to ride the rough sea, and Agata hoped it would not sail but remain safely anchored near the shore.

Carefully stepping over the rocks, a path revealed itself, and she followed it until it forced her to cross a precarious bridge. She almost turned back for fear of the bridge but reasoned it was safe, as there were no warning signs and she crossed it cautiously. Bravely she continued forward to a path leading to the beach. Reaching the sand, she took off her shoes and socks and strolled towards the boat. She witnessed a wave push the wobbling vessel in a circular position, exposing its stern. Agata saw a painted white lily and had an eerie feeling that the boat was a sign from heaven.

Agata approached the fishermen, "*Buenos Días, Señores.*"

"*Buenos Días, Señorita,*" the young man greeted.

The older man nodded his greeting and said, "I've been watching you come down the path. I hope you didn't cross that treacherous bridge. It's unsafe."

"I did."

"If you want to return to town and avoid the bridge, there on the left is a safer route," he said and pointed to a barely visible spot.

"Thank you, Señor. The ocean is so beautiful. I haven't seen it in such a long time."

"In Chile, you're never too far from the sea."

"I've been living in Santiago for nearly fifteen years without a single excursion."

"Santiago was my home, but I prefer Valparaiso and the solitude of the sea. But even *Santiaguinos* visit the ocean. No Chilean can stay away unless they are prisoners. Were you in prison, Señorita?" He winked and exposed his toothless smile.

"It was a heavenly prison," Agata chuckled. "Señor, I'm intrigued by the large flower painted on your boat. Most boats have names, but yours has only a flower."

"The boat was named to honor my niece, Lilia."

A wave of melancholy passed through Agata at hearing the name of her beloved child spoken aloud. "Señor, are you taking your boat out tonight?"

"Yes, we fish every night but Sundays."

"The sea is turbulent. It's now my turn to tell you to be safe."

The man smirked, "My son and I can't afford to stay in harbor because the sea is unruly. Magellan didn't give these waters the proper name—this monster is rarely pacific."

The fisherman's son chuckled and nodded in agreement.

"Aren't you afraid something terrible could happen to you and your young son?"

"He is not so young, almost sixteen. He is a man, and yes, things always happen. Señorita, if you fall in these waters, the cold temperature will make it a quick death."

"How frightening. May St. Brendan keep you and your boy safe." Agata crossed herself.

"We don't rely on Saints, only our safety lines and reflexes. When waves are high, we tie ourselves to metal rings screwed to the mast. We're prepared for whatever comes."

"I will pray for you!"

The man sneered, "Don't bother, Señorita. No one's listening!"

"Someone above always listens."

"My departed sister wasted her breath on endless prayers."

"Oh, I'm sure her prayers were of comfort. I'm sorry for such a great loss. What happened to your dear sister?"

"It's a long story, and we must get back to work."

The leathered fisherman motioned for his son to climb on the dinghy, and they rowed to the boat. Agata stayed on the beach and watched them as they pulled the dinghy onto the boat's deck. She heard the sputtering of the small engine and watched the boat bob into the horizon.

As the fishermen headed for open waters, the older man was lost in his memories of summer two years ago.

***

The woman walked on the thin serpentine pass between the cliffs and reached the rickety bridge. She looked down from the dizzying height at the white-crested waves as they crashed into the rocks below. The woman's eyes were hollow and dry of tears.

"Stay where you are! I will come to you!"

The man tried to run across the bridge, but it swayed and he nearly lost his balance. He slowed for fear the swinging bridge might toss him and his sister to the water below.

He continued to plead, "Wait, I beg. Please don't move."

The woman ignored his pleas. He watched as she neared the other side. He strengthened his resolve to reach her and forced himself to quicken his pace. He was almost upon her when she stretched her arm in a stop position.

"We'll find her, I swear it on my wife and children!" The man's hands trembled as he hung on to the rope handrail.

The woman's voice was calm as she asked, "Why did we leave her on such a cold night?"

"It wasn't cold. It was nearly dawn! The sun was on the horizon!" The frazzled man pleaded as he inched closer to her. "She's with a good family. She's grown up now and maybe has children of her own. We'll find her. I know she's well. I promise!"

"You cannot promise things you have no knowledge of or power to keep...I hear her cries in my sleep."

"We'll go back to Santiago and talk to Mother Superior. Maybe she's discovered a lead."

He extended his hand, hoping she would grab it. She shook her head, leaned forward and let gravity pull her into eternity, ending her pain and guilt.

Agata Finds Her Way

Antofagasta, Chile, 1945

Agata stared at her reflection in the hall mirror and thought she was almost pretty, even though the cold dry days of August had turned her porcelain skin a reddish dry hue. She had found employment on the merchant ship, *Estrella de Chile,* almost immediately after arriving in Valparaiso. The ship navigated between Buena Ventura, Colombia, and Puerto Montt, Chile.

Ferrying bananas, sugar and other tropical commodities from Colombia, the return trip was a hull full of wine, avocados and copper. In addition to being a cargo ship, it also carried a few adventurers, mostly students from the United States. Agata washed and ironed linens and was even responsible for keeping their rooms tidy. She mopped floors and did not retire for the night until they gleamed. Agata enjoyed the mindless but physical work. She slowly acclimated to civilian life, and at the same time, her wanderlust was satisfied.

Growing tired of the cold damp ocean and of working with the nearly all-male crew, Agata searched for a place to call home. She didn't care for the crew's unpolished mannerisms and foul language, but she made peace and ignored most of it. She enjoyed the casual atmosphere of the merchant ship and appreciated that the crew never intruded into her personal life by asking questions. The job afforded her time to think about her future and where she would make a permanent home. After working for two years, she missed nursing and wanted to work with patients again. At least there, she reasoned, she was helping people.

On a rare weekend when the ship was safely anchored in Antofagasta and saltpeter and copper were being loaded into its hull, Agata took advantage of a two-day layoff. She joined a guided tour of the desert, traveling 130 kilometers on a bus to see the desert in full bloom. Millions of flowers bloomed in the driest desert in the world, and Agata was captivated by its unbelievable beauty. Late that afternoon, she returned to the ship and asked to see the captain. She asked for her wages and permission to leave the job immediately.

"Are you mad, Agata? This town is small. I bet it doesn't even have a movie theater. Why would you want to settle here when there are fantastic cities to the south?" He could not hide his displeasure at one of his best workers leaving.

"The land is a contradiction to everything I know. To see such beauty in the harshest environment possible is...I can't explain it." Agata could not articulate her reasons.

"You won't find work here. They have nothing but mines."

"There's a hospital, and I was told they are in need of nurses."

"Well, I can't keep you, but I wish you'd reconsider. I'm not sure this place is suitable for a single woman such as yourself."

"It is my wish, Jorge. I've been with you for two long years."

"Of course, Agata. I cannot stop you. I'll take comfort that you'll be a nurse again, and that's better than scrubbing decks." The reluctant captain paid Agata and wished her well.

By the time Agata had settled in the small city of Antofagasta, the flowers had safely buried their seeds before they dried up and disintegrated. The insignificant cracked patches of earth and windswept vistas would hold the seeds that waited patiently for enough moisture in the air to again stun the world with their glory. Agata too was waiting, like the flowers, for the right moment to bloom.

She was finally happy working as a nurse in the small hospital. There were only three doctors and eight nurses on the medical staff. Since there were no other medical facilities and only one midwife to loan out, the hospital witnessed every possible ailment—from broken bones to fatal diseases, including the mine accidents that occurred too frequently.

No longer queasy when aiding the sick, Agata became a good nurse. Finally desensitized to gruesome procedures, she found comfort in helping those who needed her. Although no longer part of the church, she felt that she still served God, and it gave her a sense of peace and purpose.

The unattractive and poorly constructed buildings concerned Agata, as earthquakes were common. The town lacked city amenities and decent roads, but she found the natural beauty of the Andean Culampajá Mountain Range to the east, the sea to the west and the dramatic desert made it a welcoming place to call home. The mountains never looked the same on any given day as they changed with the position of the sun or under the morphing formation of clouds above.

Even more than the landscape, she loved the people. They were friendly, lacked pomposity and arrogance and were always willing to lend a hand to anyone in need. This corner of the world was a secret gem, not likely to attract the grandiose or rich, but a haven for both native peoples and foreigners who desperately wished to work no matter the harsh conditions of mining. Agata could not wait to grow roots in a town where the sun always shone and clouds dissipated quickly.

Competitor

Santiago, Chile, 1946

The years at McKenna flew by quickly for Lilia. Every school term had been almost an exact replica of the previous one, of days filled with schoolwork and piano studies. During summer breaks, Lilia went home. Every summer vacation had been trying for both parents and child. Lilia spent her time indoors with nothing to do but study music and read books. Rarely did her parents give her permission to accompany Susana to the markets.

They insisted that she constantly improve her proficiency in music. She learned at such an accelerated rate that Professor Goretsky entered her in piano competitions. He was not surprised when she consistently placed within the top three and won cash stipends. The Villavicencios allowed Professor Goretsky to manage Lilia and rarely attended her concerts. It was not that they were indifferent; it was simply that their age with aches and pains made everything difficult.

Lilia and Susana were increasingly concerned about the couple's seclusion and the new and odd behaviors they developed. They shut down socially, even from each other. They were often ill and spent days in their respective beds convalescing from different ailments. Carmen had asked Manuel to move out of the master bedroom into his study, as she suffered from stomach pain and was up most nights. She soothed herself in her rocking chair, trying to ease her aches without disturbing the other members of the household, and suffered in silence.

Manuel's stiff joints were excruciating. Sometimes he relied on his cane, but other times he spent the day in bed unable to stand or even sit up without help. The doctor told him it was rheumatism, but Manuel feared it might be something worse. His friends, including the McKenna brothers, had passed away in close succession, and Manuel's social life came to a halt. Thankfully, the bishop visited the couple and gave them communion. Susana, the ever-faithful servant, cared for them. The bishop would send a nun periodically to give Susana respite.

As Lilia matured and graduated from school, she stopped complaining about the long boring summers and found solace in her studies. She grew to appreciate the quiet home atmosphere. A constant sorrow plaguing Lilia was her desire to own a pet to love and nurture. She prodded her father to get her either a cat or dog, but Don Villavicencio was resolute in his negative answer. Scanning the street from her tall parlor windows, Lilia continued to see the many homeless dogs wandering about with their noses sniffing the ground, hoping to find something to eat. This deepened her longing.

One summer afternoon, Professor Goretsky paid a surprise visit to the Villavicencios. He knew about Lilia's isolation and took matters into his own hands. As he had promised Lilia, he was now at their door under the pretense of talking about the upcoming competition. He wanted the Villavicencios to allow Lilia to acquire a pet. Lilia promised the professor if he succeeded, she would practice eight hours per day instead of his mandated five. She swore to the professor that she would do whatever it took to win all competitions, if only there was a pet by her side. This desire consumed her thoughts. The professor was eager to please his prized student and felt she deserved a reward. It would be a small token for the endless years of dedicated study.

When Susana welcomed the professor at the front door, the Villavicencios, still lingering in their robes, came out to greet him without bothering to dress. The professor was surprised at how rapidly the couple had declined. Susana made sure the pair and the professor were comfortable in the salon. She placed blankets over the laps of Carmen and Manuel. As the adults chatted, she served tea with finger sandwiches. Lilia stayed in her room.

"My hope is that Lilia wins the next two competitions. If so, we'll have our invitation to Poland next year."

"An invitation to Poland?" Carmen Villavicencio repeated.

"Remember, Carmen, I told you about The Chopin International Competition?" Don Manuel Villavicencio said in a soothing voice.

"If she wins the first of the two concerts, the one before the Nationals, I want to show my appreciation for Lilia's hard work and buy her a gift—with your permission, of course." The professor stirred honey into his tea.

Don Villavicencio stiffened and said, "Winning is a reward by its own right. There is no reason to spend money on a gift, Professor."

"I was thinking of a small token that doesn't cost much. It may motivate her to win the Nationals, and that's our ticket to Warsaw. That's why I want to give her this gift."

"What kind of gift?" Carmen was suspicious.

"A pet."

"We don't want any animals in the house. Do you think she can win the next competition? They are getting progressively difficult, and I don't think she can. Even if by some miracle she gets through to the next one, I doubt very much she can win the Nationals. I hear her mistakes all the time—I have a good ear." Don Villavicencio took a tiny bite of a sandwich.

"She has a chance! I know it. She can win the Nationals, and that is an honor regardless of how she finishes in Warsaw. If she doesn't win, she'll still have other chances for the title in later years, and eventually, she will win. She'll only get better. So, are we agreed that if she wins the next competition, I can bring her a dog?"

"I told her a thousand times they don't belong in homes; they belong outside." The Don was adamant.

"Well, what about a tiny kitten that can stay indoors?" Professor Goretsky did not wish to lose the chance for Lilia to own any pet.

"Absolutely not! Cats will tear the upholstery," Carmen interjected.

"Then let's rethink a small harmless puppy. He can live outdoors in Lilia's courtyard," the Professor's voice remained calm.

The Don looked at his wife for any objection. She seemed to slip in and out of the conversation. Manuel uncharacteristically replied, "Señor, we agree, but only if she wins can you bring her a puppy."

Professor Goretsky covered his elation by answering monotonously, "Thank you, Don Villavicencio."

"Will she make the papers if she wins?" Carmen came out of her fog.

"Señora, oh yes! It will even be on the radio."

Lilia, eavesdropping and unseen in the foyer, heard the entire conversation and nearly gave away her discreet position by screaming out. She thought about the fun she would have playing with the dog outdoors. She would do whatever it took to win.

Lilia worked harder than usual. The extra practice was worthwhile as she easily won the next competition. Professor Goretsky was once again at the Villavicencios' front door while the couple was taking their nap.

They heard Susana invite the professor into the house but neither bothered to rise from bed to greet him and soon slipped back into their siesta.

"Good day, Susana." Professor Goretsky held a small brown dog in his arms and sported a huge smile.

"Oh, Professor, the puppy is so adorable! Lilia will go crazy when she sees it. Is it male or female?"

"Male."

Susana motioned for him to be quiet and led him to the hallway outside of Lilia's room. Lilia played on her new upright Steinway. Susana knocked on Lilia's bedroom door.

"Come in, Susana," Lilia did not stop playing and had not heard the doorbell. The professor tip-toed behind Lilia and moved close enough for the dog to instinctively sniff the back of Lilia's exposed neck. Lilia flinched at the feel of the cold nose, turned and saw the puppy cradled in the professor's arms.

"Is it mine?" Lilia's eyes glistened as she jumped from her seat.

The professor nodded.

"You've kept your promise. Thank you, Professor!" She reached for the puppy and held it close.

"What are you going to name this little boy?" Susana was eager to know.

"I don't know yet. I love him so much already." Lilia sat down on the piano bench and placed the dog on her lap. Tears welled in her eyes, "Finally! My dog."

"No tears! This is a happy moment," the piano teacher chided.

Professor Goretsky pulled out a leash from his jacket pocket. "He'll need to be walked at least twice a day. I think he may need one now. Take him to the market and buy liver or whatever inexpensive cuts you find to make him dinner. He'll also want a bone."

"I'll make sure to do everything right, Professor. I'll take good care of him. How can I ever thank you?"

The professor answered without hesitation, "You can win the Nationals!"

The Boarding House

Antofagasta, Chile, 1947

On a hot, dry day, Agata stopped a miner on the way to work and asked, "Good morning, Señor, is there a boarding house nearby? There are no street signs in this part of town."

"There's a boarding house on the very next street. Instead of walking all the way around, there's a shortcut through the alley between the bakery and the grocers. You can't miss the house. It's the largest one."

The tight alley reeked of urine, and Agata quickened her steps to pass the offensive odor. Desert winds loosened Agata's hairpins, making her stop to pull out the pins that dangled in her locks and save them in her purse. The now-loose hair whipped by the wind caused Agata to pull out a scarf and wrap her head. She was grateful to have hair again, and not the extremely short hair mandated for life in the convent. Now dark brown, the golden hair of Agata's youth was gone.

The stone house seemed out of place among the small cottages, and Agata assumed it was the boarding house. Remnants from the local quarries, the building stones were stockpiled and inexpensive and used for both homes and paving the streets. She glanced at the house and appreciated the orange clay tiles typical of roof coverings. The tiles were fastidiously laid in a pattern resembling rows of lapping waves, lending character to the house. Agata knocked on the door.

A woman in her fifties answered, "Good morning."

"Pardon me. Good morning. I hope I'm in the right place. I'm looking for the boarding house."

"Yes. Please come in and get out of the heat."

Agata stepped inside and found the house surprisingly cool.

"I'm Alejandra Reyes. My husband, Maximillian, and I are the proprietors."

"Agata Elizalde. Pleased to meet you. I was sent by Graciela Marino from the hospital. She told me about your lovely house and its reasonable prices. She said that meals are included. Is this true, Señora?"

"Yes. A typical breakfast and dinner, six days per week. You'll have to fend for yourself on Sundays."

"That sounds wonderful."

"Are you also a nurse?"

"Yes."

Señora Reyes motioned her to follow as she spoke, "We are fortunate to have a hospital. I remember when there were only a few scattered doctors in the entire region."

Agata followed the woman and climbed a set of stairs. They reached a long hallway with doors on either side. Señora Reyes stopped at the third door but pointed to the end of the hallway, "That's the only bathroom for women. Go on and look while I unlock the bedroom door."

Agata was pleased with the tiny but very clean bathroom.

Señora Reyes held the bedroom door open for Agata. "All the rooms are the same size and fully furnished."

Agata entered and again was pleased. "This is much lovelier than I could have imagined. If it pleases you, Señora, I would be so grateful to be your tenant. I've been living with three women in one room for a few years and would love to regain my privacy."

"Well, before you decide to take the room, I must confess that I've rented a room to a man." Señora Reyes saw the disappointed expression on Agata's face and explained, "I need help, as my husband's health is declining—not only to help me lift him out of bed to his chair but also for fixing things around the house. The tenant works at the mine and is an accountant. He's very quiet, barely speaks to anyone. He won't use the women's bathroom upstairs, only the one downstairs. I assure you he is like a ghost. Can you accept the situation?"

"Yes, of course. I will take the room, Señora Reyes."

"It will be great to have two nurses in the house. I have so many questions about my husband's condition. You can move in immediately if you have the one month's rent."

"I do. I'll pack this very day. I have very few personal effects."

"I'll give you a tour of the house." Señora Reyes led Agata down two flights of stairs to a kitchen located nearly underground. The cellar was almost completely buried but for windows placed near the ceiling allowing for light and ventilation. "Max and I sit mostly in the kitchen during the summer months."

"I've never seen a kitchen below ground. Why is that?"

"The heat can be unbearable and the nights very cold. Having this part of the house practically underground tempers both the heat and frigid nights. The residents may use the kitchen to boil water for tea, but no cooking is allowed."

"I won't miss the kitchen, as I used to be responsible for breakfast for a large number of people."

"Is that so?"

"Before I became a nurse, I was a nun."

Señora Reyes' eyes widened, "A nun?"

"Yes, I cooked for the children and all the sisters. Now, in Antofaghasta, I share part of a room without kitchen privileges. I survive on fruit and bread from the market and eat many meals at the café."

"Why didn't you leave sooner, especially with a nurse's pay?"

"I vowed to pay back a debt to dear friends who helped me when I had nothing but a few items of clothing. My friends didn't want the money returned, but I forced them to take it. It could be used elsewhere if they don't wish to keep it."

Agata roamed the room and pointed her finger at a small door in the wall, "What is that?"

"A dumbwaiter." Señora Reyes pulled on ropes lifting the small elevator towards the ceiling. "It takes food upstairs to the dining room. It keeps the food warm, and I don't have to carry anything up or down the stairs and risk falling. Max made it for me."

"That's genius."

Señora Reyes and Agata toured the dining room and parlor on the main floor. The windows, like those in the bedrooms, were covered with wooden shutters that blocked out the sun while still permitting air to flow. She showed Agata the small terrace outside in the backyard where sometimes they would eat dinner, weather permitting. The two-room casita in the yard was the Reyes's private residence, and it included a bathroom.

The tenants who lived in the congenial boarding house were a diverse group. All were single and hard-working. Graciela, who worked at the hospital, was from Peru and like so many others, had come to Chile looking for better wages. Another resident from Bolivia had arrived for the same economic reasons and was a secretary at the mine's office. Only one tenant was native to the area and taught elementary school to the poor miners' children. The male resident, Jacob Liebeskind, was a refugee and recent arrival from Poland.

Señor Maximillian Reyes was much older than his wife, Alejandra. He was somber, unlike his boisterous wife with a chatty disposition. Max had been a biology teacher in a secondary school in Arica, Chile. His interest in winged insects continued to keep him engrossed long into retirement, and he spent most of his time drawing his beloved creatures with his colored inks.

Moths, butterflies or any insect species were not an attraction to Señora Reyes. She preferred to spend her time photographing the Atacama landscape. She saved her money to buy the expensive new Kodachrome film to test on her Zeiss Icarette camera but was disappointed when it became impossible to find the processing chemicals in the desolate area of northern Chile, so her photographs remained in black and white. Between Alejandra's photographs and Max's colored drawings, every wall of the boarding house was filled with art.

Jacob

Moving into the boarding house and the companionship she found there lifted Agata's spirits. The rules created by Señora Reyes were easy to follow. One such rule was that the dining room be kept in a state of pristine cleanliness where not even the tiniest of breadcrumbs could be found. This rule was appreciated by all and especially the nurses. Agata cleaned and swept the room after every dinner.

Agata, Señora Reyes and the women residents became good friends. All found themselves appreciating their friendships. Señora Reyes was now addressed by her first name, and she proved to be a kind and knowledgeable friend. She freely gave advice about everything, whether it was solicited or not—even telling Agata where to buy a natural bristle brush to keep her newly long hair untangled.

On many nights when the owners retreated to their casita for the night, the housemates spent hours listening to each other's ideas and dreams while congregating in the parlor. Life in the Reyes household was affable, and the housemates considered each other family—all but the lone male resident.

The reclusive resident, Jacob Liebeskind, rarely smiled. His frown lines were etched deep in his forehead, giving him the look of a harsh man. Only thirty-eight years old, he looked more like fifty. He seldom initiated conversation except with Alejandra and Max. Although his native tongue was Polish, he was fluent in Russian and Yiddish and now was speaking Spanish almost like a native. He taught himself Spanish from a grammar book and a Polish-Spanish dictionary. Jacob denounced his Polish citizenship of his homeland and accused his country of treason against its Jews. He could not reconcile why he survived the Holocaust when his family had not, and he swore never to speak Polish again.

Jacob came to dinner most evenings, eagerly eyeing the meal, but most often did not taste the food. Alejandra's staple was cabbage soup steeped in pork sausages. Jacob refused to ingest even a spoonful. He abstained from almost every soup or stew Alejandra cooked, such as the *sopa de langosta*—a concoction of shrimp and fish—or beef stew with sour cream. Often, Jacob would sit, stare at the serving bowl and without a word leave the table. He frequented the local café.

"What's wrong with the food?" Alejandra would ask, but Jacob did not want to concern her about Kosher laws. Even a simple pasta dish would not be eaten to the displeasure of Alejandra.

Jacob would apologize, "Nothing is wrong, no, no, I'm so sorry I cannot eat it, but the food smells delicious."

"Sit down, Jacob, it's only a harmless lasagna," Alejandra picked up a plate and placed a square of the lasagna on the plate. Jacob continued to stand and told her a shortened version of his dietary restrictions.

"You can leave the meat behind and just eat the cheese and pasta." She circled the plate under Jacob's nose, tempting him to take a bite. Jacob inhaled the aroma and salivated but shook his head, "I cannot. The meat and milk have melted together."

"I suppose. Do you know how hard it was for me to find this cut of noodle?"

"Thank you, Señora Reyes. I know how hard you try." Jacob nodded.

Alejandra's face showed confusion, and the boarders looked impatient. The Catholics around the table had never heard of Kosher laws. They thought him to be finicky and wasteful to not eat food already included in the rent.

"It's complicated. I'm already guilty of breaking my dietary laws by eating out of the same set of dishes, but I think God would understand. I realize I'm only a renter in your lovely home. Please forgive me; I mean no disrespect."

"Sit down, Mr. Liebeskind. I'm sure you can partake in the salad and bread." Graciela tapped on the empty chair next to hers.

Jacob still did not sit. His face blushed, and he unconsciously bit his lower lip. The tenants often gossiped in hushed tones about him. They wondered how the doddering man with an enormous quantity of quirkiness was working as an accountant in the largest mine in town.

After the war, Jacob landed in the port of Antofagasta, thanks to money sent by good Samaritans in the United States. He was an intelligent man but did not appear so, as he seemed always at the point of a nervous breakdown.

"Señor Liebeskind, do you have a favorite dish? Perhaps something your mother made on special occasions?" Agata tried to engage him in conversation.

"*Zacusca*," Jacob's face turned redder, and his eyebrows furled.

Señora Reyes jumped into the conversation, "If it's easy to prepare, perhaps I can make it for you. Tell me the ingredients."

"Señora Reyes, it's only grilled eggplants and peppers."

"I'll buy eggplants when I see them at the market."

Jacob's reaction was slow, further cementing the housemates' dislike of the man. Jacob managed to say, "Thank you."

Agata noticed Jacob's deep, hooded blue eyes and thought he might be handsome if he shaved his scraggly beard. At times when Jacob was out of the house, away from its familiarity and comfort, he displayed a severe idiosyncrasy. He would take a few hurried steps and then quickly turn his head and look back as if someone was following him. The residents and local townspeople noticed his quirkiness and snickered behind his back. They wondered what imaginary figure was chasing the strange Señor Liebeskind. It pained Agata to see the odd behavior. She empathized with his perpetual distraught state and wished to calm his soul.

Agata did not know much about him or how he had arrived in Chile but knew he was Jewish from the yarmulke he wore on Friday evenings. Tales from Jewish survivors of horrid atrocities had recently surfaced in the newspapers. As much as Agata wanted to learn about the Jewish genocide, her compassion did not allow her to finish articles about it, as tears blurred her vision, and she could not continue reading.

Jacob always wore black trousers and a white shirt as if it were a mandated uniform. He had several sets of the same outfit hanging in his armoire. On cold days, he added a black wool jacket. His round glasses covered his cornflower blue eyes and bushy eyebrows. When Agata heard disparaging remarks about him from the residents, she reprimanded them. The perpetrators always apologized, as they never argued with Agata once they discovered she had been a nun.

Alejandra tried to vary her menu, but the residents often complained, "Please, can you make something besides oatmeal or toast for breakfast? Perhaps hot buns from the bakery?" Or at other times they would ask, "Why can't we have dessert, Alejandra?"

The reply from Alejandra was always the same, "You're welcome to buy whatever you wish at the bakery with your own money. If I buy it, I'll raise the rent. And as for dessert, we have a fruit bowl that is never empty, thanks to the figs and cherimoyas in my backyard."

One evening when the residents returned home from work, Agata noticed that Señor Liebeskind's skin had an odd pallor. She did not see him the next morning and asked Graciela and the other residents, "Has Señor Liebeskind been down for breakfast?" No one had noticed his absence. Agata climbed the stairs to his room, lightly tapped on his door and waited for a reply. None came.

Agata knocked again and called out, "Señor Liebeskind?"

"Yes," a croaky, whispered voice replied.

"We haven't seen you since yesterday, and I noticed you missed breakfast. Are you ill?"

The man coughed and wheezed, "No, I am well, thank you."

"You don't sound well."

"My throat is a bit sore."

"Can I get you something from the kitchen?"

There was a pause of silence before he replied, "No thank you, Señorita Elizalde."

"It's Agata. I think I should bring you tea. It might help."

"No thank you...Agata."

The concerned ex-nun ignored his reply and descended two flights of stairs to the kitchen where Alejandra was washing dishes. "May I make tea for Señor Liebeskind? He's not feeling well."

"You don't need to ask about tea."

"But I would also like to fix him something to eat."

"You may. There's plenty of *pan amasado* in the basket. I'm sure he'd enjoy it."

"Thank you," Agata kissed Alejandra on the cheek.

As Agata waited for the water to boil, she sliced two pieces of bread, melted butter on an iron skillet and toasted both sides. When golden, she removed the slices and spread Alejandra's homemade black currant jam thickly on each slice. After fussing over the placement of the cup and saucer and a matching plate for the toast, she admired her lovely presentation and placed it in the dumbwaiter. She pulled the rope until it would go no further, signaling that it had reached the dining room.

"Why don't you run out and pick some figs? They are perfectly ripe."

"Splendid idea, Alejandra." Agata nearly skipped to the first floor and exited the back door to the garden, where she chose two plump figs from a low branch. She washed the fruit in the outdoor basin and returned to the dining room. She placed the figs on the tray before lifting it out of the dumbwaiter. Agata found a festive yellow napkin in Alejandra's sideboard and covered the plate. She carried the tray upstairs and knocked on Señor Liebeskind's door with her elbow, nearly spilling the tea. She waited for his reply. Again, he did not answer.

"Señor, may I come in? The tea is ready!" Agata waited patiently and knocked again. "Señor, I'm warning you. I'm entering the room."

Agata pushed the door open a few inches and peeked inside. Not hearing his objections prompted her to walk in. The man flushed. She noticed he was still tucked under covers that reached his neck. He looked softer and more approachable with his disheveled hair, overgrown beard and eyes not covered by glasses.

"May I place this tray on your lap?"

Jacob nodded.

"You know I'm a nurse? You shouldn't feel uncomfortable by my presence."

Jacob was mute.

"Why don't you sit up before I place the tray on your lap?"

Jacob complied but kept one hand on the blanket, making sure it did not slip from his neck. "When I see the doctor at work this morning, I'll ask him to accompany me home at the end of the day and pay you a visit."

Jacob shook his head.

"I will respect your wishes, but I would like to check on you."

"Jacob shook his head again and whispered, "No, thank you. I will be alright."

"The tea should help, Señor Liebeskind."

"Jacob," he pronounced it, Yacob.

"I'll be back in a minute to pick up the tray and then rush off to work."

"I will bring it downstairs."

"As you wish, Jacob."

Jacob sipped the tea. Agata turned to leave and for a second lost herself in the hue of his eyes and wondered how charming he might be if he attempted a smile. He looked up from his tea, and their eyes met. Agata quickly turned away and mumbled, "Good day."

After only one day of convalescing, Jacob was well enough to join the residents at the dining room table. He talked a little more than usual, started to eat the meals Alejandra served without questioning the food and began to socialize with the residents after dinner. And then one day, Agata came home from work and was greeted by his smile.

Baltito

Santiago, Chile, 1947

The alarm clock rattled and jolted Lilia awake. Baltimore lay curled at her feet. She rose and turned off the alarm and watched her dog's foot twitch. "Get up, Baltito," she whispered. He yawned and sniffed the air. Lilia threw open the door to the courtyard. "Baltito, it's time to go. Hurry, before you get caught in the house." Baltimore wagged his tail but did not obey and whimpered. Lilia picked him up and carried him outside. Even though it was winter, the sun's warmth felt great on Lilia's skin. "I'll bring breakfast in a few minutes, so don't bark."

The Villavicencios forbade the four-footed creature to sleep indoors. Lilia always waited until her parents were asleep to sneak him onto her bed. She worried when she was out of town due to concert schedules that Baltimore would not understand why she was not home. On those trips, she stayed in a hotel with Professor Goretsky. He would always book two adjacent rooms and was an excellent chaperone. At home Baltimore missed Lilia and whimpered. The Villavicencios ignored the dog's yelps. Susana tried to calm the agitated puppy but was unsuccessful. She, unlike Lilia, was afraid to disobey the Villavicencios and never brought the dog inside the house during her absences.

The neighbors complained about the dog, prompting Don Villavicencio to commission a carpenter to build a doghouse. When the barking continued, he solved the problem by purchasing a muzzle that Baltimore wore all night. When the Villavicencios napped, Susana placated the dog by taking him for long walks.

Lilia had shortened Baltimore's name to the more affectionate Baltito. She chose his name on the day he arrived because she was reading a book on Lord Baltimore and liked the sound of his name. Since his arrival, Lilia had learned all she could about dogs. She visited the library and found out her dog's breed was a *ratonero* (rat hunter), a true Chilean Terrier, and the only type of dog recognized as a Chilean breed. It was a cross between a Fox Terrier from Europe and a native breed that existed in her homeland before the arrival of the Spaniards.

Endless hours were spent in the courtyard with Baltito and Lilia enjoying each other's company. Susana joined Lilia whenever possible and fell in love with the spirited dog, but it was obvious that Lilia was his master. Lilia treated the dog like a baby and even knitted a blanket she kept on the floor of the doghouse.

Lilia entered the kitchen to fix Baltimore's breakfast and found Susana already pouring hot water into their silver teapot. She kissed Susana on the cheek, "Good morning!"

"Good morning, sweet girl. I bet you were too excited to sleep because of your big trip."

"I was up most of the night and finally fell asleep when the alarm went off. I've got a knot in my stomach, either from excitement or nerves. I'm sad to leave you and Baltito." Lilia reached for Baltito's bowls.

The doorbell startled Susana. "Who can be calling this early? Please check, Lilia."

Lilia placed the bowls on the table and peeked out the parlor window. "It's the professor!" Running to open the door for her beloved teacher, she greeted him with a smile. "Professor, I wasn't expecting you but so happy that you came."

"I couldn't let you leave on your first trip alone without saying goodbye."

"Thank you, Professor. Come in. I'm about to feed Baltito."

The professor removed his hat and placed it on a hat rack in the foyer before following Lilia into the kitchen. "Good morning. I'm sorry to come so early, but I didn't want to miss Lilia."

Susana carried a large tray. "It's always a pleasure to see you, regardless of the hour. Please excuse me, the Villavicencios woke up early this morning and want their breakfast in bed."

"Can I help you carry the tray?" Lilia offered.

Susana pushed the kitchen door with her back, "No, thank you, but make the professor feel at home."

"Sit down, please." Lilia filled Baltito's water bowl.

"Tell me more about your trip."

"I'm a little scared to travel alone and leave the country. I had to get a passport. May I offer you tea, Professor? The water is hot."

"Yes, thank you. Your parents told me a little about your trip to Argentina."

Lilia gathered two cups and poured water into them and added a small teaspoon of tea to each. "I'm most excited to cross the mountains. They say the Andes are a pathway to heaven. Have you crossed the *cordillera*?"

"When I came from Poland, I crossed the Atlantic by ship and stopped in Venezuela. I transferred to a smaller ship and went through the newly built Panama Canal and traveled along the coast to Chile. I'll have to see it through your eyes. I can't wait for you to return and describe every detail. Which friend of yours is the bride?"

"Monica."

"Oh, I remember her. She'd come to the piano studio telling you it was time to stop practicing and go to dinner."

"Yes, I remember. My roommates were a year older and graduated last year. I didn't keep in touch with them because I was too busy with the competitions. It never crossed my mind that some of my friends could be getting married. The first time I heard anything about her fiancée, Miguel, was from the wedding invitation. I don't hear from her for months, and then she asks me to play for the ceremony." Lilia placed almond cookies on a plate.

"Your mother said you're invited to stay at the groom's house."

"Yes, Monica and her parents will stay there too. Apparently, the Riccios have a huge home."

"Your parents were cautious about allowing you to go. They asked what I thought about it. I suggested they should let you spread your wings and learn to be independent. I explained that playing at the church is also a learning experience. The more you perform, the better prepared you'll be for the upcoming competitions. And I want you to have some fun. What could be better than a wedding?"

"Thank you, Professor!"

"Now, Lilia, promise that you'll be careful while traveling so I won't worry."

Susana returned and heard the professor's concern. "I agree, Professor, make her promise. I also worry."

"I wish everyone would stop treating me like a child! I promise to be careful and stay mostly in my sleeping car." Lilia sighed. "When I get back, I'll practice non-stop for the competition."

"You need to win. Lilia, it'll be the most important night of your life."

"Yes, yes, I heard it all before! If I win, we're going to Warsaw, where we'll be so close to Chopin's birthplace and near your home as well." Lilia pretended to yawn. "So boring!"

"Lilia, the competition is serious business! If you win just one more, Poland is yours, and it will change your life regardless of whether you win or lose. Don't be nonchalant about it."

Lilia watched Baltito trot into the kitchen.

Susana noticed, "Take the dog out, Lilia. Your parents are up."

"He'll follow me back outside when I bring him his food. My parents will linger in bed for a long time."

The Professor continued, "If we go to Poland, I'll show you off to the world—my prodigy. How proud I am that you are a girl in a man's world."

"I won't win. There's another girl, a Russian, and she's better than me." Lilia filled Baltito's bowl with cooked liver from their new refrigerator.

"Bella Davidovich is a great talent, but I think you can beat her!"

Lilia peeked under the table and rubbed Baltito's ears. "Okay, let's go now! Breakfast is ready. C'mon, don't dawdle. You'll get us both in trouble if Papá finds you." Lilia carried the bowls out and Baltimore followed.

The Professor sipped the last of his tea, placed the cup back on its saucer and brought it to the sink. Lilia returned from feeding Baltito and was surprised when the professor stretched out both his hands for a hug. The professor pulled her close, planted a kiss on top of her head and then still holding her close said, "You are like a daughter to me. Enjoy your adventure but come back rested. We'll have a last push to win the Nationals."

"I will, Professor. *Adios.*"

Lilia accompanied him to the foyer and blew him a kiss as he reached for his hat. He bowed to Susana, winked at Lilia and let himself out.

"Lilia, eat breakfast. You're running out of time."

"I'll eat later in the diner car. I'm not hungry now."

They walked into the kitchen and sat at the table.

"Do you have your father's silver ticket safely tucked into your purse? He'd be furious if you lost it and would never let you borrow it again."

"Yes, I have it. I'll guard it with my life!"

"Are you nervous about playing in such a large cathedral for Monica?"

"No, it's much easier than a competition. The organ is on the balcony, hidden from view. Everyone's attention will be on the bride and not on me. There are no judges in the crowd, so there won't be pressure."

"What will you play?"

"It's so cliché, but Monica chose the 'Wedding March.'" Lilia rolled her eyes.

"That's all?"

"No, I'll do Chopin's 'Prelude in C Minor' when the couple walks out of the church."

"Is that all—two pieces?"

"I'll play 'Ave Maria' in the middle of the ceremony when the couple signs the registry, but that's it."

"The Ave Maria, that's played at funerals."

"Not anymore. Did you know that Franz Schubert first wrote it for an opera based on a poem, 'Third Song'? It's based on one of my favorite books, *The Lady of the Lake*. He didn't originally intend it to be a religious piece."

"Your head's full of trivia. I wish I could hear you play it on the organ."

"You'll have a chance when I play it here. Papá made an agreement with the bishop. In exchange for allowing me to practice on the cathedral's organ, he is forcing me to play for the congregation when I return. Can we sit outside and keep Baltito company? I will miss him so." Susana nodded and they walked out to the courtyard.

Baltimore licked his empty bowl. Lilia and Susana sat on metal chairs.

"Did you buy a dress for the wedding?"

"No. I'm wearing my concert black. I'll pair it with the pretty drop earrings the conductor gave me when I won the Puerto Montt competition."

"You can't wear black to a wedding. It's bad luck," Susana scolded.

"We're not in the dark ages, Susana. I'm not superstitious."

"Find another dress."

"I don't have another that fits properly. I think I've gained weight. I guess it's nervous eating from competing."

Susana shook her head, "I hope the Riccios are nicer than their future daughter-in-law. I do not like Monica."

"What do you mean?"

"When I visited you at the McKenna, Monica once asked why I bothered to visit you."

Lilia gasped, "You never told me. Did she mean because you are the housekeeper?"

"Yes."

"I don't think she meant to be rude."

"She was very belittling. I was not going to explain to her that you are my family. Like the professor, you're the daughter I always wished for. I hope Monica will learn that being rich doesn't make you a better person. We're all equal in God's eyes."

"The girls from school talk nonsense, always thinking poor people deserve their condition and that it can be easily remedied by working harder."

"There are so many advantages the rich have. I hope she learns compassion before judgment day at St. Peter's gate."

"There's no gate or heaven. I read that God is dead. God remains dead, and we have killed him. Yet his shadow still looms. How shall we comfort ourselves, the murderers of all murderers?"

"Stop that nonsense!"

"That was a direct quote from Nietzsche."

"Who?"

Lilia laughed, "I don't believe in God."

"Lilia!"

"I came into this world alone, without a mother. What God would create such circumstances?"

"Everyone's born to a mother."

"She was merely the soil where a seed buried itself, and I grew into existence. That is all. Another woman, Mamita, was a mother, but I was taken away from her too. I realize she was not really my mother, but just the same, I still miss her."

"Mamita, Carmen and I are your mothers. How lucky for you to have three mothers."

"I suppose, but there's always a feeling of emptiness inside."

Susana frowned, "I'm sorry."

"I'll always wonder why I was chosen to go through life with so many pieces missing. Do you understand, Susana?"

Susana wiped a tear from her eye and enveloped Lilia in an embrace, "God brought you to this house as a gift not only to the Villavicencios, but for me. Forget your past, concentrate on what you have now and the future. God's grace brought us together."

"Let's stop talking about God," Lilia pulled away.

"Hush, the angels will hear."

"Religion was created by people who were afraid to face their mortality. They created a lie for self-comfort. I want a normal life without the nonsense of religion, and I don't want to feel guilty about it."

"Oh, Lilia, if I didn't love you so much, I'd be angry."

"I love you, and the professor, and of course, Baltito."

"You've left out your parents!"

"I'm grateful for them, but I don't love them the way I love my dog."

"Shame, Lilia!"

"Papá and Mamá don't think of me as their daughter."

"Of course they do! They are from an age where you don't show emotions, but they love you."

"I overheard Papá say that paying for my piano lessons was a mistake—because I can earn a living." Lilia contorted her face and spoke in a husky voice, imitating her father, "She's going to have a career and leave us. She won't take care of us!" Lilia reverted to her normal voice, "I was brought here only to take care of them."

"Not true!"

"They are so old now."

"Yes, they're aging, but that's normal."

"One day I caught Papá wandering around the house. He couldn't find his bedroom. I guided him down the hall to his room. He was like a child."

Susana looked at her watch. "It's late, Lilia, you're going to miss your train!"

Travel

Gathering her parents for a quick goodbye, Lilia felt remorseful. An uneasy feeling settled in her chest, and she regretted the awful things she had said to Susana. She tried to atone for her misdeeds by giving her mother a tight hug. When feeling Carmen's ribs through her cotton dress, she loosened her grip. Lilia had not noticed the amount of weight her mother had lost. Carmen's cheekbones now protruded, making her nose appear sharper. A perpetual shadowing around her eyes cast a macabre look. Her skin was freckled with age spots, and a huge mole seemed to grow larger by the day on the side of her neck. As her mother's fragile appearance stirred sadness within her, Lilia kissed Carmen on the cheek.

Lilia shook hands with Don Villavicencio, who was losing his imposing height from aging and curving of the spine. He no longer was an intimidating figure. When he walked, his hips gyrated with each step, and his loosened joints made him resemble an old doll whose elastic has stretched. Often, he used two canes to support his legs. Because of Don and Carmen's weakened state, they did not accompany Lilia to the train station but allowed Susana to take their place. Lilia felt tears forming but wiped them with a handkerchief before anyone noticed.

On the way to the station, Susana held Baltimore's leash while Lilia carried the heavy suitcase. Susana noticed that Lilia's excitement had faltered since saying goodbye to her parents and wished the week would pass quickly and she would be home again. Lilia had a presage that her parents would soon depart the world. She promised herself to be kinder to them.

The summer sun drenched the train station in a hazy light. A man busily polishing the brass fixtures stopped his work, as he recognized Lilia from her many trips to school through the years and held the door open for them. Lilia stepped into the cavernous lobby, but it no longer impressed her. The aroma of coffee, baked goods and fine cigars did not lighten her mood.

"Remember your promise to stay in your sleeper car! Don't wander about talking to strangers."

"I'll sleep all night and wake up in Buenos Aires. But before I reach the Riccios, I should stop at the Casa Rosada and catch a glimpse of Evita. I hear she comes out on the balcony and waves on a regular basis."

"No! You will do no such thing. You will head straight to their house."

"I want to do a little sightseeing."

"The First Lady is not going to appear on her balcony." Susana threw Lilia a harsh look. They stared at each other until they burst into laughter. They hugged, and then Lilia kneeled and petted Baltito. "I love you so much. I will see you in a week, so be a good boy."

Lilia boarded the train and settled in her private compartment. She enjoyed the oddness of the tiny room but soon was bored and fiddled with the water faucets in the bathroom alcove. Lilia thought about leaving her compartment and sitting in first class but kept her promise to Susana and ventured out only to the dining car for lunch and dinner. She stayed in her room curled up with a novel or her music books. When boredom became too much to bear, she stared out the window, but the sun had set, and it was too dark to see.

Lilia read the instructions on how to convert the couch into a bed and marveled at the ingenuity. At midnight she tried to force herself to sleep, but it was impossible on the uncomfortable mattress. The chugging of the engine never stopped and seemed to hammer her brain. After finally falling asleep in the early hours of morning, she woke up at seven with the sun shining on an alien view and was awed by the flatlands of the Argentine savannah. She dressed and breakfasted in the dining car and went to the first-class car to enjoy the company of other people. Most passengers there were much older and either read or slept, so she returned to her sleeper compartment to study her music books.

The Mansion

Buenos Aires, Argentina

When the train finally stopped in Argentina's capital, Lilia, curious to see Buenos Aires, was first to exit. She hired a taxi and thought about going to the presidential palace but feeling guilty about her promise to Susana, she gave the driver the Riccios' address.

Lilia was impressed by the beautiful architecture of Buenos Aires. She wondered how she would manage to get away from her host family and see more of the city. On the short ride from the train station to her destination, she realized Buenos Aires was even more like a European city than Santiago. She was happy to be in the city of "good air."

The driver pulled up to a large townhouse on a tree-lined street. Homes on either side of the lane were equally beautiful. She paid the fare and then hauled her heavy valise up the white stone steps. The height and broadness of the twin entry doors dwarfed her. A brass lion head knocker was centered on each door. Lilia banged the ring in the lion's mouth and disliked the clashing sound of metal, preferring the bells that announced visitors in her home.

A short, heavyset man opened the door and broke into a large smile, "Lilia! Welcome."

"You must be Miguel's father. So very nice to meet you, Señor Riccio."

The kind man kissed Lilia on both cheeks. Monica had warned her about the Italian custom. She found the kisses disagreeable; his thick mustache and beard were prickly against her skin. Señor Riccio called to his wife, "Constancia, Lilia's here!" Turning to Lilia he said, "I'll take your suitcase inside."

"Hello, Lilia. Please come in." Constancia extended her hand.

"Thank you for inviting me to your home, Señora Riccio."

"Please, no formalities, call us by our first names, Alfonso and Constancia," the friendly man said.

Lilia caught the disapproving look Constancia gave her husband and decided to always address her formally.

The couple asked her in and escorted her to a formal parlor.

"I'm dying to see Monica. Is she here?"

"No," replied Señor Riccio, "they are running last-minute errands for the nuptials."

Constancia offered, "Shall I have someone bring tea and something to eat?"

"No, thank you. I had a large breakfast on the train."

The unusual couple embodied Italian and Spanish culture at the same time, and Lilia noticed they intermingled Spanish and Italian words in the same sentence. She found it intriguing and admired their cosmopolitan ways.

Lilia learned that Señor Riccio's family emigrated from central Italy when he was a toddler. His family brought grape plants from Umbria to grow in the lush savannah of the Andean foothills. Their large plantation was far from the capital city, and they preferred the house in town. Although the family had lived in Argentina for over four decades, Alfonso's family had not lost their Italian customs. Lilia learned that Constancia's family was from Spain and migrated to Argentina when she was already an adult.

Lilia found the man's chubby physique pleasant. She thought that if he shaved his facial hair, he would resemble the plump cherubs decorating the walls of her church. He was short, and his face was so round it resembled a full moon. His hair fell in ringlets over his forehead. Señora Riccio could not be more opposite—tall, a thin frame and a long face. Her black hair, wound tightly in a severe knot at the nape of her neck, made her look austere.

Constancia rose. "I'll show you to your room, and I'm sure by the time you freshen up, Monica will be back. Leave your suitcase where it is, and I'll have someone carry it up."

"I can carry it. Thank you." Lilia followed Señora Riccio up the curved marble staircase, stunned at the beauty of the house. She marveled at the chandelier that seemed to float from the second-story ceiling. Lilia did not see a speck of dust on the massive light. Upon reaching the landing, she noticed the wainscoting reached above her waist. Señora Riccio led the way through a second parlor decorated with Romanesque statues, oil paintings and a fireplace so tall that a person could easily walk inside without hitting their head on the mantel. Plush Victorian furniture and two Chinese break-fronts complemented the grandeur of the room.

"This must be a ballroom. I've never seen anything quite like this. It's magnificent."

"Correct. It is a ballroom, but I do not like gatherings. I much prefer quiet to loud parties," Señora Riccio replied as she walked ahead.

A long hallway at the rear of the house exposed large windows. Lilia looked out and, impressed at the view, exclaimed, "The river is so wide."

On the other side of the hallway, Lilia peeked through the open doors into bedrooms and gaped at how equally beautifully appointed they were. Constancia opened a door leading to hidden steps. They climbed the stairs, and Lilia found herself in an enormous attic. The roof was slanted on either side with small windows jutting out. Lilia counted eight beds, four on each side of the room, all with corresponding nightstands and an equal number of dressers.

"I'm sorry, but all the guest bedrooms are taken by Monica's family. I hope you don't mind sharing the servants' room."

"Not at all. I appreciate that I can stay close to Monica." Lilia tried to hide her disappointment. "It is a bit drafty."

Señora Riccio pointed to a bed, "I'm sure you'll be warm under the covers." Lilia noticed that the paint on the beautiful dormer windows was peeling.

"Señora, may I borrow an iron, please? I'd like to press my dress for tomorrow."

"The maids keep a small iron in the bathroom cabinet." Señora Ricci pointed to a door.

"Thank you." Lilia retrieved the iron and plugged it into a socket by her bed. Lilia pulled out her concert gown.

"That can't be what you are wearing for the reception. Is it?"

"Yes. My most expensive gown."

"That may be acceptable for the ceremony since you'll be seated in the balcony behind the organ, but you'll need to change to something more fitting for the reception."

"It's all I've brought with me except for these skirts and blouses." Lilia spread out her skirts.

Constancia shook her head, "These will not do! The wedding is formal."

"Black is formal."

"Black is bad luck at a wedding. Show me another evening dress."

"I'm sorry. I heard about this superstition only yesterday an hour before boarding the train, and I didn't have a chance to shop." Lilia tried to keep her composure and not sound irritated.

Señora Riccio rummaged through Lilia's clothes. She pulled out garments and laid them on the bed and nearly screamed, "You'll have to wear something else!"

"I don't own evening dresses—only black gowns reserved for concerts."

"You'll borrow something from Monica."

"I couldn't. Monica is tall; her clothes will never fit me." Lilia watched the woman's frown deepen. "Don't worry, Señora Riccio. I'll run to a dress shop right now."

"There isn't time for any of us to accompany you to the boutiques."

"Don't trouble yourself. I can go alone."

"I will not allow you to wander an unfamiliar city. I promised your parents we would supervise you. I gave my word!" Constancia threw up her palms, "Can't you see how busy we are on the day before our son's wedding!"

"I'm sorry, I didn't mean to upset you. I will be safe. I'll take a taxi."

"We'll ask one of the servant girls. Surely they must own a decent dress."

Lilia realized her jaw had dropped. She could hear her father's admonishment: *Close your mouth or you'll catch a fly.* Lilia composed herself and forced a calm expression, although her cheeks flushed. "Thank you, Señora Riccio. Please ask your staff if I may borrow a dress."

Señora Riccio opened a linen cupboard and pulled out a towel, "You may use this to freshen up."

"Thank you, Señora." Lilia wiped sweat from her brow. "I'm sorry, I'm perspiring. Please forgive me."

"I thought you said you were cold; now you're sweating. Are you ill?" The woman's tone was fastidious.

"No, I'm not ill." Lilia slapped her arm, killing a mosquito that bit her arm. "Funny, we rarely see mosquitoes at home, especially not in winter."

"Chileans always think their country is somehow better than ours. You are even comparing bugs."

"Not at all, Señora. I'm only saying our climate is drier."

"It's the consequence of living so close to the beautiful Rio de la Plata."

"Señora, I didn't mean to cause any trouble. Perhaps I should move to a hotel."

"A hotel! How absurd and inappropriate! You don't appreciate all we're doing for you."

"I really do. I meant no harm. I just don't wish to upset you further."

Constancia's eyes squinted, and her jawline looked hard as if carved from granite. "You're a single, young girl."

"Señora Riccio, I'm not new to big cities. I have competed in many all over Chile."

"You are not listening! It's inappropriate for a single girl to be unaccompanied at such places." Constancia's eyes grew even smaller and looked like black slits. A vein bulged on her forehead.

"Because of this wedding, I've acquired a passport and have come by myself through the cordillera. Certainly, a hotel room is no different than a sleeper car."

"How dare you insult me! A pianist must have class and manners, and you lack both." Lilia took a step back. Señora Riccio continued, "You lack breeding."

"With all due respect, Señora Riccio, breeding is a word used for stock animals! People are not horses!"

"You are a splinter of the people who bore you. Monica told us you're a *guacha*, adopted by the Villavicencios."

Lilia stammered, "A...*guacha*?"

"Your parents and I corresponded. They did not trust you to attend the wedding, but I assured them that you would be safe, and now you insist on leaving us like women of the night!"

"A woman of...what?"

"You don't even know who you are. What a shame! You're not European, are you? You are of mixed blood."

Humiliation tied Lilia's tongue. The words stung as strongly as if they came barreling from a rifle. Lilia froze and thought, *I'm not Indio or European. I'm Chilean.*

"Get settled. I'll have no more of this nonsense." Constancia sighed and left the room, slamming the door behind her.

Rehashing the conversation over and over in her head intensified Lilia's anger. She was mad for not fighting back. The shocking words from the patronizing woman left her shaken and mute. *Am I shamed because I am an orphan?*

Lilia sat on the bed and debated whether she should leave. *If I leave, I'll hurt Monica. If I stay, I'll hurt myself.* Lilia could not grasp how a word like *guacha* could be uttered by a stranger as if it were a plain, ordinary word. Instead of a simple word, it was a weapon. Such words hurled at a person can manifest inside and grow like malignant cancer to eventually destroy the receiver.

Lilia rose and wiped her tears. She unplugged the iron, refolded her clothes and placed them back into the valise. Thoughts came to her of the words Señorita Silva used. She flung the strap of her purse over her shoulder and held the valise as she tiptoed downstairs and slipped out of the mansion, unseen.

Walking aimlessly, Lilia headed toward the city center keeping the river on her right and soon came upon a hotel. Feeling grateful that her father had placed money inside an envelope in her hand as a gift for the newlyweds, she exchanged the currency to Argentinian pesos and paid for a small room. After settling in, she went to the lobby and asked the doorman for directions to the train depot.

At the station she checked the time of the next day's departure to Santiago and made a reservation. Glancing at her watch and seeing it was only midafternoon, she decided to visit the Casa Rosada and forfeit her promise to Susana. Trying to forget the ugly word *guacha*, she willed herself to enjoy the rest of her day.

Joining a tour group at the entrance gates of the palace lifted her spirits. She followed the guide through the massive pink palace. Due to the absence of Evita and Juan Peron, the guide was allowed to take the tourists to the inner sanctum, the president's office.

After the enthralling visit, Lilia found a local restaurant and ordered the famous Argentinian *parrilla* without asking what the meal entailed. When the waiters approached her with a flaming grill and placed it on her table, she feared to be so near fire. She moved her chair back, causing the waiter to laugh. He returned with an astounding quantity of meat. It included a large steak, a lamb chop, a *chorizo* and a chicken leg. The restaurant patrons eyed Lilia and chuckled as her eyes widened with surprise at the large plate. They cooked the meat on the table grill as Lilia watched.

The patrons laughed again when the meat was ready and served on a huge platter. Another large plate was brought to the table with a mound of fried potatoes. Lilia ate a small portion of the steak and chicken but did not touch the lamb chop or the sausage. She nibbled the potatoes and declared she could not eat another bite.

"*Por favor*, can you bring me some waxed paper to take the unfinished meal? And please, I'd like the check."

The waiter brought the paper, wrapped the meat and collected payment. Lilia noticed that she had used almost all the money from the envelope. She didn't worry about paying for her return trip home because her father's silver ticket was safely in her purse. She returned to the hotel and on the way found a stray dog with a missing eye. She delighted in watching the mangy little beast feast on her leftovers.

The Man on the Train

The Andean Cordillera

Lilia fidgeted in the first-class car with a stack of sheet music on her lap. Overcome with the work that lay ahead, she focused on the five Chopin pieces she had chosen to perform for the Nationals. Sitting next to a white-haired woman wearing thick glasses, Lilia wondered if the woman could see anything at all. Lilia thought about starting a conversation with her but decided against it, as she wanted to concentrate on memorizing her music and was afraid the woman might prove too talkative.

Feeling hungry, she left the music sheets on her seat and went to eat lunch before having to complete the boring chore of reading and re-reading the notes on the paper. It was much easier to memorize while playing, but time was running out, and she needed to have every note locked in her memory.

The *pastel de choclo* Lilia ordered was supposed to make her feel better, but she played with the corn kernels, rolling them on her plate instead of eating them. Her thoughts were of what her parents' reaction would be to leaving the Riccio home abruptly and spending the money designated for the bride and groom. She forced herself to nibble at a wild yellow mushroom, the rare delicacy that grew on beech trees, but her angst was so great she could not swallow and spit it out. For dessert, she ordered sponge cake but after one bite, put her fork down. Not even the comfort of sweets made her feel less anxious.

The dinner failed to elevate Lilia's mood as she relived all that transpired in Buenos Aires. The word "guacha" kept repeating itself in her mind. She could not erase the memory. It seemed to shout repetitively within her head—*guacha, guacha, guacha, guacha*. Lilia assumed that the Riccios sent a telegram to her parents recounting their version of the twisted story, probably highlighting the fact that she left the house rudely without telling anyone. Her parents, she feared, mortified by the complaint, would never be on her side regardless of the facts. Lilia worried about what harsh punishment awaited her at home.

The steward approached with the check. Lilia flashed her father's silver ticket. The steward nodded and crumpled up the bill. Lilia, having witnessed this routine many times, didn't give it a second thought. First, the steward's eyebrows would lift in surprise. Second, his demeanor would change to awe which transformed into a sheepish mannerism, and finally he would retreat to the kitchen to inform the staff that an important person was onboard. The one thing she liked about being the daughter of the ex-Minister of Transportation was that on trains, she was like royalty.

Lilia ignored the European tourists sipping their drinks by the bar as they took photos of the landscape with their Leica cameras. They chatted in their native tongues and excitedly pointed at silent condors gliding upon the winds.

A group of skiers sat anxiously at a nearby table eating and eagerly waiting to reach the ski lodge and begin their downhill runs. She surmised they were escaping the summer heat of Europe and traveling to the Southern Hemisphere to keep their skills sharp.

A married couple sitting at the next table addressed their daughter, "Finish your dessert and come back to our compartment. And Clara, don't loiter." When the couple left the dining car, the young woman eagerly approached Lilia and said, "Do you know who those men are?"

"No. They look like they're part of some ski team."

"Yes. They are the Swiss Olympic team. Can you imagine how lucky we are to have them on board?"

"I don't really know anything about skiing," Lilia responded apathetically, as she was not in the mood to converse with anyone.

"You don't care?"

"Well, I suppose it's exciting but not for me—I don't ski. I've seen photographs in the paper, but I'm not interested," Lilia replied, embarrassed that when it came to sports of any kind, she was oblivious.

The girl extended her hand, "I'm Clara."

"Lilia."

They shook hands and Clara continued, "I suppose you are not staying at the ski lodge?"

"No, I'm going home to Santiago."

"They're dreamy. I'm sure I'll meet them at the lodge."

"I'm sure you will."

"We're staying for an entire week. My parents and I come every year. The skiing is fantastic, and we love to skate on the lake. It's great to relax before school starts again in February."

"I hope you enjoy your holiday, but please excuse me, I need to get back to studying." Lilia rose and walked away.

The train linked two southern capitals—Santiago and Buenos Aires. Most train routes in Argentina and Chile run from North to South, but the tracks between the capitals run east to west. Passengers who cross the Andes are primarily wealthy tourists, perennial ski enthusiasts or merchants who negotiate trade between the two countries.

Lilia walked to the front of the train to the sleeper cars and thought about taking a nap. She no longer bothered to gaze at the view. In fact, the dizzying altitudes and serpentine tracks through the rugged Andes did not help calm her. On the trip east to Buenos Aires, she did not see the treacherous landscape since they traversed at night. Under normal circumstances when Lilia was in a better frame of mind, she would have loved the exciting train ride through the mountains with its frightening gorge passes. But after the mortifying events at Monica's fiancé's house, her adventurous animus was missing, and she desperately wanted to be home snuggling with Baltito.

Lilia remembered she had left her music in the first-class car. She reversed direction and headed for the caboose, which had been modified with large glass windows for better viewing of the mountains. Changing her mind about the nap, she decided she would study for an extra hour before closeting herself again in the sleeping car. When she reached her seat, it was occupied by a man who was engaged in conversation with an elderly woman sitting in the next seat. The heel of his shoe was planted on her now disheveled sheet music.

"Excuse me, Señor, you've taken my seat!"

A little startled, the young man replied, "I didn't know it was your seat. I thought it was empty."

"And look what you've done to my music—pushed it all under the seat in a disorderly fashion!"

The frail older woman sitting next to him interrupted, "He did not put them there; I did. I asked this gentleman to sit awhile and relieve me of this dreadful boredom. It's a very long trip."

"It's quite alright, Señora, they are not damaged," Lilia softened.

"I'll return to my own car," the man stood and allowed Lilia to regain her seat. He was about to take his green army-like duffle bag from the shelf above when the woman said, "Leave it here, and stay in this car."

"I will, thank you. I'll stand by the windows and admire the remarkable view." He walked to an open space without seats and stared at the landscape.

Lilia whispered to the old woman, "What a rude man! He didn't even apologize."

"I was hoping you would let the young man keep your seat, since you don't like conversing with anyone. Maybe you can move to another seat or perhaps return to your sleeper car," the woman said in a sarcastic tone.

"I left my music on this seat because I was returning. I left for a quick lunch, and I do not have time to chit-chat when I have serious studying to do."

"I don't mind that you study, but please don't ignore me as if I do not exist at all. My name is Gertrudis."

Lilia did not give her name, wiggled in her seat, sorted her sheets and glanced over at the man. She did not like his smirk and thought him rude and believed he was eavesdropping on their conversation. She addressed him, "Perhaps you should go back to your own paid seat."

The older woman interjected, "I beg your pardon, young lady, don't speak to him in such a manner. What are you implying, that he doesn't belong in first class?"

"It's alright, Señora. The young lady is correct; my seat is in third class. It's so noisy there. That's why I tried to get away from it. This caboose has much bigger windows to see the peaks and sky," the man said, avoiding looking directly at Lilia, "and the seats are so comfortable." He approached them, leaned over Lilia and extended his hand to the older woman, "Thank you for the pleasure of your company. I'll go back now." He turned to Lilia, "I apologize if I've caused you any frustration."

Lilia ignored his apology. The woman threw Lilia a warning glance and said, "Young man, please, I insist you stay and enjoy the view. I'll speak to the conductor and tell him I so need you to keep me company. There won't be a problem."

"Thank you, Señora." The man stayed in the car and continued to admire the panorama.

Lilia was about to challenge the woman, knowing she held the mighty silver ticket that would easily trump anything the woman could possibly say, but decided to drop the issue. She felt it was not necessary to further agitate the old woman.

"You haven't bothered to even look at me. You keep your nose deep in those sheets of music, yet you have the nerve to complain because a handsome man and I are enjoying a conversation to try and pass the monotony of travel."

Lilia did not bother to look at the woman as she replied, "That man is not handsome. I don't mean to be rude, but I have important studying to do."

"Dear girl, you lack manners!"

"I'm sorry, I'm not myself today. I better get back to my work. I'm in an important piano competition, and I can't afford to be distracted by mundane things."

"Young lady! Kindness and civility are never mundane!"

Lilia glanced at the man and noticed how uncomfortable he looked in his cheap ivory suit and brown tie, listening to everything she said. She peered at him again and agreed with the old woman—the man was handsome. He had a Roman nose, straight with a slight bump on the bridge centered between thick brows shadowing hazel eyes. His sandy-colored hair was straight and combed back from his forehead, kept neatly in place by a drop of Brilliantine. She noticed the color of his vermillion lips with the top half having a double curve resembling Cupid's bow as it peered out of a well-groomed mustache. Wondering why she had not noticed his appeal, she was now curious as to what brought the man to South America and deciphered his accent as European, assuming correctly he was one of thousands of immigrants flocking to the Americas looking for work after the devastating war.

Lilia continued to study Chopin's *Ballade no.1 in G minor, Op. 23*. She looked at the black dots on the page and tried to memorize them but could not. Her mind usually morphed every note, chord and bar into vivid colors and geometrical patterns, but now they did not gleam or luster in any way. She concentrated harder, attempting to weave a new intricate story that would imbed in her memory the thousands of notes needed for the performance. Again, she failed to do so. Her usual acute focus dissolved as her eyes wandered to the man. She stared at him and saw he wore a smile that seemed plastered to his face. As he gazed at the mountains, his expression was of being awestruck at the grandeur of the view. His impish grin disappeared when he yawned and moved his jaw side to side as the increasing pressure of the high altitude muffled his ears.

Lilia's attention was drawn to the large snowflakes outside as if they were in a frenzied dance. Frozen crystals fell to Earth and rose again as strong currents seized them and threw them back to the sky, and then once again gravity pulled them to the ground. Within minutes a snowstorm raged.

Although snow fell throughout the year on the mountain peaks or in the southern tip of the country, most citizens lived in the warm protection of the central coast. Lilia felt uncomfortable watching the snow obscure the scenery. She wanted to give up her studies and let her mind wander to the attractive man. Her eyes were drawn to him, and when he caught her stare, he winked. His smile grew as one dimple appeared on the right side of his face. She avoided his eyes by quickly looking down at her music. Chopin was now lifeless. The image of the man burned in her mind and although no longer looking at him, she could see his magnificent cleft chin imprinted on her memory.

As uncomfortable as she was, she peeked once more in his direction, and again he caught her stare. This time she did not shy away. Lilia pointed her finger at him and beckoned him closer and was surprised at how quickly he was by her side.

"Won't you be more comfortable in your own car where at least you have a seat?" she said mockingly.

"I don't like to sit for very long periods, and I detest noisy places," his smile ever-present as he spoke. "There are too many men there guzzling beer at an alarming rate. I don't drink beer unless it's on a terribly hot day, and never in winter. Do you, *Signorina?*"

Lilia realized by the way he addressed her he was Italian. She did not know what to say to force him back to his own passenger car. The woman next to Lilia again interfered, "Señor, I'm going to get a bite in the dining car and wonder if you'd care to join me."

"*Grazie, Signora* Alvarez, but I've brought food with me. It's packed in my duffel bag."

"I love the Italian language and don't mind when you revert to it. I can understand a little. You're a charming man, *Signore* Della Corte."

The man laughed, "And I've got you speaking Italian, *Signora,* but please call me Enzo."

"Enzo, will you please keep my seat warm while I am gone?" The woman smiled and rose from her seat.

"*Sì. Grazie.*"

Lilia could not hide her displeasure that the woman dared to give him her seat.

"Enzo, may I have the pleasure of introducing this young lady to you? Oh, but I'm sorry, I don't know her name. She hasn't bothered to introduce herself during all the time we've been sitting together."

"My name is Lilia."

Fortunately for the old woman, looks do not kill. For if so, poor Señora Alvarez would have died on the spot from Lilia's hateful gaze.

"Lilia, meet Enzo," the woman said. Enzo extended his hand, but Lilia hesitated to shake it until she saw Señora Alvarez's angry eyes. Lilia moved over to the window seat as Enzo took the aisle seat.

"Thank you, Enzo. I'll be back in an hour. Talk to each other. It might be fun," she commanded.

After many years of service, Señora Alvarez could remember only a handful of children. Her mind blurred them, but she thought of a child named Lilia. The social worker remembered that the tiny girl had something special about her—perhaps it had been the child's piercing eyes.

Before leaving for the diner car, she turned to glimpse at the young woman and did not see any resemblance to her little charge of many years ago. She remembered the girl had freckles, and this young lady did not. For a moment Alvarez tried to calculate how old the child would be now, but it was hard to remember, and she dismissed the thought.

Señora Alvarez spent her life overseeing hundreds of orphans, and the years had taken a toll. The new protocol she helped create to place orphans in foster homes was a change that did not completely work as planned. Many children still languished in institutions due to the lack of foster homes. Municipalities could not find enough foster parents because there was still a stigma in caring for them. The persistent idea that orphans were inferior stopped many upstanding families from burdening themselves with these children. Another problem plaguing the system was that the number of abandoned children grew every year at a much faster rate than government funds could support.

Lilia tried once again to bury herself in her music, but the musky redolence of the man was disturbing. She slammed her book closed, gave up studying and pretended to rest. She shut her eyes and avoided engaging with the Italian.

"*Bello*," Enzo pointed to the window, pronouncing the word with an 'l' sound.

"The word is pronounced *Be-yo*."

"Have we crossed into Chile yet?"

"I'm not sure. The border runs along the peaks of the mountains."

"It is so beautiful here. My country is beautiful too."

Lilia did not respond, hoping to discourage the man.

"*Signorina*...oh, no...*Señorita*. Where do you live in Chile?"

"Santiago."

"I'm from Italy."

"I know."

"Yes, thank God," he chuckled. "I see the Vesuvius, how do you say, smoke, yes, smoke from my rooftop. Do you know about Italy?"

"A little."

"Our history is great and very old. The art is in every corner. Caracas is not like that."

"If you live in Venezuela, why are you now so far away?" As soon as the question left her lips, she regretted continuing the conversation.

"I was on holiday to visit family in Buenos Aires. Franco, my cousin, suggested I see the Andes because I may not pass this way again. I'm happy I listened." Enzo spoke slowly as he was still uncomfortable speaking Spanish.

"You're an experienced traveler. This is the first time I've been outside of Chile. I'm a pianist and have studied Italian art and especially its music."

"I've not studied art or music. I left school when I was in the sixth grade."

"Why so young?"

"Because my father was a soldier and fought in the war of Ethiopia. He was killed there. It was up to me to help support my mother, my younger brother and sister. I work with my hands, not so much my head. It's a good way to earn a living. Not everyone can attend school." Enzo showed his rough callused hands.

"I knew a family when I was a very small child. They were farmers who could hardly read, but they were wonderful, hard-working people. I loved their humble life. The family was always together, whether in the fields or relaxing by the fire at night. It was very special."

Enzo listened and nodded in agreement. "My family was like that, but now we've moved far away from one other. I own a small construction company, and when it prospers, I'll bring my brother on board. He now works construction in Austria. Both of us send money back to our mother."

"What kind of construction?"

"I build houses. My clients are the newly rich from oil."

"Did you fight in the war?"

"Yes."

"Are you a fascist?"

"What kind of question is that? I am not, but I was a Mussolini's, oh, how you say? I was a red beret. Later I became a soldier for the Royal Italian Army."

"You were on the wrong side."

"Wrong side? To a soldier, there is no wrong side, only one side!"

"One side!" Lilia said in a scolding manner.

"*Sì*! One side. A soldier can take only one side and that is his country's side! You follow orders and protect your comrades and never ask why. I was a driver and had to bring men to the front line."

"To join the Nazis?"

"Not then. I'm sorry we first sided with the Germans because of the *l'in-glese*, their unfairness of *colonialismo*. The British have a rule for themselves and another for everyone else. We abandoned the Nazis when we got our heads on straight."

"You were a fascist with a gun," Lilia sneered.

"Actually, I did not have a gun," Enzo spoke almost in a whisper. Lilia looked at him unbelievingly. "I lost my gun in battle but still the commander ordered me to drive the troops to the Gothic Line." Enzo stared ahead, and Lilia noticed his demeanor changed. She realized the young man was not a happy-go-lucky nobody as she assumed but a complicated man who had a history.

"What is a Gothic Line?"

"It's where the German troops were trying to take my country."

"Italians should have protected the Jews," Lilia said as she stared at the continuing snowfall.

"Do you think, *Signorina,* we knew what was happening to the Jews? Or the gypsies? Or even some of our own priests?"

"Men never take responsibility!"

"I had no choice. I was a soldier."

There was a pause in their conversation while Enzo gathered his thoughts. "Italians and Jews have lived together in peace for hundreds of years. We had no idea of the truth."

"Have you forgotten the Inquisition?"

"Please! We were not Italy at the time of the Inquisition. We were divided states. Italians did not want to join the Spanish Inquisition and were the last to do so under extreme pressure. We did terrible things, but that was the past. Let's get back to modern times."

"Hmm," Lilia retorted, "and the concentration camps?"

"Italy did not have concentration camps. We didn't know. We are kind and Christian people!"

"Stop talking about the war. I don't want to hear anymore. I stopped reading the papers. It's unimaginable."

"Do you prefer to keep your head buried in sand?"

"I'm grateful that Chile is on the other side of the world and was not involved in that stupid war."

"But certainly, Chile was affected. You must understand we are one people on Earth sharing the same sun and moon. We're connected. If you drop a stone in the water in Salerno and cause a ripple, it will be felt in China as a tidal wave. Understand? Our lives are intertwined."

Lilia rolled her eyes and said, "Next, you're going to start talking about religion!"

"You're naïve and ignorant."

"I'm a graduate of a prestigious private school. You said you only reached the sixth grade. You were dragged into a dirty war, a simple puppet of a regime."

"We are all puppets! Even you! Is music all that's important to you?"

"Yes! Music! Music is important and heavenly."

Enzo shook his head and became silent.

Lilia buried herself in her sheet music. She decided to ignore the annoying man and hoped that the rightful owner of the seat would return from the dining car.

Enzo tried to relax but could not stop the images flooding his mind of that fateful day, November 21, 1943. He shuddered at the memories, closed his eyes and was back in Emilia-Romagna, Italy.

The Gothic Line

Emilia-Romagna, Italy, 1943

Freezing rain pounded the muddy road. A lone green army truck of the Italian Royal Army zigzagged over the slick pavement and nearly toppled into the overflowing drainage ditch.

"*Ah, Fa Napoli!*" Enzo cursed, gripping the steering wheel tighter.

"Get us to the goddamned Gothic Line in one piece!" grunted Pasqual, a tall lanky nineteen-year-old. Even with his hair cut nearly to his scalp, black curly ringlets framed his face. His olive complexion had turned to winter pale. His sleepy brown eyes drooped on the outer edges, giving him the impression of laziness, but he was the opposite—fierce and alert. Enzo envied three traits belonging to the boy from Calabria: his kill record under fire, his imposing height and his rank of corporal. Enzo was only a soldier, the lowest rank possible. Pasqual continued his rant, "I hope we find those bastards before they find us."

"Stop talking! You'll give us the evil eye. Say a prayer!" Enzo demanded.

Before Pasqual could finish making the sign of the cross, he yelled out, "Shit! Slow down!"

Enzo's temper flashed, "It's getting lighter out. Got to get you dickheads off this truck. I got a bad feeling."

"Give me one of your American cigarettes?" Pasqual contorted his face in a pathetic plea.

Enzo pulled a cigarette from his pocket, "My last one."

"Thanks." Pasqual lit the cigarette. He took a couple of drags before handing it back to Enzo. "Leave it to the Italian brass to send a twerp like you up here without a rifle. Officers are so fucked-up."

"*Cristo Santo!* There's the Foglio River on the right. I've gone too far north. I need to turn around when I get to a wider part of the road. We must be north of the Gothic Line. Better dump you sons of bitches."

The sleet bombarded the window with clattering force, grating on the soldiers' nerves. Enzo felt guilty that he was warm inside the cab, thanks to the heat of the engine, while behind him under the thick green tarp twenty-three men tried to keep from freezing.

Enzo felt the truck hit a pothole and he lost control. The vehicle veered to the left, careened into the bank, tipped on its side and finally rested. Fragments of glass pierced Enzo's scalp above his ear. Warm blood oozed down his neck. He managed to get his handkerchief out of his pocket while screaming at Pasqual, "Get the hell off me! Climb out through your door and help me out." Enzo pressed the handkerchief on the wound, surmising it was only a small flesh wound as it barely stung.

The men lumbered out and checked themselves for injuries. No one had more than a few bumps and scrapes, but their nerves had taken a hit. Enzo commanded the men to get the truck back on all four wheels. The heavy ice on and around the lorry made it impossible, but with no alternative, they kept trying. On the fourth attempt, a shot rang out. Enzo saw his friend, Tonino, fall to the ground with a round hole in the middle of his neck as blood spurt out in a rhythmic fashion. Enzo yearned to help the boy but knew if he did, he would be next to fall. Dozens of rifles were pointing at the Italians from the dense forest, and Enzo heard two tanks roar behind. The Nazis crawled down the hill a few meters above the mangled truck. Their barking Rottweilers snarled and showed their lethal teeth. A tall German with a craggy face shouted in Italian, then a translator demanded, "Don't move, you're surrounded! Put your guns on the ground!"

"Hey, *Paisano*," said a brave soldier standing next to Enzo. "We fought with you, side by side—we are friends, no?"

"Quiet! Weapons down! Hands up!" the translator's voice grew raspier.

The Italians slowly placed their weapons on the icy ground.

"Line up, single file!"

The bewildered men lifted their arms and fell into a line. German soldiers patted the Italians for concealed weapons. A German pulled a charcoal pencil from Enzo's pocket and looked at it, prompting Enzo to say, "It's only a pencil for the maps." The German placed it back in the Italian's pocket and continued to pat him down.

The Germans counted the weapons, found they had one less than the number of soldiers and recounted. The translator shouted, "We're missing a weapon. Where is it?"

Enzo stepped out of line, "I don't carry a weapon. I'm only the driver."

"Search the cab!" a German ordered.

A soldier, barely old enough to attend high school, searched the truck and called out to his commander, "*Alles ist klar!*"

The Nazis ordered the captured men to place their hands on top of their heads and marched them up the bank away from the road. Upon reaching the top of the bank, Enzo looked behind him at what he thought was a pothole that caused the accident and saw instead planks with four-inch studded nails, confirming the accident was planned by the devilish handiwork of the Germans.

The Nazis continued to march the Italians through the woods. They reached a clearing where a stone farmhouse with a large, detached barn stood. Enzo assumed the owners were killed when the Germans confiscated their property. Two Germans opened the barn doors, and the Nazis steered the prisoners inside.

The barn gave off an iron stench. There were no animals left in the outbuilding, but a bloody carcass of a pig hung from a rafter with its belly and shanks cut out. Droplets of blood still dripped on the ground below.

"Place your hands behind your back and sit on the floor. Any sudden moves will cost you your life!" Three Germans systematically tied the hands of the Italians to the many posts that supported the barn's roof.

The prisoners tried to find comfortable positions on the hay-filled floor. They spent the morning staring into nothingness. They avoided the Germans' faces but memorized their bodies from the waist down to their iron boot buckles. They checked their tears when thinking of Tonino's death. Airborne dust particles floated, illuminated by a single ray of light filtering through a crack in the roof. As the day wore on, the Italians relaxed a bit. The Germans shifted into less-stiff postures, bending their knees or even squatting.

Enzo whispered to Pasqual, "I think we're safe; they'll negotiate some sort of bargain. They'll release us soon."

"Keep quiet," Pasqual commanded but seconds later whispered, "I will kill the bastards!"

In the relative quiet of late afternoon, the captives had begun to drift into sleep when they heard an approaching vehicle's brakes squeal to a stop. The huge barn doors opened, alarming everyone. The translator stepped inside, his eyes searching the captured men. Finding Enzo, he approached him and untied the frightened soldier from the post but kept his hands bound. He motioned him to rise and ordered, "Follow me!"

Enzo caught Pasqual's stoic face telegraphing to stay strong. He admired his friend's coolness. Before exiting to the frigid outdoors, Enzo turned to Pasqual and winked at him. Pasqual's gaze followed his friend and did not even blink until the barn doors slammed shut and separated them.

The sleet had stopped, but the temperature dropped. The translator walked Enzo to the house where two men standing guard opened the front door allowing them to enter. They entered through a large dining room and stepped into a butler's pantry, where the translator knocked on the kitchen door.

"Enter," said a man with an unusually high voice.

Enzo was escorted in, where an oversized fire roared in a brick oven. He inhaled the enticing smell of coffee mingled with roast pork. The translator extended his right arm into the air with a straightened hand and shouted, "*Heil Hitler!*"

The field marshal did not return the salute nor rise from his seat.

The translator continued, "Field Marshal, this is the man claiming he was unarmed."

"Who are you, boy?" A muscular man with pale blue eyes asked.

Through the interpreter, Enzo answered all the officer's questions. "Soldier Lorenzo Della Corte."

"You're disobeying protocol—a soldier does not give his name. Are you making it up?"

"No sir, I don't know all the rules. I did not attend training."

"Why were you not carrying a weapon?" the marshal queried, never taking his eyes off the young soldier.

Enzo kept his stare on the floor, nervous to be in such proximity to the powerful man but too prideful to disclose the truth that an exploded grenade had sent his gun flying over a cliff. And when he returned to the makeshift camp, the Italian Army could not replace his weapon. The Italian magazines were long empty of rifles and ammunition.

The translator's staccato voice blasted, "Answer the question!"

Enzo's instinct told him to mitigate his infantry skills. His gut warned that every word he uttered could decide whether he was afforded another breath. Enzo felt his left knee trembling and tried to stop it by pressing his foot into the floor. He recited a prayer in his head, and at the same time, listened to every word spoken by the translator. He also heard the faint hoot of an owl in the distant woods.

The interpreter stabbed the point of his gun into Enzo's shoulder, prompting him to answer, "I've never carried a rifle. I haven't learned to shoot. The army recruited me only to drive troops."

The marshal laughed, "You tell such funny lies!"

Enzo kept his voice from quivering and smiled, "I learned to drive in a single morning and was handed keys. I'm the first in my family to drive anything other than mules."

The field marshal was intrigued.

Enzo continued his act, "I'm not a real soldier. The army came to my village and told us farm boys to 'fight for our fatherland,' and so here I am. They didn't even care that I'm the only son in my family."

"How old are you?

"Fifteen."

Enzo had turned nineteen only a week before but did not look his age. He was always one of the shortest boys in his class, and his angelic face gave him the appearance of someone extraordinarily young. A few years prior, Enzo was a proud youth wearing the red beret for Mussolini before joining the Army.

"I'll be sixteen soon," Enzo added to the lie, hoping the man would not see through the fabrication.

"Where's home?"

"Castel San Giorgio."

"Province?"

"Campania."

"You're not a typical southern boy with your pale skin and green eyes. You were blonde as a boy, and you can even pass for German."

"My mother has red hair."

"Unusual." The field marshal stood and towered over Enzo. "Soldier, I want you to do something for me."

"Yes sir! I am an admirer of Germany. I also have great respect for my leader, Mussolini. I first wore the fasces on my beret when I was eleven years old, and now I wear it on my sleeves." Enzo wore his best innocent expression.

"Ah, the fasces. Sticks with an ax carried over from Roman times. Do you know what it means?"

Enzo smiled as if he were proud to answer a teacher's question, "The man that carries it has the power to wield life and death."

"Do you hold such power?"

"No sir."

"It is not as impressive as our swastika, but I respect the tradition," the marshal nodded at the attractive youth. He sipped his coffee while he analyzed Enzo's perfect features. His demeanor changed, "You have a strange air about you. It's uncanny how you remind me of my son, but my boy is much, much taller." The field marshal gulped the last swallow of coffee and smacked his lips. "I'm sending you back to your army immediately."

"Thank you, sir."

"Tell them your comrades are keeping us company."

"Will you release them soon?"

The field marshal chuckled.

"I'd like to say goodbye to my friends."

The man did not answer.

"Sir, how will I get back without a truck?"

"You'll find a way."

The field marshal waived his hand, alerting the translator he was done, and refilled his cup. The interpreter motioned Enzo to walk out as he pointed the gun at his heart.

Three guards joined the translator as they marched Enzo towards the road. They reached the overturned truck, now only a shell stripped of tires and battery. Even the green tarp over the trailer was gone. Tonino's body lay lifeless on the ground, his skin a bluish hue.

The guards stopped, and the interpreter ordered, "Go."

With his heart pounding, Enzo walked at a fast clip for about a thousand meters until he reached the edge of a wood where he sprinted and disappeared. After trudging through the difficult terrain for an hour, he spotted a clearing with another farmhouse and similar barn. He dared not knock on the door, fearing it too might be housing German soldiers.

Shaking from dread and cold, he waited behind raspberry bushes for any movement or sound. When time proved it was unoccupied, he sneaked into the empty barn that once was home to cows. He was grateful for the shelter that would warm his body.

Enzo's pupils widened as they adjusted to the dim light. He found dried corn still on its cob in an aluminum bucket and bit into the kernels. The corn was as hard as pebbles, and he spit them out. Searching the barn for anything that might be useful, he found a tiny paper bag holding tacks. Dumping its contents on the ground, he folded the bag, put it in his pocket and waited.

When darkness fell and the three-quarter moon peaked through clouds, Enzo left the barn. Retracing his steps through the same patch of woods, he neared the barn where his brothers were captive. He circled the barn and house from a safe distance, at times snaking on wet snow as he surveyed the area.

The rear of the barn was empty of guards, unlike the front where German guards congregated. Enzo hid behind a tree, tore a piece of the paper bag and wrote a note with his pencil. Hunched low to the ground, he dashed towards the barn with a roof sloped downward, climbing it easily thanks to an old wisteria growing beside the structure. He prayed for the thick vines to hold his weight. Climbing onto the roof, he quietly tiptoed, hoping his footsteps would not give him away. Enzo found the crack in the roof he had spotted when he was tied to the pole. Through the slit he saw Pasqual below. He folded the paper and stuffed his message through the crack. The paper flew down to the ground, but he could not follow it to where it landed. Hoping someone from his company had seen it fall, he listened for movement but heard only snoring. He was about to climb down from the roof when the door to the house opened, casting a long, yellow glow on the snow.

The field marshal, along with a squadron of soldiers, sauntered towards the barn as calmly as if it were a hot day on a balmy shore. Enzo laid his body flat on the roof, hoping not to slip as he watched the procession. A German stationed outside the barn slid the door open and shouted commands. After a few agonizing minutes, Enzo watched as the Nazis walking in an arrogant gait shuffled the drowsy Italians out in single file with their hands still bound behind them. Five Germans formed a firing squad, and before Enzo realized what was happening, they released a fusillade of bullets.

The Blizzard

Valle Nevado, Chile, 1947

"*Valle Nevado! Valle Nevado*," yelled the steward, pulling Enzo back into the present moment.

The train pulled into the station that was covered in a sheet of white snow. The winter storm picked up its pace, and the famous ski lodge was barely visible. Señora Alvarez returned from the dining room. Enzo jumped up and held her elbow as he guided the frail woman to her seat.

"The scenery is mesmerizing. I feel a wizard has placed me inside a Christmas globe." Enzo's smile was wide.

"It is magical," agreed the Señora.

"I've never seen snowflakes the size of butterflies...I've been thinking it will be best for me to end my holiday and return to Buenos Aires tomorrow. I will not go as far as Santiago."

"I'm sorry you will leave us," Señora Alvarez said.

"I'll enjoy this winter's night before returning to the hellish heat of Caracas." Enzo pulled his luggage from the overhead shelf and extended his hand to Señora Alvarez. She shook it, but Enzo pulled her hand to his lips and kissed it.

"I wish you safe travels." A slight flush appeared on the Señora's face.

"Thank you. It was a pleasure meeting you." Enzo let go of the Señora's hand and faced Lilia, "And, of course, meeting you as well." Enzo extended his hand but not to shake Lilia's, but to reach for his brown fedora.

"Goodbye, Lorenzo." Lilia's voice quivered, surprising herself that she felt sorrow at parting so abruptly. Enzo smiled before turning away, and Lilia saw the single dimple on his cheek.

The doors of the train opened, and a gush of cold wind entered the car. Lilia shuddered and watched Enzo maneuver the slippery path toward the lodge. Another gust of wind caught Enzo's fedora and sent it flying downhill before it rolled under the train. He turned to locate where the hat might have landed, could not spot it and continued his walk up the path. Lilia wanted to run out to find the hat and bring it to him but didn't. She felt foolish and chose to remain in her seat. She stared at Enzo's back until snow obscured his image.

The hotel mimicked the architecture found in the German Alps, specifically the town of Garmisch-Partenkirchen. Enzo had seen a postcard of the local homes and hotels in that village near the famous mountain, Zugspitze. The steep gables of the roof allowed gravity to pull accumulated snow to the ground. Planters adorned each window, although now empty and covered in snow. Enzo imagined the bright flowers that would grace them in spring. The white stucco exterior walls of the lodge were hand painted with scenes from German folklore.

The lobby was even more impressive than the outside, with whole timber columns stained in dark walnut varnish that connected with perpendicular wooden beams on the ceiling. It gave the impression of great trees spreading their branches, and such a feature lent the structure a fairy-tale-like quality that could have come right out of fables by the Brothers Grimm. A lounging area boasted huge windows opening to a view of the Andean peaks.

The style of the hotel along with its splendid views captivated Enzo. He gazed at the snow falling sideways in the fury of the wind before making his way to the front desk and asking for a room. When he heard the herculean price, his face flushed, and he whispered, "Sir, I dare not spend that much. I've overextended my holiday budget. I'm afraid I won't be able to stay. What time is the next train to Buenos Aires?"

"There's only one train going east and one west per day. The one heading for Argentina left a few hours ago."

"Is there a less expensive hotel nearby?"

"Not for a hundred kilometers."

"Will I be able to spend the night in your lobby and wait for tomorrow's train?"

The desk clerk smirked, "Sir, I hope you don't think we would throw you out to the elements and watch you freeze? You're welcome to sit in the lobby tonight. Welcome to Chile."

"Thank you, Señor."

On his way to the bar, Enzo noticed the snow was abating and only a few flakes now fell from the skies. The dissipating clouds provided a break in the sky, and the sun's rays reflected so brightly on the snow Enzo had to look away. He ordered a glass of Malbec and heard the whistle of the train announcing it was leaving the station.

In a corner of the room, two St. Bernard dogs snuggled side by side on a lambskin bed, each with a small barrel of rum tied to their collar. A plaque told their names—Filipe and Pedro. A document hung below the plaque explaining their duties as working members of the lodge. The enormous dogs were three-year-old brothers who came from a long line of Swiss pedigree rescue dogs. Each year they saved the lives of skiers who did not heed the warnings or rules of the lodge and dared to deviate from the designated paths.

"*Bon giorno,* Filipe, Pedro," Enzo said, reverting to his native tongue while crouched and petting the dogs. One of them yawned and the other scratched his ear. "May I join you for a drink? I'd offer to buy, but I see you already have one." Enzo touched the rum barrel on the dog's neck and chuckled. He gave the dogs a final rub on their heads.

Enzo took a long swig from his glass and was about to take a second gulp when he heard a faint hum. The dogs sprang to their feet and barked, startling Enzo. The floor trembled and the chandelier swung overhead. Guests gasped. The humming sound turned into a loud rumble as if a truck was barreling straight through the walls of the building. A woman screamed. Harsh popping sounds grew louder while the room shook and sent shivers through Enzo's body. The sounds transported him back to the war on that horrific night when rifles thundered.

"*Temblor!*" shouted the desk clerk from the lobby, "Everyone, take cover under the tables!"

Enzo obeyed and ducked under a small round table along with a skier who had returned from a run. When the staff confirmed that all the guests were safely under the tables, they too crammed underneath. The wooden floor first undulated and then violently shuddered.

"Stay where you are!" the bartender howled.

The shaking continued as everyone's nerves unraveled. Enzo tried to calm himself and mumbled, "It's not the Germans. It's not the Germans." His hands shook as he continued his mantra, "It's not the Germans." The skier by his side surmised that Enzo had suffered during the war, patted his back and said, "Don't worry, it's a common earthquake. Chile has at least one per week. It'll be over soon."

When the room stilled, the hotel staff rose and assessed the situation. The crystal wine goblets that hung from their stems above the bar now littered the floor in thousands of shards. Better planning had kept hundreds of wine bottles safely stashed on their sides and cocooned in little honey-combed-shaped openings behind a locked iron gate. They were safe as butter-flies in a chrysalis.

The skier crawled out from under the table, extended his hand to Enzo and pulled him up. "My name is Jorge. Are you alright?"

Enzo took a deep breath, "Yes, thank you. I'm Enzo."

The staff checked on everyone as they rose from their crouching positions. They were stunned and silent, except for a woman who was drenched in tears and sobbing. A staff member tried to coax her to stop crying and handed her a handkerchief. As the guests began to relax, Enzo approached the large windows and saw a cloud near the top of a tall peak, its white mist growing larger and beginning to run down the mountainside. He tried to process what he was seeing when a woman confirmed his fears by screaming, "My God, it's an avalanche!"

The side of the mountain slipped and roared. The cloud picked up speed, engulfing everything in its wake in a sinister haze as it raced down the mountain. It made loud cracking noises as it picked up more snow and ice. Women screamed, fearing the avalanche would be on them, but it steered away from the lodge, following the contours of the mountain. Only harm-less snow vapors reached the lodge, shrouding it in powder as rocks and ice tumbled a short distance away. The noise finally ceased, signaling that the avalanche had run its course and disappeared somewhere into a crevasse. The world was once again still.

A few minutes later, a staff member addressed the room. "Expect more shocks, but they won't be as fierce."

"Sometimes the aftershocks are worse," screamed Clara, who only fifteen minutes prior had departed the train to blissfully start her holidays. Her mother stroked her hair, attempting to calm the distraught teenager. Another couple stayed locked in an embrace. An older man shouted, "My grandson was skiing! Please, someone, help me look for him!"

Jorge zipping his jacket, replied, "I'll check the ski lifts."

The bartenders and servers were already sweeping up the debris. They were familiar with earthquakes and did not hesitate to follow protocol. Comfortable with avalanches created by men with dynamite to keep the slopes safe, they were more shaken by the unpredictable natural ones. To calm the guests, the bartender opened a corner cabinet displaying copper mugs in disarray and declared, "A round of beer on the house!"

As the traumatized patrons lined up for the beverage, they heard the clang of the outside bells by the lodge's main entrance. Two medics doubling as ski patrols entered the lobby. Although the dark-haired man was of average height, he looked tiny next to the much taller one that spoke with a German accent, "Attention! I need everyone's immediate attention!"

The man's thick accent grated Enzo, his memory never far from the capture above the Gothic Line, but he forced himself to listen to the man's words.

"I'm Heinz, the chief medic of this lodge. We received a mayday from the train that left our station a few minutes before the earthquake. But now there is only radio silence, and we fear the train might have been hit by the avalanche. I need all able men, both guests and staff, to form a search party! Get your parkas and meet us outside in three minutes."

A Long Day

The staff trained in avalanche and emergency protocols knew their specific jobs and moved quickly. The male workers ran to the sheds and brought out shovels. The female staff asked for help in setting up emergency cots in the lobby and pulled sheets out of the massive linen closets. The newly arrived ski team from Switzerland was first to assemble outside. Heinz blew his whistle in three short spurts. Pedro and Felipe whimpered with excitement and followed him out.

Heinz put on his skis while he issued commands to the other medic, "Domingo! Weed out the men who aren't skiers and guide them to the sleds."

When the two groups assembled, Heinz yelled, "Follow the dogs!" He blew his whistle again, and he and the skiers along with the eager dogs followed the path downhill to the tracks.

Enzo went to retrieve a sled. Domingo frowned as he noticed Enzo was wearing what appeared to be a summer suit and shook his head, "Are you crazy?"

"Sir?"

"Where's your parka? Why are you wearing loafers?"

"I don't have winter attire. This was an unexpected stop. I assure you I've been in much worse situations!"

"You'll freeze! We don't have time to outfit you! Get back inside and help the women. Stop wasting our time!"

"I can help!"

"Young man, get back inside or you will be arrested upon our return!"

Domingo piled shovels on sleds and shouted instructions. "Two men can ride each sled downhill. Follow the tracks of the skiers. There are not enough sleds for everyone, so the rest of you will have to go on foot."

The sleds glided down the mountain while the remaining men clumsily trampled through the deep snow. Enzo felt humiliated at being the only man left behind and not able to help the passengers on the train. Thinking of both Señora Alvarez and the young lady, it pained him to think they may be in trouble. He thought of the worst possible circumstance, and along with the memory of his capture, it almost paralyzed him. Breathing deeply, he regained control, pushed fear aside and became determined to be of use.

Enzo followed the rescuers with his eyes until they faded from view. Thinking about ignoring the medic's instructions and running down the mountain regardless of having improper attire and no boots, he dismissed the idea and reasoned the medic had been correct, and he would be an additional burden. He watched a tall woman wearing a fur coat coming out of the hotel and had an idea. Upon reaching her, he begged, "Please, can you lend me your coat? I need to help the people on the train."

The woman did not hesitate, took off her coat and handed it to Enzo. He slid his arms into the sleeves and fastened the eye hooks. His hands as well as his voice quivered, "Thank you."

"Wait," she said, "you'll need the hat and gloves."

Enzo placed her hat on his head and was surprised her gloves fit. His shoes were soaked, and he could feel the wetness seeping his socks. He rushed to a ski rack where skis and boots were lined up neatly in a row and chose a pair of boots that might fit. He tried them on. They were slightly too big, but he did not have time to test for a perfect pair. He put on the other boot and tried to latch it. The mechanism was unfamiliar to him, as he had never skied, but finally he managed to buckle them. Uncomfortable and heavy as they were, the boots were better than his slipper-like shoes, which he left by the skis and poles. Enzo tried to run down the hill, but the depth of the snow and the cumbersome boots made it impossible for him to move as fast as he wished. He followed the trail and eventually found the train site.

"What's that you're wearing? Fox or mink?" a man ridiculed Enzo as he handed him a shovel.

Enzo shrugged.

Another man jumped into the conversation, "It's a good omen seeing you down here modeling a Parisienne coat. It lifts my spirit. Perhaps it means we'll find people alive."

"May God hear your words," Enzo replied as he dug the shovel into the condensed snow. Another man yelled, "Look, they found an opening!"

The men were incredulous at the amount of snow, ice and stones that had broken through the windows and embedded inside the cars. The avalanche hitting the train caused some of the cars to topple sideways off the track. It seemed a miracle to Enzo that the last three cars, including the caboose, remained tethered in their upright position. It seemed like a miracle that the snow was not solidly packed inside. Filipe and Pedro were digging and tunneling into the buried train, where their powerful sense of smell guided them to the people.

Heinz had formed teams and moved the men to various parts of the track. He too shoveled as fast as his huge frame allowed. He stopped to yell out, "Don't move to another car until you have breached the one you have been assigned. Leave no one behind. Our priority is to get to the injured." At least two men were working each of the fourteen passenger cars, including the kitchen and dining cars.

Enzo asked Heinz if he could work on the caboose, as he knew the women who'd sat with him there. Heinz agreed, and Enzo ran to the caboose in hopes that Lilia and Señora Alvarez had not moved to their sleeping compartments. He heard the dogs bark simultaneously indicating they had found a person. Two workers frantically moved to where the dogs pointed. Heinz praised the dogs, "Good boys!" He blew his whistle again and yelled, *"Mas!"* The dogs understood and they moved to the next car.

Enzo flashed back and was again reliving the war and hearing imaginary gunfire. He started to tremble from both the cold and the recurring memory of his capture. He closed his eyes and prayed aloud to his patron saint, "Santo Lorenzo, take my mind away from the war. I must serve these people and find them alive."

Enzo and another guest named Juan dug snow on the outside of the first-class car until they reached the snow-impacted window and crawled inside. They continued to work in tight quarters, gasping for air as they plowed. Glass intermingling with ice shredded Enzo's pants, and the thin white gloves Enzo had borrowed from the tall woman were soaked. He pulled them off his hands and threw them into the snow.

The two men found a small clear spot without much ice and snow. Enzo came upon a man buried halfway in red bloody snow. He noticed a large splinter of glass impaled in the man's neck. His ashen face and wide-open eyes proved he was dead.

Enzo pushed towards the rear of the car where he had sat with Lilia and Señora Alvarez. Before reaching their seats, he nearly tripped on a body lying in the aisle. Juan lifted the stiff body onto a seat as Enzo continued his search for the women.

He heard a faint "help" from the front of the caboose. He found Lilia sitting on the floor cradling Señora Alvarez's limp head in her shivering arms. The old woman's face was pale and her lips purple. Lilia's complexion was red, and a tear fell slowly from the corner of her eye as she looked up and pleaded, "Enzo, the Señora! She won't wake up."

Placing two fingers on the woman's neck, Enzo whispered, "She has a pulse!" He then placed his ear below her nose, "But her breathing is shallow." Enzo patted her face and called out her name, but there was no response.

Juan took off his parka, laid it on the floor of the car and placed the older woman on top. "We've got to get her warm. I'll get a sled for them," he said as he pulled his jacket and dragged her through the aisle.

"Hurry, Juan!" Enzo turned to Lilia, "Follow me."

"I can't! My legs are so cold!" Lilia's eyes showed fear. Her feet tucked under her skirt, she moaned.

"Where are your shoes, Lilia?"

"I don't know. They must have fallen off when we tumbled from our seats."

Enzo walked to the body that Juan had lifted from the floor and took off the man's shoes and socks. He replaced his own wet socks and latched his boots again. He then put the man's shoes on Lilia's feet. She cried, "No, I can't wear these! They belong to the dead."

"They will keep you warm, and it will only be for a short time. Look, I'm wearing his socks. All is well. I'm going to get you out of here. I'll need to pull you out the same way Juan pulled out the Señora." Mimicking him, Enzo took off his coat, laid it fur side down on the ground, lifted Lilia and placed her on it. He fell to his knees and crawled through the tunnel, pulling the coat.

Once outside, Enzo saw that Señora Alvarez was still lying on the jacket, unattended. He saw Juan coming towards him pulling a sled. The weather was turning colder as the sun dipped lower in the west. Lilia tried to speak but was not coherent as her teeth chattered violently. Enzo worried her body temperature was dropping but was even more concerned at the Señora's condition. He took off his hat and placed it on Lilia's head, attempting to minimize the escape of body heat, and he tucked the long coat around her legs.

Without the coat and hat, Enzo felt his muscles stiffen from the cold. His brain became fuzzy. Juan placed the Señora on the sled as Heinz came over to check on her. The old woman did not respond to him rubbing her shoulders as she lay unconscious on the sled. He commanded Juan and Enzo to place Lilia on the sled and get them to the hotel as fast as possible and then ordered, "Juan, please return to digging. Enzo, without a coat, you'll freeze. Get yourself and these women as quickly as possible to the lodge."

Enzo had many questions for the tall medic on what he could do to help the women but was struggling with hypothermia and could not find the proper words. His mind refused to cooperate. Heinz saw that Enzo was confused and offered, "I'll tie the sled's rope to your waist. You can pull with your arms and if you slip, the sled won't race downhill."

Heinz also rearranged the fur coat, tucking both women into a tightly neat package, unraveled his long wool scarf and wrapped it around Enzo's neck. "It might help. Now hurry!"

The medic shoved the sled with his foot to help Enzo gather momentum and yelled to Lilia, "Hold on to the Señora. Keep her warm under that coat!"

As Enzo pulled on the rope, he thought he heard the medic say, "Go with God," but he was not certain if it was a human voice or the wind. He pulled with all his might following the rescuers' earlier footprints coming from the lodge until they disappeared under fresh falling snow. Even though he could not see the lodge, Enzo knew the direction was uphill. Pulling the sled became more strenuous with every step, and it was difficult to hold on to the rope with his freezing hands. Tripping over an unseen rock, he fell to his knees. As Heinz had predicted, the rope around his waist saved the sled from gravity's pull down the mountain. His hands were now raw and his body shaking. Enzo adjusted the scarf to cover his ears and wrapped both ends around his shoulders. He could feel his chest tightening and felt as if he were drowning. Trying to take a deep breath was impossible, as the high-altitude air was not rich enough.

Trudging back to the lodge seemed too distant, and he feared he might not complete the trek. Fearing for the women's lives as well as his own, he forced himself to take another step. His hands could no longer hold the rope, and he used his body to pull the sled, keeping his hands under his armpits. Enzo was so cold that he thought about taking the coat from the women and wrapping it around himself but pushed the shameful thought away and pressed up the mountain.

The fact that Lilia's shivering had eased prodded Enzo to keep fighting and bring them to safety. That the lodge was still not in sight worried Enzo, and he thought he had lost the trail. He was about to turn back and try to find another trail when he spotted lights in the distance. With a clenched jaw and determination, he pushed on.

Enzo slowed to catch his breath. The women inside crowding around the lobby windows spotted the struggling man, and six of them ran outside to help. They untied the rope from Enzo's waist and pulled the sled the remaining way. Clara, the young girl who had been so enthusiastic about the Swiss ski team, locked her arm with Enzo's and urged him to keep walking until he was safe inside the lobby. The women settled Señora Alvarez and Lilia on lobby couches and covered them with blankets. The fatigued Enzo collapsed on a nearby chair.

Camilla, a kitchen worker, brought cups of hot broth for Lilia and Enzo. She rested his soup on a lounge table in front of him. He thanked her, and she noticed he could not grasp the cup due to his almost frozen and shaking hands. She picked up the cup and brought it to Enzo's lips. He took a sip and felt the liquid travel down his throat, almost burning him, and motioned the woman to stop. Embarrassed from feeling helpless and fed by a young girl, he stuttered, "Can you help the Señora? She isn't waking up." Camilla complied and sat on the floor by the social worker. Her feminine instinct told her to hold the woman's hand and speak softly to her.

Enzo rose slowly and walked unsteadily to the blazing fire of the hearth, crossed himself and silently thanked God. Anxious to be back at the rescue site, he looked for the coat, but it was not to be found. He looked down the hallway and spotted the owner of the fur, who had retrieved it and was waiting for the elevator. "Señora, please wait."

The woman gasped at his disheveled state.

"I'm sorry, I've ruined your coat, Señora. I will send money for a new one."

The woman smiled and shook her head, "Thank you for the lives you saved today and for allowing me to have played a small role in your heroism. You will not pay for the coat."

"Señora, thank you. My name is Enzo."

"I'm Sara, nice to officially meet you."

"Sara, please, will you lend me your coat again?"

"You are not going back out. You're soaked through!"

"I've extra clothing in my bag. I will change."

The woman gave him the coat and said, "Of course."

"May God bless you, Señora."

Enzo returned to the lobby but had forgotten where he placed his duffel bag. He searched for it while sipping on the broth. He found it under the table where he sheltered during the earthquake. Rummaging through it, he pulled out an assortment of clothing, hurried to the men's room and removed the ski boots as well as his clothes that clung to his skin from perspiration and snow. It was comforting to put on fresh, dry clothes and the boots fit better with three pairs of socks.

Enzo took a long deep breath to prepare himself to face the elements again. He walked to the lobby and threw on the coat. Lilia was on the couch still wearing the fur hat. He was pleased her face was no longer white but had a rosy hue. Glancing over at Señora Alvarez unsettled him, as she had not changed position. Camilla kept vigil.

"Lilia, may I please have the hat?"

"Are you going back out?" Lilia frowned.

Enzo nodded as Lilia took off the hat and placed it on his head. She wanted to beg him to stay, insist that he had already done enough, but realized it would be selfish as people were still trapped inside the train. Enzo exited the lodge and did not see Lilia's loving smile.

The sled Enzo used to bring the women to the lodge was still by the entrance. He rode it downhill as he watched others come up with their train victims. When Enzo reached the crash site, his mood lifted as he saw the great progress. The medics did not give the order to stop excavating until they were satisfied that no one was left behind, whether dead or alive. When the rescue team finally called to stop the search, the sun was already below the horizon.

The exhausted rescuers retreated to the lodge. They had saved dozens of lives. Regardless of their effort, the death toll was greater. Thinking about the poor souls who did not survive the avalanche grieved Enzo. When he returned to the lodge, Enzo walked out to the ski rack, took off the boots and placed them where he had found them. Enzo took off two pairs of socks and slipped on his frozen loafers.

The beautiful lobby was now a medical ward with people sitting or lying in every corner. The hotel workers ran out of cots and now were issuing blankets for passengers to make a soft spot on the floor to sleep. Enzo moved his shoes and placed them near the hearth to dry. He roamed the lobby in his stocking feet and wondered where there would be enough room to lay out a blanket and sleep.

"Enzo, get something to eat. There are sandwiches in the kitchen!" Heinz yelled across the room.

"Thank you, Heinz. Where is the woman? Has she been moved to another area?"

"Which woman?"

"The first one I brought up the mountain, the older one, Señora Alvarez. She was lying on that couch," Enzo pointed.

Heinz did not answer but approached Enzo and whispered in his ear, "I'm sorry, she's passed."

Enzo felt a wave of pain. "She was kind."

"I'm sorry. It was so unfortunate that the train was right in the path of the avalanche. If it had left a minute earlier, it would have missed it."

"May I see her and say goodbye?"

Heinz nodded. "Come."

Enzo followed the medic into the elevator and watched him pull the iron gate closed. He placed his large hand on the crank, pulled it out a tad to disengage the mechanism, and then pushed the lever to the right. The elevator immediately descended. It stopped with a stomach-churning bob a few centimeters below the floor, causing Enzo to trip as he hustled out. The hallway was poorly lit. Heinz pushed open the padded, leather-covered doors of the lodge's movie theater, looked for the switch and flicked the lights on. The theater was now a morgue. Its plush velvet seats held the bodies of the dead covered with white hotel sheets. The bodies faced the screen as if enjoying a Saturday night and viewing the latest film.

Heinz was not sure where the body of Señora Alvarez had been placed. He methodically walked through the aisles peeking under every sheet. Enzo did the same in another aisle. When Heinz came across an elderly woman, he called out, "Is this her?"

Enzo nodded.

"I'll leave you with her. Turn off the lights when you're done," Heinz threw the sheet over her face.

Enzo heard the squeak of the elevator ascending, taking Heinz to the lobby. He approached the body and timidly removed the sheet. Taking Señora Alvarez's hand in his, he fixed his gaze on her peaceful face. "Ah, Señora! You look radiant tonight, and I see you're smiling. Has a loved one come to greet you? I'm sure someone has…Señora, thank you for your friendship and for what I imagine you have done to help many children in your lifetime. Rest in peace." He kissed her hand the same way he had on the train.

Señora Alvarez had finally joined her beloved Carlos in the ever after. She heard his voice call out and then escort her towards a white light as she heard the fluttering sound of angel wings.

Enzo returned to the bustle of the lobby as guests and staff continued working. Able bodies helped wherever they could. Some prepared soup and baked bread while others nursed the injured. The most severely injured passengers moaned and tossed on their tiny cots. Some were not easily alleviated of their suffering, as their injuries were too severe for the medics to handle.

Late that night, manager Señor Cabrillo found Enzo sleeping on the lobby floor. He nudged him, "Wake up, Enzo."

Enzo's eyes fluttered open, and he nearly jumped as Señor Cabrillo stooped over him. Before Enzo could ask if everything was all right, the manager dangled a key from his hand.

"I'm sorry I can't give you a room as they are now all taken, but the staff cleaned out the pantry for you and placed a cot in it."

"I don't understand."

"We're grateful for your effort, running up and down the mountain with that fur coat and hat. We all had a good laugh. The pantry locks from the outside, but I can assure you you'll not be disturbed." The manager signaled Lourdes, an assistant cook hunched over from years of chopping and kneading. She smiled and motioned Enzo to follow.

"I'm very grateful." Enzo shook the manager's hand and followed the woman.

The cook walked slowly to the pantry, and Enzo unlocked it. He pushed open the door and saw the tiny room. "It's very nice. This will be much better on my back than the cold hard floor. Thank you."

"It's our pleasure. Good night."

"Good night, Señora."

The windowless room with its small cot, fluffy pillow and wool blanket was cozy. He crawled onto the cot still wearing his clothes and within seconds was deep in sleep.

Lilia sat on the cushioned window seat of the library that doubled as her sleeping area. Since she was one of the youngest passengers and small, she could almost stretch out in the seat. Every evening the library was off limits to men as it became the women's sleep area. The men slept in the lobby and hallways.

The lodge residents, both paid guests and train victims, did not complain but helped each other. They waited for the repair of the train and tracks to take them back home. Although some did not speak Spanish, they communicated by either pointing their fingers at objects or acting out what they wished to say. Some were patient and thumbed through a translation dictionary. They used the universal language of an arm caress, a pat on the back or a simple smile.

Workers arrived on mules bringing provisions and their own sleeping mats that were unrolled nightly in the downstairs hallway outside the theater. The laborers also brought heavy rubber mattress covers that were sewn into bags and used as body bags. The bodies were moved from the lodge's theater to the outdoors near the train tracks. The freezing temperatures kept the bodies from decaying until the train would carry them home.

Lilia stared at the never-ending snow as it accumulated on the edge of the windowsill and ignored the book that lay on her lap, Volume C of the *Encyclopedia Britannica*—Spanish version. It lay open to the biography of Frederic Chopin. She had already skimmed volumes A and B searching for classical composers.

Lilia spotted Enzo petting the dogs through the library's glass doors. She loved the way he held a conversation with Felipe and Pedro as if they were human. Watching Enzo with the dogs made her miss Baltito, and she longed to be home. When Enzo turned in her direction, Lilia waved him over. He acknowledged her and motioned he would be a minute.

When Enzo approached the library, she pretended to read her book. He knocked on the glass with his elbow, trying not to spill the precious liquid steaming from two cups. Lilia sprang to her feet and pushed open the pocket doors.

"Sorry I made you get up."

"It's not a problem. Is the chocolate for me?"

"Of course."

Lilia chuckled. "I'll rise for anyone who brings me a treat. Thank you." Lilia reached for the cup and sat back on the window seat. "Enzo..." Lilia hesitated, "I haven't thanked you."

"You just did."

"No! I mean, for saving my life."

"Don't be silly. You would have managed to get out on your own. I just helped a little." Enzo pulled a chair closer to Lilia and straddled it.

"Thank you for pulling me out of the train. I'm grateful."

"Try not to think about that terrible event. I'm glad you are well and do not have any lasting injuries."

Lilia sipped her chocolate. "Why do you sit backwards on a chair?"

"It relieves my back pain. Pulling the sled uphill has renewed an old injury. I'm sorry I couldn't get there sooner. Perhaps the Señora might have lived."

"Please don't be sorry. You've done so much. I can't help but think how wonderful people have been to me. I'll not dwell on it much longer and will try to enjoy our days here while we are trapped in this beautiful lodge."

"I feel for the Señora. She was so frail to have gone through such an ordeal. She said she had worked as a social worker, and the way she spoke about the children, I know how much she cared for them."

"I didn't know she worked with children."

"Maybe because you were too busy with your music books to engage with her."

"I once knew a social worker when I was about five years old. Her name escapes me, but I did not like her. She wasn't nice. Regardless, I feel terrible about not being kind to Señora."

"Lilia, I'm sure she forgave you. You are under a lot of pressure in what you do. The important thing is that when she needed you most, you treated her with love. You were the last person to be with her."

"I was rude, Enzo."

"You took good care of her, ignoring your own pain when you were freezing. When I saw you cradling her in your arms, I thought of the Virgin Madonna, and I was touched. No regrets, Lilia."

Lilia did not want this moment to end. She loved staring into Enzo's mischievous, twinkling eyes. Feeling her face flush, she averted his stare and focused through the window on the snowy panorama.

"I'm sorry for misjudging you, Enzo. You are a hero and not what I pegged you to be." A hunger-like urge washed over her body along with an overwhelming desire to feel his lips on hers. She wondered how his muscular arms would feel in a tight embrace.

Enzo saw a tear slip from Lilia's eye. He pulled a handkerchief from his pocket and dabbed her cheek. Embarrassed, she took the cloth from him and dabbed her own eyes. She noticed it was embroidered on the corner. "It's beautifully crafted—the workmanship is divine. I like the subtlety of using white thread on white fabric. Was this made for you?"

"Yes. My Aunt. She's commissioned to make robes for the Vatican. When she heard I was leaving for Caracas, she made me a dozen so I wouldn't forget how much she would miss me. Look at the D, see that she placed two tiny roses under it?"

"Yes."

"They mean something."

"Tell me."

"Two roses represent my mother and my aunt. They are twin sisters."

"Roses?"

"Their maiden name is Rosati."

"And the D must be your surname?"

Enzo nodded, "Della Corte."

"Oh yes, I remember now."

"Keep it. You can remember me by it."

"Thank you. It's beautiful, and so is your name, Lorenzo Della Corte. Do you come from a big family?"

"Yes."

"I've always been jealous of people with big families. I'm adopted."

"You don't have siblings?"

"None. All I have are my parents and Susana. She takes care of the three of us, but I'm closest to her."

Lilia fantasized about having a family of her own starting with a walk down the aisle of a small Italian church and Enzo waiting at the altar. She pictured herself wearing a white satin gown with a veil trailing behind her. Lilia could not have imagined just a month ago that she would ever think this way. Never did she dream of marriage like her friends at school. She thought only about being a great musician.

Now, being close to Enzo, she felt constant conflicting emotions—from ecstasy to despair. Her erratic feelings could only mean she was in love. After all, it was exactly the way songs portrayed love to be. She convinced herself that she had met Enzo through a chain of events set forth by a divine plan for the sole purpose of becoming a wife and mother. It was destiny.

Lilia wished Enzo would kiss her. Unfortunately, she had no idea how to make him do it. He stared at her quizzically, almost as if he were reading her mind. Lilia blushed and began fiddling with her book and pretending to look at a portrait of Chopin.

Enzo rose and moved the chair where he had found it, "I'll see you at lunch, Lilia."

"Wait, Enzo. I'm cold."

"Would you like a blanket?"

"No."

"Move away from the window; it's drafty. Sit by the fire."

"Enzo, come here," Lilia said reaching for his hand. "Do you want to be with me?" Lilia spewed out the words while staring at the view, again too afraid to look directly at him.

"What?"

She faced him, "Are you interested in me?"

"What?"

"I want to know if you find me attractive. I think I would like to have a real date with you."

"You're still a teenager, barely out of secondary school. I'm nearly twenty-four. You're much too young!"

"I'm not a child. I'm eighteen, an adult. I even make a salary!"

"All right. We'll have a date."

"Today. We can eat at a table for two at the bar tonight."

Enzo was puzzled at Lilia's blatant request and lack of judgment. He wondered why she did not know it was the man's prerogative to decide when and where to take the initiative, and it is never a woman's choice. "Have you ever gone out with a man? I mean alone, like to the cinema, and not with your parents or housekeeper?"

"No."

He stooped towards Lilia as if he were going to kiss the side of her neck but did not. He brushed his lips, barely touching her neck. He journeyed to her face, purposely missed her mouth, and continued towards her forehead. Lilia closed her eyes and surrendered herself to his touch, his scent and the tickling stubble of his mustache. Enzo was surprised that she seemed willing to let him taunt her and did not slap him as any respectable Italian girl would do. He reached the top of her head and snapped a kiss.

"Are we a couple?"

"You're a strange girl," Enzo smirked.

"You can kiss me if you want."

"We are in a public room. You can't demand it! It will happen when and if it happens."

"I want to know what a kiss feels like," Lilia confessed.

"Why would you want one from me? Is it because you are bored?"

"Don't mock me. I didn't like you yesterday because I was busy working. I like you today. I mean, because of what you did for me and the Señora and so many others. Everyone here has said so many good things about you. They call you a hero!"

"Is that why you want to kiss me? Because of what other people think?"

"No, I mean, yes. I don't know. I hoped maybe you liked me."

"Let's take a walk, someplace more private." Enzo held her hand, and they walked through the crowded first-floor hallway until he found a door leading to a staircase used mainly by the staff. At the top of the stairs on an empty landing, he whispered, "I want to kiss you too."

They looked at each other and Lilia grew impatient, "I'm ready."

"Don't order me," Enzo lifted her chin and brought his face to hers with his eyes closed. When his lips almost touched hers, he opened his eyes to find Lilia staring at him.

"Why are you looking at me?"

"I want to see if you like it."

"For God's sake, Lilia, close your eyes."

Lilia obeyed and puckered her mouth. Enzo parted her lips with his tongue and then inserted it into her mouth.

Lilia flinched and pulled away.

"Why did you do that?"

"Didn't you just tell me...?" Enzo was too baffled to continue.

"Why did you do that?"

"Do what?"

"You know!"

"Are you expecting a kiss from an uncle? Oh, you're so juvenile! Let's forget the whole thing. This is ridiculous."

"No, let's try again." She closed her eyes.

Enzo held the back of her neck, and she pushed her face towards his. Enzo did not complete the kiss. Lilia's eyes flew open, and she gave him a displeased look and pushed him away. She ran up a flight of stairs to another landing but did not pull open the door to the hallway. There was a small window to her left, and she stopped to look out. During her short stay at the lodge, she had learned to appreciate the treeless landscape covered in white. The mountain peaks were barely visible through the flurries. Her temperament matched the barren cold space in front of her. He denied her a kiss, toyed with her and made her feel as cold as the landscape—icy and grey, weeping frozen tears. Only a minute ago she had been happy and giddy but now felt as cold as the frozen emptiness outdoors.

"Lilia, come back down. Let's go back to the library and talk," Enzo climbed a few stairs.

"No! Leave me!"

"*Dio Mio. Questa signorina e pazza!* What do you want, Lilia?" Enzo sprinted two steps at a time and stood in front of her and was about to hug her.

Lilia pushed him away and stammered, "I don't want anything. So stupid of me to think you were nice, but now I've changed my mind."

"I don't understand." He wrapped his hand around her small waist and this time, she did not push him away but let her muscles relax. He continued to hold her as they descended the stairs to the main floor. He maneuvered her through the dining room and did not let go of his hold until they reached the kitchen.

"We're not allowed in the kitchen—only the staff are."

"I have a room by the kitchen."

"Aren't you sleeping in the lobby with the other men?"

Enzo stopped in front of the pantry door. "No, I sleep in here." He unlocked it and pushed it open. "It's not really a room, but it is private and better than the lobby floor. It's the pantry. The manager had it cleared out and put this cot in for me." Enzo entered and motioned for Lilia to come in.

Lilia scanned the room but did not enter.

"It only locks from the outside, so when I'm not here, no one can come in."

"But when you're sleeping the door is open!"

"No one would be rude to enter. The staff knows I'm here."

"It smells so nice in here." Lilia took a breath, "I can smell vanilla and cinnamon. They still linger."

"Well, come inside."

"I don't think I can. I shouldn't be here at all."

Enzo reached for her hand and tugged gently, "There's nothing to be afraid of."

"I don't know," she giggled. "There isn't even a window."

"We don't need a window. I'll turn on the light." Enzo flicked the switch, and an overhead light bulb filled the room with a harsh yellow glow.

"I prefer it dark."

Enzo flicked the switch again. "Sit on the cot with me."

"I don't know, Enzo."

"You're safe here. Remember, the door doesn't lock from the inside. You're free to leave when you wish."

Lilia was about to leave but hesitated. His dimpled and brilliant smile drew her to him. She stepped into the room and let the door swing close. In the windowless room where only a sliver of light shone through the bottom of the door, she made out a shadow-like figure of Enzo's silhouette. She watched as he took off his shirt and approached her. She trembled. He kissed her on the lips as he unbuttoned her shirt.

The Red Cross Jacket

Lilia made herself comfortable on an old worn sofa that had once been the centerpiece of the lobby, but now with cigar burns and worn-out pillows, it was permanently stationed in the laundry room. The staff loved to take a break on the couch and sometimes even take a ten-minute nap.

"Thank you, Camila. I had no intention of stopping at such a high altitude, and that's why I don't have anything warm to wear." Lilia unsnapped her purse and pulled out her few remaining pesos.

"You don't need to pay," Camila pushed her hand away.

"Thank you. I won't argue with you because my money is running low." Lilia put the pesos back.

Camila draped an old, grey wool blanket over Lilia's shoulder. "You can return the blanket when you leave."

"I will ruin it. I'm going to cut a hole out of it to make a poncho. Oh, I should pay you."

"These blankets are old, and we cut them into small squares to polish the silver. If you look closely, they have tiny holes from a moth infestation."

Lilia quickly took the blanket off her shoulders.

"Don't worry! They've all been washed in lye and are bug free. Do what you like with the blanket."

"I might need an extra one for another passenger. We'd like to walk outdoors."

The chambermaid snickered, "Do you mean Enzo?"

Lilia nodded. "Yes, how do you know?"

"Honey, everybody knows. You're always together. Be careful, Lilia. An unchaperoned girl and a man could prove dangerous."

"Don't worry, Camila." Lilia flushed. "Please lend me a pair of scissors."

Lilia cut a slit in the center of the blanket. She draped it over her head and tied a belt around the waist to keep the wind from catching it. The poncho was not fashionable, but it would keep her warm and allow her to venture outdoors.

"I'll be back to make one for Enzo."

Before Camila could answer, Lilia was out of the laundry to look for Enzo. He was not in the pantry, the lobby or the library, and not even the bar. She strolled through hallways searching for him and found him in the medic's office.

"Excuse me, Señor, may I interrupt to ask Enzo a quick question?"

"Certainly." Heinz waved her in.

"Enzo, do you like my poncho?" Lilia twirled.

"Yes, it's flattering on you."

"I'm going to make you one. We can wear the same poncho. Wouldn't it be cute?"

"No, thank you, Lilia, but I appreciate the thought! You look beautiful, but if I wore it, everyone would continue to laugh at me. They're still cackling over the fur I wore during the rescue."

Heinz mocked, "He looked like a prima donna, especially in the hat. Unforgettable."

Lilia bit her lip showing her displeasure. "But we can spend time outdoors if you have something warm to wear."

"*Bella*, I can go outside without a coat, at least in short spurts."

"All right. I'll see you later, Enzo. Goodbye Señor Heinz," Lilia sulked away.

Heinz took a long drag on his cigarette. "Enzo, where do you buy these wonderful cigarettes?"

"In Caracas—they're American, the only kind I smoke. I'll give you a few packs."

"I'd like that." Heinz seemed pleased.

"I'll bring them to you." Enzo rose to leave.

"Before you go…" Heinz opened a cabinet behind his desk, "I'd like to give you something as well." Heinz removed a jacket from a hanger. "You're right about the mink—people are still laughing over how ridiculous you looked."

"It was fox!" Enzo enjoyed the banter. "Thankfully, it's back with its rightful owner but now looks more like a rat than a fox."

"I see your little friend is eager to play outdoors. Don't let her convince you to wear that thing she calls a poncho." Heinz tossed the jacket, "Here, try this on."

"This is great! I can spend more time outside. The lodge has become so stifling and now smells like a hospital." Enzo held the jacket up with his hands, "You're so tall, Heinz. On me it will look more like a coat. People will still laugh at me thinking I stole it from a giant, but it's good enough. I'll bring it back the minute I can go home."

"Keep it as a souvenir, a memento of the mountain rescue."

"Thanks, but Caracas is too hot for such a heavy jacket. Save it. Someone else might need it. This is a Red Cross jacket, no?" Enzo followed the stitching of the patch sewn on the back with his finger.

"Correct."

"I like the large Swiss flag emblem." Enzo held up the jacket to see the cross in its entirety.

"It's not the Swiss flag. The design is the same but notice the white and red colors are reversed."

"Oh, you're right, I see."

"I worked for the Red Cross...helped evacuate prisoners from death camps."

"That must've been difficult, Heinz. Seeing those poor people in such dire condition. Walking skeletons."

"Put the jacket on and see how it looks in the mirror. There's one in the bathroom right behind you."

Enzo put on the jacket and walked into the lavatory. "It is long and not attractive on me, but it serves a purpose. Thank you, my friend. It's better than the fox and much better than Lilia's poncho."

Both men chuckled.

Heinz patted Enzo's back in a friendly gesture, "You're welcome."

"Tell me about the Red Cross."

"It's something I don't like to talk about."

"I understand. I'm the same way about the war. Words don't come easily. I had you pegged for a German when I first heard your accent, and I'm happy you're Swiss. If you were German, I don't think I could play cards with you, or eat at your table, or even have a conversation. The war changes people."

"No need to worry. I'm from Zermatt. I know how you feel. The Germans will pay a price for the horrors of their crimes for generations to come."

Unbeknownst to Enzo, all that Heinz said was a lie. Heinz was born in Hamburg and served as an elite member of the Gestapo, many of whom were also members of the SS, the *Schutzstaffel*, under Hitler. His unit of the dreaded Gestapo escaped together immediately after Germany surrendered. Heinz and his comrades impersonated Red Cross volunteers by producing counterfeit Red Cross passports. They left Europe and hid in many corners of the world. Many Germans avoided capture by the trickery. Heinz chose to live in Chile with many other war criminal comrades close by or in neighboring countries.

It was fortunate for Enzo that he never suspected Heinz's lies. If he knew the truth, he would have had no choice but to kill the medic. He would consider it an honor to end the German's life—his deceased brothers-in-arms would accept nothing less. The men who rode to the Gothic Line with him that fateful day were always on his mind. Images of his slaughtered friends were memories he could not erase. He would have easily killed Heinz and then prayed for forgiveness for avenging his soldier brothers. Enzo reasoned the church would understand his plight and surely the priests would grant atonement and guarantee his place in heaven.

Darkness

Even though the patients injured in the avalanche loved the lodge and the hospitality of its workers, they felt trapped. They were not paying guests who had come to ski, equipped with proper mountain attire and reserved rooms. The train victims were grateful to be staying at the lodge but were uncomfortable in the crowded lobby and missed their privacy. Some were not hurt during the avalanche while others were in constant pain. For the non-infirmed the long, boring days were not as bad as nights when forced to sleep on hard cots or the even harder floor. They waited patiently for the train tracks to be cleared and for service between the two capital cities to begin. They hoped that day would arrive quickly and to be reunited with their families.

The dwindling food supply caused alarm among guests and staff alike. Food deliveries were dependent on the train working. In the meantime, mules climbed up and down the mountain bringing supplies, but they could not carry nearly enough to meet the demands of the overpopulated lodge. Everyone sent letters via the rugged mules to their families to give them news. Some passengers tried to bribe the mule runners to bring them down the mountain on the animals, but the trek was too dangerous and were refused.

While almost everyone despaired, Lilia spent magical days and nights with Enzo. With her poncho and his jacket, they spent many hours outside playing in the snow like children. On one blustery day, Enzo and Lilia borrowed a pair of skis from a young couple and tried to navigate an easy slope. After falling many times, Lilia carefully walked down the hill, lugging the skis on her shoulder, and told Enzo, "I'll never try a foolish thing like that again."

As a couple, Enzo and Lilia were inseparable, spending most of their time talking, visiting the injured passengers and listening to the hotel's collection of albums. The young girl felt she had finally bloomed into womanhood as the recipient of passion from a strong and protective man. She was in love and happy. Enzo was attentive to Lilia during their daily walks and hung on her every word. Lilia heard the sneers of envious young women, especially Clara, the girl from the train who seemed to be constantly spying on her. Clara's parents kept a close eye on their daughter, rarely allowing her out of their sight—unlike Lilia who relished her freedom. Lilia's favorite part of the day was sneaking into Enzo's room at night when almost everyone was asleep and melting in her lover's arms on the tiny cot.

Lilia lived every young girl's dream, rooted in Hollywood films she caught at Sunday matinees. Her favorites were Shirley Temple and Vivien Leigh. Falling deeply in love with Enzo, she thought of him as her own Clark Gable. She dreamed of showing him off to Monica and was sad that relationship was forever severed. But she was certain that Enzo was better looking than the groom she had not met in Buenos Aires. Enzo had surprised Lilia with his comportment, and she now understood why all the girls at school dreamed of a future with a man. Being a gifted pianist, with her mind an endless music reel, she had not experienced the luxury of thinking about men. But now Enzo was part of her fantasy of marriage and raising a family. It consumed her, and she felt lucky her man was from the music and art center of the world—Italy. She wondered why it had taken her so long to become like other girls.

One special evening Lilia invited everyone for a piano recital. The guests and staff alike were eager to hear her play and so desperate for entertainment that they had begged Lilia for a small concert. She hadn't practiced but agreed.

That evening, before Lilia even sat down to play her first note, the audience gave her a standing ovation because they were so eager to break the monotony. Although the piano was out of tune, she managed to impress everyone with her virtuoso playing. Enzo watched with an aloof expression, but as Lilia continued, his expression changed to enchantment as he realized she was a great talent. He was proud that everyone knew he was sleeping with her. When the final chord reverberated throughout the lodge, she stood, bowed and received a second standing ovation.

The following day Enzo and Lilia went out on their daily walk. A furious squall raced down the mountain playing havoc with Lilia's hair. She tried to tame it by running her fingers through her locks, but Enzo stopped her. "I love the way your hair is designed by the wind. Let it be wild."

"Like Medusa?"

"Like a Roman goddess. There's a fountain in the middle of the plaza in my village. It's of Venus, and you look like her."

"Will you show me the fountain one day, Enzo?"

Enzo pretended not to hear.

When the searing wind pierced Lilia's thin poncho and cold pricked her skin, she clutched Enzo's arm and they ran together to the haven of the pantry. They amused themselves. Enzo taught her how to please him. He was a master at pleasing her. Lilia no longer tried to hide the fact that she spent time in Enzo's pantry, causing more rumors to spread throughout the lodge. She watched the men pat her lover's back or wink their approval at his conquest. By contrast, Lilia heard derogatory whispers from women, some even sending her disparaging looks of disapproval. The younger women ogled Enzo, his good looks and charismatic personality drawing their attention. They fantasized about making love to the man while they gossiped about Lilia.

On the fifteenth day in the lodge, Enzo and Lilia ate a small sandwich and retreated to the library to sit by the fire. She automatically gazed out the window at the ever-changing light and saw Heinz walking up the path to the main entrance of the lodge. Lilia noticed he wore an atypical grin on his face as he returned from checking the daily progress of the train. He stopped outside the lodge's entrance and pulled the cord of the bell to instantly grab everyone's attention. The cold metal clang of the bell sent a shiver down Lilia's spine as if it were a death knell darkening the beautiful day. She reached for Enzo's hand and pulled him close.

"What's wrong, *Bella*?"

"I'm going to lose you!" she whispered in his ear.

Enzo reached out and held Lilia's hand as they walked to the lobby where Heinz was about to impart important news. Everyone looked concerned as they congregated.

"Attention!" Seeing the startled expression on people's faces, Heinz smiled to release their tension. "This is not an emergency but great news." He paused to clear his throat and smiled jubilantly. "The tracks are finally clear!"

Lilia's hands trembled; her fairy tale was ending. A loud cheer resounded from the crowd. Men shook hands and women hugged each other. Clara's mother made the sign of the cross and kissed her husband.

"The train will depart at eighteen hundred hours today for Buenos Aires. Our Argentinian departed souls will be loaded onto a separate car to finally go home for proper burial by their loved ones. Tomorrow the train to Santiago will work the same way. All trains are back to their normal schedule."

"I'm taking today's train," Enzo blurted out.

"What?"

"Weren't you listening? The train to Buenos Aires."

"No, you mustn't. The dead will be on that train."

"*Bella*, the dead are nothing to fear."

"We can wait a few days until they are moved."

"Nonsense, Lilia. The lodge has put up with us long enough."

"Then you must continue with your plans to Santiago. It's much closer than Buenos Aires, and you need to meet my parents and Susana. Afterwards, you can take an ocean liner back to Caracas."

"I can't, Lilia. I have a return plane ticket from Buenos Aires."

"But you've already missed that flight!"

"Maybe they can credit me. I'm sure they know of the circumstances by now. Lilia, I've run out of money. I've given the hotel almost everything I had in my wallet to help pay for our food and drink."

"My father will repay you for what you gave for me. I'm sure he'll also reward you for saving me."

"I don't want him to pay me."

"What if the airline won't give you credit for the flight? It will be better to come with me."

"No, I can borrow money from my cousins if the airline will not refund me. My partners, as well as my family in Buenos Aires, must be mad with worry, as I don't know if the letters have reached them. It would be beneficial for me to be back in Venezuela before the week's end and return to normal life. Let's get a hot chocolate to celebrate."

Lilia whispered, "I'm losing you."

Enzo headed for the bar.

Lilia followed a few steps behind him, "Did you hear me?"

He turned to face her, "What?"

"I can't lose you!"

"What are you saying, Lilia?"

"We need more time with each other. You can't leave me this very day."

"It's been over two weeks! I've a business to run, and I'm losing money."

"We're more important than money!"

"Lilia, please understand! My tiny new company struggles. We do most of the labor ourselves. I should never have gotten on this train."

"Then we would not have met."

"Stop acting like a child. You know what I mean."

"Enzo, please, come to Santiago. We can't end this today!"

"Have you forgotten about your competition? Grow up, Lilia! You have responsibilities of your own."

Lilia was stunned at his words and wondered why he was not as concerned about losing her as he was about losing money. "Walk with me, Enzo. It is no longer snowing. We'll be the first to make tracks, and we can enjoy the mountains for the last time," Lilia begged.

"I must pack! We can see the mountains from the windows."

"It's not the same. I need to feel the wind. Please, Enzo."

"Fine, if you insist! Wait here, I'll get my jacket."

As Lilia waited for his return, an overwhelming feeling of urgency spread over her, and she wanted to run after him, beg him to stay, crawl back between their sheets and feel the heat of his body next to hers. Her feelings of abandonment returned, the sensation of being suffocated, squeezed from the inside out—the same feeling she had when she was yanked from Mamita and the Maipo Valley. Dark thoughts played in her mind and circulated like condors around prey.

Enzo returned from his room wearing the large Red Cross jacket. She inhaled deeply and composed herself.

"Where's your poncho, Lilia?"

"I left it in your room."

"I didn't see it—are you sure?"

"Yes, it was on the bed."

"I'll go and fetch it. You should have told me. I'm wasting time."

"Forget the poncho. I don't need it."

"You do need it. It's freezing outside."

"I want to feel the cold air of my beautiful mountains."

Enzo didn't argue and thought she would come in quicker without the poncho. He guided her outdoors. Within a few minutes, Enzo saw Lilia start to shake. He took off his jacket and wrapped it around her shoulders. "Put your arms in the sleeves. I wouldn't want you to catch a cold."

He zipped the jacket halfway to her chest, stopped to pull out the hair about to be eaten by the zipper and then pulled it up to her neck. Lilia inhaled deeply and smelled his spicy scent. He placed his arm around her waist, and they turned to walk back to the lodge. Before they reached the front door, Lilia faced him, seized both his hands in hers and gazed into his eyes. Her lips parted, and she was about to speak but she could not formulate her words cohesively. Enzo waited patiently. She averted his eyes and stared at the middle button of his shirt, hoping it would make it easier to tell him what she felt.

"I think we should get married," she finally managed to utter.

Enzo touched her chin with his index finger and lifted her face upwards, forcing Lilia to look at him. "Lilia, you're endearing, but…"

"Enzo, don't let me ask again."

"It's impossible, my love."

"Why? I know you love me as I do you!"

"Lilia, we are not meant for one another. We come from opposite worlds. You wouldn't be happy in my life. Come, it's freezing. Let's go inside."

"No." Lilia stood firm.

"We've loved each other, and it was wonderful. Now it's time to move on. Don't look so sad. You'll be home soon to your wonderful life and competitions. You'll travel around the world. You'll win that Polish competition you're always talking about. Your life is beautiful, *Amore*."

"Don't call me *amore* while you push me away!"

"Lilia, you're meant to do great things as a pianist! One day I will buy your records, and I'll be so proud that I knew you. I know how you feel. We all go through a first love."

"You don't know how I feel. I've asked you to marry me."

"It's not that I don't want to; it's that I'm not free."

Lilia stared in disbelief.

"Let's not talk about it now. I'm going to freeze to death right here if we don't go back inside." Enzo hooked his arm in hers and pushed her towards the lodge.

Lilia unlatched from his grip, "We have to talk, *now!*"

Enzo stopped, "I…I have a fiancée…in Italy."

Lilia gasped.

"You're engaged? You never said anything. Why?"

"She is from my village. After the war, I was very sick and she came to visit me, brought me soup. She's kind and my mother encouraged me to propose to her, and I agreed. When my business grows, I'll send for her. She'll come to Venezuela and be my wife."

"Why didn't you tell me? I wouldn't…"

"I thought you wanted to be loved. I didn't think you would want marriage. I made a promise to Serafina, and I will honor it."

"Serafina," Lilia pronounced her name. "Did she share your bed?"

"No."

"I don't believe you."

"Italian girls don't sleep with men. Serafina's a virgin. There are strict rules."

"I share the same Catholic rules. I broke them for you."

"It's different for you. Your parents are old, and they're not your blood parents. They don't have to know anything, and your reputation is intact. This does not matter."

"How can you say that?"

Lilia felt the blood drain from her face. She wished another earthquake would create an avalanche so great it would shroud her in a tomb of white and bury her deep in the Andes. *What a perfect place to die among black volcanic stones and white snow. Black and white. No grey to misconstrue meaning, no grey to give you hope, only black and white, life or death.* The pain in Lilia's chest spread to her stomach, and she felt acid rise to her throat. The wind picked up and Enzo shuddered, "Come on."

Lilia followed him to the pantry and watched as he folded his clothes and placed them neatly in his duffle bag. They did not talk and barely looked at one another. Enzo stripped the army cot of its linens and found Lilia's poncho tangled in the cover. He draped it on the doorknob, placed the linens on the floor and folded the cot.

"Lilia, I'm returning Heinz's jacket, and I'll say goodbye to him and some other people that have become friends. I'll be back shortly. We'll go to the bar and order our last chocolate. Cheer up, *Bella*."

Lilia nodded but sat motionless on a chair. As soon as Enzo closed the door behind him, she pulled out the handkerchief he had given her from her purse. With her new ink cartridge pen she purchased in the Buenos Aires train station; she scribbled a note on the white cloth.

> *Enzo,*
>
> *The awful things you said to me cannot be true. I'll never love another person. I am more to you than a cheap girl to pass time with. I know you have a kind heart.*
>
> *Lilia*
>
> *Calle Victoria 22221*
>
> *Santiago, Chile*

Lilia waited a few minutes to let the ink dry and then folded the handkerchief and placed it in a corner of his duffel bag. She took off his jacket and picked up her poncho from the doorknob and put it on. She scanned the room while images of their lovemaking flashed in her mind. She caressed his duffel bag with one long stroke, left the pantry and shut the door behind her.

The kitchen was unusually empty of staff, and Lilia wandered through it. She passed the giant stoves to a door that led outdoors to a small hidden yard. She exited and was aghast at the trash piled up in pyramid-like heaps waiting to be burned when the weather was drier. The glacial temperature froze the piles, and the smell was barely noticeable.

Lilia walked to the end of the refuse heaps but could go no farther, the snowdrift a barricade. Since she could not go beyond it, she hid behind one of the trash mounds and waited for the train to depart and separate her from Enzo. She hoped that he, not finding her for their last hot chocolate and a final goodbye, would not board the train and prove that he too was in love.

After weathering the cold temperature for close to an hour, she heard the first whistle of the train. She waited a few more minutes for the passengers to board and heard the final whistle. She listened to the lonely sound of the chugging train as it distanced itself from the station. Nearly frozen, she ran inside and rushed through the pantry door, hoping she would see Enzo sitting on the cot. The room was empty. Even the dirty linens were already picked up by the staff. He was gone.

The next day Lilia boarded the train and headed home. Thinking of Enzo, she tried to make sense of the past two weeks. She was numb and no longer sad but felt as if someone had removed her insides. Even the dead traveling on the same train, including Señora Alvarez, no longer bothered her. She envied them as they would not be disturbed from their sleep, and she sat for hours mired in her thoughts until the train reached Santiago.

When she arrived home, she found Susana and the Villavicencios to be overjoyed.

"I knew you would come home soon. God is great." Carmen hugged Lilia.

"We'll go to mass tomorrow and show our gratitude." Susana crossed herself.

Lilia told them every detail of the accident and Enzo's rescue but failed to mention she had fallen in love. The repercussions she feared from her parents on her Argentinian deportment did not come. She was surprised and relieved that there was never mention of it.

Aftermath

Christmas and the New Year were spent practicing. It did not feel like a holiday, but Lilia welcomed the rigorous routine. It helped push out thoughts of Enzo. She managed to get home in time to compete in the National Chopin Competition in Santiago and, to everyone's disbelief, won. The invitation to the International Chopin Competition in Warsaw came by telegram. Lilia, still brokenhearted, showed no excitement over the great feat. No one questioned why she wasn't elated at the win. Professor Goretsky made plans to accompany Lilia to Poland in six months and was sorry the parents were too elderly and sick for the journey.

Lilia's state of confusion and immaturity did not allow her to comprehend what was happening to her. Her mood swings were unpredictable—one minute she was emotional and teary, secretly wishing for Enzo's love, and the next, angry at his betrayal. Believing that finally she understood Chopin's complicated volatile music was about love and loss, it was useless trying to forget Enzo and to close that chapter. She would use her pain to interpret Chopin even better. There was a nauseous pit in her stomach that never went away, and she now feared she was carrying his child. Lilia kept this secret to herself and did not even disclose it to Susana. Hoping an apology from Enzo would come by mail and, therefore, his address would be on the envelope, she would then travel to Venezuela and tell him about the baby. Of course, he would make her his wife upon such news.

The Professor set up an interim concert to benefit the young pianist's travel expenses. Lilia had doubts about telling Professor Goretsky of her pregnancy, but because she would show in six months' time, she would be forced to resign from the competition. The Professor saw the decline in her concentration and that she had difficulty memorizing the music. "A pianist needs not only emotional strength, but also physical and mental strength, to endure the long hours of practicing," he would constantly remind her. Lilia failed to improve in all three aspects. The queasiness did not abate, and she lost her appetite. No one noticed she was losing weight. Wondering if it was hurting the baby, she spent many nights awake worrying, and dark circles shadowed her eyes.

It became extraordinarily difficult to memorize Chopin's *Concerto no. 1 in E minor*, and Lilia knew she was not ready for the upcoming benefit performance. Professor Goretsky was embarrassed that she would perform with sheet music and was anxious his prodigy was failing him.

Determined to figure out how to raise the baby without a father, Lilia toyed with the idea that perhaps Professor Goretsky might help her. Most women did not work outside the home when pregnant, and unmarried ones were sent away to deliver babies in houses of shame. These were bleak refugee homes, places to hide from society until the baby was born and then put up for adoption. Lilia tried to be optimistic. *If Enzo doesn't write, I'll earn my keep by teaching piano after the birth. But am I pregnant? Why haven't I bled? I can't confide in Susana; she would tell.*

Lilia was warming up with scales as her thoughts continued to consume her. The grandfather clock chimed a quarter till noon, prompting her to stop and listen for the letter carrier. She took a book to the parlor and pretended to read while positioning herself to be the first to pick up the mail dropped through the slot in her front door. Every day she waited for a letter from Enzo.

After the train accident, the Villavicencios softened their attitude toward the dog and allowed him to stay inside the house. Baltito, feeling her agitation, rubbed his nose on Lilia's skirt, attempting to console her. Gloom attached itself to her as if it were a ghost, and her sensitive dog whimpered— his tail sagging sympathizing with his master.

Baltito's ears pricked up and yelped when he heard the mail carrier opening the garden gate.

"Let Mother get the mail this time, I've waited for three weeks, and I now know he will never write," Lilia addressed the dog and she rose and beckoned the dog to follow. "Let it be, Baltito." She yelled across the house, "Mother, the mail is here!"

Lilia went back to her room to continue studying and resumed her scales. Carmen called out from the dining room, "Lilia! A letter came from Caracas. It's probably from the man who saved you. I'm so glad he wrote to us. We can now send him a thank you letter and repay him for his kindness."

Lilia ran to the foyer, her heart pounding. "Mamá, a letter from Enzo?" She pulled the envelope from her mother's hands.

Carmen was shocked. "Lilia! Don't be rude! Give me the letter and let me read it."

Lilia was already down the hall to the entrance of her room. "No, Mother, it's addressed to me."

"I'm sure he meant it for us. Men do not write to girls!" Carmen shuffled to Lilia's door and tried the knob, but it was locked.

"Give me a minute, please."

"Open the door, Lilia. Let me read it first!"

Tears of joy were already rolling down Lilia's face before she tore open the envelope.

"Lilia, open the door." Carmen Villavicencio clenched her jaw.

Lilia devoured the letter's contents. Carmen's knocking continued, growing louder. "Open the door immediately!"

"A minute! Mamá, please! I'll be right out."

Lilia read the letter again but still could not grasp its meaning. She slowed down to try and grasp Enzo's intention.

December 28, 1947

Dear Lilia,

I hope this letter finds you well. Where did you go? Why didn't you say goodbye? You are more than a passing thing. The trip through the Andes was a mistake, as I should not have extended my holidays. I never thought I'd be stuck in Valle Nevado, but at least I met you and Señora Alvarez.

My partners didn't finish the houses on time, and we paid a terribly high price for it. My plans are now on hold, and I will not send for Serafina. My life is difficult. Every night I come home to a cold sandwich and a single glass of wine before soaking my aching body in Epsom salt. All I desire is a family and to be a settled man.

I hope you won the competition and your dream of Warsaw is now a reality.

Enzo

Lilia was perplexed at Enzo's message. She felt the letter was more than an apology and scrutinized his words, reading between the lines. *Enzo will not send for Serafina because he loves me. I'm more than a passing thing. He's saving me. He wants to settle down. My baby will not be illegitimate.*

She scanned the stamped postal date on the envelope and knew that he had waited two weeks to write to her after leaving Valle Nevado. *Why did he wait so long?* Lilia breathed a sigh of relief that it finally came, late or not. She read the letter many times. Her eyes rested always on the sentence, *All I desire is a family and to be settled. Enzo is proposing marriage.*

Lilia fell onto her bed and thought about her options—a career as a concert pianist or to be wife to Enzo. Although the performance at the Santiago Symphony Hall was fully booked, Lilia decided to choose her love and not attend the performance. Lilia formulated a plan. It would begin by leaving Chile and traveling to Caracas. It was an easy decision to make since she was not ready for the upcoming recital. The thought of freedom and Enzo delighted her, and she was now certain that fate was on her side. She and her baby would have a happy family.

Her parents would be mortified at her marrying someone from so far away, and a man who would impregnate a young girl would never have their approval. She feared they would force her to give up the baby and stop her from going to Caracas. *I'll have a family of my own, blood from my blood.* Her lips formed a smile as she imagined her future. As for music, it would always be part of her life, maybe not as a performer but as a teacher.

Lilia came out of her room and found her mother still in the dining room. "Mamá."

Carmen was attempting to thread a needle under the bright lights of the chandelier. "So, you've finally come out. Will you explain yourself?"

"Oh, Mamá, don't be mad. Can't you see I'm happy?"

"Why did you choose to behave so rudely, snatching that letter from me? Thread this for me while we talk about the letter." Carmen handed Lilia the thread and needle. "You should have thrown the letter in the trash. A man should not write to a girl. He should have written directly to us. And for God's sake, Lilia, your benefit concert is tomorrow night!"

Lilia pulled the thread through the needle's eye and handed it back to her mother. "I'm marrying Enzo."

"Lilia!"

"His name is Lorenzo Della Corte. I love him. He was a soldier and fought in the war—a hero."

"Lilia, why did you not mention anything of this before? All you said was he saved your life by pulling you out of the crash site. What's happened between you two? Are you still pure?"

"Mamá, I knew you wouldn't understand, so I kept quiet. I wasn't sure he wanted to marry me, but now he's confirmed it."

Carmen shook her head, "Enough! Let me read the letter."

Lilia pulled the letter from her pocket, and Carmen read it.

"This is not a proposal. Put these childish thoughts out of your head. What will your father say when he hears this nonsense?"

"Father will get used to the idea. I know Enzo isn't as educated as Papá, but he too is intelligent. He designs houses and builds them, just like an architect. And he has his own business."

Carmen lost her temper but kept her voice hushed so as not to alert her husband or Susana, "Stop talking and never tell Emanuel any of this. We'll spare him this ordeal."

"Yes, I agree. Papá is old and will not handle this well. I'm sorry, Mamá, but I'm going to Caracas to marry Enzo. I've made up my mind, and there's nothing you can do to stop me."

"Don't disrespect me! We will never allow you to marry him. We don't know this man who has taken advantage of you. He lives as far away from us as possible while still on our continent."

"Mamá, he'll be a good husband—"

"Stop talking, Lilia. Go practice your piano."

"I won't perform."

"Don't even say that. That man does not love you."

"I'm not performing tomorrow or ever again!"

"Stop your craziness! Tickets have been sold and money collected! Have you gone mad?" Carmen lowered her voice and tried to reason with her daughter, "Besides, who will take care of us? You'll be married someday but not with him. Don't we mean anything to you?"

"I won't stay to care for you. Susana's your maid. It's her job to care for you both." Lilia's face flushed, and she was about to blurt out that she might be pregnant but refrained from doing so.

"Susana is not our daughter. We don't have much time left in this world. We need you." Carmen's voice trembled.

"That is the only reason you adopted me, Mamá! It was your plan from the first day you brought me here."

"You're wrong, Lilia. I don't know why the Lord keeps us on this earth and has not taken us home, but that is not for us to question." Carmen's face distorted as she tried to stop herself from weeping. Lilia was surprised at her mother's vulnerability, and her anger eased.

"I would take care of you if I hadn't met Enzo. I'll fix this and come back, even though the Bible says a woman must leave her parents to follow her husband, and that's what you believe. I promise to come back."

"Keep your voice down! Your father will hear you. That Italian does not love you. We gave you everything. Don't throw it all away. After we're gone, you will inherit our wealth and be better prepared for your own family."

"Is it why I was adopted?"

"No! We weren't blessed with children and didn't think about adoption until a kind social worker approached your father. What was her name? Oh yes, Señora Alvarez."

Lilia shuddered at hearing the name and the fact that she had not made the connection. The woman she had always hated for taking her away from Mamita brought her and Enzo together. Feeling dizzy, she reached for the wall to steady herself.

"Lilia, sit down. You look as if you will faint. As I was saying, I hoped that one day you would marry Godofredo."

"Uncle Godofredo? But he's old, and he's family."

"He's not related to you, only to me."

"He's old and fat! He walks shuffling his feet as if he were entangled in a skein of yarn. The thought of it sickens me."

"Stop your insolence. Remember your place. We rescued you—a *guacha*."

"No! I'm not insolent, and *guacha* is a horrible word." Lilia hated saying the awful word. It was painful hearing it from others, but it was much worse when it escaped from her mother's lips. Her eyes stung as she fought back tears.

"Leave me and finish your practice! Don't make a fool out of all of us." With a flick of her hand, Carmen dismissed Lilia.

Lilia ran to her room, slamming the door, and realized she was holding her breath. She exhaled and released a flood of tears. She tried to stop them and return to her stoic self, but it was impossible. She felt alone in the world, wanting to run into Susana's arms but could not, as she would not side with the Villavicencios and they, in turn, would dismiss her and she'd become destitute.

In an instant Lilia calculated the enormous price they would all pay. Professor Goretsky would lose money from the concert that would not take place. The Villavicencios would not have their daughter as caregiver, and Susana would miss the person she loves most. Even Baltito would not know why she had left him, and these thoughts made her very sad.

Lilia packed her suitcase.

L ilia wrote a note to her parents and Susana telling them she loved Enzo and was leaving for Caracas. She placed the note in the breadbox where Susana would find it in the morning while preparing breakfast. She kissed the top of Baltito's head, stroked his fur and whispered, "I promise to send for you when I am married to Enzo. Susana will surely bring you to me."

Lilia crawled into bed fully dressed. She turned off the light and set her alarm clock to four o'clock and placed it under her pillow so Susana would not hear it. Lilia stayed awake all night, and minutes before the clock alarm would rattle, she turned it off. Hearing Susana's steady breathing and soft snoring through her bedroom wall, she rose and quietly tiptoed out of the house. Lilia felt as if stones were pressing on her chest and wanted to cry to shed their imaginary weight. She controlled her emotions and walked in darkness with her heavy valise towards the train station. Feeling the brunt of her decision, she stopped, looked at the house and almost ran back to beg her parents for forgiveness. But the thought of her child, safely cocooned in her womb, forced her to stick to her plan. She hyperventilated as she turned the corner of her block.

The hours passed as if in slow motion as Lilia sat on a hard wooden bench at the train station. She placed her suitcase in a paid locker and waited for the banks to open at nine. Lilia was grateful to Professor Goretsky, who insisted on opening a savings account for her. He dutifully deposited her winnings from competitions and recitals. When the large clock stroked 8:45, she rose from her bench and went to the bank. She closed the account and was surprised to have such a healthy balance.

Lilia returned to the train station, retrieved her luggage and bought a ticket to Valparaiso on the same familiar route taken when she attended the McKenna. During the ride she recalled many details of her past commutes. She cried silently as she already missed everyone and especially Baltito. When she reached Valparaiso, she headed for the port and bought a one-way passage on a cruise line to Caracas. Luck was on her side as the small, fully booked ship had a last-minute cancellation and Lilia secured a room. She felt a momentary relief, thinking it was a sign from heaven that her decision was the right one. The ship departed that afternoon, and Lilia spent countless hours imagining her new life with Enzo.

On the eighth day of the journey, the ship navigated through the Panama Canal. Lilia watched the locks fill with water and float the ship to a higher elevation before moving out of the lock to the lake and on to the next set of locks. The process repeated itself many times until the canal opened out into the Caribbean Sea. Relieved to be near her destination and rid of the long anxious journey, she spent the rest of her time on a lounge chair on the lido deck. The days were uncomfortable as they were humid and hot. It seemed that she slapped her skin continuously in attempts to stop the endless attacks of mosquitoes. Though the deck was unbearable, the airless cabin was much worse.

The following day the ship docked in Puerto La Guaira, thirty kilometers from Caracas, and Lillia waited for the captain to give the order to unload the passengers. The heat and humidity became more oppressive as the sun climbed higher. Lilia perspired heavily with drops of sweat rolling into her eyes, causing them to sting. She squinted at the brightness of the sun and bought a pair of sunglasses. Thinking there might not be a restroom on the route to Caracas, she paid a last visit to the bathroom. As she washed her hands, she noticed the armpits of her dress had round wet spots. Embarrassed at her appearance, she changed her clothes before leaving the cabin.

The large port reeked of petroleum. Cargo ships carrying unrefined oil to all parts of the Americas and Europe used the busy port. Exchanging Chilean pesos to bolivars in a bank by the pier was easy. Lilia found it strange that at the exchange office all the tellers were men, unlike in Chile where women held varied types of office positions. She slipped the money into her purse and walked towards the small bus terminal. Carrying her heavy valise, she boarded an express that took passengers from the port to Caracas. The ride seemed endless while the temperature inside the vehicle rose as the bus traveled away from the Caribbean.

Once she reached the Caracas terminal, she hailed a dilapidated rusty cab and slid into the back seat.

"Señorita, where to?" The cab driver placed her suitcase next to her on the back seat as the car did not have a trunk.

"*Hotel Alba Libertador*," Lilia answered, hoping the cab driver would not see the recurring sweat spots under her arms. The heel of her shoe went through the rusty floor of the car. When she jerked her foot out of the hole, she saw the pavement below. She wiggled in her seat as the leather was cracked and uncomfortable. The car reeked of smoke and sweat.

"The Alba is a lovely hotel, but are you aware of how expensive it is? Do you have a reservation there?" The cab driver eyed the girl from his broken rear-view mirror.

Lilia ignored him and hunted for lipstick in her purse. She had learned of the hotel from an elderly couple sharing her dining table aboard the ship. They gave her much-needed advice, warned her to stay away from any hotel that did not post their official registered certification at the front desk and highly recommended the Alba.

"I can bring you to a quaint hotel. Don't waste money on the Alba."

Lilia glossed her lips.

"Did you hear me, *muchacha*? I am giving you advice on a better place to stay."

"Sir, with all due respect, I wish to go to the Alba."

"I was trying to save you money."

"It's none of your business."

The cab driver ignored the remark. "You have an accent. Where are you from? You are not from here."

"No sir, I'm not!" Lilia gave him a dirty look.

"You are a tough little girl—very deceiving as to your sweet exterior."

Lilia ignored him.

"Did you come from the port to Caracas?" the cab driver spoke louder.

"Yes, I came from Chile."

"Ah, a *Chileana*," he commented as he kept his gaze on her through the mirror. "We don't have many Chileans in Venezuela. You know, as I was saying, I can save you money and get you a more affordable place. I can take you there right away."

"Señor, I asked you to take me to the Alba. I will not waiver. Please don't speak to me."

"Don't talk to me with such disrespect. Girls should not talk to any man the way you do. I should teach you a lesson and drop you off right here for your insolence. See how far a girl carrying a big suitcase will get in a place like this."

Lilia realized she could be in peril and was now fearing the taxi driver. She didn't answer him and looked out the dirty car windows at the sprawling city. The city felt rugged and masculine-like, built of steel and concrete. She confirmed that the area was run down, understood the man's insinuation and decided to hide her fear, saying in a stern voice, "Do so, and I'll go directly to the police."

"You're not in Chile anymore. The police won't care, but you'll give them a good laugh."

"Then I'll tell my husband! He's from Italy. He fought Nazis in the war, and he won't be afraid of you."

The girl has spunk. She's one of those bitches belonging to the Italians. I should take her to a deserted back alley—show her what a real man can do. Whore! Smearing herself in lipstick! These girls think life is like an American movie...like they all are Lauren Bacall or some other tramp. The cab driver remembered an ugly incident that happened to his friend, another taxi driver, when he was accused of rape by an Italian girl. After the police issued a statement declaring no crime had been committed, his friend mysteriously disappeared. *Better leave her. Italians can be dangerous when you mess with their women.*

The driver pulled up by the sidewalk in front of the hotel. Lilia let out a sigh of relief. She paid the driver by throwing bolivars into the front seat, did not wait for change and hustled out with her suitcase.

The driver yelled through the open window cynically, "Perhaps I can show you around the city? Ask for Marcos," he laughed.

Lilia was happy to be safe in the hotel lobby and proud she had managed to avoid a potential incident. She thought about how only eight weeks ago, she had set out on a lone trip to Argentina and now was a seasoned traveler to a country much farther away. Satisfied she had accomplished her mission and was now close to Enzo, she reveled in her autonomy.

The indifferent front desk clerk complied with Lilia's request for a single room away from the noisy street. The bellhop, dressed in a red velvet jacket and black pants, brought her luggage upstairs and waited for a tip. Lilia overtipped.

It was sunset when Lilia stepped out of her bath and dressed. She was certain Enzo would be home after a long day of work at the construction site. She could not contain her smile or giddiness about seeing him. She let her mind wander and imagined his surprise and happiness when he saw her.

She took a shower, brushed her hair until it shone, parted it on the side and added a red bow. She then put on one of her new pearl earrings. Pleased at her reflection, she donned the second earring and smiled. Remembering a conversation with Enzo about his favorite color, she chose a red pleated skirt and a white button-down blouse. To finish her look, she added a whimsical red cardinal brooch to the collar of the blouse. Twirling in front of the mirror, she liked her womanly hourglass figure.

The elevator ride from the fifth floor to the lobby stopped on every floor, making Lilia anxious. She approached the bellhop and asked him to hail a cab but to be certain the driver's name was not Marcos. Within minutes, she was riding once again in a taxi and feeling her heart flutter with anticipation.

Lilia glanced at the cityscape and admired the tall palm trees lining the streets. The towering buildings were much higher than Santiago's, and she guessed that Caracas, unlike her city, could afford to build towering structures since they did not have as many earthquakes. Although many of the newly constructed edifices were strikingly modern, they often sat next to crumbling older buildings. The dichotomy between old and new baffled Lilia. After a twenty-minute ride on potholed streets, the driver announced in a loud voice, "We're here."

The driver stated his fee. Lilia hunted for the right amount in her purse but, due to her excitement, lost track of counting and had to start again. She chatted uncharacteristically with the driver, "That's funny. I'm paying with *bolivars,* and we are on Bolivar Street."

The driver smirked, "There are a million places named Bolivar."

"The same in Chile, but our money is called the peso, not the bolivar. It's funny how the bolivar doesn't feel like real money," she said while paying him.

"It's all what you're used to," the cab driver laughed at her naiveté.

Lilia exited the car and held on to her purse tightly. The surroundings made her nervous. This was far from the elite downtown area of her hotel.

She feared the dark streets and noticed they were void of streetlamps. Facing a single-story multi-unit house, she verified the address and looked for unit D. She spotted the black metal letter nailed to the center of the door and approached it. She felt her heart skip a beat. She breathed deeply to calm herself. She knocked. Hyperventilating from the eagerness of seeing Enzo, she tried to slow her breathing and could not wait till his lips were on hers. She knocked again.

"Stop already, I'm coming. Give me a chance to put on my robe," Enzo's voice sounded annoyed.

Holding her breath when Enzo opened the door, Lilia sprang onto him, wrapping her arms around his neck and pressing her lips on his.

"Lilia! *Dio Mio*, what are you doing here?" Enzo's eyes widened. Instinctively, he wrapped his arm around the small of her back, nudged her inside and slammed the door closed. Once inside, Lilia leapt again into his arms.

"I'm here Enzo! I can't believe it. It was so difficult."

"What have you done?"

"I've come all this way to be with you. I'm so happy."

Enzo's face showed his disbelief.

Lilia giggled and caressed his face, "Don't be so surprised. Your letter... you missed my pretty smile."

"*Bella*, I'm confused." He dropped on the couch, fearing his knees would buckle.

Lilia joined him on the couch, sliding her body as close to him as possible.

Enzo held her hand. "I know when we left it was hurried and we didn't end things right. I wrote that letter to answer what you wrote on the handkerchief. I didn't want you to feel used in any way. My intention was not to hurt you. But, Lilia, you know about my fiancée!"

Lilia stared into his eyes as if searching his soul for another truth.

"I don't know how you got this idea."

"I got it from you!"

"*Bella*, you've misunderstood. We can't be together. I never promised you anything. I am still engaged to Serafina."

Lilia unlatched her hand from his. "You gave me your love."

"I'm sorry. My Serafina, she waits for me."

"In your letter, you clearly said you weren't sending for her!"

"I can't bring her to Caracas. It has become dangerous from civil unrest. They bomb the streets, aiming at Italian businesses. They don't want foreigners and accuse us of taking their jobs. I'm trying to save what's left of my business, and then I'll go back to Italy and marry her."

"No."

"Yes."

"But you can't!"

"*Bella*, listen—"

"Stop calling me *Bella*. How can you love her when you haven't even consummated your relationship? But you did with me."

"You wanted me."

"I didn't know she existed. Maybe you don't love her anymore. You haven't seen her for years."

"It's the rules!"

"I have rules too. I hate you, Enzo."

"You've misunderstood everything."

"I understand the letter completely! Your letter said you miss me, that you wish to settle down. You're a liar—a horrible liar!"

Enzo brushed away a tear that ran down Lilia's cheek.

"I'm with child, Enzo."

"No! You can't be." Enzo's face contorted, and Lilia could not read his expression. He looked perplexed, shocked and amazed, all at the same time.

"It changes everything, doesn't it?"

"Lilia, I know a doctor who can take care of it."

"What?"

"I will take you for an abortion. He can do it after hours in his office."

"A what?"

"Lilia, don't you know? A doctor can take out the baby."

Lilia gasped, "Before it's born?"

Enzo leaned and tried to caress Lilia, but she pushed him away. She moved towards the door, "Don't touch me. Get me a taxi!"

"I'll take you back to the hotel. It's too late to find a taxi in this part of town. Stay awhile and calm down. I'll pour you a glass."

"No, I want to go! Now!"

Enzo nodded. "Wine will help you compose yourself. I'll pour you a glass."

"Are you mad? I won't spend another minute with you." Lilia let out a single sob.

"Where are you staying?" Enzo's demeanor showed restraint.

"The Alba."

"Give me a minute. I'll put on a pair of pants." Enzo went into the bedroom.

Lilia looked for a handkerchief in her purse and found none.

"Enzo, please bring me a handkerchief."

Enzo, dressed in a pair of dark pants and a sleeveless white ribbed tee shirt, came out of the bedroom and handed her a handkerchief. "Here, wipe your tears."

She sat back down on the couch and unfolded Enzo's handkerchief. It was from the set his aunt had embroidered. Lilia stared at the double roses and let her tears flow past her cheeks and fall into spots on her blouse. She looked at the sparsely furnished room and remembered Carmen's warning—*He doesn't love you.*

Enzo grabbed a pair of keys suspended from a nail on the wall. "Let's go," his voice grave and his eyes bloodshot. He rubbed his temples as if doing so would kill the shooting pain in his head. They walked across the street, and Enzo mounted a motorcycle. He started the loud engine. "Hop on. Hold on to my waist."

Lilia hesitated, never having ridden a motorcycle and afraid to hold him close and feel his body. *I'll ride with him and throw myself at oncoming traffic. That'll teach him to want to kill our baby. I wish the avalanche had taken me to my grave.*

Lilia climbed onto the bike and wrapped her arms around his waist. She inhaled the scent of almonds and vanilla, recognizing the smell of Castile soap. Closing her eyes to stop the tears, she wished time would stand still so she could understand better what was happening. *Could it be a nightmare?*

As the motorcycle raced across the city, Lilia realized she did not have the courage to throw herself onto the street and be as guilty as Enzo for wanting to end a life. She had no idea what to do next but knew she still loved him. Wishing the ride to the hotel would last an eternity, she held him tighter as their baby slept safely in her womb. She placed the side of her face on the center of his back, relishing his scent. Angry at herself for teetering between love and hate, confusing messages bounced in her head. Enzo pulled up to the front of the hotel, and Lilia dismounted.

"Lilia, kiss me goodbye. Let there be no hate between us."

Enzo sounded sincere, bringing Lilia a glimmer of hope that he might change his mind. She stepped closer to him and received only a peck on her cheek. Lilia had nothing more to say. He stared at her and said, "I'll send money for the baby."

Lilia entered the lobby, passed the front desk and was surprised she controlled her emotions with no further tearful outbursts. She stopped at a window, stood behind the drapes and observed Enzo discreetly. He had not moved and was transfixed on his motorcycle—the engine of his BMW hummed. Lilia held her breath. *He's not driving away. He loves me. He will come back for me.* Gripping the drapes tightly, she waited for Enzo to run into the lobby and sweep her into his arms. The roar of the engine shocked her as the tires squealed and pulled away. Lilia caught her reflection in the glass, saw a drop of blood and realized she had bitten her lip. She had felt nothing.

The sun filtered through the wooden shutters and created slivers of light on the hotel room floor. Lilia spent the night on an upholstered chair, not bothering to remove her clothing. An uncomfortable tingling coursed through her right leg. She rose and limped to the bathroom, filled a glass with water and drank. Feeling sick from crying all night, her head aching, she thought about crawling into bed but knew it would be useless to try and sleep it off.

Lilia opened the shutters, and light drenched the room. The horizon showed ominous clouds gathering. She swept the view and knew that somewhere, in an unknown direction of the dense city, Enzo was beginning his day, and she wondered if he too had stayed awake.

Her headache worsened. She touched her cheeks and found them to be hot and damp. She wiped her face with the sleeves of her blouse. Still staring at the sky, Lilia reprimanded an unseen god, "How could you be so cruel? Why do you toy with me as if I was an ant in a colony? Why do you destroy what I worked so hard to build?" Turning away from the window, she smirked and decided not to continue speaking to an unseen being. "God is dead!"

Lilia rummaged through her purse and pulled out her wallet to see how much money she had. She stacked the bills in order of value and began to count. Halfway through, she realized she had spent too much and was sorry she had purchased useless items like pearl earrings and sunglasses. After counting the bolivars, she figured she could pay for the voyage home and have enough money to splurge on a taxi to the port and not have to suffer a bus ride.

Lilia's headache worsened and never having felt a migraine, she wasn't sure what to do. She began to feel more nauseous, and her eyes were sensitive to light. She remembered Susana had severe headaches and tried to remember what she did to alleviate the pain. Although she had not eaten, she started to gag and ran to the bathroom, making it only as far as the sink before a horrible yellow liquid came up, burning her throat. She gargled, washed her face and caught her reflection in the mirror. Aghast at her appearance—sallow complexion, stringy hair and last night's crumpled outfit—she looked away in disgust and turned on the bathtub faucet. The water was almost unbearably hot, but she remembered Susana telling her that an almost scalding bath relieved such an episode.

Removing the brooch from her collar, she caressed the tiny bird with her finger, dredging up the joyous feeling she had when she first pinned it on a mere twelve hours ago. Feelings of anger rose with memories of the prior night, and she thought herself a fool for being so happy to surprise Enzo. She grabbed the broach and pulled it off, tearing her shirt in the process, flung it into the toilet and flushed. The bird swam in circles before it forever disappeared down the pipe. Unbuttoning only the first three buttons of her blouse before sliding it over her head, she continued to undress and leave her clothes in a heap on the floor. She now felt as if she were being hammered with every slight movement.

Lilia slid into the tub and closed her eyes, trying to shut out the strong light coming from the bedroom. Her neck muscles spasmed. After a few minutes, she mustered enough strength to crawl out of the tub and close the bathroom door. She slithered back into the tub in the almost pitch-black bathroom. The steamy water helped comfort her and softened the ache.

La Sirena Del Mar

At noontime, Lilia was feeling better but not yet normal. She felt as if she were moving through a fog while checking out of the hotel. The sun vanished under a mantle of clouds, and the sky darkened as grey clouds continued to roll in. The air was heavy with humidity mixed with petroleum smells.

The front desk clerk leaned on an exterior wall of the hotel smoking a cigarette, blowing smoke rings and amusing himself while on break. He noticed Lilia struggling with her luggage and promptly put out his cigarette to help.

"Can you call a taxi for me, please?"

"Certainly," he replied and hurried indoors to use the lobby telephone. He returned to Lilia's side, enjoying the last few minutes of respite before he returned to work. "Are you feeling well this morning?" The clerk noticed the young woman's demeanor had changed drastically from the previous day. Her youthful childish glow had disappeared. She had been so attractive and jubilant when she arrived, but now her skin was drained of color and her face wore a look of defeat. He felt sorry for her and wondered what transpired during the night—her cloak of assurance was gone.

"Perfectly fine, thank you." Lilia attempted a smile.

A car pulled up to the curb and a spry driver jumped out, nodded to Lilia, placed her luggage in the trunk and opened her door.

"Puerto La Guaira, please," Lilia instructed the cab driver.

"The port is an hour away and an expensive ride," the driver warned. "There is a bus."

"I know. I can pay."

During the long ride, a bolt of lightning flashed and hit a nearby tree. Its outer bark blew away in strips while a deafening roar of thunder vibrated the car. The skies opened to a cataclysmic torrent as water poured onto the city. Lilia enjoyed thunderstorms, but the fierceness of this one shocked her.

The car felt as if it had become an island as streets turned into rivulets. Steam rose from cars parked on the side of the road that minutes earlier were baking in the sun. The driver slowed to an agonizing pace as the car fishtailed. After what felt like an eternity, the cab finally arrived at La Guaira.

"Where would you like to be dropped off?"

"As close as possible to the Castro ticket office, please. I don't want to get drenched."

The driver stopped at a dingy corrugated metal structure. Lilia thought the building resembled a shed rather than a ticket office. She questioned the driver, "Are you sure this is where I can purchase a ticket?"

The driver pointed to a small sign, "Yes, it says so right there."

Lilia paid the driver and refrained from exiting the cab as the storm still raged.

"Get your suitcase. Push the latch on the trunk handle, and it will open. I can't get soaked. I've a long trip back and will be miserable in wet clothing."

Lilia did not leave the car, causing the driver to tap his fingers on the console and shoot her a menacing look. "I must get back to Caracas. Please."

The rain was still coming down hard, but Lilia jumped out of the car and ran to the back, unlatched the trunk and grabbed her suitcase. She ran into the office with her dripping dress clinging to her body and her patent leather shoes squeaking as she walked. A young man behind the desk opened a cabinet door and handed her a small towel.

"Thank you. What a deluge! I've never seen anything like it." She dried her face and ran the towel through her hair.

"Then I assume you don't live here. This is a common occurrence in our endless summer. What can I do for you?"

"I'd like to purchase a ticket to Valparaiso on your next ship. I bought a one-way passage on your line only nine days ago. I arrived only yesterday, but I need to return as soon as possible."

"Let's see what's available on the *Sirena del Mar*. Pardon me for asking, but why would you travel so far for only a day's stay?"

"It's not important. The price should be the same as my ticket here, correct? I have enough money to cover it."

"Class?"

"First."

"It would've been cheaper if you bought a round trip ticket instead of buying a second single ticket."

Lilia ignored the comment.

"May I see your passport?"

Lilia placed her passport on the desk as the clerk checked a logbook to verify price and availability. He wrote down some figures and handed the paper along with a pen to Lilia. "You can fill out the rest of the information and sign on the bottom."

Lilia glanced at the price. "It's too much. That's much more than I previously paid."

"Because you came on a different ship. This one is more luxurious."

"I would like a passage on that ship. I saw it still anchored on the dock."

"That ship leaves this afternoon for Brazil. You can wait four weeks till it returns if that is your wish."

"I can't afford to stay in Caracas and wait for the cheaper fare. It would cost more. I need to get home. Please, what is the cost of third-class fare on the *Sirena*?"

The clerk flipped the pages of his book as Lilia thought about remedying the situation by sending a telegram to her father, apologizing for all her mistakes and asking for a loan. Almost immediately, she rejected the idea. Groveling was beneath her, and she knew he would hold it against her for a long time. Another idea crossed Lilia's mind that was as absurd as the first—ask Enzo for a loan. That idea was even more distasteful, and she squashed the thought. Never would she reach out to him, no matter how great the need. Now in a state of misery, she entertained the thought that facing death was preferable to asking for help from either her father or Enzo.

"Sorry, it's sold out. I'll check the tourist class; that's our version of second class." The clerk buried his nose again in the logs and soon bobbed up his head. "No, there's not a single room available there either. All we have left are three first-class cabins."

"I can almost pay for it. May I have a discount?"

"That's against the rules."

"That will leave me completely without any money, but I'll take it."

"Great! It leaves in two days."

"I just told you I don't have any money left. I cannot afford a hotel in addition to the fare."

"Then, good day and good luck!"

"Please, there must be something we can do. Is there a way I can owe the company money and pay you upon my return to Chile?"

"Very funny."

"Perhaps I can work on your ship to reduce my payment?"

"We are hiring cooks. Do you have experience?"

"I don't know how to cook."

"Sorry."

"Please, I have skills," pleaded Lilia. "I'm a pianist."

"A pianist," the clerk laughed incredulously. "I've worked here for six years and not once has there been a need for a pianist."

Lilia remained calm. "Please, I can learn to help in the kitchen. I'd be so grateful."

"I'm not an employment agency. Can you afford the ticket or not?"

"I cannot if I must wait two days."

"Then again, good day."

"You do have need of a pianist. My experience on your ship was awful. My teacup had a crack, and I thought it might shatter and the hot tea would burn me. The silverware was cheap aluminum. Appalling! And most importantly, your ship needs a pianist to distract your passengers from the insipid food!"

The young clerk glowered, "We don't claim to be the RMS *Queen Elizabeth*. Our clientele are not presumptuous overbearing travelers demanding frivolity. Of course, you are Chilean, and they always seem to think they are special. Pardon me, your highness, but we don't need a pianist."

"I'm sorry. I didn't mean to insult your line."

An older man with a grey beard interrupted, "Excuse me, Antonio. This is not how we speak to others."

The clerk's eyes widened, "I'm sorry, Señor. I didn't see you there."

"I have never allowed anyone to speak rudely to our guests. *Señorita*, please forgive this young man for his lack of manners."

"It's quite alright, Señor. No harm."

The man extended his hand. "My name is Jaime Perez. I manage the line."

"It's a pleasure to meet you, Señor Perez. I'm Lilia," shaking his hand.

"Señorita Lilia, I overheard you're a pianist. What kind of music do you play?"

"Classical."

"Your favorite composer?"

"Oh, there's so many. Mozart, Beethoven, but I concentrate on Chopin."

"Ah! Chopin! The king of the romantics."

"Yes, Señor."

"His work is as dynamic as his moods. They say he had a split personality and was very temperamental. Did you know that?"

"Yes, I did. George Sands said, 'Frederick is the sum of noble contradictions.' She should know; she was his lover."

"Tell me, dear girl, which is your favorite work?"

"I couldn't choose a favorite. I love all of it."

"Have you played Gershwin?"

"Only once. Gershwin's too modern for me—a jazz artist—and I'm not comfortable with syncopation. I find him fascinating and strange at the same time."

"Which of his work?"

"Rhapsody in Blue."

"Can you play it?" The man's eyes twinkled.

"Yes, but I don't play it well."

"Will you show me?"

"Of course, I would try, but I don't know if I can still recall it by memory."

"You memorized the entire work?"

"I memorize everything. My professor says it's the only way to perform."

"That's incredible! I do have the sheet music."

"But Señor, we don't have a piano."

"Come with me, please. There is a piano on the *Sirena del Mar*."

Having lost her intrepid nature, Lilia was fearful to follow the man. "I'm sorry, but I must figure out how to get a passage home."

"Come, walk me to the *Sirena*. Don't worry, there are plenty of workers around, so you won't be alone with me. I'd love to hear you play. Please humor an old man, and we'll find a way home for you." He reached for a large umbrella from a tall vase by the door and motioned Lilia to him.

Lilia grabbed her passport from the counter, slipped it in her purse and addressed the clerk, "May I leave my suitcase here?"

"Of course," the manager answered, "Antonio will guard your suitcase. Come."

The clerk did not hide his feelings well. It was obvious from his demeanor that he was agitated that his employer reprimanded him in front of the young woman. He also did not like the attention his boss lavished on her, but he managed to respond, "Yes, Señor."

The older man walked outside and opened the umbrella while holding the door for Lilia. Looking at the skies, he said, "It's just drizzling now." They walked out to the pier under his umbrella to a huge docking and the gang-plank of the *Sirena del Mar*.

The dock swarmed with workers. Men unpacked huge crates. They opened the crates to reveal stacks of boxes that were carted on hand trucks to their destination within the vessel. On the ship, crew members swept, mopped, polished and prepped for the next voyage. Lilia watched the parade of carts and assumed they contained food, wine, cleaning supplies and hundreds of different items needed for the week-long sea voyage. Two women pulled a cart filled with fresh linens to the upper decks.

Lilia and Señor Perez entered the main hall of the ship. Upon seeing the manager, the employees greeted him. They walked through many great rooms until they reached the first-class dining hall. The manager took her directly to the grand piano.

The instrument was protected with a leather cover, and the seat was tufted. The manager pulled the heavy cover off and exposed the shiny black, lacquered instrument.

"A Blüthner! It's a prestigious piano. I'm excited to test the piano's action, how it feels and sounds. My father bought me a Steinway, studio size. He put it in my room and not the salon so as not to disturb him, because I play all the time. At school, I learned on a Bösendorfer." Lilia could not hide her excitement.

"You're in for a surprise!" Señor Perez beamed, placing the piano cover on a nearby table. He lifted the heavy piano lid and engaged the lip prop to its highest position. Lilia marveled at its beauty.

"Lilia, go to that side cabinet and pull out Gershwin's music, please. The Rhapsody is on the left, piled somewhere in the stack of sheet music."

Lilia was surprised at how many books and sheets were piled on each shelf. "There are enough books here to keep you entertained for a thousand lifetimes!"

"I justified buying the piano and all this music to the ship's owners by saying it was a necessity for our first-class passengers to amuse themselves. But between you and me, I bought it because I wanted it."

Lilia giggled and found the man delightful, momentarily forgetting her grief.

"Here it is." Lilia pulled out the interleaved sheets and placed them on the music rack. The paper was fragile, yellowed with frayed edges, but still intact and readable. Lilia did not like the many distracting pencil markings on the music. She thought it had probably been marked up to help a less proficient student decipher difficult notes.

"Whenever the ship is in harbor, even if only for a day or two, I take advantage and play it. I am mostly self-taught, but the piano is so difficult. I think you need to be a child to really learn it."

"I don't think so, Señor. I'm sure you can learn anything if you desire it."

"That's kind of you, but I'm failing. I got to a point where I could not progress further. I guess that's why they invented records," he laughed.

Lilia sat on the comfortable seat and scanned the music, skimming every page before asking, "May I warm up?"

"Of course." Señor Perez grabbed a chair and sat.

Lilia warmed her fingers and played four scales and five arpeggios. The manager admired her nimble speedy fingers gliding over the keyboard like figure skaters on ice. She pressed every note directly in the center of the ivory or ebony keys, never accidentally hitting the wrong key. The sound was clear as crystal as she continued playing her warmup, written by Pischna, from memory. She glanced at the manager and said, "I'm ready."

The young pianist played the piece. Señor Perez listened intently. Although he had never learned to play anything more difficult than pieces for young players, he appreciated music and knew artistry when he heard it. The Señor not only scrutinized Lilia's fingers but also the way her body swayed. She entered a different realm, somehow able to connect with the composer through the cosmic language of music.

The older man fell captive to her precision and interpretation. He marveled at the pianist, amazed that she did not need to practice the difficult music before playing. Her memory and focus were incredible. He shut his eyes, and the music transported him to the city he loved—energetic sophisticated New York—the metropolis he dreamed of but never visited. He felt as if he knew every street of Manhattan through Gershwin's notes.

"I played it as if I were an automaton. I'm sorry, but I don't feel I am in the proper frame of mind and spirit to give Rhapsody what it deserves." Lilia was displeased.

Señor Perez's face was blissful as he was spellbound. "Nonsense! You're very special—a true artist," he managed to say.

Lilia was about to tell Señor Perez that she had forfeited the most prestigious competition in the world but changed her mind. She did not want to retell the story and risk shedding tears. She was embarrassed to divulge how she had made a series of grave mistakes and extinguished a rare opportunity.

"You know, in America they call playing the piano, uh, I'll say it in English, *tickling the ivories*," Señor Perez said, his smile still wide.

"I speak English, but I've never heard the expression *tickling the ivories*. What is tickling?"

Señor Perez tickled the air with his fingers and said, "Coochie, coochie, coo."

"That's funny, Señor. I like it. It's like making the piano laugh!"

"Lilia, I'm going to help you."

"How?"

"I'm giving you a free bunk for your trip home."

"Huh?"

"In exchange, you'll play the piano for the first-class dinner shift. You won't spend any more of your money and can go home. By not having to pay us for the voyage, you'll have money to spend for a hotel and can wait out the departure. I heard what you said to Antonio."

Lilia was astonished at his offer, tried to find proper words of gratitude but said only, "Thank you, Señor."

"You'll share a room with other women who work in housekeeping. I cannot give you a first-class room. Is it a fair deal?"

"Yes, more than fair. I'll always be indebted to you."

"Let's go to the office. Antonio will prepare the paperwork for you, and he can suggest a hotel nearby."

They shook hands and walked silently back together. Lilia noticed the clouds had completely dissipated and the sun blazed once again in the sky. She signed a contract for her services and retrieved her luggage. Antonio hailed a taxi and recommended a safe hotel where Lilia ensconced herself in a room crying over her loss of Enzo. But the tears did not wash away her feelings of betrayal, and she could not regain her will to move past him. She was ready to go home and face her father's wrath. A sliver of hope remained that one day the lonely void threatening to live perpetually inside her chest would cease.

A Fox in a Hunt

Antofagasta, Chile, 1948

The friendship between Agata and Jacob grew stronger. Daily, they looked forward to returning from work and meeting in the common areas of the boarding house. They shared their daily experiences and talked about everything, even mundane things. The couple found these moments of friendship magical and were entranced by every detail they shared. Agata asked Jacob about Judaism and was curious about how Christianity arose from it. The subject was never discussed in the convent. When she asked questions about his family, Jacob remained silent. He also questioned Agata about her beliefs and the life she lived in the sisterhood. Agata spoke often of the children in her care and more than once mentioned she loved a little girl.

Jacob encouraged Agata to read the newspaper, but unfortunately, delivery of the Santiago *Prenza* reached Antofagasta three days after printing. They even read the same books borrowed from the Reyeses and loved to discuss them.

The tenants in the Reyes house began to treat Jacob like a friend as he became more comfortable and at ease with them. No longer hiding in his room, he made a concerted effort to join in conversations as well as participate in games such as *parchis* and chess. The boarders discovered he was well-mannered and had a soft disposition.

Every night after dinner, Jacob and Agata strolled to the ocean and enjoyed the parade of boats bobbing on the sea. The peculiar pair became close friends but never crossed the line of intimacy. Although they found solace in each other, neither of them had the courage to propel the relationship to a sexual level. She loved the kind and quiet man. Jacob did not attempt to kiss her or behave in any way that Agata assumed men would. She fantasized about sex but was too timid to initiate or broach the subject. Besides, she thought, *a thirty-seven-year-old virgin would not be a catch for any man.*

"Jacob, you've become my best friend." Agata slipped her arm in his and continued their walk. She laughed nervously, "Actually, I think you're the only real friend I have."

"Nonsense, everyone at the boarding house is your friend and cares for you."

"Yes, they like me, but they don't share their stories with me. They still treat me differently because I once wore the habit."

"I don't think so. Perhaps they don't share because I steal most of your free time."

"They never talk to me about their personal lives, intimate details that women tell each other. I'm still an outsider."

"It isn't true. They consider you family. If you want to talk about outcasts, I'm the world's outcast."

"No, Jacob, the world is not entirely like the one you came from."

"My Jewishness carries a stigma. The world is a dark place."

"It'll change! Right always wins in the end. I believe that."

"Because you are a ray of sunshine and a good person. Most people are not like you. If they were, Earth would truly be the garden of Eden." Jacob turned to look behind him as this idiosyncrasy had not abated.

"Jacob, confide in me, please."

"In what, Agata?"

"Why are you compelled to check behind you all the time? Is someone following you?"

"Maybe. I find it difficult to trust that no one is trying to hurt me. I cannot separate myself from past events. I fear that I will be attacked. I try not to look back, but I can't stop. I am the fox in a hunt."

"No one is hunting you, Jacob. You're safe now. You're in Chile."

Jacob lowered his voice into a whisper, "Agata, I've seen Nazis in Antofagasta. I recognize a man who lives around the corner from my office. He was always by the side of the commandant during the *Appell*."

"*Appell*—what do you mean?"

"It's roll call. We stood for hours every day for the Germans to make sure we were all accounted for. Or they would call an *appell* for us to gather and witness punishments or deaths of prisoners."

"It's too awful, Jacob."

"The Nazis are quivering cowards. They are hiding here."

"Could you be mistaken?"

"No. He saw me too, and you should have seen the hatred still in his eyes."

"Do you think he would dare to hurt you?"

Jacob did not respond.

"Jacob?"

"I'm sorry, Agata. I was lost in thought."

"How did you survive?"

Jacob stared at the ground and again was silent.

"Listen, my friend. You're not alone. I'm here. What can you share with me? Talking will make you feel better, I promise." Agata stopped walking and faced him. "I'll never betray you. Whatever you tell me will stay locked in my heart."

"It's hard. I'm afraid of losing control if I hear my words spoken aloud."

"Only a word or two to start with."

"I can't. My guilt crushes me."

"What guilt?"

"I'm guilty of sleeping on a clean pillow, guilty of having good, unspoiled food. Even walking with you on this beautiful night, I can't enjoy it knowing my boys and my wife cannot."

Agata motioned him to sit on a bench at a deserted bus stop. "Jacob, I'm sorry. You can tell me more about them or sit in silence. Know that I'm here."

Jacob stared at a lamppost as he spoke. "Poland was invaded by Russia and Germany. Both countries wanted to see us destroyed, not just Jews but Polish culture." Light from the streetlamp fell on his cap, creating shadows on his features. The dim light stole the blue from his eyes, and they were now dark hollow orbs. Jacob stopped talking, seemingly transfixed.

"Jacob, go on." Agata patted his hand.

"We lived in Warsaw before they moved us to Lodz. Do you know about Lodz?"

"No."

"The Nazis came at night while we nestled in our beds. Thinking we had escaped the pogroms, as our family has been Polish for centuries, we became complacent. We lived under a falsehood as we watched our friends rounded up in 1940 and sent to the Warsaw ghetto. We were blessed with a German-sounding surname. We pretended to be gentiles, but they came for us in 1943. Our Jewish heritage became our crime. The Germans allowed us to take only what we could carry. The rest of our belongings became their possessions—the house, furniture, paintings, everything. They marched us to Lodz, a horribly crowded ghetto."

***

Lodz, Poland, 1943

"You came all the way from Warsaw? Why did they bring you here when there's a ghetto in Warsaw?" Olga asked the strangers assigned to their quarters.

"That's true," agreed her husband, Jerzy.

"The Warsaw ghetto is gone. The Germans burned it," Jacob said and stared down at Olga's checkered kitchen floor, trying to control his emotions. He was angry with himself for being powerless to protect his wife, children and home. Even though it was illogical for him to think he could stop the ravages of a vicious militia, he burdened himself with guilt.

Jews, fleeced out of their property and worse, found their lives to be unendurable. When the Nazis stripped Jacob of house and dignity and his family became prisoners, his angst was unimaginable. He feared that in any unprovoked instant, he or a member of his family could face immediate death. Jacob wondered how his wife could remain strong. Anita's stone face never betrayed her fears, and she was able to control her tears. Her thoughts focused only on keeping her sons alive for one more day. Nothing else mattered.

Olga listened to Jacob and deduced that the Germans burned the Warsaw ghetto not to destroy buildings and incite intimidation but for genocide. The shrewd woman did not need to ask questions to confirm her suspicion. She walked to a wardrobe and pulled out linens and blankets and summoned the boys.

"Henrik, Yad, spread these out on the floor," Olga said as she distributed blankets and sheets to Jacob and Anita's sons. "We've only one extra pillow, but the two of you can share." Her warm voice comforted the boys. They were now part of her family.

"Thank you for your kindness. The boys thank you as well." Anita motioned to the boys, hoping to prompt them for a response.

"Thank you," said Henrik, the older boy.

"Anita and I are sorry that we've been forced into your home," Jacob added.

Olga shook her head. "Did you have a choice? When a German kicks your door nearly off its hinges and pushes another family inside without saying a word, there is nothing you can do, so don't apologize. We are all prisoners, but while we're under this roof, we're going to make the best of it. We can choose to hate or choose to love. But why choose hate? There's already too much of that in the world."

"Thank God for placing us with you," Jacob said. He noticed Jerzy wore a blue-threaded *tzitzit* on his collar. He surmised Jerzy and Olga were conservative Jews and extremely brave not to have torn the tassels off while locked in the ghetto.

"We were once in your position, the new uninvited guests. The family before us tried to accommodate us. Now, it's our turn. The ghetto gets more crowded every day. It is said that about a thousand arrive daily. When the population becomes greater than the number of rats, that's when Nazis come."

"Please, don't say anymore. The children can hear!" Anita pleaded.

"What do you mean?" Jacob whispered to Olga.

"They come for us," Olga said in a hushed voice. "It's better to learn the truth because when the time comes, no one needs to make a ruckus. Even children must obey, giving them a chance to survive."

"I'm hungry," cried four-year-old Yad, not able to control himself any longer. Jacob and Anita hoped that they would be offered something to eat.

"We have a little bread the boys can share. The Germans give each family a loaf to last for the week, but it's small and lasts a day, at most, two." Olga opened a cabinet and unwrapped a small piece of bread from a dishcloth, broke it in two and gave it to the boys.

"We do have good news, though!" Jerzy said, "Tomorrow is Tuesday, when the *Kaserne* receives its potato delivery. They are always on time, like clockwork!"

"What happens?" Anita's eyes widened.

"The truck makes a left on the next corner at precisely nine in the morning, and I'll teach you how we fish for potatoes," Jerzy smiled proudly.

Olga turned to the boys, "Tomorrow, we'll have potato soup."

"Hopefully, Olga!" warned Jerzy in case of failure.

"From your mouth," Olga touched her lips and then waved her hand up towards heaven.

"One day when I failed at fishing potatoes," Jerzy said proudly, "I went to the guardhouse to rummage through their trash bins, looking for anything edible—"

"What nerve he had, to go to the gates—almost got killed," interrupted Olga as she shook her head in disbelief.

"But I didn't," Jerzy smiled triumphantly at his wife. "A guard heard me and came out pointing his gun. I threw my arms in the air to surrender and blurted out, 'I'm only looking for potato peels.' The guard ordered me to wait, and I thought he was coming out with his friends to get a good laugh and kill me. He came back alone, handed me a bag and commanded me to run. I ran faster than I've ever run, hoping I wouldn't feel a bullet tear into my back. I made it back to Olga, and we opened the bag, and in it were four potatoes and a head of cabbage. God shows himself in the strangest of places."

"He better not dare try that again," Olga admonished.

Yad stopped crying as he sucked his thumb and listened. He lay down on the wool blanket in fetal position. His brother looked on.

"How do we 'fish' for these potatoes?" Jacob said eagerly.

Olga smiled as Jerzy, from behind the drapes, pulled out a long stick with five-inch nails sprouting at the tip.

"He hides in doorways on the street. When the truck rolls by and slows down before making a left turn, Jerzy runs behind it, swings his stick and grabs a potato. One time he caught five." Olga's face showed an expression of childlike innocence.

"What happens if he's caught?" Anita trembled.

"We don't think about that possibility," Jerzy stated flatly.

***

Antofagasta, Chile, 1947

Jacob's eyes filled with tears, "I can't live with these memories."

"I no longer wear the habit, but I still believe that God is love and all who have perished are in his bosom. God ended the war. Your pain will lessen in time."

"It never will."

Agata watched Jacob's tears roll down his face. "I hope I can comfort you. I was once helped by a doctor and his wife. I won't compare my small problem to your tribulation, but...please allow me to help you. Can I hold your hand?"

Jacob stared into the air but reached for her hand. "Our lives in that small hovel, locked in the ghetto with no way to feed and protect our sons, was unimaginable. Every day we feared for our lives. I've seen things, Agata..."

"Go on, Jacob."

"Pointed guns, soldiers laughing, children dancing to their deaths, things I can't forget. People hanging from trees or lamp posts, gallows—these images are burned into my head. I can't get a moment's respite."

Agata stroked his hand.

"Food consumed our thoughts. If you were lucky to find a blade of grass, you'd chew it till it became straw-like before you spit it out. Rats ate better. And winters were so cold...my wife traded her sweater for a loaf of bread. When they rounded us up..." Jacob could not complete his sentence, weeping while his hands covered his face. Agata embraced him and silently prayed.

***

Lodz, Poland, 1943

Sirens blazed throughout the Lodz ghetto. The uniformed German soldiers were bundled in long coats, boots and gloves that kept the winter chill away. The Jews, corralled like cattle around a flagpole with its white, red and black swastika drooping in the still air, trembled from both cold and fear. The soldiers separated the crowd into groups. Those between twelve and forty-nine years old were divided into one group. Everyone else age fifty and over and children under twelve were divided into a second group. A screaming soldier moved the first group to the other side of the recently built barracks. Once the Jews were blocked by the barracks' walls, they could not see what transpired in the second group. The ominous train spewing smoke from its engine warned the Jews of something evil.

A mother attempted to peek around the corner for a glimpse of her child, but before she could spot him, a bullet pierced her neck. The soldier had pulled the trigger without warning, not losing a step as he resumed his watch. As she fell to the ground, the dying mother's eyes found her son. She was grateful that her two-year-old did not turn towards the blast of gunfire and did not witness her demise. God had granted her a parting wish.

Soldiers turned off the electrified gate and swung it open. They walked the children and elderly out of the ghetto to the waiting train. Children gravitated to the wrinkled, white-haired men and women as if they could grant protection. The youngest and oldest prisoners piled silently into window-less cars, afraid to make a sound. Some children were lucky to board the same car as their natural grandparents or familial relations. Infirm and elder Jews of Lodz, barely able to stand, reached out to the children. Strangers thrust together moved toward the train in dreamlike states, soothing one another in complete silence. Love passed among them regardless of their circumstances.

The ones left behind the barracks, assuming the fear of losing their children was coming to fruition, held on to thin threads of hope that today would not be the last time they saw them. They watched the billowing smoke of the engine climb above the rooftop and prayed the train would not take their children and loved ones away.

A soldier howled, "Form two lines! Men left, women right!"

Another soldier blew a whistle, signaling for the gates to be closed and the fence re-electrified. A second whistle alerted the Germans to bring the workers back to the front of the barracks. The Jews marched in single file and rounded the corner of the barracks, where they saw the empty space, their worst fears proven, that their loved ones were on the idling train. Some broke their lines and screamed, running towards the train. A father, determined to climb the fence and reach his twin girls, leapt onto it, but before his legs mounted the chain link, an electric current seized his body. He was not able to let go, and not even his scream escaped. His death was slow as the current held him tightly in its grasp, his body violently shaking. Others also ran for the fence despite what they witnessed, but before reaching it, bullets tore into their bodies. The lucky ones died quickly. The unlucky lay writhing on the freezing ground.

Anita did not run nor scream but stood solidly in her line. She searched for Jacob in the crowd of men. They were indistinguishable—skeletons, phantom apparitions with dark circles around their hollowed eyes. When she finally saw him, it seemed he had aged years in that short hour behind the barracks. He looked old and broken. His face was contorted with deep frowns, his body had stooped and he could hardly stand. They caught each other's stares, motionless, telegraphing each other's pain. Jacob wished he could hold his wife.

The Jews found themselves facing tables, each with a doctor, nurse and a set of medical tools. The doctors examined the prisoners as nurses jotted the doctors' utterances in a logbook. The results of the exam determined if a prisoner was well enough to work, and if too ill, they lined up at the waiting train. Jacob assumed his bony appearance would allow him to join his boys, but he received a nod from the doctor, clearing him for the labor line. His knees buckled. Jacob glanced in his wife's direction and saw her pleading eyes begging him to rise. He followed her command and rose. His fate cast, he swore to stay alive for his wife and children.

"Face the wall!" Another order screamed by a soldier.

Jacob, refusing to turn and risk losing sight of his wife, remained in the opposite direction as everyone else. The soldier walked towards Jacob and grunted, "Face the other way."

Jacob did not comply. The end of the soldier's rifle jabbed him on the side of his head. A star-like flash blinded him for a second, and throbbing pain pulsed from his spine as he fell to the ground. The German, satisfied, walked away. An emaciated man next to Jacob helped him up.

Anita, still in line to see the doctor, tried to still her trembling body. She wore her husband's coat and was guilt-ridden that he was wearing only a thin jacket. She wished she had not traded her wool sweater for the bread in Lodz. The bread had been devoured in a matter of seconds, but now she thought if she had kept the sweater, it would still be of use, and Jacob would be warm in his coat. Anita remembered that when the Nazis had come to evacuate the Liebeskinds from their home, she had grabbed her sable coat, the fur necessary in the brutal Polish winters. A soldier eyed it and took it as he said, "This would look much better on my girl."

That autumn Anita had managed to survive with only her sweater, but when the first snow came, Jacob insisted she wear his coat.

"Open your mouth!" the young German doctor demanded. Anita obeyed. He proceeded to press a spoon-like contraption on her tongue near her tonsils. He noticed her rotting teeth and grimaced. Anita's stay in the ghetto with lack of proper food and toothbrushes had caused her teeth and gums to decay. Anita gagged. She tried to manage a cough but could not, and blood-stained spittle splashed on the doctor's immaculate coat.

"*Swine!*" The doctor yelled. A burly soldier with wide shoulders saw the incident and without further instruction, grabbed Anita by her hair and pushed her to the line destined for the train. Anita rejoiced and felt a glimmer of hope that calmed her. She would be with her boys. *HaShem has granted me a chance to save my sons. My Lord will save his people.*

***

Antofagasta Chile, 1947

"That was the last day I saw them. I worked for almost a year in a factory where we filled grenade shells with gunpowder. The bullets we made were used by the Germans to kill anyone trying to free us. I kept myself from dying, regardless of dysentery and starvation, and fought for my life with only will for a weapon. I had to survive for my family, even when I didn't know if they still lived. I had to be certain, so I hung on, hoping to see them again. One of them might still be alive."

Jacob fell silent.

"Did you find them?"

"August 4, 1944, was terrifying. The Germans liquidated the Jews remaining in the ghetto. They marched us to a field not far from town and ordered the men to dig a hole. When the hole was large enough, they lined us up at the edge of it, ten at a time. The Jews fell from the impact of bullets into the mass grave they dug for themselves. We covered the gravesite, even while some were still alive, and shoveled dirt over them. It was unbearable to see people I knew—labored and starved with—spend their last hour walking through a glorious sunlit field and then watch them die. They were buried without shrouds, without dignity, huddled together side by side. When the grave was filled, the land looked as if it had been recently plowed, ready for seeds to grow. It was a field without markers. I wonder if the site is now covered with sweet grasses and clover, with cows happily grazing. I often think of the dead buried there, unbeknownst to lovers who might enjoy a picnic on the very spot."

"But why did they keep you alive?"

"To stay in the ghetto and help Nazis search the empty buildings."

"Search for what?"

"They thought Jews hid gold in the walls. Madness! Imagine, depriving me of the right to die for non-existent gold. Whatever valuables the Jews might have had, trinkets or coins hidden in the hem of a skirt, were bartered and long gone. All was traded for food. I lost hope that day. Soon after, we were liberated by the Soviets. Almost a quarter million Jews passed through Lodz, but less than a thousand survived."

"The boys?"

Jacob shook his head.

"Your wife?"

"I learned that Anita and the boys had been fed to the crematorium at Chelmno."

"Chelmno?"

"A death camp."

Agata gasped as the air was forced from her lungs.

"I ask *HaShem*, 'Why are you silent?' but he never responds," Jacob whispered through labored breath.

"We'll never understand. It's not for us to question." Agata looked up at the multitude of stars, "Only he knows." Agata pointed towards heaven. "I shouldn't even use the word 'he' because God is not human. God is a spark that lives inside every life, no matter how small that life is, and that spark never dies."

Agata bent down to pull a yellow dandelion growing between the cracks of the sidewalk. She placed it in Jacob's hand. "Look at this common weed. People labor to pluck it out of their gardens. I often wonder why all of creation is not revered. This weed is as complicated and beautiful as a rose. It's not for us to ask why it is so but to accept it and nothing more."

Jacob looked sickened, "You haven't grasped my loss."

"I cannot! It's unimaginable. What I tried to say about the dandelion is that some people will step on it, and it will die, but since it's God's creation, the life within the flower must surely return to its maker. I believe your children are somewhere safe. I have faith."

"Agata, you cannot compare that weed to my sons. Nothing can ever justify the cruelty and horror of what happened to them. I see their faces everywhere. They will always haunt me."

"But we must still live."

"It's hard."

"We can go through life together and help one another."

Jacob shook his head.

"One minute at a time."

"Agata! Don't!"

"I gave up the convent to find someone like you. I didn't think it possible, but I had to try."

"I can't give you what you want."

"If all you can give is friendship, it will be enough for me."

Jacob unlatched himself from her grip and walked home alone.

Broken

Valparaiso, Chile, 1948

La Sirena del Mar docked in Valparaiso, where the city streets and side-walks shone in the morning light after a night of rain. The sky was gloomy, but rays of sunshine promised a nice day. Bougainvillea climbed the city's retaining walls in shades of white, pink and red. Valparaiso was beautiful, and Lilia promised to catch the funicular on her next visit and discover the hilltop homes. Lilia correlated the funicular with her parents because the funicular ascends and descends the mountainside with two cars that are counterbalanced, and she concluded that was the crux of life. Good and bad are always counterbalanced, and you cannot have one without the other. All the good deeds her parents performed by adopting her and giving her an education were counterbalanced with the pain of losing Mamita. Her actions of leaving the Villavicencios for Venezuela would have to be balanced somehow.

Instead of catching the train to Santiago, Lilia traveled the short distance to Viña del Mar. She remembered the day her father escorted her to the McKenna. He had not hugged her goodbye, and now she was surprised that she longed to feel his arms around her. But that hug would wait, as she hoped visiting the McKenna would afford her an opportunity to see Professor Goretsky and begin atoning for her sins. She would start with a deep strong apology.

Lilia sat across the street from the McKenna on an iron bench by a large eucalyptus tree. Inhaling its minty pine and honey scent brought a few moments of serenity. Her memories lingered on the first day of school, many years ago, when she had first heard the organ in the chapel and it burst into her life, changing her forever.

Lilia stared at Professor Goretsky's studio window. His office shade was pulled down, which made it difficult to see who was inside. The professor always turned on the light because it helped him see better, but she could not tell if the lights were on. She watched for movement and was sad when it became obvious the professor was not in his room. Becoming more apprehensive, thinking perhaps he had become ill from the stress of her skipping the performance, she realized that because of her, his reputation had most likely been ruined. Also, he would have paid a financial price for her decision by being forced to return the money from the ticket sales and losing his deposit for the rent of the theater.

Lilia decided to return to the train station and head home. She scolded herself for not having the courage to enter the school and face the staff, her principal and her beloved professor. *How could Enzo have caused so much destruction in my life and for those around me? No, it was my fault. Only I am to blame.*

A bus honked at a stray dog in the middle of the street and barely avoided striking it. The mutt ran in front of Lilia, and she screamed, "Baltito!" The dog was the same breed and size as her dog, and it startled her. She closed her eyes and took a long, deep breath, but when she opened them, she could not find the dog. She looked all around and thought it was strange that the dog had disappeared. A wave of depression flooded Lilia. The incident felt like an omen, and she hoped nothing was wrong at home. She returned to the train station, walking as quickly as possible while carrying the hefty suitcase, and caught the next train to Santiago.

Her mood lifted as she imagined embracing Susana and the spry canine joyously jumping around, wagging his tail and licking her face. She tried to shake off her fear from seeing a Baltito look-alike almost struck by a bus and forced herself to imagine her parents, Susana and her dog kissing her a hundred times and welcoming her home.

While sitting on the train, Lilia planned on making amends to her parents. She promised herself she would take care of them till the end of their days. She and Susana would share in the duties, and she would not think about marriage until she laid her parents to rest. Lilia would overcome her ordeal with Enzo and figure out how to take care of her unborn child. The trip seemed endless, as she was ready to confess all and spend her life providing kindness to her parents, her child and Susana.

Lilia sat in first class. Memories of her father persisted along with thoughts of Enzo. Reflecting on how she had met Enzo and showed her intolerance because he did not belong in her car, she felt shame. He had wanted to leave the noisy third-class car for the quiet of first class. She wondered what it was like to ride in the lower class and decided to ride the rest of the way there. Walking to the end of her car and facing her fear of crossing the gap between cars that were attached by a flexible connector, she jumped to the other car and realized it was easy. After walking through three more cars, she reached the third-class car.

The racket was overbearing. Children ran up and down the aisles chasing one another while mothers blissfully continued their chatter, paying no attention to the din. She remained in her seat and eavesdropped on a few conversations, eager to learn about people outside her social class.

"My employer is very unfair to me. She wakes me at night when her husband comes home, after he spent the evening in a bar, because he wants a bite to eat," a petite woman complained to a friend.

Her friend replied, "But that's what is expected from us. We work for the family and that means at any odd hour they choose."

"But that is absurd! How can they expect me to rise from bed at five in the morning and still get up at nearly midnight due to one of their whims? How can I be trusted the very next day with their four-month-old if I'm falling asleep while tending to him? It is dangerous for them as well as me."

Lilia focused on other conversations, as most of the people spoke loudly enough to be heard over the cacophony of the crowded car. Most conversations seemed to be about the inequities the working class endured. Lilia realized how lucky she was to have been adopted by the Villavicencios and not forced to labor as hard as the poor people around her.

Lilia wished she could turn back the clock and undo her choices. If only she had stayed at the wedding and ignored the insults from Monica's mother, she would not have met Enzo and would have avoided the avalanche and the pregnancy. And she would have been part of the world's greatest piano competition. She remembered Enzo's analogy of how a pebble thrown into the sea in Salerno could become a tidal wave.

Retaliation

Santiago, Chile, 1948

When Lilia reached Santiago in the early evening, the sky was filled with the golden light of the setting sun. As she reached her front door, her heart raced with both excitement and fear of her parents' reaction. She took out her key and inserted it into the keyhole, but it would not turn. The old brass lock with the tarnished spots was gone, and in its place was a shiny new one. Lilia assumed the old lock had broken, so she knocked. A rhythmic tapping noise could be heard, and Lilia knew it was her father's cane as he came to let her in. She held her breath.

Upon seeing his daughter, Don Villavicencio straightened his posture from his hunched stance. His face showed surprise, but he did not say a word. Lilia wished to wrap her arms around him, kiss his cheeks and beg for forgiveness. She refrained from doing so because of his harsh expression. He stared at her as one side of his lip turned upwards in a growl-like expression, "You are not welcome in this house!"

"Papá, I'm sorry."

"Away with you! Be gone!"

"Papá, please forgive me."

"You've thrown us aside for a man! You are cheap and shameless!" Don Villavicencio stepped out and kicked Lilia's suitcase, causing it to tumble off the stoop.

"I made a mistake. I was in love, and I thought he wanted to marry me. Don't you remember falling in love and getting married to Mamá?"

"Dare not compare the sanctity of my marriage with you whoring after a foreigner to the other side of this continent! You are no longer my daughter. Get out!" He stepped back into the foyer and tried to close the door, but Lilia placed her foot between the frame and door and stopped him. Lilia pushed past him and ran to the dining room calling, "Mamá! Mamá! Where are you?"

Susana came out of her bedroom still wearing her apron.

"Oh, thank God, Lilia! You're home!" Susana extended her arms. Lilia lunged into them, and they cradled one another. "My beautiful girl, you're safe and back home. I was so worried." Susana broke into tears.

"Fetch Mamá. Why hasn't she come out?"

Susana hesitated, then held Lilia closer and whispered, "Mamá is gone."

Lilia fell out of the embrace. "To the market? At this hour? Susana, she should not be out so late by herself."

"Oh, sweet child! She's not at the market," Susana whispered as she stroked Lilia's hair.

"Don't address the whore in such a respectful manner." Don Villavicencio said his words slowly and menacingly. "She's not a sweet child. Get out of my house!"

"Señor! Please, let's calm down, I beg. We all make mistakes."

"She's a bitch, like the woman who bore her," Don Villavicencio retaliated.

The words sent a shock through Lilia, having never heard words so cruel sputter from her father's mouth. He had never acknowledged her biological mother, always had acted as if she never existed and now was calling her a terrible name. Don Villavicencio approached Lilia in a rage with his cane held in midair.

Lilia took a few steps back.

"Stop, Señor," Susana moved in front of Lilia, protecting her.

"Where's Mamá?"

"She's dead! Insolent girl! You broke her heart." The old man's vein on his forehead bulged.

"What?"

"You killed her! She cried nonstop the night you abandoned us. The wailing never stopped. When the doctor came, he administered morphine, for he feared her heart would not tolerate losing you. She slept all day. Susana and I began to relax, thinking she would heal, but when the morphine wore off, Carmen came out of her fog and again relived the horrors of your absence. We held her hand and tried to console her, but all she wanted was you! Her heart failed at exactly 3:01 the following morning. Susana and I were by her side."

"No..." Lilia teetered and was about to buckle to her knees when Susana caught her and held her up.

"Papá, I didn't know she loved me."

"Get out of my house!" Don Villavicencio screeched.

"I'm sorry, Papá. I never imagined..."

Susana saw Lilia's eyes pleading for her father's forgiveness, but she knew his temperament would not allow for a reprieve.

"Leave now or pay the consequences." He lifted his cane again and swung at his daughter. Lilia grabbed the end of the cane and pulled it away from him. She flung it across the room, hitting the large mirror above the buffet and shattering it to pieces. The loud noise startled everyone. Susana shuddered, but Don Villavicencio, still enraged, lunged at Lilia with his fist. His ankle twisted, and he stumbled to the ground.

Susana and Lilia tried to get him up, but he slapped both away and yelled, "Get out!"

"Yes, Papá, you're right. I will leave. Allow me to fetch my dog." Lilia ran to her room and flung open the back door of the courtyard. The courtyard was quiet, and the doghouse was gone. Susana ran behind her, reached for Lilia's hand and through sobbing gasps said, "Baltito is also gone."

Don Villavicencio, having lifted himself from the floor, was at Lilia's bedroom door and mocked in a calm voice, "He's dead."

"What do you mean?" Lilia could hardly get the words out.

His reply was accompanied by a terrifying smile, "Would I keep a mongrel around for your sake? That dog was like you, a cur whose mother was a bitch—trash from the streets! A worthless dog begets a worthless dog. I pray you're not secretly carrying another bastard in your womb to add to this ugly world. History repeats itself, doesn't it, Lilia? Now, for the last time, get out of my house!"

"What happened to Baltito?"

Lilia held Susana's shoulders, attempting to calm her.

"I sent him to the slaughterhouse," Don Villavicencio shrieked.

"No!" Lilia screamed as all the air left her lungs. The already unbearable pain of losing her mother was amplified by Baltito's murder. She felt as if her entire body shattered into pieces. She tried to inhale but managed only to intake small gasps between sobs. Susana held her tightly.

"No, Baltito isn't dead! Mamá isn't dead! Where are they? I need to tell her how much I love her, and I...I need my Baltito."

"You can tell Carmen you love her when you're dead and before the angels kick you out of Heaven to the gates of Hell," Don Villavicencio seethed.

Mamá is gone. Baltito is gone. Death doesn't give second chances. Lilia grabbed the wedding photograph of her parents from the wall and ran out of the house. Susana followed.

Baltito's demise had proven far crueler than anything Lilia could have imagined her father capable of doing. Lilia flew down the stoop steps and reached for her suitcase that was crushing the white gardenias her mother had planted. She cried out, "I'm sorry, Mamá. I've ruined your flowers!"

Susana threw herself at Lilia, embracing her and patting her on the back, "You're going to be all right. You'll find a way out of this."

Lilia inhaled Susana's spice and verbena soap, but mostly she breathed in the familiar scent of motherly love. Hardly able to function, she needed to concentrate on walking away, systematically placing one foot in front of the other and willing her legs to comply. The simplest task needed strategizing. Thoughts were jumbled and incoherent in her head. Susana followed her to the sidewalk. The Don came to the doorway and silently watched his daughter leave.

Susana coaxed, "Go to the McKenna. I'm sure they will give you work."

Don Villavicencio ranted, "I'll make sure there will never be a job for you there. Have you forgotten who I am?"

Lilia continued walking away.

"The devil awaits you!" Don Villavicencio screamed as he went back into his house.

"Wait!" Susana embraced Lilia again and pulled from her pocket Don Villavicencio's silver ticket. "When I heard you come into the house, I took the Don's ticket from his dresser. Use it, and when you find a place to stay, send notice. I'll come to see you as soon as I can."

"This ticket will help, as I'm almost out of money. I'll find work in Valparaiso." Lilia turned away, fighting her will to tell Susana about her unborn child. Her father had guessed correctly and had already insulted the innocent baby by calling the child a bastard. *I am like my birth mother and compelled to commit the same sin.*

Lilia reached the station and flashed her father's silver ticket. She felt the rigid metal between her fingers and knew her father was the embodiment of that ticket, cold and unbendable.

Alone

Valparaiso, Chile, 1948

Lilia took the last train to Valparaiso arriving at midnight. Peering out the window at the gloomy station, she did not want to leave the familiarity of the train and waited until all the passengers were gone. She watched their expressions of contentment, happy to be home after a long day of work, and she was jealous of them. Her back hurt as she rose from her seat and walked out into the evening's cool ocean air, dragging her suitcase. The streets were dark, as the flames in the streetlamps were extinguished when the kerosene ran out.

Heading toward a group of hotels near the train station, she veered towards the ocean to admire the full moon and listen to the gentle roar of waves. She inhaled the ocean air and gazed at the moon. It hung above the horizon over the ocean like a portal on a golden shimmering path. *How wonderful it would be to pass through to another world.*

The heavens were free of clouds, and not even the brightness of the moon obscured the swarm of stars. Lilia continued to walk on the beach instead of searching for a room in town. She let the moon follow her while tasting the salt in the air. When sand filled her shoes, she took them off and rested on a rock. With the wind constantly pounding her skin and the night air cooling, she became chilled and rummaged in her suitcase for something warm to wear but found nothing. The sheer cotton and silk dress outfits she had packed for tropical Caracas did not include a sweater. A pink silk scarf felt soft when she wrapped it around her shoulders, but it did not warm her. She shivered but did not have the will to leave the rock or move out of the wind. The rhythmical waves and the whistling wind spun stories in her head of what life could have been like with Enzo, with loving parents and without Baltito.

Staring at the moon, she watched it rise. The magical path on the calm sea disappeared. Not moving from her rock, staring into darkness and hypnotized by the sea, Lilia sat for a long time. She looked at her watch, barely able to decipher its tiny hands pointing to three. Lilia waited for a new sun to rise.

She rose from the rock, put her shoes on and wandered along the beach. No matter how quickly she walked or how wide she made her stride, it did not warm her or help ease the terrible pain in her heart. *This pain will devour me. I want to start my life again, but how? I've betrayed those I love—my mother, the Professor, Papá, my dog, Susana...I will not be forgiven.*

The small heel of Lilia's right shoe tore off as she slipped on a mossy stone. She kicked off her shoes and removed her socks, left them on the ground and continued barefoot. She walked aimlessly on the beach, still carrying her suitcase, till the eastern sky lightened.

Rays of sun squeaked through the marine layer forming golden rods through the clouds. Behind the foothills, hints of pink and orange hues sprouted in the sky, promising a beautiful day. She left the wide beach and found herself at a rocky coastline, where huge boulders jutted out from the cliffs towards the sea.

Lilia, now exhausted, searched for a shortcut to return to the area where there were many hotels. Constantly replaying all that had happened to her, mostly losing her mother and the barbarous act of her father, she became more disconsolate. *Did Baltito know what was happening? Did he whimper for me with his last breath?* At her own questions, her pain deepened. *How could I bring a child into this world when I can't even protect a defenseless pup? My child is illegitimate, a bastard, a guacha!*

Lilia's feet began to bleed from the sharp rocks, but she didn't care. Still climbing the hill toward the bluff, she found poppies growing between stones. The flowers swayed in the wind, reminding her how the crinkly paper-like blossoms had appeased her hunger as a child. Lilia aimed to reach the top of the cliff, thinking that perhaps from that height the world would look less daunting. Tired of lugging her suitcase, Lilia let it fall from her hand and watched it pop open and its contents spill out. Ignoring it, she walked toward the cliff and looked for a way up.

The poppies were still sleeping and holding their petals tightly closed. As the dawn broke and the sun's rays touched their petals, they woke and opened to show the world their glory. Lilia picked a large bloom, placed the long stem behind her ear and climbed higher.

Hidden by many rocks and boulders, Lilia discovered a small path. She followed it as the trail turned inward. At the bend, embedded in the hill, was a stone staircase. Lilia imagined a castle at the end of the stairs, a hidden refuge to call home where Enzo and their child reigned.

At the top of the stairs, a view opened to an effervescent waterfall separating the two sides of the canyon. Spray from the cascade appeared as translucent robes of angels. Below, a beautiful rivulet of fresh water gurgled down towards the ocean until it commingled with the salty sea, churning the waters into a turquoise hue. A precarious bridge built of rope and lumber stretched from one side of the fissure to the other. Lilia mustered her courage and walked to the center of the bridge. From the middle of the rickety bridge, the ocean sparkled in front of her, bejeweled in diamonds.

The sun shone on the panorama before her. *The world can be so beautiful.* She untied her scarf from around her shoulders and offered it to the wind. The playful currents caught it and danced with it before it drifted across the sky.

In the distance, a small rickety boat came into Lilia's view. The boat bobbed as it coasted on the swells, struggling to reach the shore. She viewed what seemed from a distance a beautifully painted lily on its hull, and she felt akin to the image. It felt like both she and the boat were fighting water. Lilia's brain, unable to stop the myriad thoughts bombarding her, recounted her losses and lost her will to fight. She understood that men wrap their powerful arms around a woman and pull her close, but none of it holds meaning. *Men tell lies. You can feel their arms, but you cannot feel their hearts.*

Lilia could not imagine the long days ahead, feeling only an invisible hand squeezing her insides until she could barely breathe. A shadow covered Lilia as a solitary cloud drifted overhead in the indigo sky. She studied the lone cloud, not yet burned by the sun, and imagined God sitting complacently watching her. The cloud morphed into different shapes. Lilia pointed her finger at it, "What do you want?" She listened for a response. Silence. She caressed her womb and spoke to her child, "Now the cycle will be broken."

Lilia climbed over the ropes of the bridge as a gust of wind swayed the bridge. A large wave hit the boulders below, spraying water droplets high into the air. Lilia felt the cold spray on her face and arms. She stared at the boat, now closer to shore, and saw the painted lily clearer, its detail beautiful and pure. She let go of the rope and held her womb as she fell silently into the turbulent river.

Enzo

Santiago, Chile, 1948

A week after Lilia's departure from Caracas, Enzo received a letter from his fiancée. Having grown tired of waiting for Enzo's call, Serafina had broken her promise of engagement and married a local boy. The letter came as a surprise, but Enzo was not sorry, as he never really loved her. Now, excited about not having to go through the nuptials and free to marry Lilia, he began to fantasize about the young pianist becoming his wife and carrying his heir. She loved him and that was important.

At first, he didn't like the idea of being with such a naïve girl, but she earned an income, unlike most women he knew. It would come in handy in times of trouble and could also help him with his failing business. The women from his town did not work, as their duties lay in the home. He remembered the time immediately following the war when out of necessity, his mother worked in the tomato factory against her family's wishes and helped her sons purchase passages to foreign lands in hope of employment. He was grateful for her decision.

Enzo wrote to Lilia, but the correspondence came back with a red imprint "return to sender." He phoned the Italian consulate in Santiago for help in contacting Lilia Villavicencio, but the ambassador laughed, "We understand your problem, but we don't get involved with matters of the heart."

Upon completing his construction contracts, Enzo temporarily left the business to his bewildered partners and boarded the next ship to Valparaiso. Upon arrival, he nearly missed the train. His old brown suitcase nearly knocked over a man as he hurried past the crowded platform and hopped on at the last second. The idea of becoming husband to the talented Lilia and father to their child grew more pleasant.

At the Santiago train station, Enzo searched the large city map for Lilia's address and was surprised to discover that she was a short distance away so he wouldn't need to hire a car. The walk was invigorating as he stretched his tired muscles. He smiled as he imagined Lilia's expression when she answered the door and found him standing there. He slid his hand inside the pocket of his jacket, found the handkerchief where Lilia had written her address and fingered the gold band fastened to it with a safety pin. He had purchased the ring for Serafina years ago. He hoped Lilia would love it and wear it faithfully for the rest of her life. He dreamed of his child and hoped his first-born was a male to carry on the family name.

Enzo, smug in his thoughts for having defeated death in war and an avalanche, prayed silently in gratitude. He felt a pang of guilt as he neared Lilia's house, reflecting on how she must have felt when she traveled so far, only to be dismissed. Now, believing that the end justifies the means, all would be right. He was certain she would run into his arms for a long embrace, giggling, as was her youthful way.

He stopped in front of Lilia's townhouse, surprised that she had not mentioned its opulence. He noticed the intricate wrought iron décor on the garden gate and filed it in the recesses of his mind to use later in one of his projects. He pulled the rope and initiated the bells.

A heavyset balding man opened the door. He looked angry and was about to reprimand Enzo, thinking him to be a door-to-door salesman, but then realized the stranger could be the man who had caused such havoc on his family. Godofredo's muscles tensed and skin flushed while he tried to remain cool. He stood by the open front door but did not open the garden gate. He yelled out, "What do you want?"

"Excuse me, Don Villavicencio. I'm here for Lilia—"

Godofredo cut him off, "I'm not Don Villavicencio."

Enzo wondered if he was at the wrong house. "I'm here for the *Signorina*, I mean, Señorita Lilia. Does she live here?"

"Who are you?"

"I'm Della Corte, Lorenzo. Lilia's friend."

"Lilia does not live here!"

Enzo looked at the number on the door and compared it to the scribbling on his handkerchief. "This is the address she gave me. You are not her father, Señor?"

"No!" Godofredo turned towards the house and called out, "Susana, handle this!"

Godofredo waited for Susana to come to the door and then reentered the house.

Susana guessed the man standing in front of her was Lilia's lover and almost screamed, "Enzo! Is it really you?"

Enzo sighed with relief, "Yes."

"I'm Susana."

"Of course, I know of you. Susana. I'm so relieved."

The housekeeper sprang to the gate and unlatched it. She spread her arms and prompted him to hug her and kiss both of her cheeks.

"I'm sorry to stare, Señor. I want to have a good look at you. I see why she was so enamored. Your presence makes me feel as if Lilia is near."

"Where is she?"

Susana did not answer but held his arm in support.

"Susana! What's happened?"

"I'm sorry, Enzo. We lost her."

"What?"

"She is gone."

"I don't understand," Enzo cocked his head, a look of puzzlement crossing his face.

"Sit down, Enzo, please." She pointed to the bench in the front garden. He dropped onto the hard seat, locking his eyes on Susana who sat next to him.

"She loved you, Enzo, but she chose to leave us. They found her body in a ravine in Valparaiso."

"No, no, no...How did she have this accident?"

"It wasn't an accident."

"No!"

"Her mother, Carmen, died from grief when Lilia left for Caracas. When our dear girl returned, Don Villavicencio disowned her. We found out about her suicide when the police chief came to our door a few days later. Tragedy comes in thirds. A week later, Don Villavicencio suffered a brain hemorrhage in the middle of the night and never regained consciousness."

"I've lost her and our baby," Enzo could hardly get the words out.

Susana gasped, "No! She was with child?"

"Yes."

"Lilia was like my own daughter as much as she was the Villavicencios'. I share your grief. I wish I had known and could have done more to protect her."

Godofredo approached the front door and shouted, "Susana, it's time for you to bid the man farewell. I'm ready for my supper."

Susana nodded, "Yes, Señor. Only a minute more, please."

Godofredo retreated into the house.

"Enzo, I'm so sorry, but I must leave you."

Enzo sat motionless. Susana grabbed his hand. "Lilia loved all of us. There's nothing we can do for her. We share guilt in what happened, but Lilia paid the highest price. This house, the bank accounts—all should have been hers and not Godofredo's. Most of all, you...you should have been hers, and the child should have been born."

Enzo shook his head and made the sign of the cross.

"Lilia forgives us. God Bless you, Señor. *Adios.*"

Tears rolled down Susana's cheeks, pain clearly visible on her face. Enzo's mouth formed the word goodbye, but he was not able to vocalize. Susana stroked his arm before leaving him and entering the house. Enzo rose, fumbled with the latch on the gate and returned to the train station.

Home

Antofagasta, Chile, 1949

An oversized radio covered Jacob's face as he walked into his new house. "Agata! Come quick. Look what I bought."

Agata came out of the kitchen wearing an apron and holding a wooden spoon. "What is that monstrosity you're bringing into the house?"

Jacob looked around for a place to set it down. "This machine is our connection to the world. I can't believe I found it at the second-hand store."

"A radio?"

"Not only a radio, but a shortwave, and don't look so worried. It was affordable." Jacob placed the radio on the coffee table in front of their couch. "We'll finally hear news on the day it happens and not have to wait for the paper."

"And we'll have music." Agata spun around as if dancing. "We're so far north, do you think we'll get decent reception?"

"Yes, the storekeeper said he picked up signals from both Santiago and Lima."

"Turn it on."

Jacob moved a potted plant away from a wall socket, plugged in the radio and fidgeted with the dials. Some whistling and garbled voices sprang out of the box, but he managed to find a clear signal of a news broadcast. They listened to the baritone voice of an announcer while Agata sat on the old floral couch.

"We will listen to a poem from Gabriella Mistral, one of Chile's most loved and respected poets and—" Jacob changed the channel.

"No, put that back, please."

"I'm searching for music."

"Later, I want to hear about Mistral."

Jacob turned the dial back and the voice once again boomed into the room. "*...Nobel Prize in Literature four years ago. We will be reading Mistral's poem immediately after we listen to Chopin's 'Fantasie Impromptu.'*"

"Ah, we got our music after all. I love Chopin. He is a Pole," Jacob said with melancholy in his voice.

"Let's not forget to keep it on the same channel to listen to Mistral's poem. I didn't know she won the Nobel. I remember the doctor giving me her book of poems. It makes me proud to be Chilean, as you are proud that Chopin is Polish. Mistral won it to honor all Chileans."

"But you're not Chilean; you're a Spaniard."

"No longer. I guess we're both Chileans now. This is our home. I found you here, my love, and it's where we belong." Agata planted a kiss on Jacob's lips.

"What would have become of me without you? Thank you for putting me back together like that once-shattered figurine," he said, pointing to a ceramic statue on a shelf.

"The figurine was easy to glue—you were not," Agata taunted.

"Thank you for my life."

"I didn't give you anything. It was God. We're both changed, Jacob, like *Pinocho*."

"Who?"

"*Pinocho*, the little puppet from the old fable. He became a real boy as I became a real woman."

"Oh yes, in Polish, it's *Pinokio*."

"Now, let's be quiet and listen to Chopin's magnificence."

They sat down on the couch. Agata placed her head on his shoulder as they listened.

"Oh!" Agata cried out.

"What's wrong?"

"It moved."

"Another tremor? I didn't feel it."

Agata placed Jacob's hands on her abdomen and said, "It's the baby. I felt it kick."

"So soon? Does it feel like butterfly wings? That's how Anita would describe it when she carried our sons."

"That's exactly what it feels like!"

Jacob's face showed sadness.

"My love, this baby cannot erase your pain. But when it's born, the three of us will always remember your boys. They live inside of you, and we will have joy."

"We will have joy," Jacob repeated.

When the music stopped, Agata rose and said, "I better finish cooking dinner."

The announcer's voice blasted, *"That was a recording by the young protégée, Eliana Villavicencio. She was better known as Lilia. It has been almost two years since she was here in our studio and played this Impromptu live for us. We will miss her."*

Agata, upon hearing the pianist's name, sat back down on the couch.

"May God forgive her for taking her own life. She was very young when she won a seat in the International Chopin Competition in Warsaw. A tragic end to a brilliant career. I'd like to end the show with another Chopin work in her honor, the 'Nocturne in C minor.'"

"Lilia, my Lilia," Agata said under her breath. The first hauntingly beautiful notes of the nocturne flowed from the radio's speaker, and Agata was lost in her memories. She folded her arms into an imaginary cradle and rocked. "I'm saddened by this music. It reminds me of my special girl, my Lilia. I still love her with every cell of my being."

"She was your gift from the turnstile."

"Yes."

"I'm sure your Lilia is now grown and has a child of her own. I'm sure she's happy, wherever she is."

"Can we name our child Lilia?"

"Yes, Lilia is a beautiful name. What if it's a boy?"

"He will have both your son's names. Not to replace them but to honor them. Our loved ones will no longer be ghosts. They'll come back to our loving arms."

Jacob stood and pulled Agata up from the couch. He wrapped his arms around her waist, she rested her head on his shoulder and they swayed to the music.

Jacob whispered in her ear, "Lilia, our Lilia."

About the Author

Roxanne Z. Kind enjoys writing, acting, directing plays, traveling, teaching, and experimenting with recipes. Passionate about preserving the environment, she is growing an organic native plant garden to boost the population of birds, butterflies, bees, and other small creatures.

www.RoxanneZKind.com

Book Club Questions

Dear Reader: Depending on your reading style, you may find this list to contain spoiler alerts. It is recommended to refrain from reading these questions until you have finished the book.

1. What is the significance of the title, *A Small Life*? In what ways do you find it meaningful?

2. What main themes did you trace in the book? How were they supported by the plot?

3. Why do you think the author chose three main characters or protagonists instead of just one?

4. What feelings did you have about the writing style and content structure of the book?

5. Did you think the time period of 1929 to 1949 is accurately portrayed?

6. Which location in the book would you most like to visit?

7. Were there any quotes or passages that stood out to you?

8. What did you like most and least about the book?

9. What emotions did the story evoke?

10. Did you know about foundling wheels prior to this book and that they still exist today?

11.	Who was your favorite character? How did you relate to her or him?

12.	If the book were made into a movie, who would play the lead characters?

13.	Were there times you disagreed with a character's actions? What would you have done differently?

14.	Which character would you most like to meet in real life?

15.	What scene resonated with you most?

16.	What surprised you most about the book? Why? Which plot twists and turns did you find most significant?

17.	Did the author do a good job of organizing the plot and moving it along?

18.	How did you feel about Lilia's suicide? Would you have chosen a happy ending for her?

19.	How do you feel about Enzo? Was he a protagonist or antagonist?

20.	How have Lilia, Agata, and Alvarez changed by the end of the book?

21.	Were you curious about the music Lilia played and if so, did it inspire a search for it and did you hear it?

22.	If you were sitting down for coffee with the author R.Z. Kind, what would you want to ask her?

23.	Would you recommend reading *A Small Life*?

Publisher's Note

Thank you for the opportunity to serve you. If you would like to help share this message, here are some popular ways:

REVIEWS
Write an online book review

GIVING
Gift this book to friends, family, and colleagues

BOOK CLUBS
Read it with a group of friends

BULK ORDERS
Email sales@citrinepublishing.com

CONTACT
Call +1-828-585-7030 or email:
info@citrinepublishing.com

We appreciate your book reviews, letters, and shares.